Coburn —
A Desperate Call

MAY 08 1998 970
SEP 23 1998 3346
APR 24 2000 3303

FORT EDWARD FREE LIBRARY - NY
0 00 27 0007793 2

DEMCO

SIGNET / ONYX (0451)

ON THE EDGE OF YOUR SEAT!

- ☐ **THE DOOR TO DECEMBER by Dean Koontz.** #1 *New York Times* Bestseller! Little Melanie had been kidnapped when she was only three. She was nine when she was found wandering the L.A. streets, with blank eyes. What had become of her in all those years of darkness . . . and what was the terrible secret clutching at her soul that she dared not even whisper? (181379—$6.99)

- ☐ **BLACKOUT by Seth Kindler.** Jerry Cayce is a loving husband and father, a Nashville studio musician with a second career as a successful novelist. Ron Creed is a musician, too, but he's also a diabolical killer with a score to settle—and only Jerry knows when and where Creed will strike again. (180852—$4.99)

- ☐ **SOUL/MATE by Rosamond Smith.** A psychopathic serial killer with a lover's face. . . . "Headlong suspense. . . . What if a well-meaning, intelligent woman should encounter a demonic twin?"—*The Atlanta Journal and Constitution*. "Taut, relentless, chilling!"—*Chicago Tribune*.
  (401905—$4.95)

Prices slightly higher in Canada.

Buy them at your local bookstore or use this convenient coupon for ordering.

PENGUIN USA
P.O. Box 999 — Dept. #17109
Bergenfield, New Jersey 07621

Please send me the books I have checked above.
I am enclosing $_____ (please add $2.00 to cover postage and handling). Send check or money order (no cash or C.O.D.'s) or charge by Mastercard or VISA (with a $15.00 minimum). Prices and numbers are subject to change without notice.

Card #_____ Exp. Date _____
Signature_____
Name_____
Address_____
City _____ State _____ Zip Code _____

For faster service when ordering by credit card call **1-800-253-6476**

Allow a minimum of 4-6 weeks for delivery. This offer is subject to change without notice.

Laura Coburn

A Desperate Call

AN ONYX BOOK

ONYX
Published by the Penguin Group
Penguin Books USA Inc., 375 Hudson Street,
New York, New York 10014, U.S.A.
Penguin Books Ltd, 27 Wrights Lane,
London W8 5TZ, England
Penguin Books Australia Ltd, Ringwood,
Victoria, Australia
Penguin Books Canada Ltd, 10 Alcorn Avenue,
Toronto, Ontario, Canada M4V 3B2
Penguin Books (N.Z.) Ltd, 182–190 Wairau Road,
Auckland 10, New Zealand

Penguin Books Ltd, Registered Offices:
Harmondsworth, Middlesex, England

First published by Onyx, an imprint of Dutton Signet,
a division of Penguin Books USA Inc.

First Printing, June, 1995
10 9 8 7 6 5 4 3 2 1

Copyright © Laura Coburn, 1995
All rights reserved
"Drift Away" © 1972 Alamo Music Corp. Used with permission.

 REGISTERED TRADEMARK—MARCA REGISTRADA

Printed in the United States of America

Without limiting the rights under copyright reserved above, no part of this publication may be reproduced, stored in or introduced into a retrieval system, or transmitted, in any form, or by any means (electronic, mechanical, photocopying, recording, or otherwise), without the prior written permission of both the copyright owner and the above publisher of this book.

PUBLISHER'S NOTE
This is a work of fiction. Names, characters, places, and incidents either are the product of the author's imagination or are used fictitiously, and any resemblance to actual persons, living or dead, events, or locales is entirely coincidental.

BOOKS ARE AVAILABLE AT QUANTITY DISCOUNTS WHEN USED TO PROMOTE PRODUCTS OR SERVICES. FOR INFORMATION PLEASE WRITE TO PREMIUM MARKETING DIVISION, PENGUIN BOOKS USA INC., 375 HUDSON STREET, NEW YORK, NEW YORK 10014.

If you purchased this book without a cover you should be aware that this book is stolen property. It was reported as "unsold and destroyed" to the publisher and neither the author nor the publisher has received any payment for this "stripped book."

Dedicated to my husband, Robert, for his unwavering support and encouragement, to my daughter, Katharine, for her faith in me, and to my beloved island of Bermuda, without which this book would never have been written in the first place.

ACKNOWLEDGMENTS

Special thanks and gratitude to Det. Lee Kingsford and Sgt. Glenn Varner (dec.) of the Los Angeles Police Department for all that they taught me; to Michaela Hamilton and Joe Pittman, my editors at Penguin, for their skilled guidance as I took this book to its final form; and to Frank Cooper and Donna Forman of The Cooper Agency for their strong belief in me.

Chapter One

The frantic mother called shortly after seven—her little boy was late for dinner. An officer took down the details, tried to calm the woman, then immediately alerted all units in the field. My own phone rang at ten past eight, as I settled back to watch TV and sip a soothing drink.

Missing kids aren't that uncommmon, especially when the days are warm and the evenings mellow into long and hazy twilights before tipping over into night. They forget the rules, or just ignore them, and linger at their small pursuits before they finally turn for home.

But I see it from a different angle and know that's not always what keeps a child from dinner—sometimes someone else decides he's never going home again.

I hurried to the station and went directly to the watch commander, seated at a scarred and cluttered desk. He scanned reports and swiftly signed them, sweating in the unexpected heat of early spring. A patch of dampness showed below the collar of his uniform and drops of perspiration rode upon his reddened brow.

He heard my step, laid down the pen, and wiped the sweat away.

"Tell me," I said quickly, eager to get on with it. I stood across from him, leaning forward as I spread both palms against the darkened wood.

"Kate, here's what's happening. The call came in about an hour ago from the mother. Kid named Billy Schuyler was supposed to come home at five for five-thirty dinner, didn't make it. The mother called his friends and drove around some, searching for him herself. No luck, and when he didn't show by seven, she called us. He was last seen at the school playground around three this afternoon."

Rick picked up the pen and rolled it back and forth between his hands. Then he went back to his reports, his thick broad shoulders hunched uncomfortably above the pile of papers on his desk.

"Right now, to my way of thinking, it's no biggie—kids that age are late all the time—but we've got the command post set up at Palm and Willow to start the door-knocking just in case . . ."

He paused, pulled a plastic trash can toward him, and casually spat into it before he set it down. Then he looked up at me, squinting hard against the brightness of the room.

I stared back, my hazel eyes never wavering from his face. Hastily, I raised my hand and shoved my hair behind one ear, my nails scraping sharply on the scalp. I pushed quickly back from the desk and stood up straight.

"He wasn't last seen at the playground," I told him, and I heard my voice—my calm detective's voice—speaking funny, on a half note, slightly off-key. "Billy Schuyler was in my yard till nearly five o'clock, playing baseball with my son."

* * *

A DESPERATE CALL

I drove slowly to the command post several blocks away, my fingers tapping lightly on the steering wheel. A tiny warning tightness began to gather in my stomach and my shoulders shook in an involuntary shudder.

Sure, it was early on yet, but there was something here I didn't like. Was it only that I knew the little boy? That I had one that age myself? I didn't know, but I knew I didn't like the feeling and the signals it sent up. I felt a wisp-wind sadness touch my soul.

I straightened up and concentrated on that afternoon. I'd come home at four o'clock, called out to Jonathan as he leaned across his drawing board, then hurried on upstairs when I saw his absentminded nod. The day had been a rough one and I was beat down and looking forward to a cool shower and fresh clothes before starting dinner.

My eight-year-old, Tommy, was in the garage playing with friends. I thought of going to him, as I usually did when I came in from work, but fatigue kept me from it. I'd see him later, I decided.

I kicked off my heels and lay across the bed, and the murmurs of the warm spring day began to lull me in-and-out, in-and-out, past the edge of sleep and back again.

Abruptly, small-boy voices, shrill and fierce, jolted me. It was four twenty-five. I stood up quickly, smoothing out my skirt and yawning. I looked out the window and saw Tommy, his best friend Chris Brown, and Billy Schuyler playing catch below my bedroom. They were having fun and I grinned at the all-consuming delight with which boys that age play the game.

I turned away to straighten up the bed and, as I did

so, the voices stopped. A door banged. When I looked out the window again, the yard was empty and I heard footsteps coming toward my room. Chris and Tommy stood in the doorway.

I held my arms out to my son and he ran toward them, then slowed and blushed beneath his freckles. I understood and didn't force it. He was of that certain age where the natural yearn for mother love gets overridden by the fear of ridicule by friends.

Instead of hugging him, I dropped my arms and smiled. I thought about how much I loved him and how very long I'd waited for him before he came into my life—came and helped to heal a deathly sadness that once had gripped and smothered me until it very nearly killed my will to live.

"How's it going, kiddo? Was your day a good one?" Casually, careful not to appear overly affectionate, I brushed his blond hair off his forehead, marveling as I often did how he'd turned out so very fair while Jon and I were dark.

He told me he'd gotten "B" in spelling and punched another boy at lunch.

I frowned. That was twice within two weeks he'd been involved in fighting.

"Congratulations on the spelling," I told him as I gave a little frown, "but we've got to talk about the other thing—you know that, don't you?"

I asked if Billy was downstairs and they told me, "No, gone home." I thought no more about him till the watch commander slapped a label on the missing youngster.

I zeroed in on Billy. What did I know about him? To tell the truth, not that much. He was one of a pack of six or eight kids who played together, fought together, went to the movies when they had money and fishing when they didn't.

I remembered a polite little boy with an open face that always seemed to look at you as if it believed it could learn something from you. That face impressed me—I'm used to dealing with young toughs who dare you to try to tell them anything they don't already know.

When I remembered the face I saw the whole of the child—blue eyes, straight brown hair, a slight build for his age. Altogether an ordinary little boy, not remarkable in any way except for that honest, questing expression. You could find his double on any playground in this country.

I swung abruptly back to the present when I saw a black-and-white's light bar flashing up ahead. Davey Johnson was laying out the search plan to his officers, who stood around him in a tight quiet group. His legs spread wide and bending slightly forward, he punctuated orders with a jabbing index finger.

With his slender build and horn-rimmed glasses, he looked a lot like a middle-aged professor from the junior college on the other side of town. He was, in fact, one of the toughest sergeants on the San Madera force and a man made for heroic circumstances.

I pulled over. I'd wait awhile and give him a chance to finish without a break in concentration—I wanted them to listen well. Unwrapping a stick of gum, I slid it in my mouth and looked around me.

Moonlight played across the road in softened beauty, but it didn't fool me. I knew the darkness deep behind it hid ugly secrets—the kind that tear you up inside when you find them out.

God, I hate it when a child goes missing. I hate it

because it carries with it a sadness and an anguish of immeasurable intensity. It's the toughest kind of case I ever have to face.

I worry when my own child is even several minutes late, on a bright and sunny day when there's laughter all around and no hiding places in the shadows, and I wondered what the other mother must be feeling now, surrounded by the silence and the darkness of the night.

"It's all right," I said out loud, and I spoke to her as well as to myself. "It's all right—he'll turn up safe and sound."

I looked up and saw that Johnson was winding up his speech and the men were moving out. I quickly wrapped the gum and put it in the ashtray, then started toward him, calling out his name.

The evening wind laid strands of hair across my face and I paused to grab the long brown mass with both my hands. I secured it in a ponytail with the slim barrette I always carried with me.

"I heard, Kate," he said when I finally walked up to him. "So it was your house, was it? Beats all, that. Anyway, we've got a place to start—they're heading over to Marsh Road now to do the door-knocking."

He asked what Billy had been wearing when I saw him.

I thought hard and I had an impression of a blue-striped T-shirt and Levi's. But I couldn't be sure. All I could really see was a blur of legs and the flailing arms of three kids, twining together as they played. I told him about the shirt and jeans—I also told him I could be wrong.

"Nope, Katie, you're right on the mark—that's just

what the mother said. She couldn't recall the shoes, though. Can you?"

I shook my head.

My job was done for now, but if Billy wasn't found within the next six hours, the weight would fall on my shoulders. Till then, I'd stand by, watching from the sidelines.

"You know where to reach me if anything comes up," I told Davey and I turned to go.

"How's your husband doing, Katie?" he asked softly.

I spun around and quickly scanned his face. His eyes were serious and concerned, and I relaxed.

"He's doing fine, Davey, fine now. Thanks for asking."

I turned again and headed for the car.

Ordinarily I'd have driven home and gone straight to bed, the phone bell turned on high, but not tonight. For one thing, the search was starting on *my* street and already the adrenaline was pumping hard.

But there was another reason, too—I had to talk to Tommy, to find out if he knew where Billy'd been heading when he left our yard this afternoon. I thought of letting Jon know what was happening, but something warned me not to tell him—not just then, at least—and I hurried straight to Tommy's room.

Wisps of moonlight lay across him as he slept and I stood there for a moment watching him, saw the shadow of another little boy, and felt my heart tug painfully. Sure, I'm hardened by years of this kind of work, but this one's very close to home.

He looked so vulnerable. All the innocence in the world lay in that tiny sleeping form and it's because I know how that innocence can be used and violated, it's because I remember and mourn my own lost innocence of long ago, that the sight of a child at rest never fails to move me. Especially tonight.

I shook him awake and held him tight against me a long and silent moment. He rubbed a little fist across his sleepy eyes.

"Baby, I need to ask you something—where was Billy going when he left here today?"

"Home, Mom. Why?"

I told him, not exaggerating but not minimizing either. Deliberately, I kept my voice calm.

"How do you know it was home?"

"Because he said he'd be late for dinner if he didn't go so I know he was going home."

"But he didn't actually say so."

"Nope."

I thought for a moment, rubbing my hand slowly back and forth across his shoulders.

"Does he have any friends who live along the way?"

I knew Billy lived at 219 Hollis Place, about half a mile from our house. To get there, he'd walk four blocks east and two blocks north past tidy lawns and houses, without a single candy store or video game to catch his eye and slow him down. The neighborhood was like all the others in our little city—serene, bucolic, friendly. And, outwardly at least, safe.

"No, Mom, I don't think so, but I don't really know."

"What did he have with him? His bike, his baseball glove, what?" I asked.

Tommy concentrated, picking at the edges of his sheet. Then his clear blue eyes swung up into mine—wide open, guileless, with no hidden secrets.

"Just some books but not his bike—he walked. And

no glove either. He borrowed one of mine to play today 'cause his is no good anymore. It's so old all the stitching fell off and his thumb sticks 'way out. He left it here."

"Okay, sweetie, you did real good. You go back to sleep now—I'll wake you when we find him."

I smoothed the covers over him and turned to go, then I looked at him again and wetness filled my eyes.

I blew a kiss across the room and turned around. I know he was asleep before I even closed the door.

So what did I have that I didn't have before? Not much, granted, but enough to make me happy. I knew Billy had left here on foot, alone, and I also knew he'd probably headed straight for home. That'd do for starters. I called good night to Jonathan and went to bed. I knew I wouldn't get to sleep the whole night through.

The phone rang at one-twenty—Billy was still missing. Evening watch had gone on overtime and morning watch had joined them shortly after midnight. AM watch commander Roberts told his men to search garages and outbuildings and sound out everyone they could find who lived between my house and Hollis Place.

They came back empty-handed, without the glimmer of a lead. No one had seen a boy like Billy, no garage or toolshed held anything except the hoes or lawnmowers that belonged there. Six hours had passed and the case was now mine. Responsibility for its success or failure lay with me alone.

I slipped into a lightweight seersucker suit I'd laid out before I went to bed. I chose flat shoes instead of heels and pulled my hair into a tight round bun that wouldn't give me any trouble.

"Jon," I whispered as I knelt beside my sleeping husband, "I'm going back to work," and I threw one arm around him, squeezing him hard, but he lay still as if he hadn't heard me.

Then, just as I was about to leave the room, he swung his long legs to the floor and headed for the bathroom. Without a single glance toward me, he called out "See you later" while he yawned sleepily and ran his fingers through his dark and tousled hair. I shrugged and walked away.

Roberts stood up as I came through the station door, hitching up his dark blue trousers around his ample girth.

"Something for you, Kate," he said. "Old gal out on Marsh Road saw a boy wearing a blue-striped T-shirt and jeans walking east along her street around four-thirty yesterday afternoon. She remembers him because she was out front cutting flowers to take to her sister and this boy dropped something right at the end of her footpath."

He'd stopped to pick it up and stood there for a moment looking at it before he moved on, so she'd been able to get a real good look at him. The woman had then driven to San Marcos, a small town nearly fifteen miles away, to spend the evening with her sister. She'd just arrived back home.

"All right!" I said, and I smiled for the first time in several hours. The faint crackling of a small beginning was music to my ears.

I climbed the stairs to homicide and rummaged through my desk. I wished I'd time for a cup of steaming coffee, but I didn't.

Ah well, it'd do me good to skip it. I'd had an angry ulcer just last fall and my doctor had warned me then to cut it out entirely. It was a tough one for me—I'd quit smoking many years ago and it was now coffee that got me through uneasy situations.

I quelled the urge, picked up my purse, and left to meet the woman.

Maud Divans still wore the linen shirtwaist dress she'd put on earlier that day. Its tailored lines were sharp, its pink hue glowing, despite eight hours of wear.

She was a tall, spare woman who held herself erect as her eyes pierced my face. I summed her up immediately—a correct, no-nonsense person, intolerant of mistakes, who'd take a real close look at what she saw, then tell you all about it without leaving out a single thing or adding any frills. I found I wasn't wrong.

"Miss Divans, I'm Detective Katharine Harrod from the San Madera Police Department—and I'm also your neighbor three blocks down."

We knew each other slightly, meeting mainly when I strolled past her yard on evening walks with Jonathan.

"I'm looking for a missing child and I'm told maybe you can help me."

I smiled at her, to put her at her ease. She didn't smile back, but nodded slightly and motioned with one finger for me to follow her. We entered a small room warmly lit by muted lamplight playing on the luster of a highly polished floor. Her manner, like the nod, was crisp.

"Sit down, Detective," she directed and took a seat across from me. She was calm, poised, in control of everything that happened in that room. Maud Divans might make a stellar witness, but I wasn't sure I liked her very much. No matter. I asked her to tell me what she'd seen and she gave me the same story I'd gotten from Roberts, but with a bonus added—the boy was wearing blue low-top sneakers.

"Where did he go when he started off again?" I asked, shifting slightly in my seat.

"On down the street, heading the same way he'd been going. I couldn't see him, though, once he passed the big pine in the corner of my yard and there wasn't any reason to chase out on the sidewalk looking after him—he was just a little boy walking along."

I asked her why she'd noticed him at all.

"Well, because he was right in front of my yard, only about ten feet from me. And then he picked up something from the sidewalk and stopped to look at it. At first, I believed he'd dropped the thing himself and then retrieved it, but now I don't think so. He was paying far too much attention to it, as if he'd never seen it before but was really fascinated by whatever it was."

"You couldn't see it?"

"No, it was so small his fingers almost covered it, but I remember thinking it must be something special and I marveled at the absorption, the curiosity of the very young. I was glad he'd found something that could make him feel that way. I was a schoolteacher before I retired, Detective Harrod, and I know how intense that curiosity can be when you're growing up and how it sadly dulls with age."

I found myself softening toward her—she seemed human after all.

"What did he do with it then?"

A DESPERATE CALL

"He put it in his jeans pocket and walked on, rather quickly."

She'd left right after that to drive to her sister's and didn't see the little boy again.

I thanked her and told her I'd be back in the morning with a picture of the missing child. I'd have shown her one then but our only photo was at the printer's being reproduced one thousand times.

As we reached the door, she smiled hesitantly.

"It's interesting, you being a woman and doing this," she said, almost shyly, the aura of control missing from her voice.

"Police work? It's not all that unusual in this day and age, Miss Divans."

"Still and all, I think it's nice," she told me and a smile of satisfaction crossed her lips, as if she saw me as a symbol of a victory she'd failed to win herself, in a personal battle somewhere in her distant past.

"It is," I answered softly, "it *is* nice. There's nothing else I'd rather do."

I called the station and asked Roberts to break off as many men as possible and give them to me. I could have all twenty, he told me—crime was light that night. Billy would remain top priority for now.

"The parents are on the way down, Kate," Roberts said next, belching softly as he spoke. "I couldn't keep them home."

I ignored his words.

"Stay away from that greasy spoon, Robby—it plays havoc with your ulcers."

"Katie, girl, you weren't supposed to hear that," he protested. "But you're right about the ulcer—I'm on fire."

"Tell me about it," I replied. "I've got one of my own to cause me hell."

"What would a sweet little Irish gal like you know about ulcers?" he teased me. "They're only for old devils like myself."

"They're for anyone who works and worries, Robby," I said tartly, "and by the way, I'm *Scots*-Irish—there's a difference. Now tell me about the Schuylers."

He'd phoned them hourly, to keep them posted on the search and to ask if Billy had come home. Now the waiting had unnerved them and they wanted to get a close-up look at the people who were trying to find their son.

I wasn't one bit surprised. I'd found that loved ones of a missing person believe they can force a miracle to happen if they go where they can feel the heartbeat of the action. It doesn't work that way, but I couldn't really fault them much for coming—I'd have done the same myself.

"I was just going to the house—any chance they haven't left yet?"

"Not a one, baby girl—I see them coming through the door right now."

"Then tell them I'm on my way."

I crossed Hollis and then turned south on Willow. A black-and-white, heading north to the command post, passed me quickly. No other cars were on the road. The night was at its deepest, blackest hour—that fragment of time-stop limbo before today becomes tomorrow.

No moon lightened the blackness, no wind moved within the silence around me. I could feel the heat of the following day already starting to thicken.

It was then, in the lulling stillness of that night, that

the feeling came. At first, it was a niggling edginess on the fringes of my mind. Then it quickly rushed forward, gathering momentum, arriving as a full-blown certainty.

Until that moment, I'd been searching for a missing boy who'd be found asleep in someone's garden shed—a boy who'd stayed out past his curfew, gotten scared, and hid instead of going home to certain punishment.

Now, suddenly, I feared I was dealing with a situation that would hold no good answers, no cries of joy, no loving reunions. My mouth tightened and a discouraged, sickened feeling filled my mind and body.

I recalled the tightness in my stomach as I first drove to the command post—the premonition of a case gone wrong. But that'd been no more than an embryonic worry, as insubstantial and unformed as a summer breeze. This was different—now I knew for certain. I'd been there far too often to doubt my instincts were correct.

I cross this line in every case that's not resolved within the first few hours. Often, I cannot pinpoint the catalyst of that crossing.

I'd left the comfort of an everyday world and entered the shadowed gray-black land of terror, perversion, and the sickness of the human soul—a land that would remain the backdrop for my search until it ended. I shuddered and physically recoiled against the seat.

Then I saw the station lights ahead and, in the splinter of an instant, I again became detached, professional, masking the emotions that tumbled deep inside me. The waiting parents would never know about this quick-change in my mind. I was now ready to meet the Schuylers.

Chapter Two

They sat together at a table in the sergeants' room, drinking coffee out of paper cups. Numerous flyers lay in front of them, tossed about in wild array.

I scanned them quickly, hoping none showed a missing child, and rested easy when I found only the tough hard faces of adult fugitives staring up at me.

The room was silent but the Schuylers didn't seem to hear me enter. I paused a moment, wanting to collect impressions.

Thomas Schuyler sat slightly back from the table, upright and unmoving in a folding chair. He held his long legs rigidly together, heels touching on the concrete floor. His arms were folded tight against his chest and, though the night was warm, he wore a suit with tie pulled tight against a white shirt collar.

I'd heard somewhere he was a banker, and with his rimless, clear-lens glasses, his talcum-powdered cheeks and solemn face, he certainly looked the part.

I searched that face for an expression but couldn't even start to find one—he wasn't giving anything away. Fear, sorrow, worry—whatever he was feeling—was masked out and hidden deep inside.

The mother was a totally different story. Where her husband seemed self-assured and self-contained, Joyce

Schuyler was point-counterpoint to him. Her face showed every thought that marched across her mind. Her eyes widened, closed, opened again. A pale mouth moved from left to right to left.

Slight of build, with faded hair and washed-out skin, she sat barely six inches from his chair, her fluttering fingers tearing her coffee cup into tiny pieces. Her feet crossed and uncrossed and shifted endlessly on the floor in an unorchestrated dance.

I peered at her more closely. She was one of those women one would never call pretty, even in the best of times, though no single feature could be pointed to as marring. She was simply unremarkable—a woman who could stand at a room's edge or in the center of a crowd and go totally unnoticed. I felt sorry for her and my feeling had little to do with tonight's anguish.

As I moved forward into the room, she placed her hand quickly on her husband's knee. He looked at it, then glanced away.

"Mr. and Mrs. Schuyler? I'm Katharine Harrod, the detective in charge of the search for Billy."

They rose hurriedly and clumsily, causing their chairs to tip and almost fall as they scraped backward on the floor. Both their faces now held the same expression—frightened, dulled, like an animal that's been cornered and doesn't know what's coming next. She took a little step forward and put out her hand, he stood quite still.

I didn't want to talk to them here, in this stark and dingy room with a single lightbulb glaring from the ceiling. I wanted warmth and comfort for them and a feeling of serenity. I couldn't get it all but I could do a whole lot better than what I offered now.

"Let's go upstairs to my desk," I said. "We can talk easier there."

The three of us entered the side hall, where a drunk bellowed in the holding tank and two hypes were handcuffed to the bench, needle marks raw and bleeding on their arms. We stepped around them and headed for the stairs.

The detective room was quiet and cool and in almost total darkness. The green neon of the computer screen glowed faintly from the far end of the room. I flicked the light switch and led them to my desk.

As I was pulling up a chair, Schuyler spoke.

"You say that you're in charge here?"

Challenging, peremptory, he caught me totally off guard.

"That's right, I am. Why do you ask?"

I leaned against my desk, legs crossed in front of me, and sensed what was coming next.

"You're a woman. I'm not used to women in positions such as this. You *do* report to someone else, surely?"

I'd run into this reaction several times before—of course I had—but never offered quite so bluntly. Hurled with dead-sure aim and marked by neither blush nor stammer, it rode out on arrogance alone.

"Are you questioning my competence as an investigator?" I asked in a steely even tone, locking eyes with Schuyler.

"Yes, you might say that."

"Simply because I'm a woman?"

"That's right. If this were some little folderol, I might not care, but it *is* my son we're talking about and it's got to be done one hundred percent correct all the way."

I wasn't going to argue with him. His mind was set and there was no way I could change it even if I wanted to. The truth was I didn't really care. The important thing here was that we were wasting valuable time while he bitched about my gender. It had to stop.

I slowly tucked a wisp of hair behind one ear and then leaned forward in his face.

"I'll tell you just one thing, Mr. Schuyler, and that's all you really need to know. I'm in charge of this investigation. End of conversation."

He blanched, obviously not used to being spoken to like that, at least not by a woman. He set his lips in a thin, tight line and glared at some unknown object on my desk.

Sexist bastard, I thought hotly.

He showed no sign of starting up again and I relaxed a little. This talk had gotten off to a very bad beginning and I had to get it back on track as soon as possible.

"Look, the important thing here is your little boy. Let's focus on him. You know it's early yet—there's no real cause for alarm. Billy's probably sound asleep on some old discarded mattress in a nearby garage. When morning comes, we'll find him or he'll find us or he'll just go home to face the music."

I listened to the line of easy lies and wondered if they bought it. I glanced at Joyce Schuyler. She was silent, her frightened eyes looking into mine. I knew I'd given her little comfort—hollow phrases trotted out to mask the dawning horror.

I asked what time Billy'd been expected and what they'd done when he didn't show up.

Around five, the mother told me. When her husband walked in at five-fifteen, he still hadn't come but they weren't overly concerned. At five-thirty, though, they began to worry and started calling friends and neighbors asking if they'd seen the little boy.

They'd also called Schuyler's brother Mark, and reached another dead end there.

"Billy doesn't usually go to his house," Joyce Schuyler said, "but I was desperate, trying every place I knew."

When all the phoning failed to turn up their son, they sent their fifteen-year-old daughter Nadine to bike around the school grounds while they got in their car and scoured the streets near their home. They didn't see him anywhere.

I turned toward Thomas Schuyler, who sat in rigid silence, barely moving in his chair. I was still hot from his assault but I wasn't going to let him know it.

"Does Billy have a secret hangout," I asked smoothly, "a place he calls his own where we mightn't think to look?"

He answered quickly enough, apparently having come to some sort of terms with me, at least for now.

"I'm certain not. Billy's the type who's usually with other kids or else at home in the backyard waiting for the action to begin. He's not a loner."

Leaning forward, I peered intently into both their faces.

"Think a bit and tell me this. Do you have any idea at all where Billy might be found?"

"No, Miss Harrod, none." Thomas Schuyler spoke again. He was loosening up a little, even if he couldn't bear to give me rank. "Don't you think we'd tell you if we did?"

I stood up and gave my blouse a little tuck. I'd

gotten all I needed for right now, and I told them to go on home and wait for me to call them.

"And there's something else," I said. "I want you to rest, to lie down and try to close your eyes."

I raised my hand as Joyce Schuyler began to protest.

"It's hard, I know it's hard, but you need your strength. Leave it all in our hands now—let us do the work we're trained to do."

They got up slowly, with reluctance, trying to hold off the return to that silent house where their personal nightmare had begun ten hours before. We said goodbye and I stood beside my desk and watched them walk across the floor.

Why doesn't he at least take her hand? I wondered out loud as they disappeared through the open doorway.

I badly needed to get some rest myself. The pace of the past few hours and the lack of sleep tonight had worn me down. I buzzed Roberts.

"I'm beat, Robby—I'll be in the cot room if you need me. If you don't, let me go till six o'clock, then send the wake-up squad."

"You got it, Kate. Oh, whaddya make of those two? A bit of a stiff ass, isn't *he*, and she's a mouse from the word go."

"You do pretty good with thumbnail sketches," I replied, "but keep in mind it's not their finest hour."

We hung up and I headed for the cot room, letting my hair down as I walked. I knew I'd fall asleep and never wake till dawn.

But sleep wouldn't come. Instead, I tossed and turned and thought about this crazy business I was in and how I'd gotten there.

I'd been born in this central California valley nearly forty years ago, the only child of aging parents. We lived far out of town on a dusty country road, and I hardly saw another child my age until I started school.

My parents did their best to fill the gap—trying to entertain me in their own befuddled way—but I remained a lonely little girl. I yearned to have a playmate, soulmate, best friend forever—a mirror image of myself whom I could trust and love and who'd never let me down.

I vowed then if I became a mother, I'd surround my children with little boys and girls like them and they'd never be alone, except by choice. Their lives would be spun sugar, like cotton candy at a summer fair.

My parents died when I was in my teens and I finished growing up in a rough-and-tumble sort of way. An early marriage, clearly doomed according to the watchers, ended in divorce and I was left alone again, not even blessed by that longed-for child—the child for whom I'd make a world of sunny brightness filled with never-ending music from a spinning carousel.

My first career choice—a librarian, of all things—ended abruptly like the marriage, when I found I couldn't stand another day indoors, hidden from the wildness of the wind and the sweetness of the flowers by dark and dusty shelves of volumes long since dead.

I was twenty-one and I didn't know where I was going with my life. Then I saw a poster on a phone pole on a corner and in that moment my life fell into place. I began San Madera Police Academy that fall and left the loneliness of all those early years behind me. I'd found my work and friends who loved me.

"You'll go far," my counselor told me. "You're

tough and bright and you make the right moves always. You're a wisp of wind with a will of steel.

"But, Katie, more than that, you've got compassion and you're fair—you deal an even hand and you care about your fellow man. A cop without compassion isn't fit to wear the badge."

He'd been right—about the first part anyway—and, I hope, about the rest. I'd risen fast, especially for a woman—through the ranks of street patrol, then on into detectives.

I'd loved the contact with the public the uniform brought with it—the hustle-bustle, hurly-burly life of the thin blue line that stands up front.

But better yet I loved the precision of investigation—the pumping, throbbing high you feel when the pieces come together and you know you've got the bastard nailed.

My steady record of convictions over many months showed I was not some shooting star, lighting up the heavens for a moment, then shattering into tiny chips that briefly winked before they died forever in the darkness.

The brass took notice and promotion quickly followed. Head of burglary first, then of robbery, and, two years ago, the second spot on homicide.

Not that we had all that much to do. San Madera was medium size though growing fast—a little laid-back city with a heavy rural flavor, sometimes playing the part of the sophisticate but more often falling back on its country roots.

Neighbors still knew neighbors and often left their doors unlocked at night, and a crime of any magnitude impacted severely on their trusting psyches. Still, like any other town, we were not immune to murder.

Late last fall my head detective took retirement and left his badge and gun for a simple cabin in the High Sierra, where a silver creek ran freely through the meadow and a riding horse or two stood in the corral.

I was named chief of homicide—the first time a woman had ever held that post in this department—and I knew that I was home at last. I felt my life was touched with sundust sparkle that would never fade away.

Grumbling and head-butting rumbled through division when the promotion was announced. Some believed themselves more qualified—others simply thought a woman couldn't cut it.

No matter. I overrode it and overlooked it and, after a little while, it all died down. Or seemed to, anyway.

A crazy business, all in all, but I held no regrets after nearly eighteen years. A crazy business, that's for sure. It can make you feel like Christmas morning. Or it can break your heart.

A young officer woke me up at six. I called downstairs—nothing going on. In just one hour the first band of detectives would show up. I checked the roster—Carl Mungers and Dan Kent were both early men this week.

Carl's an old hand on homicide and my best buddy on the force while Dan's a sharp detective trainee who's fast learning how to catch the bad guys. The three of us would concentrate on Billy while Steve Darrow, the other veteran on my squad, would work on older cases needing to go forward—both the missing and the dead. Bigger cities in California have a separate missing persons unit, but in our department suspicious disappearances are handled by homicide. Sometimes, the logic in this grim coupling becomes all too obvious.

I wanted to phone home but knew Jonathan was still asleep. I'd call later, when he and Tommy were having breakfast.

Jon was used to this by now—he didn't much like it but he was used to it. He'd been up the down side of the mountain with me years before, while I worked the morning watch for months on end, while I was a vice cop playing dirty games with Johns and he never knew when I'd walk through the door or how long I'd stay once I got there.

When I made detective, my life became a normal one again, but I wanted homicide and I grabbed the chance when it came along and bought the long hours, unsettled schedule, and the grueling wearing work right along with it.

We'd talked about it but never really worked it out. It rode along beside us with raw, uneven edges grating on us—flaring up from time to time, then disappearing underground like some silent partner in our lives. Except we always knew that it was there.

Like last night, when I'd left to come down here, and at the breakfast table only yesterday morning.

He'd been sitting there, reading the local paper and slowly sipping his coffee, when he suddenly glanced up at me and said, "Stay home today, Katharine. Look at this morning"—he'd gestured toward the sunlight streaming through the window and making little squares of light on the patterned tablecloth—"it's far too nice a day to stay inside. We'll take a drive, stop somewhere for an early country lunch, be back when Tommy comes from school."

I'd smiled, thinking how very appealing his proposal sounded but also thinking he was only teasing.

"You know I'd love to, but I can't. Got a job to do, unfortunately."

His mood had changed abruptly. He'd gotten up from the chair, tightening the tan housecoat around his waist, and moved his lanky frame toward the kitchen counter, where he poured another cup of coffee.

"You've got a job to do only because you choose to do it," he'd told me coldly, winter eyes swinging toward me, meeting mine. "You're shortchanging yourself and me and Tommy when you keep on rushing out this way. Won't you ever see that?"

Taken aback, I'd looked down at the tablecloth and traced the outline of a square while I tried to get my mind in order.

"We've gone through all of this before, Jon. You know my work's important to me, but that doesn't slight you or Tommy in any way."

He'd brought the cup back to the table and set it down, then taken me into the circle of his arms.

"Sorry, Katie, I don't mean to snap just when you're ready to go out. Rotten way to start the day. You're right—we've talked about it all before."

I'd cupped his face between my hands and looked lovingly into those deep gray eyes I knew so well.

"It's okay," I told him, grateful there was to be no fight to follow. "Someday it'll all be different—someday I'll get tired of chasing crooks, I'm sure. Till that time comes, we do all right, don't we?"

"Sure, Katie, sure we do," and we'd held each other tightly, kissing like the lovers we'd been so long ago.

A DESPERATE CALL

And still were, when things were going right between us.

Strangely, perhaps, I'd never felt guilty about my commitment to my work—he'd known how much I loved it when he married me. Never, that is, except for that time three years ago when he'd needed me and I hadn't been there. Would it have mattered? Would it have really mattered? I'd always wonder and probably never know.

"Now's not the time to think about that, girl," I warned myself sternly. "You've got other things to put your mind to."

I hoped the day watch commander would hurry on in instead of lingering over home-brewed coffee. I wanted to bring him up to speed on Billy's disappearance before he started roll call and pry as many men as possible from his patrol.

I also hoped Kenny Savitch was in command today. He wasn't one of those crackling intractable street cops who'll buck you just because you wear a gold shield, even though a child's gone missing.

I patted down my face and eyes with water, freshened up my makeup, and brushed my hair back from my face. I felt a whole lot better now. Outside, the mobile food truck blew its horn and I hurried down to buy some breakfast.

The night's heat had intensified and, even at this early hour, touched me with a heavy dampness. I wiped my brow and, glancing up, saw the sky had gone from melon-dawn to blue in the past ten minutes. It was that time of year when night turns into day and doesn't miss a beat. Ken came up the walk as I ate my scrambled eggs.

"I heard it on the way in, Katie—come and talk to

me," and he laid a hand across my shoulder as I tossed the breakfast tray away.

We agreed I could have five men, his choice.

"I'll be at roll call, Kenny," I told him. "I'd like to brief the entire watch, if that's okay with you."

It was, and I walked back upstairs to wait for Kent and Mungers.

They arrived within two minutes of each other. Mungers, like Savitch, had heard about Billy on the radio. Kent had heard a child was missing but knew none of the details. I filled them in on everything I had so far, then we divvied up the work.

Carl would go straight to Willow Elementary, Dan would organize the volunteers and hand them over to patrol, and I'd pick up the flyers.

I called back to Kent as I grabbed my jacket.

"There's another Schuyler—first name Mark—somewhere here in town. He's Billy's uncle. Run a check on him while I'm gone. I'll find out if there's any more local family when I see the parents."

"Right, boss lady, and hey, take it easy there—you're looking just a little frazzled."

"You're still wet behind the ears, Kent," I shot back good-naturedly. "See how you stand up to a hard day's night when you're an old-timer like myself."

I looked at his fresh young face and eager eyes and grinned inwardly. He reminded me of a large and rollicking puppy dog—always enthusiastic, always aiming to please.

With the face of an all-American boy carried by broad shoulders and an erect stance, he was able to gain the confidence of most victims and more than one crook without hardly even trying. They found they loved to trust him.

I walked downstairs and pushed the roll call door. Savitch was alerting the troops to a "hot-prowl" suspect operating in the south end. I waited till he stopped talking and beckoned me up front.

I saw the looks and heard the whispers the appearance of a woman officer, especially one of rank, always brings. It bothered some, but it didn't bother me—I just let it roll away.

Let them have their fun, I thought. Where the heck's the harm?

The whispering stopped and they got serious when I began to talk.

I told them what I'd told my own men and cautioned them to keep their eyes open for the missing boy, to take a closer look than usual at every kid they saw. And to talk up Billy to everyone they met on their daily beat.

"Keep his name out there—dig and dig some more," I urged.

As I left the room, my mind racing far ahead, a young cop rose and followed me.

"Ma'am, may I speak with you?"

His respectful tone marked him as a rookie fresh out of the academy. His look pegged him, too—dark hair in a buzz-saw cut, eager serious eyes, the faint first show of a mustache. I hid a smile and nodded.

"I might've seen that little boy, ma'am. I finished watch a bit late yesterday and when I changed and got out of here it was almost four-thirty. I was driving home and I saw a kid with a blue striped T-shirt running, well, more like skipping, down the sidewalk.

"This same kid—or at least it looked like him—

came to my house a few days ago selling candy for the Cub Scouts. I bought some peanut bars and when he signed the receipt, I saw the last name was 'Schuyler.' I remember 'cause my brother-in-law up north is named Schuyler and you don't hear that name too often."

I asked him where and when he'd seen the boy and he told me on Marsh Street between Hollis and Willow, no later than twenty to five.

I was silent. I waited. Then I spoke carefully, rounding off each word.

"Let your mind go into slow motion. Don't force it but bring back the moment. Are you sure the child was between Hollis and Willow?"

"Absolutely certain, ma'am," the rookie replied firmly. "He was right by that vacant lot where the kids like to play."

"But he wasn't on the lot?"

"Oh, no, he was going right past it, eastbound on the south side, in kind of a hurry."

"Was anyone with him or near him?"

"No, ma'am, no one."

"Thanks, kiddo—thanks a lot. I'll fire off a flyer of the Schuyler boy to you later on this morning. Flash me a message if you can give a positive ID."

I waited till he walked away, then I spun around and slapped the wall hard with my open hand. My palm throbbed but I didn't care.

"Damn!" I exploded gleefully, "damn!"

The best clue yet and it had come from one of our own. Billy *hadn't* walked north on Hollis after all. Instead, when he reached the crossing at Hollis and Marsh, he'd decided to walk straight ahead rather than turn toward home. Why?

My stomach clutched, not in nervousness but in anticipation. The case had escalated slightly—a small break had come, a tiny opening had been made in the impasse of the past few hours. We were finally moving forward.

There was something else, too—the candy sales. Tommy, my own son, had sold candy last week for the same Cub troop. I'd thought all orders were due last Friday, but maybe I was wrong—maybe Billy had still been selling on Monday afternoon.

Had he decided, on a sudden whim, to try to score a few more sales before dinnertime? I'd find out from the Schuylers.

I picked up the flyers and drove to Hollis Place. The house was a white two-story with five brick steps leading to the front door. A cool green lawn edged with newly leafed trees sloped to the street.

Its grass was freshly mowed, its shrubbery clipped and shaped. The whole was honed to a cold perfection. I slung my pocketbook across my shoulder and started up the walk.

Schuyler waited on the top step, looking down at me.

"Anything?"

"Nothing major, no—just a few things I'd like to go over with you and your wife."

We went inside, where Joyce Schuyler stood stiffly in the hallway, like a cardboard figure in some motionless display. I went to her and looked into her eyes, then put my arm around her and drew her to me.

"I know," I said, "I know so very well what you must be feeling." My own eyes misted as I dropped my arm and turned around.

"I've just found out that Billy was spotted on the

other side of Hollis from my house, heading toward Willow. Have you any idea what he might've been doing there, where he was going?"

My eyes were clear now, my voice steady. Personal emotions were out of place here—I could keep her calm only by staying calm myself.

Nothing but puzzlement registered on their faces.

"I don't know," Schuyler answered. "I've no idea. Joyce?"

"No, I don't either. He wouldn't have come home that way and I can't think of anyone he knows who lives close enough to there that he'd think he could go to play and still be home in time for dinner."

The puzzlement had changed to fresh anxiety.

"What about the candy sales?" I asked.

"He finished Friday," Joyce Schuyler told me. "He had to turn the orders in at meeting that afternoon."

Damn, a dead end there. I'd pictured the boy knocking on the doors of strangers, stepping across a hostile threshold, hearing the door lock tight behind him. . . .

I asked about the husband's brother and if there were any other family here in town.

No, she said, only Mark and, of course, Nadine.

I'd want to see them both, I said, and told her I'd call Nadine later on that day.

Schuyler moved forward, coming within inches of my face. The haughtiness, the tight-reined self-control, had returned in full measure and were apparent in his look.

"What happens now, Detective?"

He knew I'd tell him the next step in the search—what he really wanted to hear was that I'd find Billy.

I couldn't give him that answer. Soothing reassurance may be proper in the middle of a long dark night when a case is only six hours old, but it's got no place when night turns into day and the only clues so far have led me nowhere.

I recalled that reassurance and wondered if they'd bring up my promise that Billy would be home by dawn. They didn't—they probably never had believed it.

"The search expands," I explained. "Radio, TV, and the papers will play the story hard today and we'll start to get response. Sure, the calls won't all be good ones, but some of them may help. And remember this—if anyone phones you, don't try to handle it yourself. Get in touch with us and let us do it."

I gave them this warning because kidnap-for-ransom was a real possibility, especially since Schuyler was a banker, though personally I'd just about discounted it. A kidnapper doesn't usually wait sixteen hours before laying out his wish list.

I turned to go, anxious to get back to the station, but then I remembered something else.

"You told the sergeant, Mrs. Schuyler, that you weren't sure what shoes Billy had on. Has it come back to you yet?"

"No, but I think they were blue sneakers, very faded, because I looked in his closet and those are gone."

Satisfied, I turned again and as I did so, I caught the look on Schuyler's face as he listened to his wife. It was either impatience or disgust. I wondered which and then I wondered why.

CHAPTER THREE

Driving to the station, I reflected that the Schuylers hadn't asked the question that always comes sooner or later. Some people ask it right up front while others wait, fearing that by putting the thought into words they'll give it a grim reality. They use different phrases but the meaning never changes: "Is he dead?"

No, they hadn't asked and I was glad—let it lie unspoken just a little longer.

A hot breeze entered through my rolled-down window and blue haze, sheer as gauze, hung against the mountains in the distance. Heat shimmered on the road in front of me and a gray cat fast-danced its way across the tarmac. I was looking at a glowing sun-wrapped California day.

Here's what always strikes me—the incongruity of an obscenity played out against a tranquil set. It doesn't track, it rocks the senses, it's surreal, but it happens all the time and the beauty of the background magnifies the horror.

A flash-shot suddenly filled my mind, crowding in from some forgotten corner—a memory of a day like this one several years ago, when a small plane lost its engine and crashed in a flowering garden.

Purple iris and pink sweet william flanked paths of

golden pebbles littered with torn body parts and bits of burned-off clothing. A piece of tail section dug deep into the ground and stood upright beside a marble fountain in which a figurine poured water in a bowl.

If the plane had crashed on a vacant, weed-filled lot, if the sun hadn't shown quite so brightly, it would've been just as horrible, yes, but at the same time more believeable, easier to accept as real.

Just as a day of raging storms and angry thunder would've been in keeping with the nightmare of the disappearance of a little boy, not a day like this one, that promised only sweet clear light and calm and goodness.

Kent was busy at his desk when I walked in, his boyish face serious, his dark hair falling on his forehead, as he concentrated on his work. A half-filled coffee cup stood beside him and I felt the urge to get some for myself.

Later, kiddo, later, I silently advised. As a reward.

I gave him a pile of flyers and told him to take a break and get them out to every unit in the field.

"Right away, Kate. And, oh yeah—Carl's coming back from the school around eleven. By the way, we ran a check on the uncle. Nothing. And he spells it M-A-R-C, not with a "k." I laid his driver's license printout on your desk in case you need the address."

I'd see it later but something else needed doing first. I phoned Maud Divans and she answered on the third ring and told me to come right over. She opened the door immediately and stood there, cool and crisp in a raw silk yellow dress.

"Is this the little boy you saw yesterday?"

My heart pounded as I handed her the flyer and I could feel my eyes fix steadily on her face.

She answered with absolute certainty.

"Oh, yes, Detective, yes it is—no doubt at all."

I sighed softly with relief.

"I thought it would be, but now we know for sure."

I got more good news when I reached the station—the rookie cop swore the face on the flyer was the same little boy who'd sold him candy a few days earlier.

Mungers walked in, his large plain face looking solemn, his clothes rumpled and hanging badly on his body. His big frame didn't carry suits well and the slight gut starting to appear above the belt didn't help matters either.

I looked at the honest blue eyes, the short blond hair standing up like straw sticks, and thought I couldn't have a better partner. Or a better friend.

He wasn't happy. He'd come back from the school with nothing to show for his effort—nothing, not even the tiny whisper of a lead.

"The staff knows zip as far as anyone snatching him. No strangers seen hangin' around, no problems of any sort connected with him."

"I'm fading, Carl," I told him. Breakfast and those three hours of sleep seemed a long, long time ago. "I'll work through lunch, then go home and grab a couple before I talk with the boy's uncle and sister tonight. Handle it and do me a favor—call every hour or so just to keep me current. If I'm asleep and it's imporant, have Jon wake me."

I left my desk and headed out the door. I knew the coming night could be longer than the last one if things began to break, so I'd take my sleep when I could get it.

Less than twenty-four hours ago, I'd driven this same road, looking forward to working in my garden and playing after-dinner games with Tommy. Less then twenty-four hours ago, Billy Schuyler was still in school, waiting for the final bell to ring.

If only I could turn back the clock, I thought, and make things happen differently. If I could've kept him in my yard. If, if, if. . . .

And then I thought about another if—the one I'd lived with for so long and couldn't push back in my mind.

If I'd stayed at home or worked a normal job like other people's wives, would Jon have had that breakdown several years ago? If I'd been around a little more, could I have seen it coming and gotten him some help before it was too late? If I'd been there with him instead of chasing crooks—sometimes twenty hours a day—would it have even come at all?

I'd noticed little changes, sure. My wisecracking Jon became remote, withdrawn or, at other times, unnaturally aggressive. But I was on a heavy case, working at a white-hot pace to solve it, and I rushed on by— I failed to stop and ask was something really wrong.

And then one winter afternoon I walked into my house and found him sitting there, staring silently into space. He wouldn't answer when I spoke, he wouldn't focus on my face. I found out later he didn't even know that I was there.

They diagnosed his illness as severe depression, brought on by overwork and groundless worry and many other unnamed things. He'd lived in a fragile world of high intent, and when he failed to meet his own expectations—even when the failure was apparent only to himself—that world eroded.

He was hospitalized for several months and when he came back home, we tried to live together once again, gently groping toward each other, tenderly and carefully striving to rebuild what we'd once had.

But somehow it wasn't working smoothly, or at least it wasn't like it'd been before. He suddenly resented my involvement with the force, my commitment to a job I truly loved. And this I did not understand, for I was doing nothing different from what I'd always done, since long before we met.

Jon had worked at home from the first week we were married—I'd always been the one who left the house each day. By the time we met I'd been a cop for several years and he knew I loved it and didn't want to give it up. His architectural practice was just starting out and he decided it'd be as easy to set up shop at home as to rent a suite of pricey offices downtown.

"Besides," he told me happily, "I won't have to be a part-time daddy when our children come along."

When he left the hospital, he set the pace that suited him—working a little, resting a lot, rebuilding the very core of himself.

Slowly, with counseling and medication, he grew to understand the demons that had hounded him, and one by one they fell away as they were brought into the open and exposed to full bright light.

And then this other—this one about my working—had moved in to replace them.

As I thought about his sickness, the whole of that period of my life flashed through my mind and I remembered, bitterly, how "supportive" several of my fellow officers had been of me as I wrestled with my private pain.

Some cops—not many, but certainly a few—tend to sneer at mental illness because, after all, cracking up is not a macho thing to do, and during Jon's confinement I'd heard ugly snickers and cruelly whispered words about "Katie's crazy old man." I'd walk on by, outwardly oblivious, but inside myself I hurt—I hurt a lot.

That's why I still stiffen when someone asks about him, like Davey Johnson did last night. I'm wary, on my guard, not quite sure until I look into their eyes if I'm with friend or enemy. Are they taunting me or do they really want to know if he's okay?

Also while Jon was away, I became the bitch in heat and had the make put on me more times than I could count. My fellow boys in blue saw me as a vessel of frustration, suffering immeasurably from sexual drought, and thought I'd drop my panties every time the wind began to blow.

"Anyway," the reasoning went, "she's probably never had good fuckin' from that crazy—let me show her how a *real* man can make her feel once he gets her down."

So it'd been a rough three months, on several fronts at once, but we'd come through it and out the other side. Only to find this other problem waiting for us.

I turned in the drive and saw Jon walking out to meet me. His face was grim and his eyes scanned mine with a look I couldn't read.

"Here we go again, right?" he asked me challengingly. "You're out on loan to all the rest of the world for a while."

"Not now, Jon, please. This is a tough one—nothing's breaking anywhere—and I've got to get some rest if I'm to do any good here."

"Kate, I'm sick of it"—he grabbed my arm and turned me toward him—"I'm sick of long hours, you gone, our boy running around without a mother half the time."

The sleep could wait—I needed to clear some air here. "Not fair and not true, Jon. I'm home a lot. Murder doesn't happen on a daily basis—at least not yet, not in this town. And you knew what I was before you married me—it didn't seem to bother you much then."

I could feel my face flushing hot with anger at what I perceived as purposefully hurtful distortions of the truth on his part. My tiredness dissipated as adrenaline filled my being.

He banged his fist down hard on the porch railing.

"I guess I probably thought you'd get tired of it— give it all up after you'd played cops and robbers for a while, especially once we'd had a kid. But you didn't, and each year it just gets worse. Tommy misses you. He's growing up—he needs you here more. But no, you can't see that. You had to go for homicide, which keeps you from him even more."

Surprisingly, I felt my anger lessen and I laid my hand lovingly along his cheek.

"You're blowing all this way out of proportion, Jon. Stop and think, for my sake, and you'll see it's no way near as bad as you're making it out to be. It'll all settle into place if you'll just let it and not ride on it so hard. Tommy's fine, just fine. He's proud of what I do—I've heard him brag about me to his friends."

"You're deluding yourself, Kate," he told me in a

steady tone. "The simplistic answer won't fix this one."

"Well, if it won't, at least let's let it rest for tonight. Jon, a little boy is missing—a little boy like our Tommy—and I've got to find him before he's harmed. Surely our personal problems are small compared to that."

He looked at me a moment without speaking, then turned and went into the house. A moment later, I heard the sound of a TV baseball game coming from the den.

It will pass, I thought to myself as I wearily climbed the stairs. He'll settle down and it will pass like always, or at least lie low again.

I napped for several hours, till Tommy touched my shoulder, gently shaking me awake. When he saw my eyes open, he climbed on top of me and bounced me up and down, his wiry little body springing easily from the mattress.

"Play, Mom?"

"Sorry, Tommy, not tonight—I've still got to look for Billy." His face grew shadowed, but he said nothing, just turned away. I pushed my hands beneath his arms and rocked him backward, forward, then swung him off the bed. His mood lightened and he ran laughing from the room.

I dressed and phoned the Schuylers and a strange voice answered and told me he was Joyce Schuyler's brother, Aaron Carter. He'd driven down from Stockton when he heard about Billy.

Yes, he said, Nadine was there waiting for me. I told him I'd be over within the hour.

I ate quickly with Jon and Tommy, my mind already

walking out the door. The atmosphere was cool but no longer hostile and I believed the crisis had passed. I left the house and once again drove toward Hollis Place, as the first full day since Billy's disappearance was ending. I watched its softening shadows reach toward twilight.

As I turned the corner, I saw two girls eighteen or so standing talking on the sidewalk. When I drew closer, their expressions told me they weren't just talking—they were arguing heatedly. Anger and defiance moved across their faces.

The one facing me was a petite pretty kid with translucent skin and a long blond ponytail. As I passed by, the second girl turned at the sound of the motor.

She had dark curly hair that rimmed a face of petulant insolence and the eyes, almost black like the hair, stared at me boldly. A full-lipped mouth was richly reddened with lipstick. She wore a red blouse over white shorts and held her body in an arrogant set. The sensuality, even from this distance, couldn't be missed.

She was probably way too old for it, but I'd seen younger versions of her time and time again, seated at the desk of our juvenile detective. They were products of an attitude of indulgent sensitivity on their parents' part—parents who listened closely to their wants and catered heavily to their whims, but failed to impose the loving discipline so needed by a teen. So they pushed the limits in a hedonistic gorging and sometimes went a little bit too far.

I wouldn't want to be the mama raising that one, I thought. I'm looking at a lot of trouble.

I parked by the curb and glanced toward the steps. Schuyler wasn't waiting for me this time. When I rang the bell another man opened up the door and introduced himself as Aaron Carter.

I went inside and he led me to a living room that overlooked the cool front lawn. Joyce Schuyler was seated on the sofa while her husband stood beside the fireplace, one arm resting on the mantelpiece.

He was infused with anger.

"I can't believe you're doing enough, Detective—it shouldn't take this long at all. Are you damn sure you're touching all the bases, doing everything you can to find my son?"

I'd been expecting this. Anger usually follows grief for those left waiting when a person turns up missing. By focusing this anger on me, the man could convince himself the only reason Billy wasn't home was that I simply wasn't working hard enough. If he could somehow make me do even more than I was doing, we'd find Billy and the nightmare would end.

I nodded slowly and answered quietly.

"Everything, sir—everything possible. We're working 'round the clock. It just takes time, that's all."

I saw Joyce Schuyler watching her husband and a look of—yes, I could call it anger, too—shot from eyes that suddenly sparkled hotly. But this anger wasn't directed at me—it was aimed toward him.

Then she rose and came to me and the anger mellowed, disappeared, and was replaced by warmth. Her hand at first pat-patted mine in a nervous gesture, but then it tightened in a firm sure grip that hinted at an inner strength I hadn't guessed existed.

"We know you are, Miss Harrod, we know you are. It's just that it's so terrible waiting hour after hour with nothing at all happening, seeing it over and over again on the news."

"Don't watch the news anymore," I said. "Turn it off, stay away from it. When something happens, you'll hear it first from me."

I asked for Nadine.

"She went next door," the mother answered. "She's been here all afternoon and she was feeling nervous and cooped up. She's young but she's just as worried about Billy as the rest of us. I'll get her for you."

But she didn't need to. Before Joyce Schuyler could reach the phone, a door at the rear of the room opened and a full-lipped, dark-haired girl wearing a red blouse over white shorts walked forward. This was fifteen-year-old Nadine?

My surprise didn't show, but I *was* surprised, caught off guard, recognizing her as the girl on the sidewalk. I'd never in a lifetime have picked Nadine as Billy's sister or the daughter of these parents.

She didn't fit. Her obvious sexuality jarred. She was a splash of gaudy brightness against a pale set, of razzle-dazzle in a muted household.

And besides that, she didn't even look like the other three. Her eyes, hair, bones, and coloring were all her own.

I wondered if the Schuylers knew what they had here or if they believed she was sweet innocence of youth. I felt they probably misread her, for I knew that on two other points, at least, the mother's perception of her daughter differed vastly from my own—the girl I'd seen arguing with her friend had been neither nervous nor the least bit worried.

She moved toward me.

"Hi, I'm Nadine. Are you the lady who wants to see me?"

A DESPERATE CALL

She spoke before her parents could start to introduce us. She didn't smile as she looked at me.

"That's right, Nadine—I'm Detective Harrod. I'd like to talk to you about Billy."

We sat across from each other, separated by a small coffee table. She eyed her nails and waited for me to begin.

"When did you last see Billy, honey?"

"Yesterday morning, when he left for school. I saw him first when he got up and then I heard the door slam when he went out while I was dressing."

"What about during the day?"

"No, I never do. My school isn't anywhere near his and after school I went to the library and Billy never goes there."

I asked her if she had any idea where her brother might be found. No, she said, she didn't—how could she possibly know a thing like that?

She edged forward on the chair, obviously anxious to leave. I sensed no concern, just impatience and a slight boredom with this whole procedure.

I tossed a verbal curveball.

"Nadine, what kind of little boy is Billy?"

I wasn't so anxious to learn about Billy as to find out how she perceived him.

She hunched her shoulders forward and stared at me, trying to figure out why I'd ask this question.

"Nothing special. I mean, not good or bad, just like all little boys, I guess. He can be a real pest sometimes, though."

I think the truth was she never paid him much attention, except when he got in her way—just a small annoyance scooting past.

I told her to call me if she thought of anything to

help me out. She ignored my words and glanced sideways at her father.

"I'm going out for a while. Okay, Dad?"

"Not tonight, Missy. Stay home."

He spoke sharply and I looked quickly from one to the other.

What's going on here? I wondered.

She started to retort, then stopped, tightened her lips and left the room without another word. A few moments later, an upstairs door slammed shut. I was sure of one thing more about Nadine—no matter how sexually mature she might appear, her emotions were pure fifteen.

I turned toward Schuyler and saw a face of fury. None of your damn business, his look told me when he caught me watching.

"I'd like to use your phone," I said, "to call your brother."

Marc Schuyler lived about a half mile away, on Morro Street, in a white clapboard bungalow with a short front walk and a driveway shared with the neighbor on the right. The houses on the block were small but neat. Plaster ducks mock-paraded on close-clipped lawns, marching toward bird baths with cerulean-blue bowls.

I walked up two wooden steps, my heel almost catching in a crack, and knocked loudly on the door. As I knocked, a feisty barking terrier, stiff-legged and bouncing, rounded the corner and eyed me furiously.

"Quiet, Jackie," a voice called from inside and Marc Schuyler opened the door.

"Hey, there—let me put him away. I meant to get him in before you came," and he grabbed the dog with both hands and shut him in a room inside the house. The barking didn't stop, but it became muffled, more hesitant.

"That's Jackie Day. He's okay with me, but he can be a nuisance around strangers. I'm Marc and you're Detective Harrod? A real lady detective just like on TV?"

His mocking eyes took in my legs, my face, my body. I ignored the look, but beneath the surface two emotions tangled. I rebelled against his brazenness, but at the same time I felt a musky warmth, thick and strong, suffuse me. I could feel its heat rising to my face. Unsettled and confused, I backed away.

"Yes, I'm Detective Harrod. Odd name for a dog, isn't that?"

"It's a long, long story. Come on inside and tell me about Billy."

If Nadine had seemed alien to the rest of her family, neither did Marc Schuyler take after his older brother. He was sandy-haired, blue-eyed, outgoing, and probably no more than thirty years old. With his tan complexion and broad shoulders, I took him for a bit of a jock and a framed photo of him holding a surfboard told me I was right.

"I was hoping *you* could tell *me* something about Billy, Mr. Schuyler."

"No, ma'am, no, I can't—no more than I told that cop who came around last night. I haven't seen Billy in nearly a week. We don't visit as much as uncles and nephews should and that's the truth of it. I'm just too busy with the real estate . . ."

His voice slowed and stopped. He stared straight ahead at an empty chair, then began to speak again, slowly. The eyes had lost their mocking look.

"I just don't believe this is really happening. I was

sure he'd come home—sure of it. Level with me—something's very wrong, isn't it?"

"I'm afraid it could be. It doesn't look too good right now."

I watched him throw his head forward into cupped hands and I thought I heard a sob. I forgot my warring feelings and my own throat tightened as I felt his grief right along with him. I waited several minutes, then I asked if he lived alone or if there was a wife who might've seen Billy yesterday.

Alone, he told me. He wasn't married.

I'd guessed as much. The bungalow was bachelor-decorated, with dishes stacked in random piles along the kitchen counter and rumpled sheets visible through the open bedroom door.

I saw nothing for me here so I thanked him and quickly left. What had happened in there, I asked myself when I got outside, to touch a sexual nerve and make it quicken, to draw me suddenly and hotly to this man?

I didn't know—the superstuds had always turned me off. But as I recalled that mocking face, I felt the warmth begin to spread again. I shook my head, as if to clear it out of me.

As I drove away, I wondered if Marc Schuyler would call his brother and tell him that, for the first time, I'd laid out in plain words that Billy might not be coming home. I really hoped he wouldn't.

I got to the station about eight o'clock, as darkness began to move down on the street. Mungers met me at the stairhead, coffee mug in hand.

"You've got troubles, Kate. The kid's old man's

been on to the lieutenant about you handling this case. You better go see Morris."

"I saw it coming, Carl—the bastard gave me early warning."

What a prick, I thought to myself as I walked away, as if I don't have enough on my plate right now without you stirring up this crap to hold me back.

I headed for the lieutenant's office and could see Morris sitting at his desk waiting for me. He was a prissy little man who'd look more at home in the pulpit than behind the right end of a gun. I'd had few dealings with him so I didn't know if he was good at backing up his men or liked to feed them to the lions.

"Did Carl tell you about Schuyler, Kate?" He smoothed his wispy mustache with one finger as he spoke.

"He told me. Was the complaint about a specific act of mine or was it just because I wear panty hose and have a monthly period?"

He reddened and shifted slightly in his seat. I could see this kind of talk unnerved him.

"Don't get hostile, Kate. And yes, it was the woman thing. He felt a man would push much harder. He wanted you removed."

"So what did you tell him, Lieutenant? Did you back me?"

I knew I was on the edge of insubordination, but I was steaming. The last thing I needed now was an attack from Billy's father met by spineless reaction from my own department. I didn't want my energy drained away by side issues of little import—I needed every bit of it to focus on the case.

"Of course I backed you, Kate, all the way down

the line. I told him there was simply no question of anyone else taking over—you'd remain in charge."

I relaxed and smiled a little.

"How did he take that?"

"He said he'd heard those words before and then he slammed the phone down."

"Right," I said, "he heard them from me a little while ago. Too bad he didn't bother to believe them."

I looked down at Morris and thought he had more backbone than I'd given him credit for.

"Thanks, Lieutenant—thanks for the support."

He dismissed me with an embarrassed wave and I walked back to my desk. Mungers passed me with an empty cup.

"I'm going for a refill," he called out. Then he jerked his head toward Morris. "What went on in there? Did you come out okay?"

"Sure I came out okay," I said jokingly. "You're not getting rid of me just yet."

He gave a wave behind him and I watched him walk away and thought about how much I liked him and depended on him. He didn't say a lot, but he was solid and reliable and oh so good at catching crooks. He'd been in line for my promotion but never let me know his disappointment at not getting it. That wouldn't have been his style.

The fact that I was female didn't seem to bother Carl either or, if it did, he typically kept quiet about it. He worked right along beside me and called me "Kate," not "babe" or "doll."

He soon returned with the coffee and sipped it slowly while he filled me in on the recent flood of calls. Some were washouts from the start while others,

A DESPERATE CALL 59

though a whole lot sounder, still failed to deliver what we wanted.

When he'd finished, he fiddled with his cup, eased his heavy frame forward in the chair, and stared at me with narrowed eyes.

"You okay, Kate?" he asked with genuine concern. "You look a little haggard and I'd say it's not just from the case."

"Fine, Carl," I began, and then I shook my head as if to ask myself why I was lying. Why should I even try to fool him anyway? He could read me like the good old book—always could ever since we'd met busting hookers many moons ago—and he'd been my ally through every trouble that had looked me up and come my way.

Physically, the chemistry was nonexistent. We could've lain together naked under waving fronds of palm, two people stranded on the lushest, most deserted desert isle, and nothing would've happened. But trusting friends was something else. He was the understanding brother I'd never had and always wanted.

"Ah, hell, no." I threw my hand up and shook my head again. "It's the same old tune playing out again, Carl. Jon's on my case about the job."

"I thought that had gone to bed awhile ago."

"It had. But you know it gets back out of bed after sleeping for a while, and it seems those sleeps are getting shorter all the time."

"Whaddya going to do about it?"

"Same as always. Try to make him see some reason and wait until it goes away."

"Want me to try to talk with him, Kate?" Reflectively he pushed his thumbnail against his bottom teeth.

I knew how well that would sit with Jon and vehemently I told him no.

"He'd resent it like all hell, Carl. I appreciate the offer but he'd never let another cop try to change his mind for him, especially since cops are what the problem's all about. No, we've got to work it out ourselves."

"Just remember, Kate, I'm here if you need me," he said quietly. "I know what it's like for you—I know what's going on."

His obvious concern touched me deeply, bringing tears of gratitude to my eyes.

"You mean because of Lila?"

"Yeah, because of Lila." He pushed himself up from the chair and stood a moment, staring at some unseen spot behind my head.

"Where's Dan?" I asked, getting back to business, "In the cot room?"

"Right. I'm about to wake him and go back there myself."

I saw his tired eyes and slumping stance and knew he was beat, the length and pace of the case starting to wear him down.

"Don't do it," I told him. "You two go on home— I'll spend the night here and see you guys tomorrow."

When they'd gone, I read their summaries of the day's events as well as the notes I'd made myself. Where was it, the thing that I was looking for? Had I missed something somewhere? Was there an answer, or at least a clue, staring at me that I didn't see?

Well, if there was, I couldn't find it. The notes in front of me told the whole story. We were going by the book, following procedure, doing everything we *should* do in a missing persons case. But it didn't get the job done. We were stymied.

Jon was waiting for me on the porch. "You'd better come inside," he said. "And sit down."

His tone raised a tremble in my stomach and, wondering, I followed him. I somehow knew with certainty this didn't have to do with what had gone on earlier. When we reached the hall, he turned and put his arms around me.

"Tommy's been picked up for stealing," he told me softly. "When they found out who he was, they called me to come on down and get him."

The thefts had started several weeks before, but we hadn't known till tonight. Barry Johns had caught our son taking candy from his drugstore shelf and had let him off lightly with a warning.

But then he caught him once again a few days later and then again this afternoon, but this time the take wasn't just a pack of Tootsie Rolls—it was a pricey little penknife, pearl-handled and gleaming in its newness. Johns had called the cops, who'd called my husband.

"He's willing to let it lie if we get some counseling for him and keep him out of there."

I felt a coldness in my heart, a sense of failure, a dread of unnamed things to come. He'd known better, he'd been taught different, so why?

"Where is he now?" I asked quietly.

"In his room. He won't talk to me about it."

Together we walked upstairs and found a round-eyed, trembling boy sitting still and waiting for us. I kept it low-key, even though I longed to scream at him in frightened anger.

"What happened, Tommy?"

He inched backward on the bed and pulled a small stuffed dog, worn thin and tattered, tight beside him. I sat down and took his hand.

"Tell me why."

"Because I wanted to." The voice was small but firm.

"That's not a good enough reason. You know it's wrong. You've always known that."

He looked up at me and then at Jon, and on his face I saw a sullenness, a strong defiance, that I'd never seen before. I felt alarm engulf me, and then the moment passed and he began to cry. I took him in my arms and held him and rocked him back and forth.

"I know it's wrong," he sobbed. "I don't know why I did it, but I won't do it anymore."

"No, you won't," I told him. "I really and truly do believe you won't."

I kissed him and then Jon came and took him from me and I left the two of them alone. It would be all right, I told myself, but a small doubt trailed behind me, troubling me and tearing at my soul.

I began to get out paper plates and napkins. I wanted us to be together, to do something that was fun, especially after the turmoil we'd been through. With my son and husband still upstairs, I walked outside and fired the grill for supper.

When it was hot enough, I called to them "we're going to have a picnic," and we cooked chicken and hot dogs and sat cross-legged around a checkered tablecloth spread in a corner of our yard.

Tommy smeared mustard on his shirt and Jon

A DESPERATE CALL 63

dropped a weiner in his lap. I chided both of them good-humoredly and they stuck their tongues out in unison, then rocked backward on their outstretched hands and laughed.

I reached over and pushed Tommy on his shoulder, so that he lost his balance and tumbled sideways on the grass. We wrestled with each other, rolling over and over again, till the constant surge of laughter exhausted us and made us stop.

Night dew began to fall and the sun lowered behind the trees, taking the warmth of day with it. We gathered up the tablecloth and I put out the fire.

Jon took my hand and we turned to go inside, with Tommy bouncing several steps ahead of us. Just for these past few blessed moments, I could almost pretend that things were normal and today's events had never happened.

The weather cooled abruptly the following day, dropping twenty degrees within a two-hour period. There were other, less welcome, changes also. The search party lost half its manpower as officers from the task force returned to regular duty. A few civilians kept up the hunt for a short time, but soon they, too, went back to their daily jobs.

Carl, Dan, and myself continued to check out any leads, but by midafternoon of the second day, these had dwindled to only one or two every few hours.

The week passed quickly and Monday came again. But even though the pace had slowed, Billy never left my mind and each day I called on the people who lived in the houses on Marsh east of Hollis and tried in vain to jog their minds a little harder.

Then, on a windy day in late April—ten days after

Billy disappeared—a call came in that was different from the rest.

A woman in Alto, a small town about twenty miles from us, had seen a boy in the backyard of a farmhouse near the county line.

Carol Hart told me she passed the house at least twice a day, on her way to and from work. She also told me she thought a man in his midfifties lived there alone. That is, he'd lived alone till yesterday.

On her way to work Wednesday morning, Mrs. Hart saw a young boy standing near the back porch. She thought no more about him till she reached the office. Then she saw Billy's picture in a paper ten days' old and remembered a child had disappeared.

Curious, she slowed as she passed the house on the way home, but the doors were shut and the yard was empty. Her interest grew and she decided to keep her eyes open each time she drove that way.

Going to work this morning, she saw the man looking out the side window, but no sign of the little boy. Because she was suffering from a spring cold, Mrs. Hart left her office early and drove past the farmhouse a little after two o'clock.

The boy was playing in the backyard. She again slowed her car, stared at him, jotted notes on a piece of paper, and called us just as soon as she got home.

The physical description fit Billy to a "T," but that wasn't all—the boy in the yard was wearing a blue-striped shirt. I asked her for the address and she told me 29 River Creek Road and the name on the mailbox was "Painter." I thanked her and said we'd get on it right away.

"Let's roll," I called to Kent and Mungers, and the three of us drove to River Creek Road.

I saw the house first. It was Early American, set fairly close to the road with a stand of trees rising behind it and a ploughed field at its side.

We parked our car far down the road and approached cautiously on foot. No one was on the porch, no one was in the yard. Despite the heat, the door was closed.

I knocked, then stepped quickly to one side, next to Dan and Carl. Our hands tightened on our guns. Steps approached, the door opened, and a man around fifty years old stood on the threshold staring out at us.

"Mr. Painter? I'm Detective Katharine Harrod and these are detectives Kent and Mungers of the San Madera Police Department. May we come in, sir?"

We held out our ID and he looked it over, then invited us inside. As we stepped forward, I saw the boy. He was kneeling on a blue linoleum floor, watching late-afternoon cartoons on TV. His back was to me so I couldn't see his face.

I started toward him, my chest tightening, my fingers flexing nervously against my palm. Then suddenly my heart lurched downward. Even before his head began to turn, I knew we were wrong. This boy wasn't Billy Schuyler.

Painter introduced him as his grandson from Chicago, come to stay with him for a week or so while his mother was hospitalized. He said his name was Johnny Horton, then he showed us year-old snapshots of Painter holding his grandson's hand as he rode a pony at a circus.

There was really no need. Though the boy's size and general description matched Billy's, a close appraisal showed small but obvious differences—eye color, exact height, the presence of freckles on Johnny's face where Billy had none.

We drove back to town in silence, not even making small talk. The lead had been so strong, so promising, and we'd pinned all our hopes upon it. We'd counted on it far too much and now the disappointment drained us, leaving us in emotional turmoil.

When we reached the station, I sent Kent and Mungers home, but I went upstairs to my desk. I needed a moment for myself, a time to be alone.

The next day, an isolated call gave us an address where Billy might be found. The caller sounded drunk, the address checked out bogus. There were no other calls, bona fide or not. He was gone and nothing told us where to look for him.

But all of that was just about to change. On a sun-drenched morning, as the birds trilled their clear, sweet notes and the flowers swayed in gentle dance, a farmer near San Marcos found a body in a shed.

He called the sheriff's department, who then called us. The body appeared to be that of a young boy, probably seven to ten years old. It was dressed in a blue-striped T-shirt, Levi's, and faded low-top sneakers.

Chapter Four

We drove north out of town saying little. We'd share our thoughts later but not right now. San Marcos lay fifteen miles away, in the lonely foothills of the Mariposa mountains just across the county line. The farm itself, three miles from that line, was our jurisdiction. Sheriff's men, as a courtesy, would secure the area till we got there.

The road straight-lined toward San Marcos for eight miles, then curved east-northeast and began a gradual climb. Farmland, ploughed for spring planting, bordered us on either side.

Four miles past the curve, I saw a sheriff's car, then two others, parked across the road near an opening in a fence. Another field, filled with golden grass and purple lupine, stretched behind the fence toward oak-covered hills.

A weathered shed—the only one in sight—stood far back from the road, on the field's eastern edge. Behind the shed, more oaks formed a tiny forest, and at its front door a group of men stood waiting.

Suddenly I tensed. I knew I was on the edge of something terrible. I glanced quickly at Kent and Mungers and their grim faces mirrored the feeling in my heart.

We parked behind the sheriff's car closest to us and cut our engine. A deputy got out and walked back to meet us. He nodded toward the shed. "I gotta tell you, this is not a real pretty one."

We crossed the road and he walked with us, to the opening in the fence.

"Is the farmer up ahead?" I asked.

"Yes, name of Henry Barrows. But he's not the one who found the body after all. He was down here getting ready to plough all this and he had his two little boys with him. They ran ahead to the toolshed and are actually the ones who saw it first."

"What's the weather been like up here?"

"Cold spell the last two weeks or so, just like you've had only cooler because of the hills. At night it's dipped down to the low forties—that's why this isn't even worse than it is. Though, Lord knows, it's bad enough."

We left him at the opening and started through the field, the grasses brushing against our legs as we walked forward. A purple blossom caught my shoelace, breaking near the stem.

The shed was built of aged timber, worn silver-gray by years of mountain winds and violent winter rains. Missing boards left gaps in several places while others spread open at the seams. I could've put a pencil through the softness of the wood.

We nodded to three deputies standing near the doorway. Beneath an oak tree at the edges of the forest, two boys the age of Tommy sat sobbing on the ground. A man in denims and a yellow cap hugged them to him as he knelt beside them on the grass.

We went inside. Sun rays filtered through the cracks and threw a softened light onto the hardened dirt floor and the farm tools stacked against three walls. There were no windows and just the single door.

I stepped forward and the smell engulfed me. Thick, putrid, cloying—unlike any other odor in the world—it filled my nostrils and settled on my skin. Then I saw the body and I forgot about the smell.

It sat propped against the southeast corner, legs straight out in front, its head tilted to the right and resting on a shoulder. Hoes and shovels stood in front of it, their handles leaning back against the walls. A burlap bag tossed loosely on its thighs obscured the lower torso.

We moved forward gingerly and then bent down.

"Oh, Jesus," I heard Carl murmur.

Flesh covered one cheek while the other showed bare bones. Shredded skin hung from neck and chin and touched the T-shirt ribbing while clumps of fine brown hair sprung at random from the skull.

A closed lid concealed the right eye, but the socket on the left was empty. The right hand, like the cheek, was intact and lay palm up. The left showed bones of just two fingers. The other three were missing.

Shrunken flesh inside the clothing let shirt and Levi's hang in loose folds, with little substance to support them. Mounds of nearby droppings confirmed that rats had violated the body after death.

I looked at the faded sneakers, the blue-striped shirt, the bits of soft brown hair, and then I looked away. I felt a sorrow so profound I thought that I would weep. I'd wait for the coroner's report, but in my heart I knew we'd found Billy Schuyler.

Through the door, I saw a black-and-white approaching—one of our cars, not sheriffs.

"Let's go outside," I said to Dan and Carl. When we reached the grass, I turned to them. I felt sick and torn up inside.

"It's him, you know. I have no doubt."

Carl nodded silently, Dan didn't answer.

I looked at him. His eyes were glazed, his face bewildered, his mind unable to function within the reality of the moment. His experience with homicide was limited and he'd never seen a murdered child.

And then, just as I looked away, the words broke suddenly from his mouth and fell in anguished syllables on the silence of the field.

"Jesus Christ, Kate, it's awful. That fuckin' monster. I don't know, I've never seen . . ." He waved his hands in front of him, back and forth in futile gestures. Tears left wetness on his cheeks.

I let him get it out and then I touched his shoulder.

"You'll be all right, Danny. It's always rough with one like this, but you'll be all right. Come on now, we've got work to do."

He steadied and wiped his cheeks with the back of one hand.

Carl spoke.

"Can you guess at the cause of death, Kate?"

"Not even a wild one. You?"

"It's hard to say. No obvious contusions on the skull and no weapon nearby that I spotted. We'll know more about that when we go back inside, though."

"My guess is the coroner won't even know till he finishes his tests," I replied. "It'll probably be several days before anything definite comes out."

I turned back to Kent. I wanted to get him busy.

"Go meet the car that just pulled up and tell them to string tape all the way from the field entrance to fifty feet behind the shed, then radio communications to get the coroner out here. I don't want a word to the press at this point, though."

Barrows and his sons watched me from a distance. I walked toward them and they rose to their feet, a weeping child on either side of a stolid, red-faced man.

"Mr. Barrows, I'm Detective Harrod. I understand your sons found the body."

"That's right—and I don't think they'll forget, ever. They had the day off from school and I brought them along with me. If I'd had any idea what we'd find here, I'd have left them home with their mama."

I asked him to tell me about it.

The three had arrived at the field a little before ten, he said, from their house half a mile away. He'd been late with his ploughing this spring and was anxious to get the ground tilled.

The boys—seven-year-old Doug and eight-year-old Michael—loved to play in the toolshed and ran up the path and through the door before Barrows even left the roadside. A few moments later, as he started through the field, he heard screams and saw the boys running toward him.

"They kept sobbing about a body. I could hardly understand them—they were almost hysterical. I thought they meant a coyote or a mountain lion. They wouldn't even come near the shed so I went to see for myself. As soon as I got inside, I saw it."

"Did you touch or move anything?"

"Oh no, I backed right out—the smell was awful and the boys were still screaming. We went right home and I called sheriff."

"When were you last down here?"

"About three weeks ago. I dropped off some tools

I'd need for planting and made sure vagrants hadn't carried any off since last season."

"Do the boys ever come here by themselves?"

"Never. It's too remote a spot to allow them to play here alone." Again, he put his arms around his sons and drew them close. I bent down.

"Who went inside first?" I asked gently.

"Me," the younger one whispered.

"And I came right behind. We were really both together."

"And who saw the person first?"

"I did," Michael answered.

"Tell me about it if you want to," I said, and I smiled softly into his solemn gray eyes. His voice trembled.

"It was awful. It stunk so bad. I saw the sneakers sticking out and then I looked behind the tools and saw something with the eyes all gone and bones showing. Dougie saw it then, too—he almost tripped and fell on it. And then we got out of there. I didn't even really know what it was till my dad told me after he came out."

I asked if either of them had touched anything or picked up anything from the floor.

"No, ma'am," Michael answered, "I didn't and I know he didn't either." He gestured toward his brother, who shook his head and began to cry again.

I straightened up, working a purple lupine stem back and forth between my fingers.

"Take them home," I told Barrows. "They're going to need awhile to get over this. Talk to them and let them talk to you. Get them help if they need it—their teachers can tell you where. I'll want to speak with all of you again, but not right now. Right now they need to go on home."

We walked to the car to get the homicide kit. Kenny Savitch, the day watch commander, broke away from a small group and came toward me.

"You knew it'd come to this, didn't you, Kate?" he asked.

"I was afraid so, Kenny, but you always hope."

"Is it bad inside?"

I thought of the pathetic torn body, the little hand turned palm up, the worn sneakers that had chased a baseball in my own front yard.

"You wouldn't want to see it," I told him.

We got the kit and went to work. We wouldn't touch the body—that job was for the medical examiner—but we'd turn the scene itself inside-out.

We worked for half an hour before a cop peered in the door to tell us the coroner had arrived.

"I'll go meet him," I told the other two. "You keep at it."

I stepped into the fresh spring air and, across the field of waving purple flowers, I saw a large black van pull off the roadway. Its windowless sides and rear door were marked only by two words painted in white block letters: COUNTY CORONER.

A small, gray-haired man stepped from the driver's side, smoothing his suit coat with both hands before covering it with a blue cotton smock marked CORONER'S OFFICE.

It was Howard Penross himself, chief of staff for twenty years, eligible for retirement for the last nine of those years, promising to take that retirement after "just one more case."

He was known as an infallible investigator, one who worried a question, shook it hard and turned it inside-out, until he got an answer. And even after that answer came, he worried the question some more, looking at it from yet another angle, to make sure he'd got the right one.

I smiled for the first time in several hours. I couldn't have been more pleased that Penross had chosen to handle this case personally.

I told him what we had and he nodded as he listened, then opened the rear door panels and waved to an aide to remove the equipment.

"We'll need the dental charts, Kate," he said to me, "and find out if the Schuyler boy was ever fingerprinted. From what you've told me, it sounds like ID's going to have to be made by those means."

"I'll talk to the parents this afternoon," I promised him. "It's still hush-hush as far as the press goes, so I have a little time yet before I contact them. Right now, I want to work here awhile longer."

A second car pulled up beside the van and two lab men got out. I told them what we wanted; then they, too, picked up their gear and we started back across the field.

"When can I know something, Howard?"

"You're still the impatient one, aren't you, Katharine? Well, it can't be rushed and it won't go any faster just by the asking, you know that."

Penross meant he'd do it his way, without short-cutting or shortchanging just to meet a deadline. I gave him that.

"Doing it as you wish, Howard, on your own terms, can you hazard a guess?"

"Don't even know what I've got yet, Kate, so no, I

can't. But I'll tell you one thing—I'll give you every hour I can till I bring up the answers to at least the main questions."

That was all I wanted to hear. I was satisfied.

"Fair enough," I told him.

"Steve Darrow will be joining us on this," I continued, "and he'll be the one attending the autopsy. Call him when you're ready."

Carl moved forward to meet me, his fingers snapping with excitement.

"We found one thing, Katie. There's what looks like a maroon piece of wool hooked on a nail in the door frame, as if something caught on it and then tore loose."

Curious, I followed him to the entrance. A nail protruded half an inch from the frame, some five feet up from the ground on the right-hand side. From it hung a dark strand several inches long.

Because of the position of the nail, an average-size adult entering the shed couldn't help but touch the sharp head with his right arm or shoulder if he came too close. If he wore short sleeves or was shirtless, the nail would scratch his skin—if he wore long sleeves, it'd catch and momentarily hold the fabric.

"Oookaaay," I said, "let's get that baby packaged."

One of the lab men removed the strand carefully with tweezers and dropped it into a plastic baggie. He'd analyze it later on.

"We've just started outside," Carl told me. "It'll probably take most of the day to cover the part of the field between here and the road."

I walked back inside, back to that decomposing horror in the shadows. Penross and his assistant squatted near the corpse, studying it closely. He looked up, eyes sharp behind his glasses.

"This wasn't done yesterday, Kate, but you already know that, I guess. Right now, I can't tell you anything more. There's no obvious cause of death, such as blunt trauma to the person. I've got to get it back to the lab and work on it there."

They laid out the black body bag, then lifted up the corpse, still bearing the burlap on its thighs, carefully maneuvered it into the bag, and pulled the zipper shut. A small round hollow in the dirt showed where it had rested.

I looked at the dark plastic sack. It was meant for a grown-up so the child's tiny body, lying in the middle on its back, left both ends flat and empty. My throat tightened and a tear ran down my cheek. I thought my heart would break.

Penross picked up one end and his assistant raised the other. Silently I moved forward and placed my hands beneath the center. We left that putrid building and walked outside into sunlight.

The lab men ceased their work as we passed by and Dan and Carl stepped toward us, then stood still. The golden grasses swayed in a breeze I couldn't feel and above me a single bird trilled a sweet, high-note song.

We passed through the field and then the fence, bearing an object so light I could easily have carried it in my own two arms. Without a word, Penross carefully placed the bag inside the van's open doors, then closed them firmly. He turned to me and looked deep into my eyes.

"You've got a little boy yourself, don't you, Kate?"

I nodded, and pain shot across my face.

"I thought so—I thought I remembered that."

He laid a hand on my shoulder and let it rest there for a moment, then climbed into the van and started up the engine. It turned right and headed slowly down the two-lane highway, back to town. I stood and watched the settling dust till it disappeared around a curve.

At that moment, I saw a green sedan speeding toward the field. It slowed, then parked across the road. A small sign in its front window read PRESS.

My heart sank. I knew I couldn't hold the story in for long. I'd have to leave the field and see Billy's parents sooner than I'd planned.

"Damn," I exclaimed to Carl when I reached the shed, "press is here already—that means I've got to go in town. Stay with it, I'll be back well before dark."

"Roger, boss, and lab's got some good news. They found a footprint near the east interior wall of the shed. They're casting it right now."

I waved to Kent, who was on his hands and knees crawling through the field, and walked back to my car.

Chapter Five

It's never easy telling a missing person's family that a body has been found.

When I started homicide two years ago, I believed the impact on my senses would lessen each time it happened. God, was I naive. It'll never get any easier and why should it, for what I am is a killer of hope, crushing it so forcefully and so finally it can never rise again. And this act, this destruction of one of the most joyous emotions a human can feel, haunts me long after the moment I commit it.

I turned my car around, headed south, and thought about that afternoon last week, when the three of us had ridden to another farm on another two-lane country road to ask a man about a boy.

The boy had not been Billy Schuyler but, while we left that farm discouraged at a lead that didn't deliver, at least our search could still go on. Unlike today.

I wondered if Billy Schuyler had still been alive when we talked with Mr. Painter. I doubted it, but it didn't really matter, did it? Even if he'd not been killed till yesterday, I'd failed him. I'd found him much too late.

Discouragement, rooted in a feeling of futility, took hold of me and my eyes filled with tears.

A DESPERATE CALL

I drove slowly, soothing my emotions and considering the best way to break the news. Schuyler was probably at his bank right now, she most likely at home.

Up ahead, I saw a gas station with a pay phone outside and I pulled into the graveled lot. Two pumps stood idle and a mixed-breed hound lay stretched full-out beside them. It didn't even twitch an ear when I opened my door. I dialed the number and a secretary put me straight through.

"Mr. Schuyler? Katharine Harrod. Could you please meet me at your house in half an hour, with your wife?"

A silence followed and then he asked tersely, "Why, Detective?"

"I've got some information, but I need to see you privately."

"Have you found Billy?"

I heard the strain of a voice held tightly in control.

"I must see you privately."

"If you say so. I'll be there in half an hour—my wife's already home."

I hung up and left the booth. As I walked back to my car, I saw myself reflected in the window of the station. My face was grim and my eyes tired and rimmed by lines that seemed to have deepened since that morning. My hair had escaped its bun and hung wildly around my cheeks.

Suddenly, urgently, I longed to see Tommy—to hold him and hug him and toss him high in the air in a room that echoed laughter. I wanted to feel the warmth of his clean small body pressed against my chest, to see his soft blond hair and clear blue eyes. But I'd have to wait, perhaps for hours.

There'd been no more problems that we knew of,

although at times he seemed unnaturally quiet and withdrawn, as if he felt a weight we couldn't see.

I'd tried to probe, to find out what was bothering him, but he'd shrugged me off and told me, "nothing." I had some vacation time coming, and after this case the three of us would go away together and my little boy would talk to me about himself.

Again I drove slowly, this time to make sure Schuyler reached the house before I did. I was coming to open country now, leaving the rolling foothills behind me. The valley land spread out before me, flat and dry and patched with squares of red clay and ochre stubble. It hadn't rained since March.

The air was brisk, the far-off mountains sharp against the deep blue sky. I knew the cold spell would soon break—it always did at this time of year. Already, I thought I felt a warming of the wind.

I began to wonder how the body had gotten to the shed. In what kind of car or truck? Covered by a blanket or exposed in a trunk or rear seat? Surely it had traveled northbound in the lane beside me. I didn't know of another road leading to San Marcos.

Later today, or tomorrow, we'd talk to everyone who lived along this road, within several miles either side of the shed. I'd go back to the gas station I'd just left, to ask if anyone'd noticed anything unusual that April day two weeks ago or on the days and nights that followed. But for now, that would have to wait.

I passed my own house, drove four blocks east and then turned north. I hadn't been to Hollis Place since the night I saw Nadine and I wondered if she'd be there now. Schuyler's car, a tan four-door sedan, was in the driveway. So he was home—good.

I parked on the street and got out. Behind a front

window, a curtain swung shut, as if someone had watched for my arrival, then stepped back when I drove up. The door opened before I reached the steps and the Schuylers both came out to meet me.

"Let's all go inside," I said.

I hadn't seen them in two weeks. He'd changed little, except that his inanimate expression now showed a haggard set. She'd lost at least ten pounds.

Her eyes were large and frantic ovals in a thin and drawn face. Her blouse hung off her shoulders like an oversized man's shirt and the bones in her feet stood out sharply in her sandals. Her movements, always nervous, now seemed almost overdrawn in their constant darting manner.

When the door closed, I turned to them. I felt hollow inside, hollow and alone, but I couldn't give in to my own private grief. The dirty job had to be done.

"A body has been found. We don't know if it's Billy's. It *is* a little boy about Billy's age. I'm sorry."

Joyce Schuyler stumbled forward and her husband caught her by the arm. The hint of strength I thought I'd seen that other day now seemed nonexistent. It was as if, for just a moment, something long-subdued had tried to surface, but then, not finding sustenance to nurture its fragility, had died away again.

"It mightn't be your son," I continued. "We've got to do some tests before we know."

"Why can't we just see him and we'll tell you if it's him?" she cried, and I knew in her mind she saw a dear sweet child who looked as if he slept.

"It's best my way," I told her gently, and Thomas Schuyler hushed her when she began to protest. He understood the awful words I hadn't spoken.

"Where was it found, Detective?" he asked calmly.

I gave them very little, only that the body was discovered in an outbuilding on a farm near San Marcos. The positive ID would have to come first—the whole sad story could wait till later. It would have been cruel and pointless to upset them any more than I already had.

"I'll be in touch this evening," I told Schuyler as I left. "It may be tomorrow before we know if it is or isn't your son, but I'll call tonight anyway."

I walked away, and a high-pitched keening sound began behind me before the door finally closed. I left them with their grief. Only then did I realize I hadn't seen Nadine.

Schuyler had given me a set of Billy's fingerprints—made last year with his church group—and I'd picked up the dental charts from the family dentist.

Once I got them, they were like fire in my hand and I couldn't wait to give them to Penross. I wanted to hear the official irrevocable answer to the question—was the body Billy Schuyler's? Once that was laid behind me, I could get on with my investigation.

I found him in his office, blue-smocked as before, studying data on his desk. Despite a full day's hard work, his appearance was impeccable.

"Can I wait?" I asked impatiently.

"Kate, I'll call you. Even with these, it takes time. Where are you going now?"

"Back to the shed," I told him. "I'll be working there till dark—probably seven-thirty or so."

"All right. *You* call *me*, then. Phone me here when you're through. I'll try to have something to give you."

I drove back toward San Marcos, anxious now to work the field and shed for clues. Traffic was breaking

A DESPERATE CALL

from the city as the workday ended and the first few miles were slow ones.

Gradually, the cars thinned, turning left or right off the main road, and I was able to gain some speed. The brightness of the daytime had dimmed and the approaching foothills lay in languid purple shadows as the sun lowered in the sky.

Dan and Carl were still searching the field inch by inch, bending the grass carefully as they crawled forward, minutely examining and probing each square foot before moving on. I called out to them and Mungers came to meet me.

"That piece of yarn's all we've got so far," he said. "That and the footprint. Lab's packed up and gone— you probably passed them on the way."

"Okay, we'll just keep on looking," I said firmly, "and we'll come out here again tomorrow. But remember, even if we can't walk off easy with a pile of evidence from the scene, there're lots of other ways to put it all together."

I brushed a blade of grass from Carl's shoulder, then began to scan the ground around me. We searched till dusk, bending over till our backs and knees ached with deepening pain, staring till our eyes strained and watered. We found nothing.

"Let's wrap it up for now," I told the other two. "We'll come back tomorrow. One of you can finish this while the other starts talking to the neighbors. I'll call on Mr. Barrows and the kids."

We left two cops to guard the field and drove away. The press corps, aware the action was over for the night, dispiritedly disassembled their gear and began to move it toward their trucks.

"Damn it, Katie, it's been a long one and not

much to show for it," Carl said wearily, slumping forward so that his large frame filled the seat beside me. With his coarse features and florid coloring, he looked just like a prize fighter who'd had a bad night in the ring.

Dan lit a cigarette and leaned forward. Even after hours of searching, his tweed coat was creaseless, his face was clean and bright.

"Learn anything from the parents, Kate?"

Good for you, I thought. The rookie who'd lost himself earlier today had gotten it back together again.

"Dunno. Nothing obvious, anyway. Never heard Tommy say Billy had any problems but, of course, a lot of times kids don't talk. It's the right place to start, though."

"Son of a bitch. Why would he put him in that shed instead of burying him?" Carl asked furiously. "And why behind those tools? They certainly didn't hide him."

"You're right," I agreed, "but maybe whoever left the body there thought if someone just gave a casual glance, he'd never notice anything. Same reason he threw the burlap over the thighs—to give a little cover-up. But that would've worked for only a short time, till the odor started."

"And the animals," Carl continued. "He sure as hell must've known the rats would get him if he wasn't buried."

"Maybe he wanted them to get him," I pointed out. "Maybe he hoped even bigger animals would come around and totally destroy the corpse before anyone could find it. One thing, whoever our fella is—if it even *is* a man—he doesn't know much about spring planting or he'd know that shed would soon be put to use. We might have a real city type here."

We exchanged more thoughts, probed more possibilities, let questions form free-will as we neared the city lights.

"I'm calling the coroner," I told them, "then we'll all go home and try to get a little rest. Let's meet again at daybreak."

We parked behind the station and walked upstairs. The clock showed eight-fifteen. I picked up the phone and dialed Penross. He answered right away.

"This is very preliminary," he said, "and I don't want it released just yet, but it looks as if we've got the Schuyler boy here. There're just a few more matches I need to do before I can give an official ID, but between you and me, it's him."

I didn't feel a thing. I had not, even in my deepest being, held any hope that Penross would give me different news.

"What about the cause of death, Howard?"

He paused.

"More tests on that one, too, Kate, but if I'm right, we've got a real brute here. He had to kill him twice."

I frowned in puzzlement.

"How do you mean?"

"It seems the boy was killed by some means of ligature strangulation and then, just to make sure, the murderer choked him manually till he broke his neck."

Disgust welled in my throat and sickened me.

"The bastard!"

"I'll have all of it for you by ten tomorrow, Katharine. Now I've got to get back to it."

I hung up and faced Dan and Carl.

"It's him," I said, "and we're looking for a monster."

I left the room and walked to a lonely corner of the building. The tears came and wouldn't stop. I remembered Billy as I'd seen him on that sunny April afternoon nearly three weeks ago and as he'd looked this morning in the shed, and I thought about the ugly tortuous road he'd been made to travel to get from one place to the other.

I splashed water on my face and neck and then went back inside. I'd have to call the Schuylers. Surprisingly, Joyce answered. I used my best professional voice, even-toned and noncommital.

"The tests aren't finished quite yet, so I've nothing definite I can tell you. The lab's working full-time and should know something by midmorning and I promise I'll call you then."

Schuyler's voice broke in.

"I was listening on the extension, Detective. We'll be waiting for your call."

I hung up, thankful that they'd asked no questions. I thought about the dreadful secret I carried and about their blessed ignorance of that secret.

"Let's go home," I called out suddenly and we walked outside together.

A slow and lazy breeze caused the leaves to move slightly and carried with it the sweet strong scent of spring flowers and moist earth. High above, the moon formed a curved splinter in a blue-black sky and ice-chip stars sparkled with a rare clarity. It should have been a lovely night, but instead it tore my heart out.

* * *

A DESPERATE CALL

I turned on the radio and the powerful rolling rhythm of a '60s rock song filled the car. It took my soul and soothed it and, as always in times of black reality, let me lose myself in rock 'n' roll. Its beat, its mood, its joyous raucous message uplifted me and gave me strength to carry on. True rock, after all, celebrates hope and faith and life itself in a gospel outpouring of the depths of our emotions.

I turned the volume high and drove on slowly. I wanted a moment's space between the day behind me and the family waiting up ahead. I needed time to let the tarnish of the crime diminish before I put my arms around them.

The lights in the houses along my street signaled warmth and normalcy. I, more than anyone, knew unspeakable horrors can exist behind such exteriors but sometimes, like now, I willingly and purposely let myself be fooled, just for a moment.

I thought of the Schuylers' house, looking like the ones I passed now, and how this was the last night any small bit of hope for Billy would ever exist there. Their lives had changed forever on that April day and now change would strike those lives again with an even harder blow.

I saw my own house up ahead. The front door light was on and all the downstairs lights as well. I turned into the drive and coasted to a stop while the last sounds of a heart-bending, blues-touched song of celebration wrapped their rhythm right around me—

"Oh, give me the beat, boys
Free my soul
I want to get lost in your rock 'n' roll
And drift away...."

Jonathan stood on the top step and Tommy leaned against him, hugging his legs with both his arms. I looked at them and loved them and opened the door fiercely and went to them. I was home.

Chapter Six

It was still dark when I awoke. I showered and dressed and headed toward San Marcos well before first light. I ate some toast and drank cold juice and hot black coffee while I drove.

A pink-tinged sky behind the hills began to cut the darkness. Dew, like gleaming webs of silver, shrouded grasses in the fields. I parked in gravel off the road. As I turned the engine off, the other two arrived.

"I'll work with you till eight or so," I said, "then I want to go see Barrows and be back in town by ten."

The morning's search turned up nothing new. When I knew we hadn't left a blade unturned, I sent the men to try to sniff out something from the neighbors and I set out to see Barrows.

The farmhouse stood behind a white rail fence less than a mile from the field, its woodwork gleaming in tones of green and white. An L-shaped porch held a wooden swing and random flagstones set in scattered pebbles formed a pathway to that porch. It could've been the cover shot for a book on rural America.

I was certain breakfast had ended several hours ago, but the full sweet smell of bacon and honey-laden biscuits still lingered on the air coming through the open window.

Smoothing back my hair, I knocked on the screen door and called out. A small woman, neat in a brown-and-white-checked dress, set a broom against a wall and walked toward me. Barrows appeared behind her, wiping his hand across his mouth.

"Good morning, Detective, I wondered when you'd come."

They opened the door together and I went inside.

"How are the boys?" I asked.

"The big one's okay, I think," he told me, "but the little one woke up screaming last night."

"Keep an eye on both of them," I said, "even the one who seems okay."

I asked him if he'd ever noticed anyone hanging around the shed and he told me he'd chased a persistent vagrant away a year or two back, and occasionally saw some hunters and the odd courting couple trying to find a little privacy.

How about two or three weeks ago, I asked.

He frowned, then answered.

"Nope, haven't even noticed a car stopping for some time now, but you've got to know, Miss, that I'm not usually down that way. Oh sure, I pass it on my way to or from the city, but except for planting and reaping times, I don't do a daily check down there."

I nodded and went on to something else.

"There's a nail sticking out of the shed door frame—can you tell me anything about it?"

His eyes went blank, then remembrance shot through them.

"Oh sure, that nail, meant to bang it in but didn't. I noticed it when I stopped down that way a few weeks ago. Ripped my arm on it, in fact, but then just forgot about it after that."

Unconsciously, he rubbed a small scar on his forearm.

"Tell me this," I said, "when you looked at that nail, did you see anything hanging from it?"

"Nothing—it was clean. I'd swear to that 'cause I took a good close squint at it. If I'd had on sleeves, it would'a caught them for sure, but it was during that real hot spell we had back then and I just had on a T-shirt and overalls."

"Can you remember exactly which day you noticed the nail?" I asked, leaning forward and peering into his face.

He considered, then nodded to himself in satisfaction.

"Sure I can. It was on a Friday ... one, two, three weeks ago yesterday. I know 'cause I'd been waiting for a new spade to come into the hardware and it arrived that morning. I picked it up and dropped it off at the shed. Matter of fact, that was the last time I was there till yesterday."

Three weeks ago Friday was just a few days before Billy disappeared. If Barrows was telling the truth, that meant the maroon strand had been plucked from the clothes of someone other than himself, at some point in time since that day. I doubted that traffic was heavy through the shed door so there was a real good chance the yarn belonged to whoever laid the body in the corner.

"I'd like to see your little boys now," I told him, and his wife went to get them. A screen door banged and they came into the room, holding onto their mother's hands as their bare feet moved soundlessly on the cool linoleum floor. Michael smiled at me, but Doug stared blankly, with no sign of recognition.

"I want to thank you boys for your help yesterday and ask you if you've remembered anything else you want to tell me," I said softly. They shook their heads.

"You reached the shed before your father. Did you see anything moving around it, like maybe trees bending or something you thought might've been an animal in the bushes?"

Again, they shook their heads. They had nothing more to offer, so I stood up to go.

Suddenly, Doug broke away from his mother and came and stood in front of me. He looked directly up into my face, his eyes wide and frightened.

"That'll happen to me, too, won't it?" he asked.

"No," I answered, bending down to touch him, "no, it never will. Why do you say that?"

"Because he's a little boy and I'm a little boy, too, so sometime if I'm bad maybe that'll happen."

And he began to cry in low rolling sobs. I quickly hugged him. Then his mother rushed over and took him from me and held him in her arms. Henry Barrows wiped his hand across his eyes and pulled his other son onto his lap.

"We'll be all right, Detective," he said sadly, "but maybe we *will* need some help after all."

My sadness of the day before was spent. The unconsciousness of sleep had let me cross a barrier between deep depression and positive aggressiveness. I'd rallied 'round myself and now I felt that questing, scenting feeling—that instinct of inquisitiveness—that meant I was eager to begin the hunt. I grinned—I felt damn good at last.

A DESPERATE CALL 93

Anxious now to reach the city, I drove quickly, spinning the wheel with one hand as I took the curves. I'd decided I'd phone Penross from my desk rather than stop at a public call box along the way.

"Careful, kid," I warned myself giddily, "don't put it in the ditch."

The wind had shifted and a heaviness of heat, unlike any I'd felt for nearly three weeks, permeated the air. I rolled up my windows and cut on the air conditioner.

Earlier, a cooling fog had drifted hazily across the mountaintops, like clouds of powder shaken from the sky. Now, above the trees, I saw only clear and brilliant blue. The summer drought was on for sure.

I reached the station and hurried through the door. By some miracle my desk was clear. It was as if a vacuum had developed in the past twenty-four hours, and I was glad. I didn't want messages unrelated to this case, other problems that diverted me, unimportant bits of flotsam to catch my mind and slow me down.

At ten o'clock, I phoned Penross. He was ready.

"It's Billy Schuyler, Kate," he told me, "no doubt. Prints and dentals are a perfect match. I'll send you the complete report in several days, but here's what you need to know for now.

"The cause of death was ligature strangulation from behind. The neck-breaking was an extra touch after death occurred. Postmortem lividity suggests the boy was killed somewhere other than the shed and then moved to that location. Time of death was probably two to two-and-a-half weeks ago—it's hard to be more precise. Without that cold spell in the mountains, I couldn't even give you that much.

"There's no evidence of sexual molestation, but

there *is* something funny I can't identify at this point. The corpse's right arm, both above and below the elbow on the outside, shows round dark marks approximately three-eighths inch in diameter and one-eighth inch apart, as if something burned the flesh or made an impression by forceful contact. I'll work on them awhile longer."

"What about his clothes?" I asked.

"I've got them here—you can see them anytime you want. And Darrow's been with me all morning—he'll fill you in if you come up with any questions later."

"Thanks, Howard, I'll be down shortly."

I hung up and sat in silence, my chin between my hands. The next call was the tough one, but I had to make it.

"Mr. Schuyler, I'm coming over," I informed him in a voice devoid of feeling. "I'll be there in less than ten minutes."

I didn't have to tell them—they knew the minute they saw my face. Joyce Schuyler gasped and stared at me wildly, then she fainted. Thomas Schuyler carried her to a nearby sofa and laid her down.

He turned to face me, his cheeks wet with tears. Before, his self-containment had kept him quiet—now, he tried to speak but couldn't find the words. I helped him to a chair.

"We'll talk about this later," I said quietly, "several days from now. Is there anyone who can be here with you?"

He mentioned Marc Schuyler and his wife's brother from up north.

"The body should be released in two to three days," I said, talking almost in a whisper. "You could plan

A DESPERATE CALL

the funeral for the end of next week. There's just one thing I want to ask you now—is there anyone you know of who might've done this to your son?"

He tried to answer and an awful gurgling sound came from deep down in his throat. He waved a hand in my direction in a futile gesture and shook his head violently from side to side.

"I'll let myself out," I told him. I doubt he even heard me.

I walked to the sofa and knelt beside Joyce Schuyler. I clasped her hand and stroked her hair for several moments, then I bent and kissed her gently on the brow.

"I'm so sorry—so very, very sorry," I murmured, and I heard my voice begin to break. Her hand tightened slightly on mine but her eyes didn't open.

I stood up straight and walked away, and left the two of them alone in that room of grief. As I passed through the hallway, I heard a radio playing somewhere upstairs. The sound was loud and it was brassy. It wasn't my kind of music and it seemed especially tasteless at a time like this.

Of course, Nadine didn't know her brother had been murdered. I wondered who'd tell her and how much she'd really care.

When I got outside, I stood on the steps for a moment and gazed, unseeing, across the lawn and into the deep-blue distant sky. I thought about life, death, and the sadness that surrounded me, and wondered why it had to hurt so much. Then I thought about the job I had to do, and I quickly shook the sadness from me and headed toward my car.

* * *

I was halfway to the coroner's office when I got the urgent message to call home. Alarmed, I found the nearest phone and dialed my number. When I heard Jon's words, they paralyzed my mind and drained my body's strength.

Tommy—my child, my love—had disappeared, had not been seen since eight o'clock that morning when he'd left home to bike the short distance to a friend's house.

He'd gone off without his baseball glove, so Jon had phoned to say he'd bring it over ... and learned Tommy had never arrived at his destination.

He'd traced the route our son would've traveled and called other kids he knew, and now, three hours later, he was calling me.

I hurried home while terror—dull at first, then sharp with pain—built inside me. This could not be happening, this could not be what I thought it was. Billy Schuyler had been an isolated case, the one-time action of a madman who wouldn't strike again.

But why wouldn't he, I asked, why wouldn't he? Suppose Billy hadn't been his first and suppose he'd developed such a liking for it that he'd hunted down another little boy to maim and mutilate? Suppose he'd seen my Tommy and wanted him, to feed his fever for a kill?

I could taste a thick foul taste in the back of my throat and my tongue felt dry and hot inside my mouth. I saw my hands tremble on the steering wheel.

The car had barely stopped before I was running toward the house, hoping all had changed, all was now all right. It wasn't. Jon, his face gray and drawn, met me and asked, "What now?"

"We've got to notify patrol," I said. "I won't wait any longer."

We drove downtown and laid it in the lap of Kenny Savitch. His face grew tight and I knew that he, too, was remembering Billy.

"We'll find him for you, Katie, don't you worry—we're cracking on this one right away." And he picked up the radio and put the word out.

I took Jon's arm and pulled him toward the door. He walked through it as if living in a daze. When we reached the car, he turned to me and drew me close, almost hurting me with the intensity of his hold. I felt the heat of his breath warm my neck as he buried his head on my waiting shoulder.

"Katharine, Katharine, I love you both—you know that, don't you?" he whispered in a voice so low I hardly heard him. "If anything happened to my family, I couldn't take it, wouldn't want to go on without the two of you."

"Nothing's going to happen, Jon." I held him just as tight as he held me and felt a grateful strong delight that I could comfort him. "They're going to find our baby soon and we'll all three be together again."

But the afternoon went by and then the early evening, and patrol didn't find Tommy—didn't find a trace, didn't find a clue. I tried to take it over, as I'd done six hours after Billy disappeared, but the captain wasn't having it.

"You're too involved, Kate, you know the rules on this one. I'm calling in a southend unit to take charge."

I nodded, knowing he would override me if I argued, but knowing, too, that Jon and I would never stop our own search.

We rode the streets and walked the fields and playgrounds but, when darkness fell as the new-moon night became pitch-black, we finally turned for home, hoping, knowing, then totally believing he'd returned while we were out and we'd find him tucked tightly in his bed.

But he wasn't there, and the absolute silent emptiness of that little room wrenched at me and overwhelmed me, and, sobbing, I collapsed in Jon's arms and our tears ran together. The nightmare that had been the Schuylers' was theirs no longer—it was ours.

We lay down, exhausted, but neither one could rest. From time to time, I got up and called the station and then lay down again. Finally, I drifted off in a fragmentary daze of semiconsciousness before I finally, wearily, slipped deep beneath the surface.

And then the dreams came, the vivid powerful shattering dreams of torn arms and empty sockets that wouldn't let me sleep, that tore me from my slumber and left me wet and stinking with a cold and running sweat.

At dawn I couldn't take it any longer and I dressed and left the house, telling Jon to stay beside the phone. I drove toward the station, then swung north when I saw a line of searchers starting toward the woods. The sergeant broke away and came to me.

"Go on home, Katie, we're doing all that you could do."

"The bastard's got my little boy, Robby—I'm going nowhere."

He shrugged helplessly, not knowing what to say, and then he came to me and put his arm around my shoulders.

A DESPERATE CALL

"You can't know that, Kate, you can't know that. You can't allow that thought to get inside your mind."

But of course it *was* inside my mind and it wouldn't go away. I tried to keep it hidden from my husband but soon realized the futility of that endeavor. Of course it filled his thoughts, too. The horror that a monster had snatched Tommy and used him for his own perverted pleasure.

"Kate, tell me about the Schuyler boy," he begged. "Tell me everything you can about his murder, in case I can pick up on something you missed that'll help us find our son."

I looked into the anguished eyes of my beloved husband, sitting on the edge of his favorite chair, as he twisted a piece of thread nervously between the caring fingers whose caress I knew so well.

I went to him and knelt beside him and smoothed his hair back with my hand.

"We've got to have faith this isn't the same, Jon. We've got to believe there's no connection between the two. We can't afford to think like this because if we do, we'll go crazy—we won't survive."

How could I order him to do that, I wondered, when I couldn't will myself to do the same? Why couldn't we indulge ourselves and share our worst nightmares instead of trying to pretend we were exaggerating?

But even as I asked myself the question, I found I knew the answer—because I wanted to shield him from all evil, I wanted to make things right for him, I wanted to protect the one I loved.

Jon took my hand and led me quietly toward his study. My words seemed to have calmed him, given him some sort of solace. He pulled a desk drawer open and withdrew a little box. Turning to me, he placed it in my hand, then kissed me tenderly on the forehead.

"I bought this for you several days ago, for no special reason. Just as a little present. Somehow I want for you to have it now."

Wondering, I carefully untied the yellow ribbon, then lifted off the top and saw a slender silver bracelet engraved with my initials.

"It suited you, I thought," he told me as he slipped it on my wrist. "I know we've had our differences but you also know how very much I love you."

Wordlessly, I put my arms around his waist and we stood together, giving silent comfort to each other as the pulsing warmth from both our bodies flowed and mingled as if one.

A retching child at Sunday school brought it to an end. A teacher noticed William Harding crying in a corner of the classroom and as she went to him, he bent his head and vomited into his hands. And then he told a story, now sobbing with relief to get it off his chest.

He'd been hanging out the day before with a ragtag group of boys deep in Sanchez woods. There'd been five or six of them—two older bully boys and a couple of younger kids like himself who knew they shouldn't be there but could not withstand the lure of the forbidden.

The older ones had smoked a little dope and offered it to William, who shook his head in silence and wished that he were home. Then they'd pulled a wide-eyed alley cat from a burlap bag they'd carried with them, and begun to torment it.

A that moment, another little boy, riding on a bike and pedaling hard, came along the path beneath the pine trees. When he saw the group, he braked, bewildered at the scene in front of him. It was Tommy and he was about to meet his hell.

He didn't know the other boys but he knew he'd stumbled onto something very wrong. And he knew he needed to get out of there right away. He tried to turn around and bike away, but the biggest bully grabbed him and knocked him to the ground.

"Let's have some fun with this one," he called out. "Hell, it beats skinning cats any day."

According to the Harding boy, Tommy somehow managed to break away and began running through the woods—tripping, stumbling, racing blindly toward escape with the pack in close pursuit.

But suddenly he'd pitched forward and dropped into a little canyon, an arroyo seco, that split the woods in half. And when the bully boys reached its edge and peered over, they saw a bloodied body lying down below—a silent, broken body that never moved, although they watched it for some minutes.

And then they left and scattered toward their homes, a wordless pact binding them to silence so that they told no one about the body in the woods. Until today, when an honest little boy could bear the guilt no longer and had to let the story out.

We rushed to find him, our minds closed against the possibility of death. A protective mental barrier came down and wouldn't let us look ahead.

We crossed a field and entered woods thick with

underbrush that lay in shadow. A single path ran beneath the trees and we quickly followed it, the rescue team coming close behind.

Suddenly I felt my heart tear and I gave a little cry, stopped short, and grabbed Jon's arm. Tommy's bike was lying on its side against a pile of rocks, its wheel and bars twisted as if it had hastily been thrown down. We raced past it and didn't stop again until we reached the edge of a small cliff that dropped sharply from the forest floor.

Sick with fear, I looked over. He was flat on his back, his eyes closed, his left arm flung out beside him. Blood and dirt and leaves covered his upper body and his face was pale and still. I could not tell if he was breathing.

"Tommy, Tommy," I cried out, although I knew he couldn't hear me.

I scrambled down a rope hoist rigged up by paramedics and ran to him along the canyon floor. One rescuer who'd already reached him turned to me and said, "He's got a pulse—he's unconscious but he's got a pulse."

Tears, so tightly contained till now, ran down my cheeks as I whirled around into Jon's encircling arms. We stood in tight embrace and poured our thanks out from our hearts.

"He's safe, Kate," Jon whispered in my ear. "Our prayers were answered—our boy's alive."

I bent to touch him, pushing past the paramedics. And then I saw it. Beneath the dirt and leaves and blood, a spike protruded from his forearm. In falling, Tommy had impaled himself on a six-inch metal rod used to tether cattle in a long-forgotten canyon pen sometime in the distant past.

* * *

He'd never be all right, not completely. He'd lost a lot of blood, though not enough to be life-threatening, and he drifted back to consciousness that evening in the hospital.

But the spike had pierced a tendon, and even after months of therapy, it would still hang partially useless by his side.

When he could talk, I asked him why he'd gone to Sanchez woods instead of to his friend's house. He'd run away, he told me calmly, his eyes staring straight ahead, because I didn't love him anymore.

Stunned, I took him in my arms and squeezed him hard.

"You cannot believe that, Tommy, you cannot think that's really true."

"It is!" he yelled, suddenly calm no longer, "it is, too! You're never home, you're always gone, you love Billy more than me."

He balled up a little fist and struck my shoulder.

"I love you, and if you don't believe it, I'll have to prove it to you harder. And I will."

Later, Jon and I drove slowly home, saying little. I wanted him to hold me, to comfort me, and, foolishly, I thought he'd do that once we reached the house. Instead, when the door shut behind us, he turned to face me and his words slapped me hard and turned my world around.

"I want you to take some time off, Katharine—I mean a good, long time. We've talked about this before, but you've never taken it seriously—'it'll all settle into place,' you tell me. Well, it hasn't and now it's reached a crisis point. True or not, Tommy apparently believes what he's saying and he needs you here, at least for now."

I sat down heavily on a chair and felt a dreadful emptiness inside me. Even though we'd touched upon it, talked about it briefly, I'd never seriously believed Jonathan meant I should give up my job. I'd fooled myself about his depth of feeling because I'd wanted him to feel another way.

But I believed him now, and I'd finally have to face the fact and deal with it straight out.

I set my lips and sat up firm and straight.

"You know I cannot do that, Jon. You know I love it—have loved it since long before we met—and I cannot walk away from it. There's got to be another way and I am going to find it."

He wheeled around and left the room without another word.

Chapter Seven

I went back to work the following day. In all good conscience, I could not give up the case, could not withhold my help from that grieving family. I was good at what I did and personal considerations would have to stand aside, at least for now. I had no choice, there was no other way.

Carl, as usual, had noticed and put his hands on both my shoulders as he asked the question.

"Beast get out of bed again, Kate?"

"Never really did go back after last time, Carl."

I looked at the silver bracelet and started to retract my words, but then I stopped. Nothing had changed after all. I told him about the ugly confrontation of the day before and then I asked him something I'd been curious about—something that suddenly seemed to have more relevance to me than it ever had before.

"Did it begin like this with Lila, Carl?"

He looked steadily at me, then he answered.

"Nope, nowhere near this drawn out. She left me after very little conversation. Just said she couldn't take being married to a cop and off she went."

I knew she'd moved out nearly seven years ago and Lila, who'd been a high-flying fancy girl from all I'd heard about her, never had come back. Her tastes had run toward fun and flash—quite the opposite from Carl's—but, I guess, he'd seen her as a shining ornament of beauty and desire and had fallen heavily, completely, in love.

He lived on his own in a small apartment right around the corner from the station—clean, austere, no stamp of personality anywhere upon it. To my knowledge, he'd never dated since she left—all that he took home at night were the grisly murders he was working on.

"I kid you not, it's rough right now," I told him, "but I can't believe Jon and I will ever get that far—he'd never let these feelings end our marriage."

He looked at me a moment, with an odd expression in his eyes. I tried to read it but I couldn't.

"Have you seen Betsy lately?" I asked, as I broke the growing silence. His face grew bright, excited, and quickly the look was gone as his mind moved somewhere else.

"Yesterday. And I think, just for a moment, she knew me. We played for nearly half an hour."

The ill-starred union had produced a little girl—a dreamy-eyed redhead who'd steal the hardest heart away. But she'd been born severely retarded and had spent nearly all of her eleven years in a local institution. I knew she never recognized her father—not even for a moment—and he'd told me once that any sort of play was far beyond her capabilities.

"It's not easy, is it, Carl?"

"Not easy, Kate, not easy ..." his voice trailed off. "But it's the hand that I was dealt and I am going to play it."

Hastily, he walked away and I got back to work.

I'd gone downtown and checked out the plaster cast

of the footprint made inside the shed. While there, the lab boys filled me in on what they'd found out about the piece of yarn.

It was a worn acrylic fiber common in clothing made for export in Korea or Taiwan and had once been part of a thicker length of thread—the type woven into heavy garments, not lightweight shirts or blouses.

Which made it highly likely the body hadn't been dumped in the shed till some time following the sudden drop in temperature, at least several days after the dead boy disappeared.

But there was another possibility, too—that the killer had entered the shed much earlier, maybe on the very night Billy vanished, and had worn dark clothing to hide himself inside the darkness of the field. Perhaps a heavy sweater was the only camouflage he owned so he put it on despite the smothering heat.

Whose was it, I wondered, and where was it now? Who owned a maroon sweater with a torn strand missing from its sleeve? And did the murderer know that strand was missing and guess where he had left it?

I took the cast to Barrows's farm and asked to see his footgear. Willingly, he handed over two sets of boots and some rubber galoshes.

I carried them to my trunk and took out the plaster cast. I didn't want these shoes to match. I'd no cause to suspect the farmer killed Billy, but even if I had, I wouldn't need a footprint to tell me he'd been around his own field.

No, I wanted this cast to hold an alien print—one belonging to a stranger who should never have stood inside that shed.

I examined the galoshes first—their pattern was totally different from the imprint. A set of black leather boots came next. I turned the left one over and cursed what my eyes were seeing. Damn—a match, no doubt about it. Line for line, groove for groove, length and width, the shoe fit. The plaster cast belonged to Henry Barrows.

I'd take the boot back to the lab, to let the experts see it, but my own reading was good enough to bring me cold despair. One of our few possible clues, one of the tenuous trails we'd thought to follow, was shot to hell—the intriguing footstep had been made by a farmer placing tools inside his own toolshed.

I turned on the car radio and dialed in the news. A satin-voiced announcer speculated on the identity of the body in the field and assured her listeners that positive ID would come that afternoon.

She was telling it true. Now that I'd informed the Schuylers, the whole world could know and it wouldn't matter. Enough of that—I tuned out the satin voice and kept on turning till I found the music, then I settled down to driving and sifting through my thoughts.

Had the killer known about the shed, I wondered, or had he stumbled on it accidentally as he searched for a spot to hide the corpse? And what about the missing schoolbooks? They'd not been found with Billy's body—were they with the murderer or were they somewhere else?

I gave a deep sigh—we had so damn little. I'd called my men together for a two o'clock meeting and the first thing I wanted to do was sort out exactly what we *did* have to work with and where we'd take it.

I wasn't worried—the clues were there. They always

are and we'd find them. And, when I finally put the cuffs on, the case would be so tight I'd know he'd never walk away from it in court.

"You bastard," I said out loud, and my fingers tightened on the steering wheel, "that's the day I'm waiting for."

Darrow's coat was hanging on the rack when I reached the station and when I moved around a cabinet I saw him being briefed by Kent and Mungers.

He'd been tied up out-of-town on a double murder from ten months ago or he'd have been with us from the start. Now that he was back, I'd let the rookie go.

"Come on, guys, let's go in here," I said, and led them to a private room and shut the door behind them.

"Okay, let's hear it." I nodded toward Dan and Carl, and as I spoke, I thought of Tommy lying in the hospital and wondered if he hated me.

"Nothing we can use," Carl began. "No one on that road saw or heard a thing. A few reported backfires after dark, but they can't remember any other sounds, like car doors slamming or people's voices. No one saw a car parked near the field at anytime or any strangers in the area."

"What about the store and gas station?"

"Store closes at six, station closes at nine, but neither reports anything unusual during business hours. No customers who stood out in any way or made a big impression."

I turned to Dan and thanked him for his help. He rose and left the room reluctantly, pausing at the door before he went.

"Anytime you want me, just holler, boss lady—it's been a pleasure."

I waved him off and looked at Darrow.

"So what did they tell you?" I asked.

"Not that much. They were just beginning when you walked in."

"Fill me in on the autopsy—I'll catch you up later on all the rest."

"Nothing major that Penross didn't give you on the phone. They touched all the bases, that's for sure. Those odd marks are what we can't pin down. There's something about them that looks familiar, but I'm damned if I can grasp it yet. Like he told you, they're going to work a whole lot more on that downtown."

Steve Darrow wasn't one of my all-time favorites and it wasn't just because I looked at him through a woman's eyes. He was smart and he worked hard, but he was also arrogant and sometimes hasty.

Too often, he'd shortcut where I'd take the longer route. When his shortcuts worked, he made himself look brilliant, but occasionally they didn't and then we wasted precious time unraveling the mess. We'd never had any real run-ins, but privately I didn't like his style. He had too much flash.

I don't think he liked *me* much either. I sensed that he, unlike Carl, resented working for a woman. A ladies' man at heart, he believed in the days when ships were made of wood and men were made of iron and women stayed at home in the kitchen.

I could not deny his handsomeness, if you liked a certain type. Dark thick hair, combed back carefully with a high side part, framed a well-tanned face with deep brown eyes and straight white teeth.

A former football player, he worked hard at keeping his physique in all-male shape, and his broad shoulders, moving easily on a six-foot frame, caused eyes to roll around like sets of dice at a Las Vegas gaming table. He loved it all and played it to the hilt, all the while pretending not to notice ... until it suited him.

Once or twice he'd started to get fresh with me, but I'd spurned his moves and quenched his fires with withering disdain. When Jon had had his problems, Steve had been one of those lurking in the background waiting for his moment. It never came.

I quickly brought him up-to-date on Billy's disappearance and the finding of the body. When I finished, I broke down what we had into two lists—solid leads on one hand and, on the other, facts that could go somewhere with hard work and bits of luck.

I split up the work and handed it out. I'd concentrate on the Schuyler family, Carl would check out Billy's teachers and coaches, and Steve would go over the sex offenders. Though Penross had found Billy hadn't been molested, that didn't mean the murder wasn't sexually motivated. Perhaps the frightened little boy had screamed and the killer panicked before he could do his dirty tricks, so he choked him to shut his mouth and keep it shut forever.

We pushed back our chairs and went to our desks; I thought about my plan of action. I didn't need to talk with Joyce or Thomas Schuyler or with Nadine to get to know them—I'd let the funeral come and go before I went one-on-one with them.

At this point particularly, I preferred what I call the oblique approach, talking all around them to neighbors, bankers, teachers, and friends of the family.

I'd tackle the Schuyler brother straight out, without

beating around in the bushes, but with him, too, I'd wait till after the funeral. I didn't want to intrude on his grief.

Minutes later, my phone rang and I snapped the hand-piece from its cradle. A woman's voice asked if I was Katharine Harrod. I said I was, and Maud Divans began to speak.

"I heard it on the news," she told me, "about the body being Billy Schuyler."

Frankly, I was surprised she'd called. She hadn't struck me as the type who'd keep in touch just because she'd seen the dead boy walking by her house. But that surprise dissolved the second time she spoke, and she had me sitting forward in my chair.

"I find this incredible, Detective," she continued in a low, cool voice, "but I passed that field the night he disappeared, when I visited my sister, and on the way home I saw a car parked there, right beside the opening in the fence."

Damn, I thought, I should've been on top of that—I should've remembered Divans and her trip to San Marcos. If I was letting my personal worries distract me from my work, I'd better recognize that fact and make it stop right now.

"What time was it?"

"It must've been around eleven-forty. I know I got home shortly after midnight and I usually try to leave Vera's by eleven-thirty or so."

"Did you get a license number?"

"Oh no, there wasn't any reason then to do so. I noticed the car, though, because it's unusual to see one parked along that stretch of road so late at night, away from any houses."

I asked her to describe it for me.

Light-colored, she said—maybe tan or cream or even pale yellow—a sedan, probably American make. She didn't know if it had two doors or four.

"Any distinctive features, like a bent fender or a vinyl top?"

"If so, I didn't notice, but my impression would be no."

Had she seen anyone around the car or moving about in the field?

No, no, she hadn't. From all appearances, the car had been unoccupied and the field had been empty.

"Frankly, Detective," she explained, "I thought either no one was in it or that it was two lovers parked there and lying horizontal."

Maud Divans was adamant about the location. She told me she knew the field well because it was one of the few along the road that hadn't yet been ploughed.

"I always slow to see the flowers," she explained.

She'd heard about the body yesterday, but hadn't called earlier because she hadn't known it was Billy's. Today, when she learned the identity of that body, she knew a car seen near the unploughed field on the night he disappeared could be important. I thanked her and hung up.

Bingo! I snapped my fingers gleefully. I could taste the acid bite of high excitement rising in my throat. Thousands in this city couldn't give us anything on Billy's murder, yet Maud Divans had scored a bell-ringer not just once but twice.

She'd spotted Billy walking east on Marsh and now she'd given me a possible description of the car itself—the car that carried that broken little body to the field.

My phone rang again. It was Penross.

"I can tell you more about those marks, Kate," he said. "Not what caused them, but this much anyway. They're definitely burn marks and they were inflicted posthumously, but I haven't a clue as to how they got there—we may never know that.

"Another thing—Billy's stomach was almost empty. He hadn't eaten for at least five hours prior to death, except, perhaps, for a small snack."

I bit my lips while I considered his words. The marks were curious but I'd let them go for now. The empty stomach could mean the boy was killed shortly after Divans saw him walking down Marsh ... and shortly after he'd left my house.

I'd always had a rock-bottom hunch he'd been killed the same day he disappeared and, if this were true, I could now narrow the time of death to late afternoon or early evening, before he'd had a chance to eat another full meal.

I moved to the computer and began to do some homework. I'd checked the Schuylers once before, just to see if either had a record. Now that we'd found the boy murdered, I had to know a whole lot more.

I ran the parents for warrants, aliases, previous addresses, but nothing showed. Then I asked if either one had ever been a suspect in a crime and the machine began to chatter back to me.

What it said stunned me and made my eyes bug open—Thomas Schuyler stood accused of beating up his wife in June of '93 and then again just nine months ago.

I ran downstairs, pulled the reports from a records file drawer, then stared at the pages in my hand. You could never tell—no one knew that better than I— and yet I admit I was totally surprised. What had I

A DESPERATE CALL

thought that night while driving home? That horrors can exist behind exteriors of normalcy? Well, here was proof.

Both times a neighbor had called the cops after hearing screams coming from the Hollis Place address. The officers saw no bruises on the victim, though Mrs. Schuyler told them her husband had slapped her repeatedly on the head.

He, in turn, admitted touching his wife but denied using any violence. He said he merely grabbed her to calm her down after angry words between the two.

Joyce Schuyler had refused to prosecute, despite the urging of authorities, so the charges were eventually dropped.

I dialed the number of the neighbor who'd called the cops and a recorded voice came on and told me that phone had been disconnected.

I called a family two doors up from the Schuylers and asked did Robert Wellmont still live next door?

No, a Mrs. Burns replied, he'd been transferred to Visalia one hundred miles south nearly three months ago, but if I wanted, she could give me his new number.

I told her to keep my call confidential, depressed the button, then released it and dialed the Wellmonts.

A woman picked up the phone and spoke against the laughter of children in the background. I asked to speak with her husband and when he came on the line, I told him who I was and that I wanted to talk with him about his former neighbors.

He readily agreed and we made a date for six-thirty one evening later on that week. I didn't ask him any questions and he didn't offer any information—it would all keep till then.

* * *

I visited Tommy in the hospital every chance I got. Physically, his wounds were healing nicely, except for that limp and useless arm, but psychologically he'd sustained a lot of damage.

The chase and the ensuing fall had terrified him, and the memory wouldn't go away. On top of that, his feelings of hostility toward me had hardly lessened, despite my constant reassurances of love.

When he came home, I thought, I'd find a therapist who'd work with both of us together, who'd make him understand I really cared.

One night Jon joined me. Though he, too, saw Tommy every day, he usually visited in the early afternoon—maybe because he knew I wasn't likely to be there then.

We sat stiffly, on either side of the narrow bed, while our son lay quietly between us.

And then—I don't know who started it—one of us began to run our fingers underneath the covers, making little humps like a mole scooting in a burrow, and the other grabbed the humps and stopped its progress.

Tommy saw the game—it was for his benefit, after all—and began to laugh despite himself, and soon the three of us were cutting such a caper, just like old times, that a nurse poked her head in the door and told us to tone it down.

"Katharine, go again—she's down the hall," Jon whispered conspiratorially, and, much to our son's delight, I made another "mole" beneath the spread and felt Jon's hand tighten down on mine. This time, though, he did not release me but looked deep into my eyes.

"I love you, Katharine Harrod," he told me in a

A DESPERATE CALL

caressing voice. Caught off guard, I gave a little nod but didn't answer.

He hadn't pressed me any further about my stopping work, but there was an unspoken understanding that I would come to a decision soon. I put it off, I couldn't do it—not the way he wanted, anyway—so I became adept at avoidance of the subject whenever I could see it coming. His increasing coolness toward me, save for this evening's unexpected burst of tenderness, told me that he knew what I was doing.

Chapter Eight

I'd dropped in on Billy's teacher, to find out more about the little boy. Helen Hornsby was a large woman with long thin legs and thick-lensed glasses that rested on a short round nose. She was also the best-loved fourth-grade teacher at Willow Elementary.

"What kind of child was he?" I asked.

"He was a sweet child, Detective Harrod, and I don't mean that in a nicey-nice way. He never tried to be teacher's pet, but you couldn't help but like him. He was on the quiet side, very polite, and yet there was nothing sissy about him. The other children, both boys and girls, seemed to like him, too.

"He was just an average student, but he always took such an interest in everything we studied...." Her voice trailed off and she was silent. "He could be very funny," she finally continued. "Sometimes he'd make a little joke and when everybody laughed, he'd be a little bit embarrassed and then extremely pleased."

I asked her if she'd ever noticed any mood changes in Billy.

"Do you mean moment-to-moment or for longer periods, Detective?"

"Either way—anything at all you can tell me."

Miss Hornsby thought for fully thirty seconds, then she answered me.

"There was only one time I noticed anything and afterward I even wondered if I'd been wrong. Last September, shortly after school started, Billy seemed especially quiet, withdrawn, very serious.

"I would've thought it was the newness of a different teacher, a different class, or else it was the child's natural personality, but I'd taught him in music the previous spring—I knew him and he knew me."

I asked how long the mood had lasted, and she said about a week, as best as she could recall.

"Then he started coming out of it and soon he was the Billy I'd known before."

I turned my attention to the family, asking if she knew them well. She told me she saw the mother only at parent-teacher meetings, but that she'd known Thomas Schuyler for years.

"Well, let's more correctly say I've known *of* him, Detective. I've met him several times, of course, but the Schuyler boys were raised here in town and so was I, so I've been aware of their existence for a long, long time."

"Did Billy get along well with his parents?"

"Oh, I think so," the teacher told me openly. "At least, I never had any reason to believe otherwise."

Finished now, I rose to go and she walked through the hallway. She stood a moment before she said goodbye and when she finally spoke, her voice began to break.

"I've never lost a child before," she sobbed. "I feel it very personally." Then, before I could start to comfort her, she quickly shut the door behind me.

* * *

I found Darrow busy working on the sex offenders.

"Katie, baby, I might have a possible," he told me, looking at me with a raised eyebrow. He'd propped his long legs on the desk, his feet in their charm-boy Gucci loafers crossed casually at the ankle.

"Remember good old Harry Hansen, the pervert who spread peanut butter on his victims' privates? His specialty was little boys between the age of six and ten, though he'd do a little girl if all else failed. Well, get this—computer's showing Harry was paroled last month."

"Very interesting," I answered. "Get an address on him and check it out. If it's a good one, we'll pay a little visit."

If I remembered right, Hansen had a sister who lived just east of town and he used to stay with her occasionally.

"I always wondered if he found the smooth or chunky spread worked best," Darrow wisecracked, smiling.

My head jerked up. I stared straight at him. I wasn't amused, but he didn't seem to notice—he was absorbed again in Hansen's rap sheet.

I sat down and rested my chin between my hands. What was the meaning of those battery reports anyway? Had Schuyler actually struck his wife or was she adding high drama to a couple of basically innocent incidents?

If he *had* struck her, why, and were these the only times he'd done so? How many batterings had occurred when there was no neighbor nearby to hear the screams?

If a man beats his wife, he'll often beat his kids—

that's the way it seems to work. I've seen the statistics and I've handled too many grim cases to disagree with them.

Had Schuyler ever battered Billy? I didn't know that, but I did know he drove a tan Oldsmobile. Light in color, American in make, like the car seen at the field the night Billy disappeared.

The detective's name on the follow-up was Niles and he'd transferred to the San Madera east end about four months ago. I'd ring him up and try to jog his memory on the Schuylers.

Suddenly I was tired. I felt a depth of weariness that even coffee couldn't cure. I knew a lot of it was emotional, stemming from my personal situation, but I was worn down physically, too.

I could feel my sharpness dulling, my mind involuntarily gearing down. If I didn't break the pace, I'd soon begin to miss things, to fail to pick up on facts I'd have grabbed at two hours earlier.

I told Darrow I was leaving and to call me if he got a good address on Hansen.

I meant to go straight home, but instead I drove along Hollis, turned east on Marsh and parked beside the vacant lot. It ran fully half the block and was bordered on both sides by tall hedges.

Across the street, only three houses faced it directly. Of those three, just one—a split level—gave a clear view of the street and the property beyond it. The other two were California ranch style, with mature trees and bushes creating a screen of privacy against their windows.

An abductor could easily stop here, entice a child into his car, and drive off without ever being seen, even at four-thirty in the afternoon. Of all the blocks in the area, this one probably offered the best setup for a pickup.

Is that why we'd found no trace of Billy past this point? Because he met his killer here and didn't walk one step farther east? I glanced again at the houses with the hidden windows. It seemed highly likely.

No one called out when the screen door banged behind me, then I heard Jonathan's voice talking on the phone.

"Wait a minute—I think she's here now."

Silently, he handed the receiver to me.

"I've got a good address on Harry Hansen," I heard Darrow say. "That one of the sister's checked out. I've talked with several people who say a guy fitting his description's been going in and out of there for a week or so at least."

"Great," I replied eagerly, my tiredness suddenly slipping away. "Let's go do some cage rattling on him early in the morning."

"Wait a sec, babe, there's more—I found something that looks really promising. A man was pulled over for speeding at three forty-five on the day Billy disappeared, less than two blocks from where he was last seen. He showed ID belonging to a James Lord of Los Olivos and said he was passing through town on a business trip. I haven't run him yet, but here's the hooker—he was driving a white '86 Chevy."

"Nice going, Steve. See what else you can dig up on him."

We agreed to meet at six a.m. to go see Hansen.

"Hallelujah," I cheered as I hung up, "the ball's beginning to roll at last."

Tommy would be coming home from the hospital in several days and by then I'd have to find a way out of my dilemma. Relations with Jon were straining toward a breaking point.

I'd tried to set a plastic bowl up on the shelf as I was doing the dishes after dinner. Somehow—perhaps because of soap left on my fingers—it'd slipped away and bounced down on the floor. Jon, coming up behind, grabbed it from my reaching hand and placed it high above the sink where it belonged.

"If you weren't so damn tired that wouldn't have happened," he snapped at me. "You'd have been able to hold onto it instead of dropping it."

Stunned at this unfair attack, I admit I lost it.

"Jesus Christ, Jon, I'm not tired and that's not the reason it fell. Anyone can make a mistake like that, even you. I don't want to hear it if you can't be civil—you'd never have talked to me like that a month ago."

He moved his face in close to mine till I could feel his hot sweet breath fan my face.

"This is not a month ago, Katharine, this is now. And everything has changed."

I didn't answer—what was left to say?—but silently put away the other dishes, then left the room.

A marriage that had seemed solid for so long had suddenly moved to unfamiliar hostile territory, and now I wondered if it had ever been as sound as I once believed.

Perhaps Jon's resentment of my work had always gone far deeper than I thought, and Tommy's accident had lit a fuse that had been smoldering just beneath the surface for many, many years.

Oh God, I thought, I love him so. I love them both, but I can't believe I'm wrong.

I felt alien, on the outside, a person unjustly accused. I'd never thought I'd slighted Tommy, never felt I'd let him down emotionally.

Just bear with me through this case, I thought. Then I'll find a way to make it right for everyone, including me.

"What did you find on Lord?" I asked when I picked up Darrow at the station.

"He's squeaky-clean, not even an outstanding warrant. According to DMV, he's lived at the Santa Barbara county address for nearly eight years. I wanted to check with you before I did any phoning."

Maybe Steve was learning something. It wasn't like him not to plunge ahead without a word to anyone.

"Sure, we'll ring him up when we get back from Hansen," I said breezily, "see what Jim-boy's got to say for himself. You never know."

Steve shifted in his seat till he was looking straight at me. His brown eyes danced and held a teasing look.

"Jon seemed a little tense when I phoned you yesterday. Is everything okay at your house?"

"I appreciate your interest, Darrow, but everything's just fine," I lied.

"Uh-huh," he said knowingly. "Well, maybe it's just male menopause, then. I could a' sworn he was a bit out of sorts about something."

I didn't answer but I boiled inside at his nosy persistence with a subject that I'd really like to sidestep. Deliberately, I led him away from it.

"It'd be great if we could at least place this guy near his old hangout, the schoolyard, sometime that afternoon."

"Yeah," Steve agreed readily, "the owl sure don't go to the mouse picnic to pitch horseshoes."

We drove east, passing through the business district and coming to the other side of town. The houses were small with unkempt yards, and junker cars sat parked in several driveways. We stopped beside a bungalow with yellow paint that peeled from dried-out wood.

"It's three doors down," I said. "Let's walk from here."

It was only twenty after six but that suited me just fine—I like to get a suspect nice and early in the day. Tumbling out of bed, still filled with sleep and facing me, he doesn't have the time or wits to polish up a lying story. His mind can't cull and sort and put together a pretty presentation for my ears. I'd rather try to get the truth at daybreak than at any other hour.

We knocked and stepped aside. Somewhere in the back a dog barked and then was quiet. I heard a shuffling sound inside and saw a short woman with sallow skin and a toothless mouth peering at us past a curtain.

"Police," I called. "Let us in."

She opened up the door and stood beside it and we went past her quickly, to the rear. The house was single-story with five small rooms, all of which I could see from where I stood. The door to one was closed. We pushed it open.

Harry Hansen had heard the noise and was climbing out of bed, hurriedly pulling boxer shorts past his buttocks and around his bulging belly. His fingers fumbled as he tried to do the fastener on the waistband, his eyes were glazed with interrupted sleep. He tripped forward in a stupor, then grabbed the bedpost to support himself. He knew exactly who we were.

"Fuckin' cops," he seethed, "bustin' in like this."

Then he looked at me and sneered. "Oh, pardon me, dear lady—sure hope I didn't hurt your pretty ears."

The blue-black lines of prison house tattoos showed on both his arms against the pallor of the skin. His gray hair stood in jagged greasy spikes above his scalp and angry weasel eyes glared at us with hatred. I'd seen him or others like him till I was sick of them.

"Sit down, Harry," I began, "and tell me all about yourself."

"What's to tell? You know it all—you and your fuckin' computers like Mother Russia keepin' track of everyone."

"So tell us anyway. When did you get out?"

"Three weeks ago, maybe four. I don't know."

"Oh sure you do. You've got that date engraved on your heart, Harry, so don't give us that jive."

"Okay, it was April thirteen."

"Your lucky number, that one," Darrow chimed in. "Where've you been since then?"

"I got a job up north and I was workin' it."

"We told you to give it to us true, Harry. You've got no job up north. I bet you didn't even stop to take a piss before you straight-lined it right down here to home sweet home."

"Okay, so I got a job here."

"Doing what?" I asked, picking up the beat.

"Over at a carwash."

"Names and addresses please, Harry. I'm not into pulling teeth this early in the day."

"Simpson's, third and Alvarado." He grumbled to himself and slid his bare feet back and forth across the floor.

"When did you start?"

"Two days after I got out. My sister got it all lined

up." He jerked his head toward the hallway where the little woman stood listening.

"Okay, Harry, you're doin' just fine so far. What you been up to in your spare time?"

"Nothin'. What's this all about anyway? Why're you roustin' me?"

I ignored the questions and gave Darrow the nod to take over.

"Tell us about the weekend of April seventeen, Harry—what did you do for amusement?"

"I worked all day Saturday and Sunday I was right here. Ask the sister."

"No walks around, no visits to the parks or playgrounds?"

"Motherfuckers," he exploded and spittle flew from corners of his mouth. "I see where all of this is leading. Some weeny-wagger somewhere shakes it at a little cunt and everyone comes lookin' for Harry."

"You've got that wrong, Hansen—we know you're not a weeny-wagger."

I moved forward.

"Forget the weekend, Harry—tell me about the following Monday."

"I went to work."

"So when did you get off?"

"Four o'clock."

Steve and I exchanged glances.

"And then?"

Harry Hansen broke into rolling laughter. He edged backward to the bed and sat down so forcefully the mattress creaked and sagged. The weasel eyes showed triumph and exhilaration.

"Oh, I know now for sure. I watch TV, I saw about that Schooler kid. And I got one for you stinkin' dicks—I was with my parole officer. How's that for an alibi?"

Hansen told us he got off work early, to keep an appointment with parole, the first since his release.

"You don't think I'd be dumb enough to miss that date, do you? I was there from four-thirty till nearly six. They always crowd up at day's end and I had to do some waiting."

We took the name of the person he'd seen and, just to be on the safe side, phoned from Hansen's house while we still had him in our sight. I dialed a special number for nonbusiness hours and an employee told me Harry Hansen had signed in at four twenty-five and hadn't signed out till five forty-three on the day in question. The interview itself had started a little after five.

I'd call tomorrow, to make sure Hansen had actually stayed in the office the entire time, but it didn't really matter. Even if he'd stepped out, he wouldn't have had time to pick up Billy, murder him, hide the body, and return by five o'clock.

We left without much ceremony. Like he said, for abibis you couldn't get much better. As we walked down the footpath, I saw the sister back a car from the garage. It was a dark blue compact, probably Japanese in make.

CHAPTER NINE

"Call James Lord," I told Darrow when we reached the station, "and I'll sit in on the extension."

The number was with Santa Barbara information. Steve dialed it and Lord himself picked up the phone. He was obviously surprised to hear from us and thought it concerned the traffic ticket.

No, Steve told him, it concerned another matter—where had he gone following the stop by our traffic guys?

He didn't hedge. Jim Lord told us straight out he was coming from a morning meeting at his company's home office near Sacramento and was heading to a four-day convention in Los Angeles when patrol spotted him.

"That's the reason for the ticket," he explained. "I had a lot of distance to cover and I was bearing down a bit too hard."

He told Steve he continued driving south, arriving in L.A. a fast four hours later. Apparently, the citation had only temporarily slowed him down.

Darrow asked him where he'd stayed and he said the Bonaventure. He thanked him and hung up without further explanation.

Steve called the Bonaventure Hotel and spoke with

registration. He asked the clerk to pull a record for the night of Billy's disappearance and tell him exactly what time Lord had checked in.

Some staff can be rigid and unbending and will insist they can't tell you anything without a subpoena while others will cooperate as if they wished you'd asked them something harder.

Steve got lucky—he laid the charm on the young lady desk clerk and she gladly told him everything she knew. I liked her willingness but I didn't like her words—James Lord's registration card showed he'd checked in at seven forty-five p.m. He'd been much too busy driving fast to murder little boys.

Steve was on the phone again, but he wasn't talking to hotel staff, he was chatting up some woman for a date that night. His rough and arrogant manner, the persuasive grin that played below the boldness in his eyes, had a sure effect on other females, if not on me.

I'd never seen him with the same one twice, but you could count on two things—Darrow's girls would be beauty-pageant pretty and they'd hang on him adoringly. He liked the challenge of the chase and he liked a date that made him look good. No matter they were easy-come, easy-go, like so much small change in his pocket.

I sighed and told myself to walk on by. This was none of my business anyway, except that he was doing it on my time. Besides, if I said anything he was vain enough to think I was jealous.

I decided I'd head on over to Hollis Place and sniff around the Schuylers' neighbors.

I started door-knocking at the north end of the street and found most people were willing, even eager, to talk to me. The problem was they weren't telling me anything useful.

Again and again, I heard they knew the Schuylers but didn't know them well. The families nodded as they passed on the street or did their yardwork, but no intimacy was involved.

It seemed the Schuylers were a fairly average bunch, not given to troublemaking, who kept pretty much to themselves—in other words, good neighbors.

I heard a discordant note only once, but it played out full-blown.

I'd rung the bell at the house across from Billy's and a thin blonde with upswept hair and large brown eyes invited me inside. She wore a pink-striped playsuit and explained that she and her husband were barbecuing in the backyard. We went through the house and onto the patio, where Paul Miller was shaping raw beef into burger patties.

The Millers listened intently to my questions, then exchanged slow glances before they answered, obviously reluctant to talk about their neighbors.

"Believe me, this is all in confidence," I told them. "I'm only trying to get a picture of Billy's background, just for me to know."

The blonde began to speak.

"It's nothing definite, Detective, just a feeling that he doesn't like them very much."

"Who?"

"The dad. I've never seen him smile or say one kind word to his wife. Or to the kids, for that matter. He always seems so cold and so detached."

"A pompous ass is what you mean," Paul Miller contributed, "let's call a spade a spade. Got a board stuck up his backside, takes himself so seriously. Excuse me for my mouth, ma'am, but that explains it best."

"Have you ever seen him hit Joyce or the kids?"

"Oh, heavens no, nothing like that, Detective. Please don't misunderstand me." Rose Miller seemed genuinely shocked.

"They've got a daughter," I went on. "What kind of girl is she?"

"Have you seen her, Detective?" Miller asked.

I nodded.

"Then you know."

"I'd like to hear your opinion."

"It can't have anything to do with Billy," he parried.

"Just tell me."

"She's trash—hotter than a gypsy dancer. Up till two years ago, she was a cute kid but then she changed. She grew up but in the wrong direction. Ask the wife."

Mrs. Miller nodded in agreement.

"All you've got to do is watch her walking down the street to know she's asking for it," she said, "and finding it, too, from what I've seen her with on street corners."

"How did she get on with Billy?"

"I never saw her with him," Rose Miller continued. "I doubt she even knew he existed."

I decided I'd take a break. I thought of calling Jon, but I didn't know if he'd be glad to hear from me. I was riding down a road I'd never ridden down before, and I had to go gingerly, carefully, and always stay a little bit on guard. I wasn't in the mood for that right now so instead of going home to eat, I headed for a coffee shop several blocks away.

Marty's served the strongest, hottest coffee in town. That was reason enough for me to forget about my ulcer for a while. The bonus was that the food was first-rate, too—ample, fresh, and tasty. A Marty's sandwich would carry you to dinner and occasionally beyond.

I sat at the counter and lost myself in the menu. I was hungry and I intended to indulge. A hand on my shoulder broke my concentration and Pete Blackwell eased himself onto a stool beside me. He ran a small hardware store in town and we'd known each other casually for years, ever since I'd walked the beat around his neighborhood.

He told me his wife was out-of-town, so he'd decided to treat himself to Marty's.

"And treat it is, Kate," he said in a slow, deep voice. "I could've eaten at the sister's, but somehow she never got the hang of it. Her food just lies there"—and he patted himself below the waist—"you practically have to ask it to get up and leave."

He wondered if I was working or if Jonathan was away, too. Working, I said.

"The Schuyler boy, I guess."

"Right. We're just getting started on it."

"You know, Kate, I jumped right out of my chair when I saw it on TV. Not the disappearance—I don't mean that—but where they found the body.

"Few years back—oh, three or four, I guess—I was lookin' to buy some property, thought I'd start me up a farm. Must've seen everything available from here to Bakersfield and back—felt like it, anyway. But here's the thing—that farm was one of them. Gave me the creeps when I recognized that shed and all."

"So what did you buy instead?" I asked. I hadn't known Blackwell was a farming man.

"Nothing. After all the looking, the wife decides country life won't suit her, so it just fizzled out. I don't know, though, someday, maybe . . ."

I enjoyed Pete Blackwell. He was big and he was slow and some thought him a hick who lacked the city polish, but I found him straight and unassuming and liked the fact he came with no frills attached.

We talked through lunch and through a final cup of coffee, then we got up and paid our bills and said goodbye. I could feel my ulcer getting angry, but I was full and satisfied and didn't really care.

I was out of bed by five-thirty—there'd be nothing but early days for me from now on. Driving to the station, I mentally laid out my plans. I'd check with Penross and Detective Niles, and get on down to Schuyler's bank. In midafternoon, I'd head for Visalia.

I poured a cup of coffee and set it on my desk, then dialed downtown. Penross wasn't in but his aide told me the body could be released on Tuesday. I phoned Thomas Schuyler. The conversation was succinct and to the point. He informed me the funeral would be held at two p.m. Thursday.

I sipped the hot brew and dialed the east end division Niles had transferred to several months ago. He was just walking in the door—his partner told me to hang on.

He came on the line and we talked shop for several minutes, then I told him what I wanted. He vaguely recalled the Schuyler cases but couldn't give me any details on them.

"They're the parents of the murdered boy," I told him, explaining my interest.

"No shit," Niles exclaimed, "I never made the connection."

"Don't worry about it," I said, "I'll check with the cops who took the calls."

Officers Alvarez and Hickson had responded the first time, Alvarez and Geer the second. I called the watch commander and learned both Hickson and Alvarez had transferred out of division, but Geer was still with us. He worked nights but the WC would leave word I needed to see him.

Half an hour later, much to my surprise, Officer Wayne Geer stood before my desk.

"I have court today," he explained. "Just happened to walk in as the WC was taping up your note."

I handed over his report.

"What's the real skinny on this?" I asked. "Can you give me anything that isn't here?"

He took a moment to read it, then nodded to himself.

"Sure, I remember now. Mainly because he's with the same bank I do my checking at, so I took a personal interest at the time. What do you wanna know?"

"How did you see it? Was it a righteous crime or was she just acting hysterical?"

"We couldn't see any injury," he told me, "but personally I believed the woman. We talked with her alone and she told us she screamed because he slapped her hard on the head. Wouldn't say why he struck her, though, and didn't want to sign the report.

"I saw him look at her when we were leaving and anger was blazing in his eyes. That's when I warned him if we had to return that night, I'd take him into custody. He was a cold bastard and as high-and-mighty as can be with us, but I've no doubt he did her just like she said he did."

I asked him if anyone else had been at home.

"Didn't see a soul," he said, and left for court.

The bank couldn't have looked more conventional. In a time when financial institutions do business in modern structures of glass and chrome, Westside Savings was a throwback to the forties. Standing on a corner and built of granite block, the open space inside stretched two stories above its marble floor.

I was shown into Wilson Royce's office and inwardly I smiled. With his white hair and rimless glasses, the bank president was right in keeping with the architecture. We chatted amiably for a few minutes, then he began extolling the virtues, both personal and professional, of Thomas Schuyler. When he started to repeat himself, I asked to see some other staff, leading off with Schuyler's secretary.

Marion Gibson was all business—she must've pleased her employer tremendously. It soon became obvious he pleased her, too.

To Miss Gibson, Thomas Schuyler was the perfect boss—an organized, efficient man who functioned on a precision schedule of predictability. I doubt she ever looked beyond his business self or wondered at his life outside the office—her only interest was the way he handled finance from nine to five o'clock. I asked her to send in the next employee.

By early afternoon, I'd finished with the lot. I'd gained no startling revelations about Thomas Schuyler, but a consistent picture of the man had steadily emerged from all the chatter—he was a highly motivated, low-key person who kept his business life and personal life strictly separate.

Ready to leave, I thought a moment, then asked Royce to show me Schuyler's office. I knew he'd taken some time off so I wasn't worried about running into him and having him wonder why I was nosing around. The banker unlocked a dark oak door and stood nearby while I walked in.

"When was he last here?" I asked.

"On Friday afternoon around two-thirty. He left right after detectives called and asked to meet him at his house."

I looked around. The desk was clear of work, the blotter straight against the leading edge. A stack of papers sat neatly on a table, a crystal paperweight placed squarely in their middle. The obligatory photo of wife and children was framed beside the phone.

"I suppose Miss Gibson tidies up for him," I said.

"Oh, no, she doesn't," Royce replied, "he makes sure he's the one who does the tidying. He trusts her implicitly but he won't let anyone touch this office but himself."

The call, of course, had come from me, telling Schuyler a body had been found, so he'd either worked till then in a clutter-free environment or he'd taken time to straighten his office after I phoned, despite the gravity of my message. I believed the latter and this action told me much about the man.

I reflected on the duality of Schuyler as I drove back to the station—the fast-rising financier to whom appearances were paramount, the wife beater who did his battering behind closed doors. An icy, calculating man of self-containment on the one hand, an emotionally volatile being on the other.

Except I didn't believe that for one single minute. I believed Schuyler always acted right in character, with calculated moves. If he'd struck his wife, he'd done so with cold deliberation, not in heat of passion, and neither shame nor remorse had followed that act.

I collected some items from my desk and headed for Visalia. Sun-drenched flatland stretched for miles beside the freeway, till distant mountain ranges stopped it cold, and swirling dust rose in small beige clouds as pickup trucks made turns in nearby fields. I was in the heart of California's agricultural district—the long and sprawling valley called the San Joaquin.

The road ran straight, north to south, through county after county, a thin white band baked in searing heat. I settled down to driving and the miles clicked off as gleaming eighteen-wheelers surged past me heading for Los Angeles.

Most people call this road boring, but I found it invigorating. The open space around me and the high blue sky above, the golden ground and faded purple mountains, let me shake off the closeness of the city. Pervading warmth and penetrating brightness soothed me. I felt enveloped in California sunshine that gave me the illusion it could last forever.

I neared Visalia around five-thirty. Wellmont had given me detailed directions to his house and I found it easily, then backtracked to a coffee shop for early supper.

It was a poor relative of Marty's and I thought of his healthy sandwiches and how I wished I had one now. This omelet wouldn't stick by me for long and I'd not get home till after ten tonight. Then I forgot about my hunger and concentrated on the reason I was here.

* * *

Wellmont was watching out for me and opened the door as my hand was reaching for the bell.

"We've just finished dinner," he said, "but will you join us for coffee and dessert?"

I readily accepted and we settled ourselves in a comfortable den. He was a skinny homely man with a long, sharp nose and crooked teeth.

His wife, on the other hand, was a pretty blonde with perfect skin, pale blue eyes, and a few extra pounds that showed but didn't matter. I sighed in envy and wished I could be so lucky—"pleasingly plump" wasn't a style that fitted me well.

A little girl who looked just like her read a book and pretended to ignore me. Her father introduced her as Wendy and told her it was time to watch TV upstairs. Obediently—almost eagerly—she left the room.

"If you're wondering why no protest, Detective Harrod, it's because we told her she could use the set in our room and bounce all over our bed," Wellmont explained. "To a six-year-old, that's a special treat. We decided we'd rather speak with you alone."

"Good," I said, "we can talk more freely that way. And I've got an eight-year-old so I'm familiar with the little bribes."

I asked if they knew about Billy's murder and they said yes, they'd seen the story on TV. Then I told them I knew they'd called the cops on Schuyler.

"As I understand it, you heard a woman you believed to be Joyce Schuyler screaming, but you couldn't make out any words and you didn't actually know if anyone was beating her or not."

"That's right," Wellmont said, "but I wasn't taking

any chances. I'd heard him yell at her before, but never heard her scream back like that."

Carol Wellmont excused herself, then returned with plates of apple pie and ice cream. She served them, then left to get the coffee. After pouring it, she joined us again, sitting straight up on a footstool with one leg tucked under her.

I asked if they'd ever seen any marks on Mrs. Schuyler.

"Never," Wellmont's wife insisted, "and we looked for them. After the trouble that first night, every time we saw her we sort of looked her over. It wasn't being nosy—it was more protective than anything else."

"Did you see much of Billy?"

Carol Wellmont nodded.

"Wendy's six—a lot younger than Billy—but he was a friendly kid who didn't like to be alone and when he had nothing better to do, he'd drop by and play with her. I think he liked to act the big brother bit. He was very sweet and she adored him."

"Did he ever mention his parents' fights?"

"No, he didn't, but sometimes he'd be quiet and kind of sad. That's how he was for several weeks both times after the cops came and that made us dislike Schuyler even more—because we believed the fights affected Billy."

She was probably right. The last time Wellmont called police was four days before school opened last fall and that visit coincided with the depression noticed by Helen Hornsby.

I considered my next question carefully, looking down at the rug and then at them.

"Did you ever see any marks on Billy?"

Hurriedly, Mrs. Wellmont answered first.

A DESPERATE CALL

"Detective, little boys always have marks on them—they fall, they bang themselves. You're a mother, you must know that."

"I mean marks that may not have been caused the usual way—bruises or cuts that made you wonder how they got there."

"Look, Detective," Wellmont broke in, "I don't like the man but I can't be saying I think he killed Billy just because we saw a bruise."

"I'm not asking you to say that—far from it. I'm asking you only about any obvious sign of injury. You did see some, then?"

They looked at each other, then he nodded to her and she began to speak.

"We talked this over before you came and we decided if you asked we'd tell you, even though we don't know if it means anything. Twice in the past year, I noticed bruises on Billy. Robert didn't see them himself but I told him about them.

"Neither time was close to when we called police, so I don't think they had anything to do with what happened to his mother. In fact, the last time was right before we moved, just three months ago."

"Where were the marks and what were they like?"

"Last summer they were on his upper arm, as if someone had grabbed real hard and squeezed the flesh hard enough to make it turn black and blue. Then, near Valentine's, his cheekbone was red and puffy."

"Did you ask him what happened?"

"Not the first time, but the second time I did. He told me he ran into a doorknob. He didn't seem overly concerned about it."

"And what did you think?"

"About his arm? I thought probably someone had

grabbed him hard enough to hurt and, like with the mother, I watched out for other bruising but never saw any for nearly seven months.

"When I saw the cheek and he told me about the doorknob, I noticed his face *did* come right to that spot on a door, so the injury could've happened just like he said it did. We moved right after that, so that was the end of it. There simply wasn't enough to go on either time to make a fuss about it, Detective."

We sat in comfortable silence, eating the last of our pie and sipping our coffee. Then I set down my cup. I'd just about run out of questions—meaningful ones anyway—so I left and began the long drive home to San Madera.

The stars were gone tonight and the moon was covered by moving clouds. Only the lights of oncoming cars brightened the roadway. The heat of the day had dissipated, replaced by waves of coolness. I rolled my window up and began to think about this whole sorry mess.

Had Schuyler murdered Billy and if so, why? I didn't have all the answers—all I had at this point were some clues that held together, some arrows pointing to directions to explore. When I learned his alibi for the hour Billy disappeared, its checking-out would go a long way toward telling me if Schuyler was the killer.

I shivered and it wasn't from the cold. How could a father strangle his own child and then break that child's neck? How could anyone kill a nine-year-old, for that matter?

The shiver passed and I stopped asking questions no one sane could answer. I switched on the radio and lost myself in the music.

A DESPERATE CALL

* * *

The showdown came later on that night—a nasty brutal scene unlike any other in my marriage.

It was nearly ten o'clock when I got home but I saw the light still on in Jon's study. He met me in the hallway.

"We've got to talk about this, Kate. I've got to know what you're going to do for Tommy. He needs you now, he needs you here."

I was ragged from a long day's work and longing for my bed. I felt beat-down and vulnerable and in no shape or mood for an emotional encounter. I slung my purse into a chair and collapsed beside it.

"I will work it out with Tommy," I told him wearily. "I will spend more time with him and prove to him I love him, but first I've got to do this case."

"You just don't get it, do you?" he snapped at me. "Later isn't soon enough. Something else might happen."

I stared at him in disbelief. My God, he actually blamed me for the accident, he blamed me for the fall and the torn tendon that would never fully heal.

"That's not fair," I cried. "I didn't make him run away and I didn't make him pitch over that cliff. For God's sake, Jon, think of what you're saying!"

Silence suddenly lay between us as we breathed heavily and paused a moment, like two weary fighters taking respite from a battle.

"So you won't give it up?" he finally asked, "or at least take a slot that lets you work some regular hours?"

I shook my head no and then he exploded.

"You know what, Kate? I think you never really cared about our little boy—you fuckin' never cared.

Oh sure, you say you do and sometimes you even act like it, but down deep inside you probably wish you'd never had him.

"Give you a crime to chase, a crook to catch, and you're off and running and leaving him behind. And then you wonder why things happen—you wonder and you weep but you never really change. And it's you who's got to change to make things better."

I'd never seen him this way before—yelling I didn't love Tommy—and I didn't know how to make it right because I could not do the thing he asked of me. Startled by his anger and wounded by his accusations, this time I was the one who turned and walked away.

Chapter Ten

Darrow and Mungers came in together the following morning.

"How was the trip south?" Carl asked.

"Very productive," I told him, "let's go in here," and we returned to the small room we'd used before.

I recounted the Wellmonts' tale of battery and bruising, then asked the pair how they'd made out yesterday.

"No damn good. We've gone through every adult we can find who had any sort of relationship with Billy," Darrow said, looking at his notes. "We worked our tails off and everyone's an angel. There's not one iota to check out further on any of 'em—no records, no gossip about them, zero."

I asked Carl about the lab and Billy's clothing, and he told me they'd picked up some fibers that could've come from some sort of blanket and also other fibers similar to those used in auto upholstery.

"If they got a sample from a suspect vehicle, they could try to do a match, but right now they're just on file till we give them something to compare them to."

Steve went on about his business but Carl followed me to my desk.

"How's it going, kid?" he asked as he sat down

heavily beside me, looking at the badge riding on his belt as if to check that it was polished to its usual standard.

"Like hell," I answered him succinctly.

"Care to talk?"

"He tells me I must hate Tommy, wish I'd never had him."

He raised his eyebrows.

"You got a real problem going there, Katie. That man's pulling all that crap out of some refined high-mountain air. He's reaching, but God knows for what or why. At least Lila didn't stick around tormenting me with a bunch of baggage like you've got to take."

"I'll work it out, Carl," I assured him once again. "It'll all work out eventually."

He looked at me a long moment before he walked away.

"You think so, huh? You really do? Well, Katie, I only hope it will. But remember this—you deserve far better than you're getting now."

The day had not been easy. I'd put up a good front at work—except for now with Carl—but inside myself I felt raw and scalded, my feelings raked by my husband's words, my emotions tumbling and tossing in confusion.

Was there any truth in what he said? Was I denying something to myself that really held validity?

I walked down the hallway to the little room and went inside and shut the door. I needed to hold communion with myself, to try to sort things out. I sat there for nearly an hour and when I left I wasn't sure I liked myself much anymore.

I saw myself as a fractured individual who'd come

A DESPERATE CALL

through childhood lonely and who'd vowed early on that any child of mine would never know such pain.

But was that vow held only in the abstract, and when I had my own son and faced the real-life demands of a growing boy, did I love him yet resent him, even though I pretended otherwise? Did I feel deep down he interfered with the work that I adored?

I thought of Billy Schuyler and my near-obsessive quest for his killer, a quest that threatened the whole fabric of my personal life. I began to fear I saw him as a symbol of my younger self and felt if I could make it up to him by punishing his murderer, I'd also make it up to that lonely little girl of long ago.

It was so easy to be kind and caring to someone who could no longer make demands on you, unlike the son I had at home.

And, if all of this were true, then I, who thought I knew myself inside-out, had been living with a stranger deep inside me all these years—a stranger who kept her real feelings masked and hidden in the inner chambers of her soul.

In all honesty, I didn't know what to think, but I suspected there might be some truth lying here somewhere, and I was left deeply perplexed and unhappy with myself.

Our son came home the following day, his arm in a protective sling, his face tired and pale. He seemed reserved, subdued, and he fell asleep shortly after we reached the house.

When he awoke, I held him close and told him that I loved him, but I felt strangely awkward and ill-at-ease. The words, the emotion which I'd thought so true before, had been perceived by him as false and now I'd started questioning them myself.

But I knew this much—I knew my heart turned over when I put my arms around him and I could not imagine a day without him in my life.

Jon and I maintained a tone of light civility in front of him, but behind his back we were barely speaking. He was adamant that I take some time off now and then step down as head of homicide.

I was just as adamant in my refusal. I'd told him I was going to think it all over once I'd worked this case through, but that answer wasn't good enough for him.

"Look," I'd said, "this isn't just some little office job that can be easily filled by some other typing pool girl. There's a real responsibility here and I've got to keep on going till it's finished."

He'd stayed silent and I'd walked over to him and laid my hand upon his shoulder.

"You could help me out if you only would. You know I love him and you could reassure him on that score. You're here with him all day long—you have a world of time to be on my side and tell that little boy he's wrong about me."

"I don't think he needs my words," he'd said. "I think he needs you here beside him."

And the evening ended coldly, as the morning had begun.

I'd planned to wait till after the funeral to talk with the parents and the uncle, but now I didn't see why I should hold off on Marc Schuyler.

I gathered his relationship with Billy had been more in name than actual fact—sporadic, absentminded, well-meaning but not intense. While he'd be understandably disturbed and shocked by his nephew's death, I didn't think he'd be in such intense emotional upheaval that I couldn't talk to him without a breakdown coming.

I knew he was a realtor and I found his work number and dialed it. The receptionist asked me to hold and, in a moment, Marc Schuyler came on the line.

He was showing property at four, he told me quietly, but he could meet me at his house at five o'clock. We agreed and I hung up. I remembered Jackie Day and smiled. I liked that peppy little dog and hoped I'd get to see him.

Then I remembered something else—the sudden intensity of that unexpected sexual surge that had coursed through me the first time we met. I could feel myself blushing even though I was alone, but at the same time I was curious to see if it happened the second time around.

I was ten minutes early so I parked across the street and waited. Precisely at five o'clock, a bright red convertible came down the block and swung into the driveway. Marc Schuyler got out and, looking neither left nor right, went directly to the front door and let himself in.

I stayed where I was for several moments, then followed him. My first knock brought a round of raucous barking and I could hear sharp nails hitting the floor in canine quick-steps. I knocked a second time and Schuyler came to the door. He'd taken off his sports coat and was toweling off his face.

"Come in, Detective, I was just freshening up," he told me. He stuck out one leg to hold the terrier back while he tossed the towel onto a chair, then bent to scoop up the little dog with one arm.

"Let him be," I said, "we might get along real good."

Jackie Day pranced forward and, after delivering a few growls to test me, began to sniff my shoes. Billy's uncle waved me toward the living room.

"In here, Katharine," he said jauntily. "I *may* call you Katharine, right?"

I stiffened.

"Wrong. Detective Harrod's just fine."

He arched his eyebrows but said nothing further.

We sat across from one another, in two well-worn armchairs. Schuyler leaned toward me, his elbow on his knee, his hand cupping his chin. The jauntiness had disappeared.

"It's so dreadful I can hardly take it in," he said. "I dreamt about it all last night. I always believed, despite everything, that we'd find him alive." His blue eyes held mine as he spoke.

"Of course you did," I sympathized, "that's not unusual at all. Sometimes hope's all that keeps us going and we've got to hold on to it very hard."

His face contorted and, as he'd done the first time I met him, Schuyler shielded his expression with his hands. I let him have a moment, then I spoke.

"I need to ask some questions. They're strictly routine and have to be asked in circumstances such as these. I'm sure you understand."

"Of course."

"What was your relationship with Billy?"

Schuyler started, as if he hadn't expected me to be so nosy in a personal way, but he answered readily enough.

"Not real close, I'm afraid. I always meant to spend more time with him, but the days slipped by and I'd

A DESPERATE CALL 151

find I hadn't done it. Then I'd swear to do better, but I'm ashamed to say I rarely followed through. Now, of course, when it's too late, I wish I'd acted differently."

"Did you like him?"

"Did I like him? You've got to be kidding, Detective—of course I liked him. He was my nephew, my own brother's son—just a child."

"How did he get along with his parents?"

"They adored him and he loved them right back. My brother was always bragging about him."

I set that one aside to ponder later, then I asked him the main thing I'd wanted to find out all along.

"Where were you the afternoon Billy disappeared?"

Marc Schuyler stared steadily at me for a moment, then dropped his gaze and stroked the sleeping dog.

"I suppose I should resent that," he said finally, "but I don't. I know you have to ask the question. Well, I was working—in fact, I was showing property most of the day."

"And you can prove it?"

"Sure I can. Want some names right now?"

"Uh-uh," I said, "later will do. Just so I know I can get them if I need them."

I stood up to go and he stood up beside me, hands thrust deep into his slacks pockets. With my heels on, I was almost at eye level with him and he looked at me a moment, then stepped forward till his face was close to mine.

"Do you have any leads?" he asked in a warm and easy voice while his eyes gazed steadily into mine.

It started all over again. I felt his breath touch my cheeks and I sensed an invitation to an intimacy I didn't really want, but which powerfully lured me all the same.

I was mesmerized by his sexuality. I could feel its rawness reaching out to me and radiating through me. I rebelled against it and felt hatred at myself for responding to it like a randy tart, but I could not deny it.

"A few."

I gave my standard cautious answer as I eased myself slightly to one side, but I could hear my voice cracking nervously and I knew my face showed my confusion. I was behaving like a schoolgirl and I'd lost control of the situation.

He knew it, too. Nodding slowly, he watched me while an amused expression played across his face, then he turned and walked away. The moment broke and we both walked toward the door, the little terrier moving with us like a rolling toy.

As I went, I looked around the bungalow. I saw no photographs of females, but I doubted Marc Schuyler led a lonely life.

I passed an open door and a handsome silver band set with oval turquoise stones caught my eye. It was a woman's bracelet and it rested on the nightstand beside the double bed. I couldn't say I was one little bit surprised.

The closet door was standing open when I walked upstairs, and when I looked inside I saw Jon's clothes were gone. I gave a little cry, then whirled around when I heard a sound behind me.

"I haven't moved far, Katharine—only to the guest room—but I can't stay in here right now."

He looked sad and drawn, but he made it clear to me that he'd have left the house entirely except for Tommy.

I asked him if he wanted a divorce—asked him with

A DESPERATE CALL

bravado while my heart crumbled in my chest. No, he said, not now, perhaps not ever. He just needed this separation of the two of us for a little while.

"But if I ever did, Katharine, you know that Tommy would go with me."

Stunned, I stood there, trying to take it all in. The thought of losing my son had never even occurred to me, simply because I'd never admitted the possibility that our marriage might totally disintegrate. I'd always optimistically believed the two of us would work our troubles out.

But I couldn't take that blind-faith ride any longer, could I? Not with the undeniable fact of Jon's move from our room staring at me through an open closet door.

"But he lives here," I cried. "They'd never let you have custody—you're the one who would be leaving, not me, and this is home for both of us."

"You're right, Kate, I couldn't take him with me right at first, but I think you're dead wrong if you believe I wouldn't eventually be awarded primary custody.

"You see, it's the nature of the beast we're dealing with here. The courts like a stable atmosphere for the child and I stay home all day to work while you don't. I've been the constant in his life every morning, every afternoon, and sometimes in the evening. If you had him, Tommy would be left with some stranger for many of his waking hours and the courts would never stand still for that as long as I'm home—even if it's not in this house—for twenty-four hours a day."

The blow of his words and the sudden realization that he could very possibly be right punched me in an almost physical way and I felt sick and weak inside.

"Damn you, Jon, how could you even think of doing this to us?" I hardly recognized my own voice. It quivered in a broken huskiness. "You know how much I love that little boy and how much it would upset his life to leave here."

"Think about it, Katharine, just think about the possibility. Because I'd never just walk away from him. I love him, too, and I'd fight to have him just as hard and in every way that I possibly could."

Sickened and shaking, I watched him close the door behind him.

Oh my God, I thought as I sank onto the bed, how did it ever get this far?

CHAPTER ELEVEN

We got to the cemetery long before two o'clock but kept ourselves well out of sight.

"Ah, God, Kate," Carl told me softly, "I feel so sorry for this family, losing their little boy, their little son. You had a close call with Tommy, but he's all right now and both of us should be so thankful—our children are alive but theirs is never coming home again."

His voice choked and I turned to him, surprised. Carl rarely showed emotion but this display was not what startled me. Rather, it was my sudden realization of the way in which he regarded Betsy.

Guilt swept through me and engulfed me as I admitted to myself that I'd never really thought of Betsy as a child—certainly not in the same way I thought of Tommy and his playmates. I'd seen her as some poor impaired creature who perhaps burdened Carl with her continued presence in this world and I'd felt sorry for him.

But I now saw that, clearly, he thought of her as his beloved daughter—different, yes, but just as dear and close to him as Tommy was to me. Not a burden, but a wonderous blessed child. In that moment, I loved him deeply and I nodded, my throat too tight to speak.

Soon, I saw headlights near the entrance gates and then the hood of a long black hearse followed by a line of limousines.

"They're here," I told the others quietly.

We watched the procession as it came toward us down the driveway. When it finally stopped and mourners ringed the grave site, we moved forward one by one and placed ourselves at different points throughout the crowd.

I saw the blueness of the sky and felt the warmth around me and remembered that the day Billy disappeared had been warm and sunny, too.

I guessed the crowd numbered nearly two hundred. Family and friends, sure, but I knew some of them were strangers who'd come only out of curiosity, because a murdered child was being laid to rest. I watched as eyes fixed in dreadful fascination on the small white casket embossed with golden angels.

Occasionally a murderer will stand among those strangers, keeping an unnatural alliance with his victim, and that's why we were there—to watch, to photograph discreetly, to be on hand in case anything unusual went down.

I stood a little distance from the Schuyler family, across the coffin from their shaded seats beneath a canvas canopy. They sat in silence, looking straight ahead.

Joyce Schuyler, dressed in a dark print suit, wore a plain hat and tinted glasses so large they covered half her face. She seemed extremely subdued and I guessed she was sedated. Her brother sat beside her, to her right, and as I watched, he placed his hand on hers.

Nadine was on her mother's left, wearing glasses just as large but even darker. A black veil fell from her forehead to her throat and through it I could see the pouting crimson lips. Her dress, black also, was cut low and tight at the breasts and from time to time, she raised her hand and slowly stroked the edging on the neckband just above them.

She crossed and uncrossed her legs and I saw she wore black pumps with sling straps and narrow heels at least four inches high. Gold link earrings hung almost to her shoulders and as she moved her head, their glitter sparked the shadows that surrounded her.

Knowing what I did about Nadine, I suspected she'd seized the drama of the moment to put herself on bold display. She might mourn for Billy, but she'd make darn sure she looked seductive while she did it.

My glance moved on to Thomas Schuyler, seated in the chair beside his daughter. His eyes weren't concealed behind dark glasses and I watched as he stared in front of him. I could read no expression whatsoever on his face. His brother Marc leaned toward him and whispered in his ear. He listened, then nodded but didn't speak.

I looked toward the little casket but I didn't shed a tear. I was working now—all business—and I couldn't afford the luxury of unrestrained emotion.

I began moving through the crowd, taking pictures when I thought I could do so on the sly. I knew that somewhere near me, Carl and Steve were circulating also—looking, listening, hoping for a lead to help us out.

The service started and I scanned the solemn faces. I saw sorrow and simple curiosity, but couldn't find a one that drew me to it and made me want to find out more about it.

Once again I focused on the family. Joyce Schuyler

was crying now. I could see her shoulders shaking as she wiped her eyes behind the glasses.

Aaron Carter placed his arm around his sister and drew her close. Nadine and Thomas Schuyler glanced at them, then looked away, while Billy's uncle bent his head and shook it slowly, side to side.

The sermon lasted only twenty minutes and then the little casket was lowered to the grave. As spades of dirt began to fill the open spaces, Thomas Schuyler rose abruptly, took his wife's forearm, and raised her from her seat. He quickly turned her back to Billy's coffin and led her from the canopy and across a sloping lawn to their waiting limousine.

Marc Schuyler stood up also and approached Nadine and Aaron Carter. They followed Billy's parents without a backward glance.

The limousine moved forward toward the gate and other cars soon fell in behind it. The remaining crowd dispersed. I watched the workers filling in the grave, till a corner of the coffin was all that showed above the dirt. Then I, too, turned and walked away. Billy Schuyler's funeral was over.

"Looks like that was a total waste of time," said Darrow as we scrutinized the photos the following day. "I can't see anyone who bears investigating."

He knew it didn't work that way, but I went ahead and spelled it out for him.

"Hey, hey, don't be so hasty. You and Carl go take these pictures and show them to the people on Marsh Street and along the San Marcos Road, to jog their memories on who might've been around there the day Billy disappeared and afterward. Get out there with them this afternoon."

A DESPERATE CALL

He ignored me and held up a shot of Nadine to the light.

"The daughter looks like a hot number," he said, leering. "That one might need a little investigation by the old pro himself. How old is she anyway? About eighteen?"

"She's only fifteen," I told him curtly and let the rest of his remark slide by. I piled up the photos and handed them to Carl.

"Take care of it," I told him, "and don't let Steve sneak any out for his personal use."

I walked slowly back to my desk and thought about the funeral, as I'd done ever since it ended yesterday. I admit I was disappointed—no matter how often I ran the mental freeze-frames through my mind, I could find nothing that demanded follow-up.

The family had been stoic, except for the mother's gentle weeping, so there was no bizarre emotion to pique my interest. No one had seemed out of character, as if he'd come for any reason other than curiosity or a genuine desire to pay respect.

I'd even driven past the cemetery nearly an hour after the service ended, to see if someone else had also returned or, perhaps, just arrived.

I found nothing. The grounds were empty except for two remaining workers patting down the dirt around the tiny mound. Oh well, perhaps the photos would bring a clue—I'd know later on this afternoon.

My talk with the Schuylers could wait no longer. When I called to say I was coming over, Aaron Carter answered and told me Thomas Schuyler was out, attending to some postfuneral details.

That suited me just fine. I'd have spoken with Joyce alone regardless, but with him gone we'd have even more privacy and hopefully a more relaxed atmosphere so she'd feel she could talk without restraint.

The brother opened the door and welcomed me cordially, despite the signs of deep strain showing on his face. I imagined it wasn't an easy house to live in at the best of times and would be even more trying now because of Billy's death, and I wondered if he regretted his decision to stay down here for several weeks.

"How's she doing?" I asked.

"Better than expected. Last night was rough, of course, but today I didn't even have to give her a tranquilizer—at least, not yet. She knows you're coming."

I heard footsteps on the stairs and Joyce Schuyler came down them slowly, holding to the banister. She walked toward me and gave me her hand, seeming more composed and in charge of herself than at any time since I'd met her.

It was possible once the funeral ended she'd finally been able to reach inside herself and somehow find a strength sufficient to sustain her as she tried to deal with Billy's death and the way in which he died. I hoped so.

"Dear Miss Harrod, I know you want to talk with me though I'm really not sure I know why, but we can go in here."

She motioned toward the living room and I sensed that Aaron Carter wanted to join us.

"We need to talk alone," I said, "and then I'll want to talk with you."

He nodded and turned away.

"Joyce—may I call you Joyce—I'm not here to cause you unnecessary pain," I began, "and I wouldn't

A DESPERATE CALL

have come so soon after the funeral if I didn't have to, please believe me."

"I know you have your reasons," she replied. "You've been so very kind from the beginning that, of course, I believe you."

I treated her gently, as if she were a fragile object that could be nurtured only in an atmosphere as soft as summer breezes. I knew if I scared her in any way, I'd lose the bond between us.

"Let's go back to that first afternoon—the day we met," I said. "Tell me what you were doing from four o'clock on."

"I was preparing dinner. I usually start around then and that night I had to peel potatoes and cut up some beans. I remember I was busy at the sink and listening to the radio while I worked."

"Did you go out at all during that time or did anyone come here?"

"No, I was all alone till Nadine came home around five o'clock and then Tom came in at five-fifteen."

"Does your husband always get in then?"

"No, no, he doesn't. He's usually earlier—he gets off at four-thirty—but I imagine he had some work to finish up."

She spoke calmly, in control, and I hoped I could keep her on this even keel.

"And Nadine?"

"She was at the library that afternoon—she goes there once or twice a week."

I hesitated and gauged my next words before I spoke.

"Mrs. Schuyler, how do you and your husband get along?"

Her head jerked up and she looked at me with large

and frightened eyes. I'd seen the same expression on faces of animals running from a forest fire.

"We're fine," she told me, then she bit her lip. "I just don't see what that has to do with Billy."

"Are there ever any arguments?"

"The usual, Detective, that's all. After all, we've been married nearly eighteen years—everybody disagrees from time to time."

"Joyce, I know something. I know the police were called to this house twice within the past two years. Please tell me what happened."

She crumbled visibly, as if I'd closed my hand on a stiff piece of paper and crushed it, reducing it in size and strength. She didn't fight me with denials.

"My fault, my fault both times," she wailed, "and that's why I wouldn't go to court—I brought it on myself."

I'd heard this pathetic guilt acceptance from a thousand other victims of domestic violence—they were always the ones to blame.

"Tell me how," I said, and I reached over and took her hand and held it. My heart turned over for this frightened little woman.

Again she bit her lip, and her face flushed deeply.

"Must I?" she asked pleadingly.

"I wish you would, yes."

"If Thomas even knows I'm talking to you like this or it gets out about those cops coming, he'll be furious. His job, you know—his position—it's so very important to him."

"This'll just be between the two of us," I reassured her, and I gave her hand a little squeeze.

"Sometimes I drink, Miss Harrod—I don't know why, but sometimes too much. Both times we'd been

A DESPERATE CALL

at a party given by another person at the bank and Tom thought I overdid it. I embarrassed him. He was angry and when we got home, we argued."

"Did he hit you? Did he hurt you, Joyce?"

She began to cry and I heard the door open quickly behind me.

"Not now," I told Aaron Carter sharply and waved him away, "we're all right." The door closed again.

"Yes, but I deserved it. I shamed him and made him mad and then when he tried to talk to me about it, I was silly and began to cry."

"Were there other times?"

"No, never," she said quickly, with strong denial. "Only the two you know about."

I'd leave that for now. If he *had* battered her more frequently, she wasn't about to admit to it today.

"Did he ever strike Billy?"

"No," she replied, but I saw the lie behind her eyes.

"Tell me about it," I said gently.

Again, she cried.

"Only a few times, when Billy did something wrong, just like any father would do. And not hard—never hard."

"Then why are you crying when I ask you about it?"

Her defenses went totally down.

"Because I felt so sorry for Billy. Tom never showed him he loved him, though I know he did. He just seemed to ignore him all the time and I could see Billy ached for his father's affection and felt so hurt when he didn't get it. I tried to make it up to him."

"Can you guess why your husband acted that way?"

"It's just his nature, Detective, to hold things in. And then he's so busy with his work."

"Does your husband hit Nadine?" I asked.

"Nadine? Oh no, not for ages. Nadine's different. She's so ... I don't know," and she waved her hand listlessly in the air, as if she honestly couldn't describe her daughter to me—probably because she didn't understand her well enough herself.

"I know this has been a strain on you," I told her, "but I'm almost finished now. Just go back to the night in April, after your husband came home. You called friends and then what?"

"We called, we rode around, we sent Nadine to the school grounds, then we came home and called some more and then Tom went out alone to search. He told me to wait here till he came back and if he hadn't found Billy we'd call the police, but sitting here all alone I got so scared for Billy I just couldn't wait any longer so I phoned myself, before he got back."

Whoa, I thought, wait a minute—this was the first I'd heard of Thomas Schuyler being out alone that night. I remembered the call had come in about seven-twenty.

"When did your husband leave?" I asked casually, "and when did he get back?"

"He left around seven o'clock," she told me, "and came back about a quarter to eight."

So there'd been a period of forty-five minutes when Schuyler had been on his own, supposedly looking for Billy. I mentally filed that fact away for future use.

Then Joyce Schuyler asked the question I'd known was coming.

"But why do you want to know all this, Detective—you can't think we had anything to do with what happened?" Her eyes grew wider and then crinkled shut in pain. "Oh no, that's just too cruel."

A DESPERATE CALL 165

"It's only routine, Mrs. Schuyler," I answered. "I'm sorry I hurt you but the questions had to be asked. It's a normal part of the investigation but now we can leave it alone and go on ahead."

She seemed satisfied by my explanation and regained her composure.

I asked if I could see Billy's room. I'd examined it several weeks ago, shortly after he disappeared, but now, in light of his murder, I wanted to see it again. Perhaps, among the toys and books and baseball cards, I'd find a clue I'd missed the first time around.

Joyce Schuyler led me upstairs and down a hall, then stopped when she reached a closed door. She turned the knob and pushed it slightly open.

"It's not been touched, Detective—go on in. I'll wait downstairs." She turned away.

I stepped inside and looked around.

A single bed stood beneath a window that faced onto the deep backyard. A bright blue rug was laid upon the floor and white wood bookshelves stood along the walls. They held a few adventure stories and some board games, but were mainly filled with the odds and ends all small boys collect—those little treasures that mean nothing to a grown-up but mean all the world to them.

I started to go through the shelves, then through Billy's bureau drawers and closet. I found clothes and shoes and several packs of chocolate creme-filled cookies squirreled away behind a pile of socks, but nothing that would help me solve his murder—no scrap of paper with a name or address, no alien object that defied a ready explanation.

I bent down and peered beneath the bed—more

games, a pair of skates, a ball of knotted twine. Nothing else.

I stood up and swung a final glance around the room. I saw a baseball shirt with Little League insignias tossed across a corner chair. I saw a small stuffed rabbit, its ears worn flat from years of pulling. I saw a place that looked endearingly familiar to anyone who had a growing boy.

And then my throat tightened and my heart clenched as if a sorrowing hand had cupped it and squeezed it hard, and I saw Tommy—saw him as clearly as if he'd been standing there in front of me.

The fear of losing him to Jon, never far beneath the surface since his threat, now hit me full-force, swept over me again and overwhelmed me, leaving me feeling weak and nauseous.

No, he wouldn't be dead like Billy Schuyler, but he would still be gone and I, like Joyce, would be a mother without a son. I couldn't bear the thought. I simply couldn't bear it. I felt the tears starting and I fought to push them back.

I stood there several moments, trying to compose myself. Then I gave another look around, paying silent homage to the youngster who'd once lived here, pulled the door behind me, and went back downstairs to where his mother sat, hands resting quietly in her lap.

I thanked her and told her I'd finished talking with her, but wanted to wait for her husband's return.

"And what about your daughter?" I inquired. "I'll have to see her, too."

"Nadine's at school," she answered. "You might think it odd, the day right after and all, but she said she'd feel better going—it'd take her mind off Billy—so we let her."

CHAPTER TWELVE

Aaron Carter waited for me in the hall. The stiffness of his stance and the stern look he gave me showed his anger.

"You were rough with her," he told me. "She doesn't need that now. You're a woman—you should understand. I don't think I really want to talk with you, okay?"

"Suit yourself, Mr. Carter, but I wish you would. I need to sort things out. I need to know all there is to know before I can decide what's important. Sometimes I touch on tender areas, but that can't be helped—they've got to be explored. That's what happened here. But it wasn't about Billy, if that makes any difference to you."

He was obviously startled and momentary confusion shot through his eyes.

"What, then?" he began, but faltered and continued weakly. "I can't imagine what else."

His shoulders dropped and the stiffness left his body. He waved me ahead of him into the kitchen and we sat at a small round table.

I was sorry he'd overheard his sister's crying. I needed Aaron Carter to trust me, to confide in me, to feel relaxed enough to tell me things about the

Schuylers that only someone close to them, but not one of them, could tell.

I asked if I could have a cup of coffee. I didn't really want one, but I thought if I could steal a few moments before we talked, I'd try to establish a rapport.

He nodded and walked to the sink and then the stove. He was a good-looking man of average height, with an easy smile and kind warm eyes, and I found myself wondering if he was married.

He took two cups from the cabinet and set them on the white tile counter, then he turned to face me.

"Look, I'm sorry. I shouldn't have gotten on you like that—I know better. I'm just making your job that much harder. Let's start again."

"Good," I told him, "I'd like that," and I took the unwanted cup of coffee from his hand. I was going to drink every single drop of it.

"How often do you see the family?" I began.

"Not often—maybe every four to five months is all. My job keeps me up north."

"Then you can't tell me much about the relationships here?"

"Can you be more specific, Detective?"

I hesitated, then decided to plunge right in.

"Has your sister ever mentioned any problems in her marriage?"

Aaron Carter began to shake his head, then paused and frowned.

"What sort of problems do you mean?"

"Physical abuse," I said quietly, all the while holding his eyes with mine. "Do you have any reason to believe your brother-in-law ever used physical force on your sister or the children?"

"Oh, come on, Detective," he responded, with some degree of astonishment. "If that wasn't so funny, I'd wonder what all this is leading up to. You're just fishing, aren't you? Tom would never do that even if he wanted to—it's not in keeping with The Image."

He laughed heartily and got up to set his cup down on the counter. I let it go. If he didn't know about the violence, I didn't need to tell him.

"Did Billy seem a happy child?"

"Always," Aaron Carter answered. "A happy-go-lucky little kid—a typical little boy but with a special way about him. I loved him and it kills me that he's gone." He looked away.

I heard a door click shut.

"Tom's back," the brother said. "Do you want to see him, too?"

"Yes, I do," I told him, "and thanks—thanks for talking."

He nodded silently, then glanced up as the kitchen door swung open and Thomas Schuyler walked toward us. He looked right past Aaron Carter and stared into my eyes.

"So soon, Detective?" he asked.

I caught the stare and threw it back.

"I'm sorry, sir, it has to be. Shall we sit down?" And once again I settled into a chair at the rounded table. Aaron Carter winked at me and moved toward the hallway, leaving the two of us alone.

"I'd prefer my study. If you'll follow me, please?"

Ordinarily, I'd have seized control, but I wanted to cut some slack for Schuyler, to let *him* set the pace and tone and believe *he* was the man in charge. When I'd laid back long enough, he'd know about it—till then, let him treat me like one of his secretaries at the bank. I wanted to see what tale he had to tell and I wanted him at ease while he was telling it.

I rose and followed him. The hall was empty and the living room as well. Through a large glass window I saw Joyce Schuyler sitting on a garden bench, her brother standing close beside her. From time to time, he bent to kiss her hair and stroke her shoulder gently.

We entered a small study, uncluttered like the office at the bank. He sat behind the desk and waved me toward the leather chair that faced him. He laid one hand in front of him and lightly tapped the blotter with his fingertips.

"Well?"

I spoke rapid-fire.

"Tell me about the day Billy disappeared. I want to know where you were, what you did, the works. Start with that morning."

My directness shook him, for his eyes momentarily widened, but that was all—he gave no other sign of his surprise. He continued to tap the desktop, in a slow and rhythmic motion.

"I got Billy off to school. His mother wasn't feeling well so I set out his breakfast, saw to it he had his lunch money and so forth. He dressed himself, of course."

"Did you eat with him? Did you talk?"

"No, Detective, he ate alone—or maybe Nadine sat with him, I don't know. I have coffee in here while I read the morning paper and brief myself on the day ahead. I need the quiet."

I thought of that poor little boy eating by himself in the silent kitchen. It seemed such a lonely way to start the day and I wondered if it'd happened often. I imagined that it had and I sighed.

"Did you see him or speak with him again that day?"

"We've been over that, Detective. The answer's still the same—no."

"We've not been over all of it," I snapped, getting down to the fine-lining. "Were you at the bank the whole time?"

"Yes, I was."

"When did you leave work?"

"At four-thirty—I always do."

"And you got home when?"

"Around five-fifteen, just like Joyce told you at the station that night."

I paused a moment and let the silence lie, then I continued.

"How long's the drive home, Mr. Schuyler?"

"Twenty minutes," he answered brusquely.

I waited. He looked at me haughtily.

"If you want to know why it took longer that night, I'll tell you, but I'm hoping this is leading somewhere. I had something on my mind—a business matter—and I needed time to think. I drove around some."

Suddenly, he became agitated, upset. I saw his mouth quiver at one corner and a look I can only call fear passed quickly through his eyes.

"Does this happen often?" I asked quietly.

"Very seldom, Miss Harrod—I normally come straight home."

I let him wait a moment, then I spoke.

"Now I'm going to ask you something I want you to reflect on before you answer. Take your time, think about it. Did you see any child, even from a distance, who resembled Billy in any way? Maybe in another part of town where you wouldn't expect to see him and so it didn't register immediately?"

He didn't take his time—he answered right away, with sharp impatience. He was in control again.

"No, and I wasn't in another part of town—I was mainly in this neighborhood, just circling."

"All right, but now you can see where this was leading," I told him calmly, ignoring the fear and agitation I'd noticed. "There was a chance that you might've seen something or someone that could help us—a remote chance, sure, but worth looking into. You didn't, but I had to ask. Sometimes the mind's strange—it doesn't recall events till long after they've occurred."

My words soothed Schuyler and allowed me to gloss over and slide past the golden nugget of importance I'd gained—for forty-five minutes, at the very time of day Billy disappeared, his father had no alibi. And, by Schuyler's own admission, his behavior of that afternoon didn't fit its usual pattern.

"Now let's move forward to the evening. You arrived home, your wife told you Billy was missing, then what?"

His fingers stopped their tapping and I saw his body relax slightly. Even his voice lost its icy edge.

"We called friends and rode around and called again and then notified police."

"Mrs. Schuyler notified police."

"Well, yes, but it's the same."

"Not quite. Where were you when she made the call?"

"I was here. No, no, you're right"—Schuyler smiled and nodded quickly—"I was out again. Of course. I wanted to look some more for Billy and I told myself

A DESPERATE CALL 173

if I couldn't find him, we'd call when I got back, but Joyce jumped the gun and phoned herself."

"But you'd just returned from looking."

No one spoke for several moments, then he took up the slack.

"I mean to be cooperative, Detective, and now I'm playing games with you. But this is unimportant, it's small, it can't matter.

"You've met my wife. She's easily agitated, loses control in any crisis situation. She was getting on my nerves—I couldn't calm her. I'm ashamed to say it, but I had to leave to get where I could be alone. And, of course, I *did* search for Billy while I drove."

"I'm a married woman—I know relationships can sometimes be difficult," I said, playing him along while I reflected on the truth within my words. "Tell me more about your wife—do the two of you get along well together?"

My approach failed. He looked at me warily, his guard up. He was no fool and he'd probably figured out I knew about the police reports. Even so, he still decided to fence with me awhile.

"We do just fine, Detective. We've been married eighteen years and only little problems."

"Then why were the cops called to your house twice in the past two years?"

He sat up ramrod-straight and his eyes narrowed.

"Don't play me dumb, Miss," he snarled. "If you know that, you've read those lying reports and you know what they say. But I told them then and I'll tell you now it wasn't true—I never struck her."

I gave him a moment to cool down, then I spoke.

"I've handled domestic violence," I told him, using

a sympathetic tone again, "and I know every story has two sides. Tell me yours."

He softened. Maybe my technique was better or maybe he was easily conned after all. More likely, Schuyler was enjoying the emotional charge that comes from confiding in another person—a rare feeling for him since he normally allowed no one to get close to him, but I'd forced my way in and now he found he liked it.

"Joyce is difficult, Detective. I told you she's highstrung—well, the truth is she drinks a bit too much. I don't know why. She never used to but then, about four years ago, I became aware of it.

"On the occasions you mentioned, she'd embarrassed both of us at a party and when I tried to talk to her about it she got hysterical. Some busybody stuck his nose in and called the police."

"I understand," I said soothingly, feeling like a Judas. "I'm a woman myself but honestly, sometimes I get sick at my own sex. They just go all to pieces and you have to take some action to get them to pull themselves together."

"Exactly," Schuyler eagerly agreed. "I couldn't tell those cops because *they* wouldn't have understood—I knew that right away—but the truth is I *did* slap her once or twice just to calm her down. It was the only way. I'm surprised and gratified you understand. You're a most unusual woman."

I looked at the rug so I wouldn't have to look at him. I'd gotten what I wanted, but I couldn't trust myself to hide the deep disgust I felt. He made me want to vomit. I waited a long moment, then glanced up.

"Does the drinking affect your home life?" I asked calmly.

"In the mornings. Sometimes she can't get up when she should. That's what happened the day we last saw Billy. That's why she couldn't tell the cops what kind of shoes he had on—she didn't know because she was lying upstairs drunk and wasn't here to see them."

Now I knew why he'd looked so strange that night several weeks ago when I'd asked his wife about the shoes.

"Why doesn't she get some help?" I queried.

"Oh, it's not that bad," Schuyler said with quick denial. "We'll work it out ourselves—no need to bring outsiders into it."

Right, I thought wryly, in case the word gets out.

He got up and walked away from me toward the window, his right hand thrust deep into his pocket. I understood the gesture and watched with great interest—I'd had a young professor who'd entertained himself the same way.

Sure enough, when Schuyler turned around again, I saw a slight bulge beneath his zipper.

Why, you old masturbator, I thought with some amusement, take your pleasure where you find it.

"Tell me about your son," I said, lifting my eyes to his face while I hid a smile, "did you enjoy him?"

"Enjoy? That's an odd word to use, Detective. He was my son—I felt what any father feels. I thought he was a little immature at times, but he was going to turn out all right."

I'd never heard a nine-year-old called immature before and the rest of his description made Billy sound like a model rolling off of an assembly line.

"Did you play with him much, do activities together, talk with him?"

"I don't play games, Detective, and I don't like activities, so no to the first two, and frankly I found conversation a bit limited with one in his age group. You have a boy yourself, I believe, so you can understand."

That hit real close to home, but I didn't offer comment. My relationship with Tommy was none of his business.

I asked if Billy needed discipline from time to time.

"Not much," Schuyler told me, "but when he did, I never hesitated. I don't believe in that liberal line—what's the term, 'giving them their space'?—but I was never harsh, never. Only a few quick smarts on the bottom and that took care of it."

The bruises seen by the Wellmonts hadn't been on Billy's buttocks, but I doubted Schuyler would admit to more, at least not now. I did a quick right turn.

"Nadine's a pretty girl," I said, and let the words hang out there.

Schuyler frowned.

"She's going through a hard period," he explained, using the same confidential tone I'd heard earlier in his voice. "The teens—I don't really understand them, but both my wife and I hope we can see them through."

He laughed with forced heartiness, then we stood up and shook hands across the desk. He smiled at me and his voice was friendly.

"It seems strange to say this, Detective Harrod, especially since we got off to such a bad start earlier on, but I enjoyed our chat today. I think we understand each other—you're not like the other women I know."

A DESPERATE CALL

I fooled you good, I thought. I know *I* understand *you*, but don't bank on the reverse.

He saw me to the front door and pushed it shut behind me. I walked slowly toward my car while two facts kept pounding at my mind—Schuyler used violence on other human beings and, for two separate periods in those critical first hours following Billy's disappearance, he had no alibi.

CHAPTER THIRTEEN

While Jon and I continued to exist in hostile tolerance, I felt my son and I were making some progress.

We'd attended our first therapy session together and he'd begun to open up tentatively to me, without the angry outbursts that had marked his words immediately following the accident.

I talked to him about Billy and how my searching for his killer in no way diminished or replaced my love for him.

"If Billy's mother was a detective, I'd wish with all my heart she'd do the same for you if need be, and that her son would understand and know she still loved him all the same."

He wasn't buying it just yet, but I could tell that he was listening—taking it all in to be digested later.

I knew—I truly believed—we could work it out together if we stuck with it long enough. And if Jon didn't try to take him from me, especially before he'd had a chance to really understand me and grow totally confident and unquestioning of my love for him.

There it was again—the fear of losing him, the ugly specter of the aching emptiness of life I'd know if I were forced to live without him. Jon had never again mentioned taking him away, but the haunting thought rode close beside me every single moment of my waking hours—sometimes lying back a little, other times rushing full-force forward to consume me and wrench my soul with sadness.

"You're still working, Mrs. Harrod?" the therapist asked as the session was drawing to a close.

"Yes, I am," I said defensively.

"Does it mean a lot to you?"

"Yes, yes, it does. I love what I do and I think that it's important."

"Good—then I'm glad you haven't quit."

Confused, I stared at her. Wasn't my working supposed to be the root of all the problems?

She smiled at me in apparent understanding.

"Perhaps you'd like to talk about it sometime, just the two of us. Maybe you could come in a little early for the next session."

I told her I'd look forward to it, and, indeed, my curiosity and interest were aroused. Why had she said "good" instead of scolding me and telling me I'd better give it up?

I was still mulling over her words when I dropped in on Helen Hornsby later on that afternoon. I wanted to talk with her again, and decided the question in my mind demanded a face-to-face meeting.

I found my way to her classroom and as I reached it a bell rang, her door flew open, and children raced past me giggling and poking one another as they ran. She was standing at the blackboard, erasing figures. I didn't want to startle her, so I waited till she turned around.

"Detective Harrod, this *is* a surprise. How may I help you?"

"I want to ask you something. I want to know if

you ever saw any bruises on Billy—bruises that seemed unusual for a boy his age to have?"

She flushed.

"I debated to myself if I should mention it," Helen Hornsby told me, "and I decided not to, but now that you ask, of course I'll tell you.

"Once last fall—long after his funny quiet mood went away—I saw a bruise on his forearm that looked as if someone had grabbed him and held him hard. There were separate little dark spots like pressing fingers make. I asked him what happened and he told me a playmate had squeezed him in anger.

"Then sometime last winter—in February, I think— his cheekbone was all puffed up. He said he'd run into a doorknob at home."

I asked if she'd believed him both times.

"I had to, Detective. We're required to report suspected child abuse, as you well know, but I didn't have enough here to report. There was no continuous pattern—only two isolated instances of bruising that could've happened just like he said they did—so I would've been way out of line to take any formal action.

"I decided instead to keep an eye out, but I never saw him hurt again. I forgot all about it till his murder stirred it up in my mind, but it's been bothering me this past week and I'm glad you asked—I feel as if a load's been lifted from me."

"But there were only those two times? You're sure?"

"I'm absolutely certain."

I said goodbye and started driving to the station. I now knew of three separate injuries to Billy within a six-month period—the cheekbone swelling and the double bruising of his arms. If three injuries had been spotted, chances were he'd suffered others that had gone unnoticed, perhaps because they'd been hidden by his clothes.

I'd no proof that Billy's father had been the one who hurt him and, even if I had, there'd still be no tie-in to Billy's murder. What I did have, though, was a strong alert—a warning bell telling me to keep on looking hard at Thomas Schuyler.

I'd done a lot of introspective thinking about my feelings for my boy, and I'd concluded that, in the flurry of emotional uncertainty following the fall, I'd asked myself far too many questions, analyzed myself far too much.

I didn't know that then, of course, but I knew it now. Time had let me get a little distance from those questions, so that I could stand a bit apart and see myself more clearly.

Instead of letting my brain provide the answers, I now rode with my gut feelings, and they told me I'd always loved Tommy, always wanted him, and would die if I had to so that he could go on living.

But in all honesty I also knew that sometimes I *did* resent him, *did* feel that he demanded too much of my attention when I wanted to be working on a case. And when I could finally admit this to myself, I felt a guilt I thought I could not bear.

"What the hell did you expect?" I asked myself, "when you went ahead and had a child?"

I couldn't give an answer to my question—not one that pleased me anyhow.

* * *

Darrow and Mungers were at their desks, fiddling with a toy Carl had bought for his sister's kids.

"I think I'll get another one for Betsy," I heard him tell Steve. "I think she could maybe see how to make it work."

Sadness gripped me. He'll never give up hope, I thought, nor should he. I cleared my throat to let him know I was standing there.

"Nothin' doin' on those funeral photos," he told me. "We showed them along Marsh Street and out the San Marcos Road, but no one recognized a soul. We worked our butts off."

I wasn't surprised. On TV cop shows, a mystery man appears in snapshots and turns out to be the killer. Sometimes it works that way in real life—that's why we took the pictures, after all—but not too often.

"Okay, put them in the file," I said, "we may need them later."

I poured a cup of steaming coffee and sipped it right away, not caring that the liquid bit my lips with a quick and stinging burn. It tasted good and the heat gave me a jolt I badly needed.

The phone rang as I was setting down my cup, and I found Marc Schuyler on the other end. When I heard his lazy, teasing voice, I didn't need to see his face to know it held that mocking grin.

"I thought maybe you and I could have dinner tonight."

Just like that. No preliminaries.

"Maybe you didn't know, but I'm a married woman." My heart pounded loudly in my chest.

"I didn't, but I wasn't sure it really mattered."

The insolence aroused my anger but it also aroused

A DESPERATE CALL

another feeling deep within me. I knew I should've said no, but I heard my voice saying yes.

I tried to tell myself it was all part of the investigation, but finally I sighed and gave up the pretense.

Quit conning yourself, Katharine, I thought. You know exactly why you're going.

I'd never met such sexual magnetism before and I found it difficult to resist. I'd no intention of getting involved with him—oh, no. I just wanted to titillate myself a little further, to dip a little deeper into that white-hot heat he generated and feel it swirling all around me. I wanted to stand on the edge of that steaming cauldron without falling all the way in.

I was playing a dangerous game I'd never played before—I knew that—but both the urge and the lure to do so were irresistible. I couldn't draw back and I wasn't even sure I really wanted to.

He picked me up at seven o'clock, at the station, and we drove to a restaurant on the other side of town. The talk was light, almost perfunctory, yet I felt a nervousness, a tenseness, totally alien to my nature. I was certain he could see right through me, as if I were the most transparent pane of glass, and know exactly how he moved me.

We drank some wine and I felt myself relax. He smiled at me and nodded.

"You needed that—you were wired up tight. It must've been a hard day at the office." The white teeth gleamed through the mocking smile as he let his eyes play around my face.

"Not particularly," I told him. "I don't know—I just felt a little tense before we came here, but you're right, I'm feeling better now."

He tried to fill my glass again, but I laid my palm

across the top. Silently he took my hand in his and held it, then went ahead and poured. I didn't stop him—I let him do just what he wanted, pushing warning signals far back in my head. I was becoming reckless, not caring, completely mesmerized by this man sitting next to me.

We ate our dinner slowly as we sipped our wine. We talked, but very little about Billy. It was as if both of us wanted to avoid that painful subject. Finally, after coffee and dessert, he told me it was time to go.

We drove back toward town and I believed we were heading for the station. I'd pulled it off after all, I thought, giddy from the wine—I'd teased myself with my private titillation and no harm had come of it.

Then he spoke—casually, easily, the words rolling out without restraint.

"I've got to drop in to feed a friend's cat. It'll only take a moment—you'll come with me, won't you?"

I nodded. What could possibly be wrong with that?

We pulled up in front of an apartment house, two stories high and set back from the street. I followed him as he let himself into a unit near the corner.

"Buddy's gone away and I promised him I'd do the honors," he explained as he poured some kibble into a plastic dish and set it down.

I turned around to go—suddenly starting to feel uneasy, suddenly knowing I'd walked out on this limb too far—and then I saw the light go out and I felt his arms around me. I tried to pull away, but he caught me back and held me to him tightly.

Without speaking, he began to kiss me and caress me and in the darkness, in the warmth and strangeness of that place, I began to feel as if I drifted in another world—a world of liquid sensuality, of primal urges, of raw hot cravings of the flesh.

"Katharine," he murmured to me, "Katharine," and his voice was soft and filled with longing, his touch firm yet gentle, undemanding. It was as if he waited for my cue, wanted *me* to lead the way. Gone was the cocky smile, the brazen band of self-assurance.

I moved even closer to him and I felt desire engulf me and pound through every portion of my body. But then an inner voice, from somewhere deep inside me, began to dampen that desire, began to push it back as it demanded to be heard. This wasn't me, it said, this wasn't who I was, and I could not consummate this act I longed to finish.

I pulled away from him and stumbled backward—shaken, weak, yet still desiring this man who stood in front of me. He seemed to sense what I was feeling and he came to me again and took me in his arms.

But this time he only stroked my hair—stroked it with a loving hand and soothed me with caressing words until I settled down.

"I'm sorry, Katharine," he murmured to me now. "I should've known better. When I came close to you I simply couldn't help myself."

Again his gentleness surprised, confused me. He took me by the arm, opened up the door, and led me toward the car.

The following morning found me at my desk, reflecting on my foolishness. As I thought about the night before, I felt a flush fill my cheeks and I shook my head slowly back and forth.

And then, woven in with all the rest, another thought came to me—I'd never checked Marc

Schuyler's alibi. I picked up the phone and dialed his office, just to do the routine thing. I asked for personnel and a man's voice answered on the first ring.

I told him who I was and what I wanted, and he asked me for a call-back number and said I'd hear from him in five minutes. I hung up and waited for his ring, sipping at another cup of coffee and relaxing in my chair. The phone rang shortly.

"Mr. Schuyler checked out at three-thirty that day, ma'am. My records show he wasn't feeling well."

I verified the date and asked him to keep my inquiry strictly confidential. He told me he'd do that for sure.

Well, well, well, I thought, what have we here? Is someone playing games with me or just remembering poorly?

I'd find out but not right now. It was a little after three, and if I was going to see Nadine tonight, I'd need to leave here soon and take a break at home. Earlier, I'd felt the air's sweet warmth and now I longed to get out in it. I'd clip my roses, take a shower, and maybe grill some hot dogs with my little boy.

My tiredness suddenly fell away. Perhaps it was the coffee, but I believe it was the thought of the simple joys that lay ahead.

I didn't clip the roses because, by the time I reached the house, I'd become too intrigued with the possibilities surrounding Thomas Schuyler.

Billy's father admitted using violence on both his wife and child. He'd downplayed that violence, calling it just a slap or two, but I had only *his* word on that—others had seen swelling and bruising on the little boy.

Billy had suffered at least one period of depression—something not uncommon with a child who's abused or is otherwise unhappy in his home.

Schuyler seemed indifferent to his son, lacking any feelings of warmth and love and making no particular effort to hide that lack.

And, finally, Schuyler had had the opportunity to do the killing—he didn't have an alibi for two different time periods in the afternoon and evening after Billy disappeared.

True, he couldn't have met and murdered the boy, driven him to the San Marcos shed, hidden the body and returned—all within forty-five minutes—but suppose he'd divided the work into two parts, killing Billy in the afternoon and placing the body nearby, then retrieving it two hours later and driving it to the lonely field as twilight dimmed the area?

I slapped my hand down hard as this strong possibility dawned on me.

"Let's think a minute here," I murmured. "Could someone pick up a body, drive to that field, carry the corpse through the grass and prop it in a corner of a shed, then get back to Hollis Place in three-quarters of an hour?"

I recalled my own visits to the spot and felt it probably could be done. I'd check it out—after I saw Nadine I'd drive it once again and time it, at roughly the same hour of day Schuyler would've made the trip.

As I thought about the two unalibied periods, I remembered Schuyler's nervousness and fear when he'd talked about the first forty-five minutes—yet, he'd been relaxed and glib when he'd confessed to going out alone later on that night.

If both time periods were connected to the boy's death—and such would have to be the case if Schuyler were the killer—why did his reactions differ so markedly? What scared him so much about four-thirty to five-fifteen but not about the later time span?

And what about a motive? Why would Schuyler kill Billy anyway?

I trusted my earlier judgment that the man ran on tight control and didn't act on impulse, so I ruled out a crime committed in the heat of anger, a murder done when racing blood pushed emotions past their limits.

No, if Schuyler had killed his own son, he'd done so with a cool head and clear intent.

I began to pace the room and think out loud, wrapping a strand of hair around my finger as I walked. Suppose he *had* battered Billy? Was he an abuser who'd have struck no matter how the boy behaved or had his son done a deed so very terrible it fueled the father's hatred time and time again, until that hatred finally found its ultimate release on that sunny day in April?

If so, what could that offense have been? What in heaven's name could a young boy do that's so awful death becomes the final punishment?

I wasn't worried—if there was a motive, I'd find it. First I wanted to make the drive out the San Marcos Road and when I saw how the time fit with Schuyler's absences, I'd go from there.

Chapter Fourteen

"I've loved it from the day it all began," I told her. "It's been my life."

"But now you have some questions, don't you?"

I looked quickly at her, in anticipation of the onslaught.

"Sure I do. Who wouldn't, after I've found out how my son thinks I feel about him?"

"And how *do* you feel?"

I drew in my breath and trembled, as I stood ready to admit to another what I'd only recently admitted to myself.

"I know a lot of things I never stopped to think about before. I know I love him, but I also know that sometimes I resent the demands he makes on me."

As I spoke, the tears rose from somewhere deep inside. I don't think I'd ever felt such regret or guilt before.

"Would you be surprised if I told you your feelings are entirely normal and not to be denied, not to be ashamed of?"

Her question stopped me cold and I listened carefully, leaning forward in my seat.

"You're a career-oriented woman and from all I hear, you do a fine job in your work. You cannot deny yourself the person who you are, for if you do, you'll become someone you dislike intensely and that someone will react adversely to the people closest to her, for she'll blame them for changing her and taking her away from something very dear to her."

Puzzled, I asked her what to do, how to resolve the conflict tearing at me from two sides.

"Ah," she said, gesturing with an index finger, "what we must do here is get your son to realize your work takes nothing from your feelings for him, and, in fact, makes you a better mother because it fulfills you as a person. And we will do that."

I parked in the drive, behind the tan Oldsmobile, and looked at it and wondered. As usual, Schuyler answered the door. I didn't see his wife or Aaron Carter anywhere around.

"Nadine's waiting in my study, Detective," he said pleasantly. "I thought we could talk in there."

"That's just fine," I answered, "but I'd like to speak with her alone if that's all right with you."

He hesitated, then agreed.

"Certainly."

Nadine was seated on the sofa, legs together, hands folded neatly and resting on her skirt. She didn't speak, but looked at me expectantly.

"You remember me, Nadine—I'm Detective Harrod. I don't believe I've spoken with you since your brother's death. I want to say I'm very, very sorry."

She shrugged her shoulders and continued staring at me.

"It must be rough on you," I said.

"Not so much—I'll get over it." She paused, then "What do you want with me? What can I tell you?"

"How did you get along with Billy?"

"Okay, I guess. We used to fight when he got in my way or used my stuff—like he used to go in my room sometimes and mess around. I kicked his butt for that."

"But no really big problems?"

Again she shrugged.

"Nothing big, no. He was so much younger we didn't even fight like brothers and sisters. It was more like I was his baby-sitter."

"How did Billy get along with your mom and dad?"

"Fine. Mom spoiled him."

"And your father?"

"He wouldn't spoil anyone"—she spat the words out—"not me, not Billy, not anyone."

"Did your mom and dad spank Billy when he needed punishing?"

"Dad would give him a good wallop from time to time—enough to make him yell."

"On what part of Billy's body?"

"Across the butt."

"Nowhere else?"

"Nope, not that I ever saw."

Nadine's legs were crossed now, the right foot swinging with obvious impatience back and forth above the floor.

"So you wouldn't call the punishment excessive or out of line?"

"No way—Dad's not a beater. And you only get it if you ask for it."

"And what about you? Does he hit you, too?"

"Not for years. I'm sixteen, almost—he wouldn't."

Her look of scorn told me I was dumb to ask the question. She got up and walked past me and sat on a corner of her father's desk, her legs dangling loosely in front of her.

"When I visited here last month I saw you on the corner talking to a girlfriend. Who was that?"

"Jan. She moved in next door, where the Wellmonts used to live."

"You were arguing."

She thought about it several minutes, then agreed.

"May I ask what it was all about?"

"I don't remember, really."

She was lying. I'd been around the track far too often not to know when I was being jiggled.

"It wasn't about Billy?"

She was startled.

"Billy? We never talked about Billy. Whatever would we argue about him for?"

"I don't know," I said. "It was right after he disappeared and I thought it might've concerned him somehow."

Nadine shrugged her shoulders, then slid off the desk and walked back to the sofa.

"I guess it was about boys or something, but not about Billy."

Maybe not, cookie, I thought, but why not tell me right up front? Why the earlier evasiveness? Something didn't hang together here—I still felt she wasn't being totally straight with me.

"Is there anything else you'd like to tell me?" I asked.

"Nope, there was nothin' in the first place, but Dad said you wanted to talk."

On the way to the car, I asked myself if I'd done any good in there. Not a whole lot, I admitted, but I had learned a few things. Like the fact that Schuyler's

A DESPERATE CALL 193

own daughter didn't call her father an abuser, and a teenage girl could stand around and argue over boys the very day after her brother disappeared without a trace.

I headed for the field, checking my watch as I pulled away from Hollis Place. The time was seven-forty. I turned west on Marsh and started toward San Marcos. Daylight had dropped away but few streetlights hit the thickening dusk.

I drove evenly, neither fast nor slow but at a pace that would put the miles behind me, yet let me keep control on the dark and sometimes winding road.

There was no traffic to make me change that pace and I guessed there'd been very little on that fatal April night, for this wasn't a heavily traveled route except at daytime rush hours.

I reached the field at precisely eight o'clock and turned around and drove straight back into town. When I got to Hollis Place, I checked my watch again—eight twenty-one, a total of forty-one minutes' driving time.

If Schuyler had indeed been absent forty-five minutes, this meant he'd had only four minutes to walk the corpse through the field, dump it in the shed, prop the tools in front of it, and return to the car.

And those four minutes didn't even include retrieving the body from wherever he'd hidden it that afternoon. No, it just couldn't be done.

I tried to rework the times. Could I have driven any faster? Definitely not. Suppose Billy's mother had been wrong and Schuyler had been gone *fifty* minutes—was it possible to do the job in *nine* minutes plus driving time?

Still too close to suit me, and besides, I was pretty sure he'd been away for only three-quarters of an hour. I'd bet Joyce Schuyler had anxiously watched the clock for his return and so was accurate within a minute or two of the times she gave me.

Damn! I banged my hand on the steering wheel. Damn! I'd bought my theory before I really tested it and now, when I'd proved it couldn't work, I felt the letdown. Disappointment settled on my soul.

I looked up from my desk and saw Joyce Schuyler standing there, holding a cream-colored envelope.

"I wrote this for you, Detective Harrod. It's just a little note thanking you for all you've done and are trying to do for us. I was going to mail it, but then I decided I wanted to see you and tell you in person."

She moved as if to put the letter in her purse, but I reached my hand out and stopped her.

"Please, I'd love to have it even though you're here," I said, and she gave the envelope to me, then sat down across from me.

I tore it open and found a sheet of thick, fine-quality stationery folded once inside. It was richly embossed with the initials "JCS" twining in and out of one another, and, faintly perfumed, it bore a small raised flower not unlike a primrose beneath the monogram.

"How beautiful," I murmured. "And the paper feels so good just to hold in one's hand."

"I've always loved it," she told me proudly, "and it's what I've always used—for years and years. A small indulgence I allow myself."

The note was simple and direct and, in a sincere, even loving, way thanked me and all my squad for our kindness to the family and our doggedness in trying to find Billy's killer.

"Ah, this is thoughtful, Joyce, but with all the grief you're having to deal with, you didn't need to think of us."

"I did," she replied firmly. "You're a good person and goodness can't be overlooked or go unacknowledged."

I poured two cups of coffee and set one down before her.

"What do you intend to do, Joyce, to help yourself cope with all of this? Did you work, can you work? Even if you don't want to, it would be excellent therapy."

Her eyes fastened on mine and she leaned forward slightly, lips parted in a little smile.

"No, Detective, I don't work. I never have. Oh, I'd have liked to but Thomas put his foot down. Not fitting, he said. Do you know I once had dreams?"— here, she leaned forward even more and her voice took on an excited confidential tone—"I even had dreams of becoming a ballerina. Can you imagine that?"

She shook her head as if in wonder that she'd ever dared to be so bold, or maybe just because the dream had died away.

"So what happened?" I asked, truly curious. "Trying to fulfill our dreams is what keeps all of us going."

"Oh, this and that, I don't know. It all seems so long ago now."

She eased backward in her chair and sipped the coffee, staring wistfully in front of her. Then quickly, the words jostling and romping with each other to try to get out first, she began to speak again.

"You know, Katharine—"—she'd never called me that before—"I think I *do* know why I drink. Because I've failed and I cannot live with that fact. I used to be a pretty girl and Thomas saw me and he loved me—or so I thought—and life was going to be so wonderful.

"And then it all came tumbling down—my world, I mean, because somehow I couldn't get the hang of it, couldn't get it right. Almost from the day we married, we began to grow apart. He demanded ... so much perfection and I could never satisfy him. And now— I know it's crazy—but now I feel I'm the one who caused Billy to be murdered. Somehow I didn't take good enough care of him and so he's gone."

Her finger traced a little pattern on my desktop and I saw the tears fill up her eyes.

"I sometimes wonder why I stay here. My boy's dead, my husband left our marriage a long, long time ago, and my daughter doesn't even know that I exist."

She slumped a little in her chair and I thought I'd rarely come across a more shattered human being. I began to lean toward her, to try to comfort her.

But then the strangest thing happened. I saw a look of harsh defiance flash across her face and I caught a glimpse of a Joyce I'd never seen before—a Joyce of spirit, sudden self-assurance, and, yes, even a certain prettiness. She drew herself up straight, leaned back in her chair, then placed a cigarette between her lips and lit it with an obvious relish. I hadn't even known she smoked.

She inhaled slowly, then blew the smoke away from me in a lazy upward spiral. The ritual seemed to calm her, give her even more confidence, and I felt the cigarette supported her like an old and trusted friend.

I was certainly looking at a different woman here—not the quivering little creature I was used to but one who exuded both control and a measured strength. She'd skinned away the layers of the Joyce Schuyler I'd known up till now and given me a glimpse of the girl she must've been in that time so long ago.

"You know what really happened, don't you?" She flicked a fallen ash with a quick hard snap. "I let him wear me down instead of standing up to him. I wanted so to please him that I gave in far too much and he ended up despising me, and by the time I knew what was happening it was far too late. And for that I sometimes hate myself because I think it could've been so different with us and I let it get away."

"Does it have to be like that?" I asked, still caught off guard by the person I was seeing here. "You seem to think you know what's wrong—couldn't you begin to make it right?"

"No. It passed that point many moons down the line. Tom knows me only as he sees me now—I doubt he even remembers the girl he fell in love with when we had our hopes in those distant days and talked about our dreams."

Abruptly, she stubbed out her cigarette and as the glow dimmed and flickered till at last it ceased, the light left Joyce Schuyler's face, the defiance fled to wherever it'd hidden for so many years, and the dawning prettiness became again a face of hopelessness with eyes that dulled as they turned toward me.

"I've got to go now, Katharine. Thanks for being concerned about me, but you can't help with the mess I've let my life become."

She stood up, hesitated for a moment, then bent over, quickly kissed my head, and walked away.

Chapter Fifteen

I went to Morro Street right after breakfast, to find out why Marc Schuyler had lied to me. I hadn't seen him since our dinner, and I felt slightly gauche and ill-at-ease. But I needed to get an answer to my question and that need would power me through the awkward situation.

The red car was parked outside, its canvas top up, and as I crossed the street, the house door opened and Schuyler came out to get the morning paper. He wore only a T-shirt and jockey shorts, and I saw a tanned and muscled body his older brother might've envied. I had to force myself to look away.

He didn't see me coming and went inside and shut the door. I knocked and immediately it opened. I didn't dance around.

"You lied to me. Why?"

His guilt showed all over him. He stepped uneasily backward and blushed slightly as he spoke.

"Come in, Detective Harrod, and tell me what you mean, but first, let me get some pants on, okay? I thought you were the paper boy."

He disappeared a moment and came back dressed in faded Levi's.

I dug right in, strictly business all the way.

"I'm talking about the day your nephew disappeared—you told me you were showing property."

He rubbed the golden stubble on his chin.

"I thought I was. Why?"

"Don't fence with me—that's not a day that you'd forget what you were doing. I know you left your office a little after three, supposedly gone home sick."

He gave in.

"You're one tough cookie, lady—you don't give up. Okay, but I didn't think it'd matter. I'm sorry—really sorry—if it messed you up. I apologize. Mind if I get a cup of coffee?" and he went toward the kitchen with me following.

He spooned instant powder into two ceramic mugs and put the water on to boil.

"None for me," I told him, and he set one mug aside.

"It's a delicate matter," he explained, "and I'm sure you'll understand once you hear it. I was rendezvousing with a ladyfriend." He seemed hesitant and ill-at-ease.

"Who was it and where?" I asked, ignoring his discomfort.

"A girl I know—Ellen Dancer—and it was here. I left early, came straight home, and she arrived ten minutes later. I didn't want to trash her reputation so I told a little lie instead."

"Where can I find her, to see if she remembers it like you do?"

I knew he'd call the Dancer girl and tell her I was coming, so I decided I'd ring up Carl and have him phone her while I was still at Morro Street. Schuyler saved me the trouble.

"She's right here," he said. "She spent the night." His discomfort seemed to deepen.

He went to a closed door and quietly opened it. A drowsy blonde sat up in bed and held the sheet in front of her. Her dazed expression and sleepy eyes told me she'd just awakened. I knew she hadn't heard our conversation.

"Sorry, babe," Marc Schuyler told her, "this lady cop needs your time."

I made sure I watched him while I questioned her. He stood quietly and sipped his coffee, his face expressionless.

"Miss Dancer, do you remember Monday, April twenty—the day your friend's nephew disappeared?"

She nodded, her mouth slightly open.

"Would you mind telling me where you were that afternoon from three-thirty on?"

She smiled. If he was bashful, his girlfriend certainly wasn't.

"Right here," she told me, stretching one arm above her head, "for several hours, at least. We had such a lovely time."

A sudden shot of jealousy and envy jolted me and left me craving what she'd had and I'd missed. Hastily, I turned away. As I left the room, I saw her yawn and snuggle down beneath the covers.

We walked together to the door.

"Katharine ..." he began, then he stopped. The liquid warmth began to flow between us once again. "I'm sorry—I should've told you straight out, but surely you can see why I didn't, can't you?"

Summoning all my strength, I ignored his pleading and the rising warmth receded.

A DESPERATE CALL   201

"You've wasted time in a murder investigation," I told him sternly. "Don't ever lie to me again."

He looked embarrassed and contrite and I wondered if I'd been unnecessarily harsh. I knew my reaction hadn't been just about the case.

"Where's the dog?" I asked, trying to take the edges off my tone and end up on a friendly note.

"Jackie's shut out back," he told me, "on the side porch. Would you like to see him?"

"Some other time," I answered and I left. The dinner and the moments after it were never mentioned.

"Steve called," Jonathan told me coolly as I walked in. "He wants to hear from you right away. He's at the station."

Wondering, I dialed the number. It rang five times and I was starting to hang up when he finally answered.

"Sorry, babe, I'm up here all alone and I was in the head. Listen, I think I've spotted something in these photos after all. Skip the scolding, Mama, but I wanted to feast my eyes on that little dolly some more so I got out the funeral prints and suddenly I saw something else.

"There's this one guy who seems to be staring at the Schuyler family in all the pictures—at least in those I shot. Can you come down and take a look?"

"Right away," I told him. The screen door was still swinging when I started up the car.

Darrow had all the prints laid out across a desktop. He pointed to the upper right-hand corner.

"I first noticed him in these two that show both him and all the Schuylers, and then I looked at the other ten I'd taken—this guy shows up in four of 'em. I tried to recall the angle I'd shot from in each and realized in every single one he's facing toward the family.

"*You* took this batch"—he pushed ten to fifteen snapshots toward me—"and he's in five of them. Can you remember where you took them from?"

I sat down and scrutinized the prints for several minutes. By checking certain trees and fences and the position of the shadows on the ground, I could pretty well tell where I'd stood in relation to the man and to the family. I looked up at Steve and nodded—in every single one of those five photos, the stranger's face was turned toward the Schuylers.

At every funeral, everyone steals a glance at the survivors, but then they'll move their eyes away. This guy never dropped his stare. He was fixated—he looked at nothing else.

"Get the glass," I told Darrow.

He handed me a magnifier and I concentrated on the man. He was a tall Caucasian in his midfifties, weighing about 180 pounds, with gray hair cut military-short and dressed in a dark blue coat with lighter-colored pants. Though I tried, I couldn't read his expression in any of the pictures.

"I'm taking these to Schuyler," I said. "Do you want to come along or have you still got work to do?"

"Let's go," Darrow answered, putting on his coat.

"Can you trust yourself around the daughter?"

Usually, I wouldn't have encouraged him, but my mood had suddenly picked up.

"Think that little honey might be home? Don't worry, boss—hands off and eyes straight forward."

I knew the hands would stay in place—I didn't buy the bit about the eyes.

We drove up without phoning first and saw Schuyler getting into his car. I called out to him and told him we had something to show him, and he led us back inside the house.

"Take a look at these," I said and handed him the pictures. "Do you know this man?"

Schuyler walked toward the large glass window and tilted the photos toward the light. He studied them for several minutes, frowning in concentration.

"I know him and I don't," he said finally. "I've seen him—that's for sure—and I can almost tell you where and when, but it eludes me. Maybe I'll remember later."

"Maybe so," I told him, "and that's why I want you to keep one or two of those and look at them from time to time. If you remember who he is, please call me—you've got my home number."

"Why are you so interested, Detective?"

"Because he's staring straight at you and your family in all the prints. We want to know why."

Schuyler frowned again—he didn't like it.

"I never noticed," he said uneasily. "It's certainly strange."

We were just about to leave when Nadine walked through the hall and out the front door. She wore faded jeans and a purple halter top, tightly tied across the back and at the neck.

She cut across the yard, toward the Wellmonts' old house, and I saw Steve's eyes following her till she disappeared behind a hedge. Schuyler seemed to totally ignore her. He spoke to me, his hand on the doorknob.

"You'll be hearing from me—I know the name will come to me."

Darrow waited till we got into the car, then he let himself go.

"Oh, Katie, she's riper than I thought."

"You saw her at the funeral," I said, with obvious distaste.

"Yeah, but she stayed behind those glasses and she was sitting down. Today, all the goods were on display and I caught them set in motion."

"You know she's underage?"

Steve was too smart to get involved with a minor.

"Yeah, you told me. Don't worry, Kate, Internal Affairs won't be humping me on this one." He sighed and chuckled softly. "But I'll tell you something—if I were a long way from home and didn't have the rules to play by, I'd sure as hell grab that pretty ass. And from the way she swings it, she'd put it in my hand—I wouldn't have to do much asking."

I stayed silent, thinking I was glad Nadine hadn't seen us. I knew a charge would've shot between her and Darrow and I didn't need this complication in my case.

"You've been married a long time, haven't you, Katie?" he asked next.

"Nearly fifteen years." He didn't know about the separation.

"I tried it once and didn't like it. Didn't last more than eighteen months—now I wonder why I ever thought it would. I couldn't dream of life without the spices, kiddo. All you warm and luscious babes out there, just waitin' for the pickin'. No strings, no commitments—just the fun and lots of satisfaction."

I felt his eyes on me and when I looked at him he grinned.

"Hey, maybe you should leave the straight and nar-

A DESPERATE CALL

row sometime, boss, and come on out with me—you might find you like the action."

"You're out of line, mister—'way far out," I snapped. "Drop it now and leave it."

"Okay, okay, sweet Katie"—he held his hands up gesturing surrender—"I didn't know you'd be so touchy."

Damn him—he'd tried it on with me once or twice before, with a hint he could satisfy me more than Jon, but I'd just ignored him. Today, though, he'd really gotten to me—my nerves must be riding near the skin.

I changed the subject and began to fill him in on the Friday talks at Hollis Place. Immediately, I got his full attention.

"Do you think it's Schuyler?" Darrow asked. He watched me keenly and waited for my answer. His mind had tossed the "babes" away.

"There's sure a lot to point to him," I said, "but the drive hangs me up. The bottom line is the man couldn't have done it all in the time span I've got to deal with. And now we've got the fella in the photos who's a possible. It's just not as clear-cut as it was yesterday."

"Think we'll hear from Schuyler on the pictures?"

"You betcha—I've got a hunch the name will come to him."

The next hour proved me right, or nearly so.

I'd dropped Darrow at the station, gone on home, and just finished a light lunch when the phone rang. It was Billy's father.

"I know who he is, the man in the pictures," he told me. "He applied for a loan about a year ago, but it was denied. He came down to the bank the next day and raised a royal ruckus—we thought we'd have to call the police to calm him down."

I asked if he had a name for me, and he told me no, not yet.

"But I know the type of loan it was—I can go through my records and come up with it, I'm sure."

"This afternoon?"

"Of course."

I told him I'd meet him at the bank at two o'clock.

I watched Schuyler work for twenty minutes, then I heard his exclamation.

"Here we go," he said with satisfaction. "Randall Gilbert, 4516 Olive Street, San Madera. A small-business loan."

I called the station. Steve was gone but Carl was there.

"I need you with me," I told him, "but first check out a Randall Gilbert, last known address 4516 Olive—I'll explain later. Pick you up in less than ten."

I slowed the car outside the station and Carl got in. He looked a little down and I wondered if things were worse with Betsy. I'd feel him out after we'd taken care of business.

"What did you find?" I asked, wanting to know who I was dealing with. Mungers told me Gilbert had no record.

We drove across town, entering a section of the east end. I saw small houses, like Marc Schuyler's but with yards that weren't as neat and paint that lacked the gloss of freshness.

"There it is," I said, pointing to a blue-rimmed clapboard set close to a cracked and rutted sidewalk, "and there's himself swinging on the porch swing."

A DESPERATE CALL

We watched as the man from the funeral photos rocked back and forth, swigging on a bottled beer. He was no longer neatly shaven and he didn't wear a suit. Gray stubble frosted cheeks and chin and gray sweats clothed a flaccid body.

We walked slowly toward the porch.

"Mr. Gilbert, we'd like to talk with you," I said. I asked him if he knew Thomas Schuyler. No, he said, he didn't.

"Then what were you doing at his son's funeral on Thursday?"

"I wasn't there. I been sick. I didn't leave my house that day."

I reached into my pocket and slowly took the photos out. I held them so he could see they were snapshots but couldn't see their content.

He shifted uneasily in his swing seat and stared toward the pictures in my hand.

"What you got there, lady?" he asked, still not giving in.

"Let me lay it out for you. Show him, Carl," and I gave the shots to Mungers and let him show them, one by one, to Gilbert. I stood back and watched for his reaction.

He didn't disappoint me. His shoulders suddenly slumped and he wiped his hand nervously across his forehead. I saw it tremble as he took it down.

"So what? Lots of people went. Anyone'd deny it when cops come along asking nosy questions—makes a person get his guard up."

"Just tell us why you went."

"Curiosity, I guess." He was weaseling and I knew it.

"Let's leave it, then," I said. "Where were you on Monday, April twenty?"

He started counting on his fingers and I saw his face begin to brighten.

"Wait a minute," he told us slyly, holding up one finger, "I got something here to show you."

Wondering what was coming, we followed him inside and watched while he rummaged through a crowded drawer.

"Read this," he said and thrust a piece of paper at my hand. "I was ass-flat in Kingston Hospital. Told you I'd been sick—got my gall bladder taken out."

I read the form and felt the hope go out of me. It stated Randall Gilbert had checked into the local hospital on Wednesday, April 15, and hadn't checked out till Thursday, April 23.

I had a sense of déjà vu and I remembered Harry Hansen and his parole officer. I was getting sick of airtight alibis. We turned to go, then Gilbert caught my arm and spoke.

"You wanna know why I went to that kid's funeral? You really wanna know? Well, I'll tell you why." His voice was low and rolling. "I went to see the old man suffer. Bastard put me out of business when he wouldn't lend me money. I lost it all—everything I ever worked for. I went to see it comin' back on him."

His voice was rising and his fingers clutched the wooden door frame. His face contorted and anger sparked his eyes.

"His only son! I bet that hurt. He won't forget, not ever. I watched them all—the family—sitting there and whimpering and sniffling. They all deserve it— every bit—and I went to see them have to wallow in it."

A DESPERATE CALL

He was yelling now.

"God gives back—this proves it. I loved it all—it made my day. I wouldn'ta missed a single minute. Wish I'd had *me* a camera, too!"

The outburst over, he began to smile. He grabbed the beer and sucked a hearty swallow, letting the liquid wet his lips and chin.

I felt sickened, and a dry and dusty taste filled my mouth and settled on my tongue. I looked at Carl and nodded toward the car. Again we turned to go and this time we didn't stop. Behind us, Randall Gilbert laughed loudly and the sound of triumph threaded through that laughter.

Chapter Sixteen

The phone call came shortly afterward—a rough raw call laden with malevolence, a call that scared me more by what it didn't say than what it did.

It was going on eleven when a ring tore the silence of the night. I picked up the phone and heard a breath so close it seemed to stand beside me, a breath filled with heavy heat that rose, then fell, then rose again.

And then another sound came, biting deep into my ear—a licking, sucking sound, sometimes rolling lazily along the line, other times vibrating crazily to an urgent climax.

I just stood there, listening, looking for a clue but finding nothing, mesmerized by the evil of that tone.

Then the sucking died slowly down and the voice offered up one word—"Cunt!"—hurled at me and wrapped in filth. And then hung up.

My number was, of course, unlisted, so at first I thought the call was random, but I soon began to suspect with a dreadful certainty that it was tailor-made for me. I shuddered and climbed beneath the sheets but sleep did not come easy. Finally, I drifted off, napping fitfully till daybreak.

Now I frowned and wondered once again who'd been behind it, as I lay in bed and listened to the murmuring sounds of morning. Eight o'clock—it was Sunday and I'd give myself a few more minutes. I stretched and threw an arm across the empty spot beside me.

My son and I continued to grow closer, although that closeness wasn't coming overnight. We had to work at it, guided by the therapist, but he wanted it just as much as I did, and so the bonding grew.

Jon was another matter, though. When I told him what I'd learned about my working, he'd hooted and said it was a bunch of crap.

"A lot of wacko words from some far-out looney tune. Tommy laid it out for you—he's the one who's knowing how he feels and what he thinks went wrong."

I'd sighed and turned away. It was just no use, not now anyway.

He continued to occupy the guest room, spending days with Tommy while I went out to work and he worked, as always, in our home. On weekends, though, he became a shadow, a peripheral figure standing in the background, staying out of sight. I knew where we had been, I thought silently, but I sure as hell didn't know where we were going.

Suddenly I needed to get on with it. I threw the sheets back and stood upright in a single motion.

I passed the window and, as I'd done so often lately, looked down into the yard. Four weeks ago tomorrow Billy Schuyler had left that yard and walked to meet a monster. Today, I no longer knew where to take the case. My clues had crumbled, my suspects vanished one by one, and I was completely stymied.

"Mom, breakfast. Dad told me you'd be up by now so I came along to get you. He's already eaten."

Tommy stood in the doorway. I grabbed my housecoat and put it on.

"Let's go," I said and we skip-stepped down the stairs.

We ate waffles, browned the way I like them and smeared with amber syrup and butter melted by their warmth. A bowl half filled with creamy batter waited for the call for seconds.

Tommy didn't know about the problems Jon and I were having. He thought his dad had hurt his back and had to sleep alone, and we were careful not to let our anger show in front of him. Or, at least, we thought we were.

I poured a second cup of coffee and ate slowly, savoring the taste and the closeness of the moment, but feeling sorrow override it all the same. Would we ever be the way we were before?

Tommy must've wondered at my silence for he pinched my hand lightly, teasing. I caught his arm—the strong one—and in that instant saw the ragged cut.

"What happened here?" I asked as I turned his forearm over and looked at a three-inch laceration that still showed heavy scabbing.

"I got stabbed," he answered, and made a dramatic sweeping motion through the air. "I bled like everything."

I asked him when and how.

"I thought you knew," he said. "It happened at the picnic last Sunday, the one Dad took me to. A boy beside us was jousting with a skewer and I turned and scraped my arm across the point. Dad almost took me to emergency till we saw it wasn't all that serious after all."

I gently squeezed his hand and then released it.

"Where was the picnic?" I asked. "At the Duck Pond?"

"No, no, Mom—it was at that other little park up that way." He pointed out the kitchen window, toward the north side of town.

"Ah, right," I said, "I know the one."

And then, suddenly, I sat still and grew very quiet inside myself. I saw the park clearly in my mind and that vision opened up a door for me.

I saw a baseball field and then a dirt road running along the south side near the picnic area—an unpaved road that went into the woods, then disappeared from sight.

I watched Tommy run a finger around the shallow of his plate, scooping up the syrup. I bent and hugged him.

"I've got to go out now," I told him, "but I'll meet you after Sunday school and we'll do something fun."

I moved quickly, my mind racing as I went. Long ago, as a young rookie cop, I'd handled a dead body call on that same dusty road. The poor soul turned out to be a suicide, lying in the ditch one mile beyond the park.

I'd never seen the road before and I remember asking someone where it went. They told me it joined the main route to San Marcos several miles from where we stood. The case was quickly closed and I forgot about the road. Until today.

Again I started out from Hollis Place. The time was ten to nine. I reached the park and eased my car on to the graveled dirt. The single lane led me to a stand of willows that quickly changed to thick dark forest.

When it rained, the dirt would turn to sludge, forming grooves and peaks that would make the road impassable, but there'd been no rain for months and the pebbled surface was now firm and level, letting me maintain a steady thirty miles per hour.

The road ran straight, without the curves that marked the main route to San Marcos, and after only several miles of driving I saw an open field ahead of me and cars moving in the distance. Within moments, I joined that other route, at a point only a mile or so from the field where Billy's body had been found.

I swung a right and continued to the grassy meadow. I cut the engine, then checked my watch. Nine-o-six and forty-eight seconds—a total of less then seventeen minutes since I'd left Hollis Place. Relief and joy washed over me—I'd found a shortcut to San Marcos.

I sat back and penciled in some notes. Using the dirt road, the round trip would've taken less than thirty-four minutes, leaving at least eleven minutes to retrieve the body, take it through the field, dump it in the shed, then return to the car.

It could be done, I knew it—and with time to spare. And that meant Thomas Schuyler could indeed have killed his son or, at least, have been the one who hid the dead boy's body.

I felt a stirring on the edges of my mind and then I thought of something that would've given Schuyler even more time to perform his dirty chores.

Suppose there'd been no need to retrieve Billy's corpse because that corpse was already hidden in the rear of Schuyler's car? Suppose he'd killed the boy, then kept the body in the trunk, driving it around while his wife rode in that same car searching for her son, not knowing he lay dead only seven feet away?

I shivered. The gruesome scene was all too real.

A DESPERATE CALL

And that was how I knew it could've happened just that way.

Only one thing hung me up. Why had Schuyler worked at twilight instead of waiting for the shroud of total darkness? Sunset on April 20 came at seven thirty-one, almost smack in the middle of the time period Billy's father was away from home. His figure, while shadowed and dusky, would still have been more easily seen than if he'd waited till even eight o'clock.

Then as soon as I asked it, I answered my own question. Schuyler saw the heightened level of his wife's concern, feared she'd soon phone the police, and knew he had to dump the body before she made the call.

He had no choice—he couldn't pick his time. He had to make his move at seven o'clock and take his chance with twilight. I was satisfied.

I took the long way home, planning how I'd handle it from here on in. I'd meet with the district attorney, to see if I had enough to impound the car and search it, and I'd ask Schuyler to volunteer to take a lie detector test.

Perhaps, when it was all laid out before him, he'd tell me why he'd killed and brutalized his son. Perhaps he'd reveal to me the dreadful sin that warranted the tightening of a ligature around a little neck and then the breaking of that neck by forceful crushing hands.

I'd expected to feel exaltation when I reached this moment in the case, but I did not. Instead, I felt an emptiness filling quickly with a deepening sorrow. I saw the face of Billy Schuyler and I felt the void his death had caused.

Sure, I could make the killer pay, but I couldn't

give the victim back his life. And because I could not perform a miracle beyond the power of anyone alive, I felt ineffectual, depressed. Any way you cut it, my efforts would result in second-best.

Dejected, I turned on the radio and punched the volume up to "high." An old Jackie Wilson tune was playing and its pounding beat pushed and pummeled my emotions. Soon my sorrow started leaving and a hard resolve began replacing it. Before too long, my spirits lifted to a level where I couldn't wait to start the work ahead.

Elated, I moved the volume even higher as I turned into the driveway. My music never failed me—I could count on it to get me there every single time. It still pulsed inside my mind as I climbed the stairs, shed my clothes, and slipped beneath the covers. Exhausted, yet at peace at last, I slept the whole night through.

I got out of bed while dawn was still deciding what to wear. I'd already showered and dressed before a deepening glow of salmon-rose lit the eastern sky. I was anxious, but it was a good anxiety. I felt sharp, crackling, ready.

I drove to work and bought a bagel from the breakfast truck. I carried it upstairs, poured a cup of coffee, and was on my second refill when Carl and Steve arrived. I told them both the news.

"Think we've got enough, Kate?" Carl asked.

"I think so. I'm going to run it by the DA once he comes in and then we'll know for sure. And if Schuyler agrees to take the poly, that'll be the cap. After that, it should all unwind just fine."

"That bastard," Steve exclaimed. "Why? I don't

have kids but it doesn't matter. Why would he do this? Fuckin' cold-faced son of a bitch!"

"I hope he'll answer that one for us," I replied, "but could be we'll never know."

They went back to their desks and I started making notes for the district attorney.

In the distance, I heard Steve's phone ring, but I paid no attention. Several minutes later, he stood in front of me and his usually brash face held a look I couldn't read.

He handed me a traffic accident report—misdemeanor hit-and-run—and pointed to the license number of the suspect's car. 2JRS164. Puzzled, I looked at him.

"It's Schuyler's," he told me, "and look at the date and time it happened as well as where—April 20 at four-forty p.m., on Barham Street."

I felt my strength drain away, as if someone had physically removed it from my body.

"Where did you get this?" I asked.

"It was on my desk, in interoffice mail. That call was from a friend of mine in traffic investigation, asking if I'd seen the report he shipped me Friday. I hadn't, so I dug it out.

"He told me they're so backlogged they'd just gotten around to it, but when he ran the plate and it came back to Schuyler, he recognized him as the father of the murdered boy and thought we might be interested. He didn't even notice the date it happened, just the name."

"Has he questioned Schuyler yet?" I asked.

"Nope, and I told him to hold off on that awhile."

I called the victim and learned Molly Blevins's car was parked at the curb outside her house on Barham

Street in the late afternoon of April 20, when a light-colored sedan traveling west veered suddenly and struck her left rear fender.

The sedan then sped off and disappeared from sight, but not before Mrs. Blevins, who'd been walking to her car at the time, was able to get a license number. She filed a hit-and-run report within the following hour.

I hung up the phone and stared in front of me. Defeat hung heavy in my eyes.

"You know what this means?" I said to Steve. "It means if he was slamming into cars on Barham at four-forty in the afternoon he couldn't be picking Billy up on Marsh and killing him because the streets are at least fifteen minutes' driving time apart. It means he's got an alibi and my theory's shot to hell."

We went to Schuyler's bank. He'd just arrived and his secretary showed us in.

I held the paper in my hand in such a way he could see it was an official police report. I made sure the title, "Accident Investigation," stared him in the eye.

"Mr. Schuyler, do you want to tell me now what happened the afternoon Billy disappeared, after you left this office?"

He knew we had him. He didn't hedge, but told it straight out.

He'd been driving west on Barham, his mind on banking matters, when his car drifted sideways and grazed the one owned by Molly Blevins. Instead of stopping, Schuyler panicked and kept on going.

"And then I knew I'd made a bad mistake," he said, bending, then straightening, the fingers of one hand in a nervous gesture, "but I couldn't fix it.

"I knew if I called later to report it, they'd get me

for hit-and-run and I couldn't afford to let that happen. I'd jeopardize my position, my reputation. It was unacceptable. I didn't know anyone got my license number and I hoped it would all just go away."

Schuyler said he stopped to check his own car, found it showed no sign of damage, and then drove around in circles till he once again got his nerves under control. Nearly half an hour passed before he felt calm enough to go home.

Now I knew why he'd seemed so nervous Friday when we'd talked about this same time frame.

"And where were you Monday night?" I asked.

"I told you, Detective, Joyce was driving me mad and I couldn't stand any more of her hysteria. I wanted to do a quiet search on my own, so I left her."

I believed him. God knows I didn't want to, but I knew he was telling me the truth.

CHAPTER SEVENTEEN

Patrol had brought in two hookers, who snapped their gum and laughed while they waited to be booked. Farther down the bench, a suspected burglar was handcuffed to the anchor chain.

I passed the joyless scene and walked upstairs, where I found Patti Burke, my old partner from patrol, delivering a truculent arrestee to the detective handling sex crimes. Seeing me, she silently held out a gruesome photo.

It showed a woman who'd been raped by her onetime live-in lover—the grunting beast standing there in handcuffs. He'd returned, flamed with jealousy, and not only had taken her by force but had beaten her to a bloody mass of swollen tissue just for extras.

I went to my own desk, my mouth set, my face grim. Two new reports had come in and I picked them up and read them.

A middle-aged man was suspected by county social services of beating up his invalid father, and three thugs had jumped a woman walking home from work. They'd beat her, stomped her, and cut off her little finger before robbing her. She wasn't expected to live.

I threw down the reports and raised my hands to

my face. Ugliness was everywhere. I felt as if I wore it like skin upon my body.

That night I returned to the shed in the field near the foothills. I felt a need to connect with it again, an urge to stand within its shadows.

I drove slowly out of town, my thoughts turned inward. Once or twice I thought I saw some lights behind me, but no one ever passed me and soon I believed myself alone.

I pulled onto the shoulder and cut the engine off, sitting silently for some moments, then starting toward the path. I thought I heard another engine and a distant crunch of gravel, but I saw nothing and soon the night grew quiet around me.

The darkness of the woods stood against the twilight sky and the grasses rose high in front of me. I stepped roughly through them, forcing them aside, heading toward the shed. I saw it, small and lonely, standing in the distance beside the silent oaks.

This compulsion, this madness to return, drove me toward it relentlessly. What did I look for? What did I want? What could I possibly hope to find? I didn't know; I only craved to reunite with it, to bond once again with the scene of one of the most gruesome horrors I'd ever witnessed.

When I'd stood here before, I'd had my husband, had my child, had my ordered life well under my control. Now all that was gone and confusion and disarray replaced it. I couldn't even catch the killer of that little boy. Perhaps I thought I could sort it all out here, could use this lonely place of death as the wellspring from which would rise the answers to my problems.

I stopped before I went inside and felt the velvet

softness of the night surround me. The field and woods were silent, except for a nighthawk's shrill and cutting cry. I felt a strange and blanketing peace. I was not afraid.

I stepped through the doorway into sudden darkness. A pleasant musty smell—so unlike that smell of death on that day in springtime—rushed to meet me. Then something cracked softly just behind me and I tensed, poised on the icy edge of fear.

I turned slowly to my left and felt a breath hit my face—warm, full, moist—and then I felt the pain as something grabbed my arm, and I was falling, falling into another darkness that grew ever deeper and would not let me go....

Dawn entered slowly and brought a silver light filled with softness. It touched my swollen eyelids and pulled me back to consciousness.

Dizzily, I raised myself on one elbow and looked around me. I saw a rock behind me stained with blood and when I ran my hand along my head, I felt a large contusion ringed by wet and matted hair.

Then I looked down the length of my aching body and revulsion made me turn my eyes away. I was naked, except for my underpants, and my breasts were scraped and blackened from fresh bruises.

But that was not what sickened me. What made the vomit rise into my throat was the sight of a thick and milky substance resting on one nipple and nestling in a hollow on my stomach near my navel.

Slowly I reached out my hand and touched it ... and knew it without doubt for what it was.

Someone—whoever had hurled me down and

beaten me—had then stood astride my fallen naked body and ejaculated on me once and then again. I stared at the semen, now shining opalescent in the rising sunlight, as it stood in tiny globules on my violated flesh.

Holding back, wanting not to know, I moved my hand between my legs and underneath my panties. Carefully, clinically, I rubbed my vagina its full length, then gave an involuntary cry of thanks—I had not been raped. Not only was there no semen present, but the flesh and membranes yielded up no pain, no sign of violation that I'd have recognized if it had been there.

Clearly, the person who had done this to me had desired not sex, but rather the humiliation of my body, the total degradation of my soul. But who? And why?

Wanting nothing more than to wipe it off of me, to obliterate it and wash myself clean of it, I nonetheless took a plastic baggie from my purse and saved the semen, pushing it deep down inside. For evidence, in case my violator was ever found.

Moving gingerly, I pulled on my skirt and blouse and got slowly to my feet. A different smell was in the shed now—in the shed and on my clothes. A faint smell, diluted by the breezes since the hour of violation, but an unmistakable scent all the same. Men's cologne. Not one I was familiar with but men's cologne without a doubt. I'd not soon forget its cloying odor.

Although I ached, I found I could walk easily enough and, fighting vertigo and inner devastation, I headed toward my car. I should've looked for clues, should've checked the crime scene, but I could not be that objective now and I didn't fault myself.

The long drive home finally ended and I pulled myself through the open car door and staggered up the steps. Jon caught me as I sagged suddenly toward the wood porch floor, and I remembered nothing else till I awoke and found a doctor bending over me.

I got out of bed the following morning, now steady on my feet but still emotionally shaken from my ordeal.

Detectives from division had combed the crime scene, but found nothing. The semen had been analyzed and typed, but now waited for some further clue to tie it to a suspect. The only help that I could offer was the memory of a drifting scent—too nebulous a lead to be of any good right now.

The detective in charge laid a hand on my shoulder after questioning me.

"That was pretty gutsy of you, kiddo, packaging all that cum the way you did."

I grimaced and said nothing, recoiling from the memory.

Sitting in a corner of my bedroom, I wondered at the turn my life had taken. I'd gone to that shed seeking solace and to try to find a way to work out the problems I was facing, but I'd come away from it far worse than I'd gone in ... and I'd very nearly lost my life. I shook my head in sorrow.

And then, without warning, the freeze-frames started—vivid shots of filth and the sordid creatures who create it snapping quick to ones of foaming ocean, stands of pine, open space that didn't end at the horizon but continued far beyond.

Back and forth, in and out—in a seesaw contrast of

madness to serenity—these opposing flip cards played out in my mind.

This always happens and it is my salvation. When the world in which I choose to move begins to choke me, I start to see a place of solitude, of sun-touched peace and tranquil beauty—a place where madness stops.

Often, I cannot believe that such a place exists, though I know it does for I have been there. It's a fixed post of sanity in a world of chaos and I long to leave that world behind and go to it. Sometimes, if I'm lucky, I can do just that.

Jonathan walked through the door, carrying a tray. He'd been stunned by the assault and had stayed beside me through the night. For a few deceptive moments, the animosity, the acrimonious overlay to words, had disappeared and our relationship seemed sound and loving.

Partially because of this, I debated voicing my next words, then decided to go ahead.

"I'm driving to Carmel tomorrow. I need to get away for a while."

He set down the tray and turned to me.

"I can understand that, but I want to go there with you. May I?"

I had not expected this and my mouth dropped open slightly, but how could I refuse him? And it might be a good thing, too. Perhaps we could relate on neutral territory and find a passageway to free us from our present impasse.

"Are you sure you want to?"

"Absolutely."

We drove west, then south, then west again, picking up the two-lane road that winds across the Central

Valley toward the coastal plains. There's a shorter way to reach Carmel, but we seldom use it. We want the quietness of this country road, the beauty of these rounded hills, the sight of fat white cows and sleek brown horses running in the fields beside our car.

The pavement curved and dipped in tortuous gyrations that put us on a roller-coaster ride. Even though our speed was slow, our bodies swayed from side to side as we tried to keep our balance. From time to time, I'd steal a glance at Jonathan and wonder what was going through his mind.

The twists and dips went on for nearly twenty miles and then, although the curves continued, the road began to flatten as it headed toward the mountains in the distance. The softness of the rounded hills gave way to higher elevations and pine trees ridged the peaks above the fields of green and gold.

We passed through woods where sunlight filtered down to strike the fallen needles and create a layer of russet softness beneath the tallness of the trees. Then the road descended to another valley and only one more mountain range lay between us and the sea.

We'd dropped Tommy off at Jon's cousin, Barbara's, then filled the car with gas and headed out of town. I'd thought I felt like driving, then realized I was too weak, so Jon got behind the wheel. I poured coffee from the thermos he'd prepared and as I handed him his cup, he'd asked if I could talk about it.

I'd told him no, not just then, but now I felt I wanted to begin. The brilliance of the daytime beauty was acting as a catharsis on my soul.

"I feel very shaken, Jon, but not because of what was done to me. I can stand the degradation and the dirtiness because, contrary to what this maniac must think, this doesn't really touch my soul. I'm sort of like the snail inside the shell—my essense doesn't suffer from external forces.

"No, what bothers me is that I somehow feel this was a very personal thing, meant for me and me alone, and that's what scares me half to death. Because I don't know who and I don't know why."

I told him about the phone call I'd received.

"I don't know if there's a connection or not, but there sure as hell could be."

He stopped the car and pulled me to him and wrapped me in his arms. I folded up completely and pressed against his chest, basking in a sense of warmth I'd sorely missed for some time now.

"Welcome home, Katharine," he murmured to me. "I will never let anyone hurt you."

Futile words, if someone really wanted to get me, but I loved to hear them all the same. I didn't ask, couldn't ask, about our other problems and how we'd work them out. I didn't want to touch the moment, so budding and so fragile. I'd not push it now, but let the hours drift slowly past and find their own direction, and see where time would take us.

Finally, he let me go and, starting up the car again, drove down the winding road toward the coastal mountains.

We crossed a north-south freeway and picked up the road to Carmel Valley. The past two hours had graced me with a free and easy mind, a relaxed mood I hadn't really known for many days.

We'd driven casually, stopping when we felt like it to take a picture of a bird or watch a herd of cattle amble through a field. We'd laughed at every little thing, even when it wasn't really funny, and when we saw how silly we'd become, we'd laughed at that, too. A mood of joy was building in us and it demanded to be heard at every chance.

Again, the road began to curve and undulate, just as it had done at the beginning of our trip, but here the scenery was smaller—clumps of trees set close together, grazing fields lined with fencing, grassy knolls so close they hid the mountains far behind them.

A stream ran beside the road at many points and I rolled my window down so I could listen to its sound. A baby deer, still spotted and wearing frightened eyes, appeared beside the road searching for its mother. We stopped the car and watched it, afraid to move in case we scared it off. Then a doe moved up the hillside and took it with her through a stand of birch.

We passed through the Carmel Valley and out the other side, and I knew that in a moment the open sea would lie below us.

The road rose and dipped, and when it rose again I saw my foaming ocean, my tranquil pines, my open space that never seemed to end. I saw it and I loved it, but I knew the urgency to reach it had left me two hours out-of-town.

We checked into our hotel and put our walking shoes on, and when we walked until we tired and craved a touch of comfort, we found a timbered lounge and ordered Irish coffees. Strong and hot, thick and rich with fresh whipped cream, they soothed us as we settled back and watched the tourists pass.

We strolled slowly back to dress for dinner. The sun of afternoon touched the waves with silver glitter, and chalk-white sand, running toward dark forests, held the sea in check. A pungent salty smell swept toward us and clean cold air slapped us with its freshness.

We ate seafood at a restaurant on the wharf in Monterey and afterward drove south for several miles to see the full moon rise at Rocky Point. Then we went to bed, without question, without hesitation.

We stayed two days and filled the hours with walking and exploring and eating quantities of food I'd never think to eat at home. In the afternoons, we strolled on Carmel beach—that wide expanse of cool white sand that lies below the town.

Sometimes, feeling frisky, I ran ahead in spurts and leaps and spins of vigor while Jon walked lazily along the water's edge. Although I thought of them from time to time, the nightmare moments of the shed were fading fast behind me.

Once I caught a flash of red and swung my head around. It was just a little kid with a smile on her face and her heart all full and her hair swinging out to the left as she spun around in a wild and joyous pirouette on top of a sandpile.

I watched her and I remembered Emily, the child I'd longed for all my life, who'd died at birth eleven years ago.

That death had devastated both of us, but wrenched at me long after Jon had learned to numb the pain. For several years I'd been afraid to try again—afraid another crushing misery would bend me past the breaking point the second time around. Then finally Tommy came along and I turned a corner in my life.

On the last afternoon, as we left the beach, I saw a little dog biting at a ball and another romping with a child.

"That looks like fun," I said, with a sideways glance at Jon as he bent forward walking up the slope.

"What's that?"

"The dogs—they look like fun. Maybe we should think about getting one for Tommy."

"What kind?" he asked, throwing a piece of driftwood toward the ocean.

"How about a terrier?" I ventured carefully, pitching for a dog like Jackie Day. "Those little ones that come in white and black and tan. They're just about the right size, I think. It could go on walks with us."

"But they're stiff, Kate—they've got legs like woolly broomsticks. They wouldn't cuddle well—they'd prickle when you picked them up."

"Let's talk about the type later," I told him, so the issue wouldn't close before I made my case. "We'll take our time and think about it."

"Okay," he agreed, "and maybe Tommy needs a vote in this thing, too."

Maybe so, I thought, but in my mind I already saw a dog like Jackie Day running on our lawn.

We left Carmel the following morning, heading east on the road we'd traveled in on earlier this week. I took the wheel and found I drove a little harder than I usually did and I knew I was ready to return to work. I'd regained balance and was back on-line again.

CHAPTER EIGHTEEN

Afterward I told myself I should've been expecting it, but I wasn't so it caught me off guard and unprepared. I'd just reached home when the phone began to ring. I took the call, felt a weakness flood my body, and leaned against the wall. When I hung up, I held my head in both my hands and wept.

Joyce Schuyler had committed suicide, climbing to a lonely attic corner, laying rope across a dusty beam, and hanging from it till she died.

I raced to the scene, nearly tearing out the car's transmission as I ground it into gear. Patrol cars were already in the driveway and I saw a uniformed officer moving toward the door.

I walked straight to Thomas Schuyler, who stood helplessly near the bottom of the stairs. His face was pale, his eyes blank and staring.

"Who found her?" I barked out, softening the frenzy of my question by the laying of my hand along his arm.

"I did," he answered woodenly, moving backward from my touch. "She wasn't in the kitchen, wasn't in her room, wasn't anywhere that I could find when I got home from work."

After checking all the obvious places, he'd spied the

open attic door, climbed the narrow stairs, and found his wife hanging from a rope. He'd looked at her, determined she was dead, then picked up the little stool she'd kicked away and set it neatly to one side before he called police.

She'd left a note, written in a shaky hand and placed against a bowl of violets in the kitchen, and when I read it, my heart squeezed tight in pain and I wept again for that poor pathetic woman.

> There's no point in living any longer, so I'm going to leave the two of you. I've been no good to anyone—always so useless and getting in the way—and now with Billy gone I find I haven't got the heart to keep on trying.
>
> I'm so sorry it's come to this and that I let you down so many times, dear Tom. Believe me, I always tried so hard, but I never seemed to get it right. Now you can go on without me and it'll be better that way for you and for Nadine. I love you both so very much, but now I'm going to my little boy.
>
> Your loving wife, Joyce

I slowly walked upstairs to the second floor, then turned and climbed the wooden steps to the shadowed attic. As my head rose above the trapdoor opening, I saw the lifeless body hanging there in front of me. It moved slightly—twisting left and then right, responding to unknown forces—as the head hung slightly sideways, tilting toward one shoulder.

How could I've been so blind, thinking she'd found an inner strength once the funeral ended? Her timid personality, her emotional dissolution when the body was discovered, marked her as a person set to take her life if someone didn't step in quick and help her through the world of horrors that was hers.

Poor tormented woman—she'd been ridiculed and battered by her husband and totally ignored by her growing daughter. And then she'd lost her little boy—the only shining light in that bleak world—to a cruel and savage killer.

I should've urged that she get counseling, I should've talked to her more often, I should've seen a wounded bird that couldn't raise a wing to fly and known that it would soon give up forever.

I thought about the way she'd died, the means she chose to end her time of torment—had she purposely selected hanging, knowing it would break her neck, so she could forge a closer bond with Billy, whose neck was broken, too? My shoulders shook and a chill passed through my body.

When the lifeless form had been cut down and carried out, I went downstairs and sought out Thomas Schuyler. He was standing by the window, watching as the coroner drove away.

"I'm so very sorry, Mr. Schuyler," I said quietly.

He turned and looked at me and I won't soon forget the expression on his face. His lips lifted at the corners, like a snarling dog's, and anger filled his eyes with shining sparks.

"She was a weak-willed woman who couldn't deal with life so she took the coward's way out," he said. "I admire you, Detective, you're not like that. You're strong—you wouldn't have handled it that way at all."

My own anger rose until I knew I'd raise my hand and strike him if I stayed there any longer. I spun around and left the house without another word.

* * *

Joyce's death was just for starters. The bigger blow was yet to come.

I'd gone straight home, leaving Carl and Steve cleaning up the details, and as I wearily climbed the steps, I ached for Jon's presence and the comfort that he gave me. Since returning from Carmel, our lives had wound together once again and I believed the worst was well behind us.

Now, feeling tired and beaten and filled with such self-blame I doubted it would ever go away, I craved solace and a person who would soothe my battered spirit.

He was waiting for me in the den and, gratefully, I started toward him.

"Katie, we need to talk about the changes in your life."

Confused, not knowing what he meant, I made a stab at answering him.

"I'm doing fine now, Jon, just fine."

"No, no," he said patiently, "you misunderstand me. I mean the changes you must make that you haven't taken care of yet."

"Such as?"

"Why, giving up this job, taking something less demanding. Surely that was understood."

I could not believe what I was hearing, yet at the same time I believed it all too well. I felt as if I'd walked into the vortex of a whirling fan that sliced and cut at me with wild abandon.

"Then Carmel was just a sham," I cried. "You went there with me to deceive me and try to make me think we'd worked things out when all the while you knew better. You purposely tricked me, and that was the cruelest thing you could have done. But why? Can you really hate me all that much?"

I felt emotionally raped and then abandoned, the ragged edges of my feelings paining me with every word I spoke.

"You've got it all mixed up," he answered, as he came to me and tried to hold me. "Carmel was real, not a sham. That was what I wanted you to see—how happy we can be when we lead a normal life, when I have you with me all the time. I showed you that and I know you felt it, too. Look how close we've been the past few days."

I don't remember starting crying, but when I tasted salt upon my lips I raised my hand and found my cheeks were wet. I shook my head and wiped them dry. I was fighting for my life now and I needed to be strong.

"I was happy because I thought this was all behind us, because I believed you finally understood what my life was all about. Tommy and I are getting on just fine now, so I do not understand any of what is happening here."

But suddenly, as I spoke, I understood it all in one brilliant flash and I realized I'd been blind from the beginning.

"This is not about Tommy, is it?" I asked slowly and deliberately. "This has never been about him at any time. You just seized on that to cover up the fact that *you're* the one who's jealous of my work, *you're* the one who wants me here with you. And you've probably felt like that for a very long time."

"Damn right," he yelled. "I've hated it from the beginning. You couldn't see that—or maybe you just didn't want to—and I knew better than to come right out and ask you to give it up.

"When that dreadful thing happened to our boy, I thought you'd finally see the light and stay at home, but I was wrong. That cock-assed therapist fed the two of you some bullshit that you both lapped up like eager little puppies.

"But then I almost lost you in that shed and I saw a chance to take you to Carmel and show you what it could be like again. When we came home I thought you finally understood what you had to do."

I backed away, groping toward a chair.

"I know what I have to do, Jon, and Tommy now knows, too. I have to work, and be true to the person that I am. Only then can I be true to you. This is not my problem, it is yours."

He looked at me, both hurt and hatred filling up his eyes.

"I'm not backing down from this one, Katharine, and just in case you're wondering, I'm not cracking up this time around. I'm a stronger person now than I ever used to be."

That night he moved back into the guest room, and the open door between us was firmly shut again.

Something bothered me—bothered me a lot. Why had Joyce Schuyler used the wrong paper? The thick, cream-colored sheets embossed with her initials and a single flower were all she ever wrote on—she'd told me so herself—and yet the suicide note had been penned on an ordinary piece of typing paper.

She'd loved that other stationery—looked on it as some sort of personal signature, I thought—and I

A DESPERATE CALL 237

doubted she'd have used any other kind in the most sadly momentous moment of her life.

At first I hadn't noticed. It was only after several days, after I became aware of a nagging, prodding feeling of uneasiness resting somewhere deep within me, that I realized I was missing something. And then I saw it in my mind—that sheet of thin white paper—and I knew what was pulling at me telling me, "Look here."

What was I saying? I didn't really know, I didn't want to think that far ahead right now. I'd take it one step at a time and probably get it sorted out quickly.

There was most likely an innocent and logical explanation as to why she hadn't used the fine thick sheets. She'd been too distraught to think about them or she'd acted hastily as her depression came down deep upon her and had laid her hands on the first scrap available for penning that sad note. But I had to know and so I called the coroner's office.

"Jerry, did anything unusual turn up in the handwriting analysis on the Schuyler suicide note?"

"We'd have let you know if it had, Kate."

"Right, but do me a favor. Pull the record and tell me what it says."

He grumbled a little but went off to get the file. I waited. And waited some more. I could hear some background noise, like drawers closing, and then some lowered voices. Finally Jerry picked up the phone.

"Sorry, Kate, it looks like no analysis was done. It was an open-and-shut case of suicide by hanging and Chris saw no reason to believe the victim hadn't written that note herself."

I swore and clenched my teeth. Of all the coroner's assistants, Chris Robinson was the one I least liked to deal with. His attitude was often callous, his work sometimes sloppy. I avoided him at every opportunity.

"How did he get my case?"

"Easy enough to answer, Kate. We were logjammed here and this was suicide, plain and simple. Maybe he should've analyzed the note, but he didn't, and, in this case, I don't think it's any big deal."

"Damn it, Jerry, it's procedure and it should've been done."

"You want to go to Penross over this, then?" His truculence pounded through the phone.

"No, but I *do* want the note analyzed now, by either you or Howard."

The pause on the line became far too long.

"Well?"

"Can't do that, Kate," he said finally, and the truculence had markedly receded. "Chris released the note, along with the victim's other effects, to the husband just this morning."

I exploded, then just as quickly calmed down. After all, it wasn't Jerry's fault. If I had a beef, I should take it up with Penross.

"Tell me this," I asked him in my most civil tone, "looking at the file, are you totally satisifed that it was suicide?"

"I'm looking at the file and I was also cutting up a corpse on the gurney next to Chris when he was working on her. I'm satisfied she died by hanging from that rope around her neck. Now if you think she did all that because someone was standing there with a gun on her telling her to kick the stool aside or else—well, that's your theory and up to you to find out."

I lit into him again.

"And how am I supposed to back that theory up

when I can't know for sure if she did or didn't write that note?"

"It wouldn't really matter, would it, Kate? If someone held the gun on her and made her jump, he sure as hell could've put it to her head and made her write that note, too. Come on!" Jerry was getting just as riled as I was and it came out in his sarcasm.

"Okay, you're right. But I'd like to have it analyzed anyway. I'll try to get it back and bring it on in."

He backed off, too.

"Look, Kate, we messed up—I'm sorry—but I really don't think it would've made a bit of difference in our conclusions."

I was on my knees picking up the broken glass from a jam jar I'd dropped when I felt a little tug on my shoulder. Turning, I looked up into Tommy's eyes, only inches from my face. The smile was on his lips but it was in the eyes, too, as he moved a hidden hand from behind his back and held it toward me.

"I picked them 'specially for you, Mom—here," and, wonderingly, I took the tiny bunch of violets and dandelions with a single daisy in their middle.

"I love you, Mom," he whispered, and he fell down beside me and threw his arms around my neck.

I hugged him to me, kissing him and rocking him, smelling that special warm, sweet smell that all young children seem to have. I guess I knew then that we were going to be all right ... unlike the other mother, the other little boy, whose soft sad images played across my mind and filled my heart with unrelenting sorrow.

Chapter Nineteen

A break finally came, borne by a most unlikely messenger—Jon's cousin Barbara.

Babs lived several blocks from us and dropped by from time to time, whenever the fancy struck her. I came home the following day and found her waiting on the porch, a little smile playing on her lips. I waved her on inside.

An extroverted cutup with a soft spot for a kid, she was way out front as Tommy's favorite relative. I liked her sense of humor and her devotion to my son, but I knew I'd have found her constant presence slightly wearing—"low-key" wasn't a word that fitted Barbara well.

Her impulsive nature let her mouth run before her mind, and words spilled out in the pop of the moment, fresh and funny, but sometimes causing trouble for her later.

I wondered if she'd guessed about our situation. Probably not, or she'd have pried and probed to find out more.

"What's up?" I asked, as we walked out to the kitchen.

"I've got a juicy little story for you," she replied, and her eyes twinkled as she enjoyed the prospect of telling me her tale. "All about illicit sex with a little hanky-panky with a minor thrown in to jazz it up."

"Go on," I told her, egging her along, "my tongue's already hanging out."

"It's about a naughty boy who should've known better, but let his hormones get the best of him."

"Tell me more," I said, wondering what was coming next.

"Janie Crane's in my workout class," she started, "and a few of us go out for coffee when it's over. Yesterday, we began to talk about the murder and Janie suddenly remembered something she hadn't thought about in ages.

"A family who used to live next door to her had a teenage virgin daughter. The girl was sixteen, but truly innocent and naive—not a mover in the fast lane, by any means. One day Mom and Dad came home and found this fella stroking Susie Q in all the wrong places.

"They saw this torrid passion through a window, as they came up the front walk, and by the time they got inside the loving couple had jumped apart. The daughter actually seemed to fear the man and told the parents later he'd forced himself on her and she'd resisted. Knowing the daughter, Janie told us, that was highly likely. Anyway, the man beat a quick retreat, denying he'd even touched the girl."

"Did the parents call police?" I asked.

"Janie said no. They were about to move from here, the girl had suffered no real damage, and besides, they weren't one hundred percent sure of what they'd seen because their daughter's back was to them, so they decided to let the whole thing die down and not have sweetie's name dragged through the mud."

Personally, I thought the parents were a pair of spineless fools. If I had a daughter and thought I saw even a hint of sexual battery, I'd phone the cops so fast the wires would burn. Maybe they hadn't wanted to believe the truth themselves—blind eyes let lots of criminals walk away.

"Who was the man? How did he get inside the house?" I asked, slightly confused and still not quite sure why Barbara was telling me this story.

She didn't answer right away. I looked at her and saw a smile that smacked of wickedness and satisfaction. I'd fallen for the bait and finally asked the question she'd carefully cultivated in my mind.

"It was Billy Schuyler's uncle."

"You mean Marc?" I asked, surprised. "The surfer babe?"

"That's the one, Katie. I've never seen him but the description fits with what I've heard. These people were moving out-of-town and Schuyler was the listing agent for their property. That's why he was in their house that day. He came by to meet a client, but the client never showed. Instead, he found the girl at home alone."

"Did his employer find out?"

"Oh, yes, and that's another reason the parents didn't call police. They bitched to the boss and he told Marc he'd better take a hike—he didn't want an open zipper for a salesman. Mom and Dad felt firing would do just fine for punishment. So Schuyler lost his job while daughter's name remained untarnished."

"Does Janie think Marc knew the girl was underage?"

"Honey, Janie didn't say and I didn't have to ask. I'd seen her once or twice myself. She not only looked like an angel in a chorus, she also looked a whole lot younger than she really was. Except for the boobs, that is—they'd fulfilled their promise long before their time."

Barbara had her triumph. I admit I was surprised at her story about Marc Schuyler and I told her so. I'd sensed he possessed a strong taste for sensual pleasures, but I hadn't known he picked those pleasures from vines that hadn't ripened. I remembered the man who'd been with me—his sensitivity, his willingness to let *me* set the pace—and I could not believe what I was hearing.

But if her tale were true, then I'd been fooled and he was a randy stud who usually took what he desired when he desired it and didn't care a bit about the age. And didn't necessarily care if the lady shared his feelings either.

That bothered me a lot and I wondered if the girl had really been sweet innocence of youth. Parents often can't see for looking and sometimes friends and neighbors are easily fooled as well.

Maybe Barbara's Susie Q had done a bit of flirting or at least hadn't resisted a whole lot when Schuyler put the make on her. A trumped-up story for the benefit of Mom and Dad would sound just like the one the daughter told.

But suppose the girl hadn't wanted his attention? Suppose she *had* been taken by surprise and *had* fought back? And suppose the parents hadn't walked up when they did? What would've happened next?

If he'd tried it on with one, he'd probably tried it on with others. I had some checking-out to do first thing tomorrow morning.

* * *

I cornered the detective in charge of sex crimes as soon as he got in.

"Let me run something by you, Glenn. Have you had any reports of a man forcibly assaulting teenage girls or, at the very least, making suggestive overtures?"

Not lately, he told me, though he seemed to recall some like that from earlier in the year. He asked was I including flashing.

"No, I doubt flashing's involved here," I answered, "it gets worse than that."

"Okay, I'll dig 'em out and bring 'em over, but what's happening here?"

"Maybe something, maybe nothing. Let me look at what you have, then I'll fill you in."

"Here you go, Kate," he said a few minutes later as he tossed three reports in front of me. "I never got anywhere with these myself—couldn't find enough to go on. The girls gave good descriptions, but there were no witnesses, no car connected to the guy, nothing to help out like a tattoo or sweatshirt logo."

I quickly scanned the reports. In each one, the victim—a fifteen- or sixteen-year-old girl—had been walking alone when a man came up to her and tried to fondle her while asking if she'd "like to get it on" with him.

The first assault occurred behind the public library, the others in a recreation area near the high school. The victims told police the man tried to kiss them and stroke their breasts while cornering them against some shrubbery. In one case, at least, he succeeded.

All three girls managed to free themselves from their assailant, who didn't try to restrain them nor did he pursue them when they fled.

All three said they'd never seen the man before and gave roughly the same description of the suspect: "male white approximately 5'10"–6'0", 170–185 pounds, 25–30 years of age, blond hair, blue eyes."

Well, look at that, I thought. I couldn't have written it better myself if I'd been describing Marc Schuyler. I carried the cases back to Thompson.

"None since March?" I asked.

"Nope. Either he's blown town or the girls just aren't reporting it. Sometimes these guys are fairly harmless—just want to cop a feel and go their way. But you never can tell—it could get out of hand. We had a stakeout at the rec area for a while but saw no one the victims could ID."

I told him about Janie Crane and the girl who'd lived next door.

"You're going back how long, Kate? Several years at least. There're lots of blond-haired, blue-eyed jocks out there. I'm not sure the connection's one that's worth the making."

"Maybe not," I admitted, "but tell me this. Would you mind if I dug into it a little, see what I come up with?"

"Don't you have your plate full of murders and felonious assaults? You want to dip into my bag of fun and games as well?"

Glenn was razzing me, but I knew deep-down he wondered where I got my motivation. I decided I'd enlighten him. I owed him that much.

"The guy who jumped on Janie Crane's neighbor is the uncle of the nine-year-old found murdered last month. I'm at a standstill there so I'm flailing out in all directions trying to stir the dust a little to see what shows when it finally settles down."

Thompson raised his brows and whistled.

"Go to it, then," he told me. "Anything you do on these can only help *me* out and if you find something for yourself, so much the better. I'm betting you come up empty, though."

"Maybe so," I answered, "but at least I'll be doing something I can feel might be a tiny bit constructive."

The real truth went a little deeper. I *did* wonder if Schuyler could be the suspect in these cases, and if I spoke with the virginal victim and her story seemed solid, I'd for sure show a photo lineup with him in it to these other girls.

But I was also obsessed with Billy's homicide and any involvement with it, no matter how peripheral, invited me. I'd probably investigate the shade of Nadine's nail gloss if I thought I could justify it to my captain.

I phoned Barbara and got Janie Crane's number. I could feel the questions bubbling and breaking on the surface of her mind, but she never asked them. She was too much Jon's cousin to try to pump me about my actions on a case.

Janie Crane was home and showed surprise when I called.

"I was only trading gossip with my friends," she protested. "I didn't mean to cause an official inquiry."

"I doubt it'll develop into anything full-blown," I assured her. "I just want to ask the girl a couple of little questions. Can you tell me where the family moved to? I promise you I'll not tell them how I learned about the trouble."

"Can you hang on? I've got the address in my Christmas card box."

I waited, and she came back in several minutes and

A DESPERATE CALL

gave me what I wanted. The Warner family had moved two hundred miles south, to northwest Los Angeles, some three years ago. The daughter, who'd be about nineteen now, was named Leslie Jean.

I debated what approach to take. After all, the girl had never called the police so I couldn't pretend I was following up on anything. Finally, I decided to handle it the cleanest way—straight out. Pussyfooting wasn't really needed here.

I dialed Los Angeles and a woman who told me she was Hannah Warner held the phone and heard me talk about a crude occurrence that happened many months ago.

She seemed uncertain how to answer me and wavered back and forth as to whether I could visit her and talk a whole lot more. She asked if she could check with her husband and her daughter and I said I wanted her to do just that and left my call-back number with her.

"Anything you say will be completely confidential," I assured her as I was hanging up. "I'm not trying to make a case out of something that happened so long ago, but it's possible your daughter's trouble ties in with several recent crimes against some other girls and that's why I need to hear her story."

She said she'd call her husband right away and talk with Leslie Jean, a junior college student, when she got home from school at one o'clock. Then she'd call me back.

I got absorbed in other cases and forgot about the Warners, and when my phone rang at noon I tried to place the wispy voice that spoke to me. It was Hannah Warner.

"Leslie came home early," she explained. "I've

talked to her and to my husband and we agree it's fine for you to visit us."

I made a date for one o'clock the following day and told her I needed very little of her daughter's time. Actually, half an hour should do it. I only wanted to peel away the gossip and reach the shining core of truth that lay beneath.

I had to tread delicately here. I wanted that letter back from Thomas Schuyler, yet I didn't want to arouse undue suspicion when I asked for it.

He seemed almost glad to see me when I knocked on the door that evening and, companionably, he asked me to come in and sit.

"No," I told him as I remained standing in the entrance way, "I don't want to interfere. I just want to ask a favor of you, if it wouldn't pain you. I grew to think a lot of Joyce—we talked from time to time, just the two of us—and I wonder, if you wouldn't mind, if I might briefly borrow the note she left, to make a copy for myself just to have a record of her final thoughts ..."

My voice trailed away. I sounded phony even to myself, so how could I expect that he'd buy it? Why on earth would I want to keep, or think I had any right to, such a deeply personal and pathetic reminder? Better to have asked for a piece of inexpensive jewelery or a favorite scarf if remembering a casual friend was my motive.

He didn't seem to notice anything odd. Instead, he looked me in the eye and told me he'd torn up the note and flushed it down the toilet.

"You could've had the thing to keep if I'd known that you wanted it," he said. "Why you would, I cannot understand. It was a pathetic statement of the weakness of the woman and nothing I'd personally care to have around."

So now I'd never know if Joyce had really written that note or not. But if she had, why hadn't she used the thick cream paper? And why had Thomas Schuyler really destroyed her final words? For the reason he'd given me or because he knew we'd realize our mistake and come looking? And find out what?

Because I didn't know and couldn't know the answers to these questions, I asked myself some others. Could Thomas Schuyler, finally unable to tolerate Joyce and her weakness any longer, have goaded her into putting that rope around her neck? Could he have undermined her last remaining bits of confidence, perhaps even accusing her of causing Billy's death, so that he finally made her crave nothing more than the hangman's noose he offered her?

Or perhaps he *had* used a gun, as Jerry had sarcastically suggested, and she'd feared it more than she'd feared the plaited rope and so had kicked the stool aside. Or had thought that once her husband saw her start to struggle, he'd feel the horror of his act and cut her down in time.

I recoiled from what my mind was offering me, as I saw two darkened figures moving toward a length of hemp. I recoiled but I did not deny the possibility. Nor the total lack of proof.

No, I could never really know what had happened in that dusty attic corner on the day Joyce Schuyler died. I'd have to place the manner of her death with the wisps and clouds of other facts I didn't know for sure. But the notepaper bothered me a lot.

* * *

Los Angeles. The words shimmer with a sundance brilliance that sparks the mind and fires it with electrifying imagery. They're magnetic words, mesmerizing in their captivation. They get my full attention every time I hear them.

Bold and brassy, strutting like a gamecock, there's nothing subtle about the City of the Angels. It's a searing raucous entity that never wants to quit. Raw and vivid, hard and fast, it defies you to ignore it.

If Jon had been at all keen, I'd have thought of moving here, of succumbing to the powerful pull of this boisterous sprawling place. But he never had been, even before our present troubles, and I knew that in reality, life was better where we were. Sure, the pace of San Madera had heated up in recent years, but murder still brought feelings of horror and of shock and wasn't yet an everyday occurrence.

The city to the south, in contrast, moved always on the cutting edge, roiling with relentless fervor, playing hardball all the way. Yes, I knew better than to get involved with it, but I also knew the lure would never go away.

As I reached the city limits, I checked my watch, then swung a right and headed west. I'd allowed myself plenty of time before the meeting and I decided to pick up the coast road and ride with the ocean right on into town.

I drove through narrow canyons flanked by jagged mountains that flaunted colors blazing with a heat and light the cooler tones of northern California don't possess. Ochre, umber, rose, and burnt sienna mixed and matched and ran in rampant patterns in a glorious melee.

I followed a twisting road along a canyon floor, until it ended at the ocean's edge, and then I followed the road beside the ocean until it reached the city.

I found the Warners' house without much trouble. Standing in a cul-de-sac high on a mountainside that overlooked the valley floor, the one-story ranch house sat in a risky perch on a narrow point of land.

I wondered if they ever worried about tumbling down the hill during violent storms and then I realized they probably did, for I'd read about the winter mudslides common in this area. I thought about my two-story on its firm and level lot, but I still felt slightly wistful.

Two cars were in the driveway, a third was parked inside the garage. I was several minutes early, but I'd bet the daughter and her parents were ready for my visit. If I'd been in their place, my curiosity would be running wide open.

A dog barked as I rang the bell. The sound was deep and gruff but not entirely unfriendly and, as the door opened, an Irish setter pushed forward and nosed my outstretched hand. I wiped off the hand and gave it to the man who stood behind the dog.

He told me he was Kendall Warner, the father of the girl I came to see. He led me to the living room and introduced me to his wife and, as he finished, his daughter entered from a side door and he introduced the two of us as well.

Leslie Jean was nineteen now and three years may have seasoned her naiveté a little, but I could still see why Barbara had called her an angel in a chorus.

Fine blond hair set off a heart-shaped face devoid of any makeup, and pale blue eyes gazed straight at me with a look of total trust. The girl possessed a quality of innocence I'd noticed only in small children and sisters of the cloth.

Her parents, on the other hand, seemed neither innocent nor worldwise. Rather, they impressed me as faded, timid persons, fearful not of anything specific but of everything in general. They sat there, hands clasped and resting in their laps, waiting placidly to find out what I wanted.

I started gently.

"Leslie Jean, I understand that several years ago, right before you moved down here, something unpleasant happened between you and a local realtor, is that right?"

She blushed.

"Does everybody know?"

"It's not the talk of the town, no," I told her. "In fact, I heard about it only because of the job I do."

"Yes, it's true, but why are you asking now?"

I explained about the other crimes involving teenage girls and told her I was checking out every lead that came my way. I didn't tell her about my obsession with the Schuyler case and my desire to stay close to anyone connected with it.

"What do you want to know?" she asked meekly, twisting a curl around her index finger.

"Everything. Please start at the beginning."

"It's been so long I'm not sure I can remember all of it."

"Just do the best you can then."

Her parents must've thought I was doing just fine, for they both sat quietly and didn't try to prompt or silence or otherwise interfere.

"I was home alone," she started, "and the doorbell

rang. I knew the realtor by sight and I could see him standing on the steps so I let him in. He said he was supposed to meet someone there in ten minutes so I left him in the living room and went upstairs.

"About fifteen minutes after that, I came back down and he was still alone, walking back and forth. He told me he'd wait a little longer and if his client didn't show up he'd leave and come back another time."

She paused for breath and coughed slightly.

"Finally he decided to go and I started to walk him to the door. We'd almost reached it when he put his hand on my shoulder and turned me toward him."

As the girl spoke, color rose to her cheeks and she kept her eyes focused on her loafer tips.

"And then what?"

She glanced quickly at her parents and I sensed her discomfort in their presence. I turned to them.

"Perhaps it'd be better if I spoke with Leslie Jean alone. Sometimes people find it hard to talk about sensitive things in front of those closest to them."

The Warners instantly agreed and rose and left the room, patting their daughter's shoulder as they went.

"Thanks," the girl said gratefully. "It still embarrasses me a lot in front of Dad."

"I'm sure it does; that's only natural. What happened next?"

"He tried to kiss me. I was so surprised I jerked away, but he put a hand on my other shoulder and backed me up against the wall. I kept telling him to stop and struggled with him, but he was too strong and he started kissing me all over my face and neck and pressing his body against me really hard."

One corner of her upper lip rose slightly, as if disgusted at the memory.

"And then my parents came home and I got away."

I looked at her quickly. I felt as if we'd gone on fast-forward and I'd missed a crucial part.

"Did he do anything to you besides the kissing?" I asked, recalling Barbara's version of the story.

Again she blushed.

"He touched me."

"Where and how?" I kept my voice low and spoke as softly as I could. I knew this talk was tough for her.

"On the breasts."

I could barely hear her. Then she lifted up her chin and I saw a tear roll down her cheek.

"There, and then he tried to touch me down below as well, but that's when Mom and Dad came home."

"Did he say anything while he was doing this?"

"Some things."

"Leslie Jean, I've heard it all many, many times before. I won't be shocked. This is girl talk here—you can trust me—and if you feel up to telling me, I'd really appreciate it.

"You see, a guy will sometimes use a word or phrase that's not too common and if he talks the same way when he does another crime, it helps us to catch him and put him away."

She drew in her breath and sat up straight.

"He asked me if I wanted any and told me he was ready for me. He tried to push my hand down and make me feel him. He told me he was going to stick it in me till it hurt and still I'd beg for more. Then he called me 'bitch' over and over again."

Her face was glowing scarlet now, but once she'd cried she'd gotten her composure back and showed no sign of losing it again.

"Thank you, Leslie, you did just fine," I told her.

"You've helped me even more than I'd hoped before I came here. Would it upset you if I showed you a photo, to make sure we're talking about the same man?"

She shook her head no and I showed her a duplicate of Schuyler's driver's license picture.

"That's him," she said. "He looks a little older, but basically the same. I think his last name was Schooler or something like that."

I told her to ask her parents to come back in and in they came, hesitant, quivering smiles on both their faces.

"Thanks for your cooperation," I said. "But why didn't you call the police when this thing happened?"

Hannah Warner looked at her husband in confusion and listened as he answered me.

"Nothing really *did* happen to Leslie Jean," he said, "and we felt it'd be too embarrassing to make a lot of fuss about it. Fella lost his job, after all, and that was good enough."

His wife smiled her little smile and nodded in agreement.

No, nothing happened except near-rape, I thought, and I turned to leave. I'd stripped away the gossip and reached the hard core of truth I'd come to find. I believed every single word of Leslie Jean's disturbing story.

But I still could not forget the sensitive, passionate, caring man I'd known for those few moments in that darkened room.

"It's worth a shot," I told Thompson when I saw him. "Schuyler's right in line with the description and he did a job on Leslie Warner, that's for sure. You can't overlook the possibility."

"I'm overlooking nothing, Kate—I'm just thinking it's a real *long* shot. We're talkin' about a description that fits a lot of people and we're talkin' about three long years between the crimes. But of course do a lineup. If you don't, I will. I'm just saying I'm not gonna hold my breath waitin' for the answers."

I put together a photo lineup and called the three victims to the station. One by one, they arrived and one by one I showed the lineup to them, cautioning each to take her time and carefully study all the photos, then tell me if she saw the face of her assailant.

By four-fifteen, the third and final victim had seen the lineup, said goodbye, and left me looking at a case that wouldn't come to life. Not one girl had fingered Schuyler as the suspect. In fact, all three had stated positively he wasn't the man we sought.

Angrily, I tossed the cases on my desk—I'd hand them back to Thompson in the morning. I'd taken Barbara's story and given it a run and it had teased me with its promise, then led me up a dead-end trail. I told myself to turn around and walk away.

CHAPTER TWENTY

I couldn't do it. A compelling questing urge drove me toward Marc Schuyler. I didn't kid myself that this had anything to do with Billy's death, but he was Billy's uncle and his complexities intrigued me.

He hadn't merely flirted with a younger girl—he'd brutalized her in a crude and ruthless manner to satisfy a selfish sexual urge. I'd found this one dark chapter in his life and it made me ask if there were others.

Who was he really? I saw a good-time Charlie right up front, but what lay behind that flashing smile of self-assurance? I felt a powerful need to find out all about him and flesh out this figure standing on the edges of my case.

I'd play with this one on my own time, a hobby tailor-made to keep me linked to Billy's family. I'd ask some questions, check some facts, and gradually build a picture of the man, and when I finished I'd step back and take a look at what I'd put together. A deep-set hunch told me I'd turn up a few surprises.

Then Darrow took my hobby and changed it to official business.

I'd returned from lunch and found him looking through the murder file.

"Just going over it again," he said, "searching for that missing link."

"Be sure to tell me when you find it," I answered wryly.

"You checked the mom was home that afternoon?"

"I did," I said, thinking of that poor, sad woman. "A bank employee talked with her at ten to five. Phoned to speak with Thomas on a business matter—knew he usually walked in around that time."

"Little sis says she studied at the library—satisfied with that one?"

"Enough to let it go for now. She doesn't drive, she doesn't own a car, and, like her mother, she didn't have the time to kill and do the moving even if the first two were a go."

Darrow leafed the pages quietly, his chair tilted backward, rocking on its legs. Suddenly it lurched downward with a bang and leveled with the floor. I jerked up my head and looked at him.

He was leaning forward, both elbows on the table, holding a report of mine in front of him. Narrow frown lines gathered on his forehead, and his eyes focused in unbroken concentration on the written page he held.

"This is all a crock," he said indignantly. "Ellen Dancer—what a joke! Sorry, babe, I'm not buying that one."

He pushed the page across the desk and I reread the words of Billy's uncle after I'd broken his original alibi.

"What's wrong?" I asked, genuinely puzzled.

Darrow eyed me closely, then he spoke.

"The fella says he didn't want to—how did he so

daintily put it—'trash' his girlfriend's reputation, so he lied to you at first, correct?"

"That's right," I said, "and I can understand that, Steve, even if the lie was ill-advised. Where's the problem?"

"Kate, Ellen Dancer's the hottest lay in town. She's a gorgeous cookie, but she'll spread for anyone who'll do it to her. That's baby's reputation *can't* be trashed because she lost it in the sheets a long, long time ago."

"You're saying?"

"I'm saying something's wrong here. Schuyler's got to know her for the party girl she is. If he told you he lied to you to keep this dolly clean, that's bullshit and it means he's lying to you now."

I stared at him. Darrow knew his ladies and if he said the Dancer girl was common property, I'd bet my bottom dollar he was right. What was going on here anyway?

"Can we be sure Schuyler's got her pegged?"

"Damn sure, Kate. Every guy in town knows Ellen Dancer." He paused and threw a mocking sideways glance. "Except for some old married men like Jon who maybe keep the blinkers on."

I let that one pass right by and walk on down the road, and when he saw he couldn't bait me he turned serious again.

"Marc's a single boy just like myself. He knows the score. That little tramp could never fool him."

"Does Dancer work?" I asked, rising from my chair.

"Off and on, but I don't know which it is right now. I've got the home address, though, if you wanna try her there."

My expression must've showed surprise.

"Don't worry, ma'am," Darrow reassured me, "this

babe's not one of mine—I just happen to know these things. I'm a little bit more choosy in my women."

"Let's go, then," and I motioned toward the doorway as I slung my bag across my shoulder. "We'll turn it over on the way."

"I wouldn't think of going back to Schuyler yet," I said, talking to myself and letting Darrow listen. "He lied at first and then he lied a second time, when I exposed him.

"I want to know what's going on before I even try approaching him again, so that next time *I'll* be holding all the cards. We'll get this girl to tell us what she can, then we'll take it on from there. And we'll put the fear of God in her, to keep her quiet about our visit."

Ellen Dancer lived in a condo on the northern edge of town—an area known for its singles bars and flashy cars as well as for its transient tenancy. It wasn't a settled neighborhood by any means.

We checked the street for Schuyler's car, then drove around the block and down an alley. Unless he'd parked it in a garage or gotten there some other way, he wasn't on the scene.

The buzzer panel showed us Dancer lived two floors above. We waited till a mother and her little girl left the building, then caught the swinging door and stepped into a lobby tiled in black and white.

A staircase to the left took us to the second floor and a tiny card embossed in silver told us when we found the door we wanted.

I knocked and waited. Nothing. I knocked again and then once more. As we were just about to walk away, a sleepy voice asked us who we were and what we wanted.

I ID'd myself and told the voice to open up the door. It swung slowly inward and the drowsy blonde I'd seen at Schuyler's place looked out at us, a flimsy negligee tossed loosely on her shoulders.

I'd wondered on the way here should I play it hard or easy, and I'd decided hard.

"We've met before, Miss Dancer," I reminded her, and I stepped quickly past her with Darrow close behind. "Do you recall the meeting?"

I turned and caught her gaze and held it till she answered.

"At Marc's, yes—about a month ago."

Suddenly she was wide awake and her eyes were asking questions.

"On the money, kiddo, now let's try something else. Tell me what you said to me that day."

"I said I was with Marc when his nephew disappeared—for several hours at least, late that afternoon."

Her tongue responded quickly, but a tone of caution overlaid the words and her eyes showed gathering uneasiness.

"So you did, Miss Dancer, so you did. Now I'll ask you once again—where were you on the afternoon of April twenty?"

"With Marc, in bed, just like he told you. He thought it would embarrass ..."

"Cut it. Cut it right there. You're lying to me now just like you lied to me the day I saw the two of you together."

I snapped the words out like a whip and she gave a start and stepped involuntarily backward. Frightened eyes flicked from me to Steve and back again.

"Let me lay it out for you," I said, moving toward

her as I spoke. "You're playing games with us but you're the one who's coming up the loser. We're slapping you in jail on charges of withholding information. Get your clothes and come along."

"Wait a minute—no. I'll level with you. You know, you act pretty mean for a lady cop."

I ignored her observation.

"Promise?"

"Yes, I promise, but how do you know about before?"

"We know," I bluffed.

"We've known all along," Darrow added for good measure.

It worked. She folded visibly before our eyes. The fun and games were over and the laughs were echoes in the distant past.

"I didn't think it mattered," she told me weakly.

"I'm sure you didn't," I began, my tone quick-changing to a soothing stroke. "Perhaps you told a little lie or gave the truth a twist it shouldn't take, because you truly thought it couldn't hurt that much."

Her head bobbed up and down excitedly and she tossed her hair behind her shoulder in a quick and nervous gesture.

"That's exactly how it was," she said, and I heard relief fill her voice.

"I think we understand each other now," I told her, "so let's begin again. Tell me where you were the afternoon Billy disappeared."

"I was in Reno, actually."

"Reno? That's a long way from Morro Street."

"I know. I lied to you because Marc asked me to. When I got back in town he called me and we did some partying that night. We arranged that if you

A DESPERATE CALL 263

asked me where I was on April twentieth, I'd say I'd been with him."

"Just how did this arrangement come about?"

"I'd lost a bit of money gambling—not much but I was in a temporary bind. He insisted I take some cash and then he told me there was something *I* could do for *him*.

"I said sure, anything, why not, and that was when he asked me. I told him you'd find out I lied, but he said you'd be satisfied and not check any further."

"Do you always lie when someone asks you to?"

"Well, no, of course I don't, but Marc and I are old, old friends and he'd just helped me out. I knew it had no bearing on the murder so I couldn't see the harm in playing you along."

"You knew it had no bearing? How could you be sure?"

"Because I asked him right up front why he wanted me to alibi. He told me he'd had someone in the sack that afternoon, but he couldn't let her name get out so he needed me to cover for her."

"And you didn't mind that he was using you?"

She shrugged her shoulders and lit a cigarette.

"Why should I? I've been in jams myself and friends have done the same for me."

"Any idea who this woman was?"

"None. I didn't even ask 'cause I knew he'd never tell me. He likes to keep things to himself. Someone's wife, most likely—Marc's always screwing where he shouldn't."

"What's *your* relationship with him?"

She looked at me and shrugged again as she stubbed out the cigarette.

"We're friends, that's all. We see each other, sure,

but nothing heavy and not that often, really. It was just by chance I was there the day you came to see him."

"Are you good enough a friend to get yourself in trouble for him in the future?"

"No way, not if I know first that trouble's coming."

"Then let me give you some advice."

My voice dropped its soothing tone and tossed the words out harshly.

"Keep your mouth closed about our visit here today. Let your boyfriend think he's got the alibi he wants. This is serious business and you're best off walking out of it right now and staying well away. Is that clear enough or shall I spell it out some more?"

Her eyes snapped open as she realized I'd put us back on fighting ground.

"Of course," she said. "If that's the way you want it, I'll never mention you were here."

"That's the way I want it—make sure I get it just like that. I'm not forgetting you lied to me and kept that lie alive long past its time. That doesn't set too well, so I'll be watching out for any other trouble you might cause me."

She bit her lip and pulled the negligee around her shoulders in a protective gesture. I left her standing there while Steve and I walked out the door and shut it tight behind us.

I didn't even say a curt goodbye. Let her fret a bit about my words and wonder what I'd do to her. Maybe I could keep her quiet till I could sort out what the heck was going on.

"You lost your voice in there," I said to Darrow as we went outside.

"It was your show all the way," he answered with

a grin, "I love to hear you talkin' tough. Besides, I got a chance to watch the scenery. She's sure a looker, that one. Too bad she spreads herself so thin."

"You think she'll stay quiet about our visit?"

"Yeah, babe, I do. The way you put it to her, she'll never say a word. Her main concern's old number one and she doesn't want us comin' through that door again."

He laughed and looked at me.

"I just realized—I gotta be the only guy in town she isn't hot to see ... except for maybe your old man!"

Jon. He'd moved out the night before, no longer needing to pretend he had to stick around for Tommy's sake. He wanted a *real* separation, he told me, not one that just involved a change of rooms, until we both could settle down and see our lives more clearly.

I could translate that one easily—it meant until I came to my senses and quit work.

I let him go—I really had no choice—and the pain that had permeated every crevice of my being during all the fights that came before was strangely absent when he finally walked away.

Not because I didn't care, but rather because the enduring hassle had finally worn me down and made me numb, and I couldn't feel a thing. My emotional sensors had been rendered silent.

With his leaving, I realized that ultimately each of us is on his own, and, for that reason, one must forge the strongest bond possible with one's inner self, so that regardless of the disappointments others bring you, you *can* go on alone.

He'd given one last parting shot as he set his bags down by the door.

"I don't know where all of this is heading, Kate, but remember what I told you earlier. If this becomes a permanent separation or, God forbid, a divorce, I'm suing for custody of Tommy. If you think that was an idle threat or one I'd back away from, well, you read me wrong. Don't ever underestimate me. I'm going to have him with me."

And so my deep and constant fears had been fed anew by the ugly, frightening fuel of Jon's intentions. I knew him well enough to know he meant everything he said.

Carl guessed before I ever told him. I'd sat atop the corner of his desk, my shoulders hunched in visible defeat, and he's just said, "It's happened, Katie, hasn't it?"

I nodded and compressed my lips. Quietly, he reached up and squeezed my shoulder.

"Sometimes love just is not enough," he told me sadly. "It maybe should be but it isn't. Sometimes we even hold on far too long. It's the good memories that keep you there, thinking they'll come back again. But when you realize they probably won't and bad memories are all that's being made, well, then you know it's finally time to go."

Chapter Twenty-one

Like the slow rising of a winter sun, it dawned on me. I think maybe it'd been there, hidden, all the time.

If I believed it possible that Thomas Schuyler could've had a strong and active hand in Joyce's death, could I still be absolutely certain he'd had nothing to do with Billy's? I knew his alibi was sound, or seemed to be, but didn't it deserve another look?

I dropped in on Molly Blevins and brought up the hit-and-run.

"You told police your car was hit at four-forty in the afternoon. Are you positive about the time?"

A big blousy woman with disheveled hair, she ran her fingers through her reddish curls and handed me her answer. Couched in comfortable profanity, it sent my mind reeling.

"Hell, no, I was all wrong about that. Must've been at least a half hour later that it happened. That goddamn little clock—little thing's been a bastard since I got it—had decided to do its slowing-down bit without telling me."

"Why didn't you let us know once you realized?"

"Didn't need to." She flashed a broad grin that let me see the gap between her teeth. "By the time I knew about it, they'd already got the fucker that rammed into my old Betsy."

She explained that the marble clock she'd looked at when she ran back inside the house was battery-operated and those batteries had started to wear out.

"I thought about them when I set it forward for the time change a week or two before the crash," she said, "thought that I should soon be getting new ones. But then I just forgot the hell to do it and it started runnin' down."

I called Nadine. It was mid-afternoon and I knew I'd get her home alone. The conversation was to the point, with no pleasantries wasted on either side.

"Nadine, when did your parents ask you to take your bike and go look for Billy?"

"After my dad got home that night." The petulance in her voice let me know she didn't want too much to do with me.

"And what time was that?"

"I don't know, really. I was listening to my radio and not paying much attention to the clock."

"Was it around five-fifteen, do you think?"

She hesitated a moment, then responded.

"I know that's what my mom said, but I always felt it was a little later. I don't know why, I just thought more time had passed than that. I remember thinking he was pretty late that night and wondering when we'd have our dinner."

So now I'd got myself a whole new ball game or, rather, the old one starting to play out again. Regardless of what had happened to cause poor Joyce's death, I did now know for sure that Thomas Schuyler could've been in the right place at the right time to pick up his son and kill him.

A DESPERATE CALL

And maybe he'd been on his way to the field to dump the body when he ploughed into Molly Blevins's car, and he'd panicked and driven home instead, calmly eaten dinner while the mangled corpse lay hidden in the trunk, then ridden out later on to do the hiding.

I'd go carefully here and give all of this a lot more thought before I made any move at all. Earlier, I'd been panting to get him in for questioning, but that had been before I'd found out about the alibi. Now, even though the Blevins woman said she'd been wrong about the time, the official police accident report still indicated Thomas Schuyler couldn't have been anywhere near his son when Billy disappeared, and any defense lawyer worth his salt would take that fact and run with it.

Also, there was no longer any Joyce Schuyler to query again about the time her husband had come home, to try to break her story with Molly Blevins's tale or at least see if she'd admit she might've been mistaken.

No, I wanted to lay back a little, to make damn sure I felt secure with what I had before I tangled up with him. Besides, there was another difference now— I had someone else in sight who'd managed to intrigue me.

Marc Schuyler, like others who lie easily to police, believed we'd buy his lies and never do a double-check.

His cocky self-assurance told him he could fool us with a glib and smooth delivery fueled by false sincerity. He'd find out just how wrong he was.

He'd handed me a lie the first time I'd asked him

for an alibi and even though I'd called him on it quickly, he turned right around and handed me another. He'd fooled me momentarily with the second try, but in the end I'd found him out and now he'd gotten what he wanted least—my full and close attention.

"They think they're so damn smart, but all they do is hang themselves," I murmured to myself. "They whip their tails around them and wrap themselves into a snazzle that they can't get out of."

I reached the house and poured a glass of fresh iced tea, and took it to a lawn chair in the corner of the yard. I set it down and traced a pattern with my finger in the moisture forming on its side, then I tried to bring some order to the mess.

Schuyler told me he'd been working, but I soon found out the lie. Next, he said he'd bedded Ellen Dancer, but that wasn't possible because she'd been in Reno at the time. And now I heard he'd claimed to her he'd been making it with some other cutie the day that Billy disappeared.

Was this indeed the truth or just another level in the mounting layer of lies? Was Schuyler really covering for a woman or did a different reason for these lies exist? And if there *was* a different reason, did it connect to Billy's murder or to something else? And if to something else, to what?

I tapped my fingers on the little metal table. I felt as if I held a tangled skein of yarn that showed a new and tighter knot behind each one that I unraveled.

Marc Schuyler held the key to all the answers, but he wouldn't let me have it. No matter—there were other ways to open up the doors. I'd get to know him inside-out and maybe then I'd learn what he was up

A DESPERATE CALL

to. Perhaps it didn't touch on Billy's murder, but I'd find that out and put his lies to rest once and for all.

Who could tell me best about him? I mused. No one person, I decided, but several different men and women who'd known him at varying stages of his life. Not his buddies, though. I'd stay away from them—stay one step removed for now—to keep him blinded to my interest.

I threw the melting ice behind a bush and got up to fill my glass again. I grinned. As usual when the quest was on, I felt a quickening of my spirits and a heightening rush to hurry the pursuit.

Helen Hornsby was leaving on vacation. I asked her to put off her packing for a moment and talk to me instead.

She was waiting for me, dressed in fine white dimity embossed with purple flowers. The summer heat had settled in for good and the dainty dress was her chosen way of coping. I doubt she even owned a pair of shorts.

"Detective Harrod, please come in." She greeted me most warmly and waved me toward the little living room. I saw the suitcase on the bed and asked where she was going.

"To Tahoe—my brother has a cabin there. It's beautiful and cool and very, very peaceful. The peace is what I need right now. This whole affair has torn at my spirit and I've got to start rebuilding."

I nodded slowly. She must still be deeply wounded by the death of Billy Schuyler. What was it she'd once said to me?—"I've never lost a child before. I feel it very personally."

She must've read my thoughts.

"Enough of that," she said as she straightened up, firmly set her lips and looked right at me. "What can I help you with today?"

I told her I wanted to know about the Schuyler men—still building background, I explained—and asked if she'd formed impressions of the two while they were growing up.

She smiled. "I thought you people only dealt in facts."

"That's true," I told her, "but we sometimes need a little help in finding where those facts are buried."

"All right, quick sum-ups then. The older one was always serious and driven—never any doubt he'd get whatever he desired. The other boy seemed nondescript and frivolous—a sort of lightweight who never really made his mark."

I asked if Marc had worked in town since high school. She couldn't be sure, she said, but didn't think so.

"I've got an impression of in and out, in and out—here for several years, then away, then back again."

Helen Hornsby placed a folded blouse beside the suitcase, then raised her eyes and stared steadily at my face. I realized I hadn't fooled her for a single moment. She sensed I was doing a whole lot more than gathering simple background information.

Her expression held an invitation to disclosure, but she never spoke the words, never asked the questions lying on the edges of her tongue.

Ignoring her, I turned my eyes away and started toward the door. When I looked at her again, the inquiring stare was gone.

* * *

A DESPERATE CALL

I knew Arnold Harper lived on Elm Street so I drove straight there. I wasn't wasting any time.

The principal was kneeling on his steps, sanding them with layers of coarsened paper. A brush and paint can sat nearby.

Harper must've sensed my presence for he swung his head around, then put the paper down and rose to greet me.

"Detective Harrod, isn't it?" he asked, and his gray-blue eyes held a question in their depths.

"You're right," I told him. "We met a year ago last winter when the Masters boy ran away from home. Now I have another child I need to talk to you about."

Harper moved the can behind a post and motioned for me to sit beside him on the step.

"Unless you'd rather go inside," he said. "I don't know how formal this should be."

"The steps are good," I told him, and we settled next to one another on the top one. I tucked my skirt around my thighs and he stretched his legs straight out in front of him. He lit his pipe, then glanced at me expectantly.

"Another missing child, Detective?"

"Not exactly, Mr. Harper. You see, I'm still involved with Billy Schuyler's murder. I know he wasn't in your school but I'm not really here for him—it's his family I'm concerned about right now. You taught his father and his uncle, didn't you?"

"That's right, Detective Harrod. Or at least I taught the father. I'd been appointed principal before the young one came along."

"But you knew him?"

"Certainly I knew him—I know all my pupils. Got to or I'd figure I wasn't doing a good enough a job.

How can I help 'em if I don't know who they are and how they're handling growing up? I make sure I read their folders till I can call each one by name and know what baggage that name brings with it."

He leaned forward, picked up a leaf, and held it toward a wounded bee crawling slowly on the steps. The insect climbed aboard and Harper lifted it and set it on the grass beside him.

"Did the Schuyler boys have any baggage worth mentioning?"

"Nothing bad, not the older brother—a good student, that one, and very, very serious. Well, look at him today, a straight line from teens to forty or whatever age he is right now. Consistent all the way."

I asked about the younger brother. Was he serious, too?

"Hardly," Harper answered scornfully. "He was extroverted and he let the good times roll. That crowd he ran with liked to party more than study. I had him in my office several times for cutting class and hanging out with other wastrels in the parking lot."

"But no major problems with his discipline?"

"None, Detective. Some might've even called his actions just high spirits."

"You didn't like him." I made the statement quietly.

"You're right, you know, I didn't." Arnold Harper turned his head and eyed me keenly. "I felt he lacked a backbone and had a jellyfish morality. He traded on his looks a lot and wasn't past a con or two. That's a type that doesn't set too well with me."

I asked him if he knew where Marc had gone from high school and he named a junior college several counties to the west.

I rose to go. Another easy walkaway, I thought, and marveled at my luck. But Arnold Harper wasn't Helen Hornsby and he'd decided it was his turn now.

"Detective, I'd be stupid if I didn't wonder why you questioned me. Does it tie in with that child's murder?"

I didn't lie to him.

"I've got no reason to believe it does," I said. "There're just some things I have to know."

He wasn't satisfied but that was really all that I could give him. After all, I had no more myself.

Stewart Crider remembered Schuyler because he'd lost patience with him time and time again.

"A lot of kids come here just to play," he told me sourly as we sat at lunch together. "They think that's what school is all about. But that one drove me up the wall—he wouldn't settle down at all.

"He was brash and rude and, on top of that, he was dumb. I mean intellectually dumb, because he could be crafty in other ways and I didn't like that one bit either."

Crider, Schuyler's junior college counselor eleven years ago, paused and wiped a crumb of muffin from his lip.

"You know the type, Detective—big and blond with flashing teeth and girls go ga-ga over them and they play it to the hilt. You look as if you'd have too much sense to get involved yourself, but some gals don't—they eat it up.

"Anyway, I finally went to him and said 'hit the beach—that's where you belong' and, by God, you know he did it!"

"I understand he flunked out," I said.

"Oh, he did—couldn't cut it worth a damn—but when he left he told me he was heading for Hawaii, working with a friend of his in one of those, whaddya call 'em, dive shops somewhere."

I asked if he'd been in any trouble at the college.

"Trouble? No, not what *you'd* call trouble. Why? Is he in some now? Is that what all this folderol's about?"

"No trouble that I know of," I answered levelly. "I badly need to get his help on something big and I want to learn the kind of fellow I'll be dealing with, to decide the best approach to take."

Crider nodded, totally convinced.

"You do your homework. Good for you—I like that. Smart girlie."

I lifted up my coffee cup and hid a smile. I liked the bristle and the bustle of this man.

He leaned back in his chair and looked at me, squinting slightly in the summer sun.

"Since you're so keen on knowing all about him, I'll tell you something else. I've been doing this for thirty years and I can size 'em up. That cocky little kid was what you saw, but underneath that bold hard front lay a lot of insecurity."

CHAPTER TWENTY-TWO

Thomas Schuyler never left my mind. I'd told Carl and Steve about my fresh suspicions and how they'd led me to Molly Blevins and the breaking of the alibi.

"But the alibi's not really broken," Carl pointed out, his large florid face seeming redder than usual, "not so any judge or jury would believe it, anyway. That official police accident report stating Schuyler was on Barham Street at four-forty p.m., when you have him somewhere way across town picking up Billy, will override the verbal testimony of your witness in their eyes. At best, they'll see her as a confused woman whose words are unreliable."

He was just confirming what I already knew. Which was why I hadn't made my move. And based on what I *did* have, which was mainly well-founded suspicion but just suspicion nonetheless, no judge would order up a search warrant for the trunk of Schuyler's car.

"And forget about the poly, too," Carl continued as if he read my mind. "You've lost the momentum on that one. He knows you've got nothing solid on him so he'd never agree to take it if he's guilty. He'd put himself too much at risk with nothing at all to gain, especially if he *did* have something to do with Joyce's death, too."

"All true, Carl, but my knowledge of what the Blevins woman told me is enough to make me keep on digging till I turn up hard evidence. Maybe I can't prove anything about his wife, but if he killed that little boy, so help me God he's going to hang for it."

I knew where I was going next. Stockton was an easy drive from here and I could be there and back by dinnertime.

I couldn't call ahead—I'd have to hope he'd be there. If Aaron Carter knew I'd made a special trip to see him, he'd lay far too much importance on my questions.

I wondered if I should take the chance. How close to home could I approach without my quarry learning I was hunting? Then I put my doubts aside. I'd bluff my way along and try not to raise suspicion.

It was worth the risk. Carter, after all, could likely lead me through Marc's life so I'd find out where he'd been and what he'd done since college. With that framework in my grasp, I could plan my next moves with precision.

No doubt about it. I had to talk with Joyce's brother.

I dropped by the station, pulled the Carter address from the folder, then headed north. Within two hours I'd reached the Stockton city limits and I stopped for lunch and phoned him while the waitress placed the order.

"Mr. Carter? Detective Harrod here. I'm up from San Madera on other business and thought I'd call and say hello."

"Detective, it's really great to hear from you." He

sounded genuinely surprised and pleased. "Can you drop by?"

"Actually, I'd like that very much. I'd like to talk with you and offer my condolences about your sister."

Driving up, I'd decided I'd lead with Billy's mother and mix in Marc somewhere with the words that followed.

His apartment was a pleasing hodgepodge of mix-and-match. It had a welcome down-home feel about it, as if it were a refuge that offered creature comforts to its owner. A pungent smell of pipe tobacco filled the air.

He offered coffee or a drink, and after serving it took a seat across from me. I found myself thinking once again how attractive this man was.

"Any luck, Detective?"

"Very little, I'm afraid, but we're working on it every day."

"And the trail keeps growing colder with each passing hour—isn't that the saying, isn't that the truth?"

"I don't look at it like that," I told him. "Sometimes nothing happens for weeks or months and then a little break comes that opens up the door, or sometimes several big breaks come suddenly all at once. No, I'm not discouraged."

He picked up a pipe and idly tapped it on a table.

"You said you wanted to talk about my sister. Well, there isn't that much left to say—she's gone."

"I felt I should've seen it coming," I admitted. "She seemed so vulnerable—the most vulnerable of all of them."

"Hindsight's wonderful, Detective Harrod," Carter answered bitterly. "I've blamed myself every single day. *You* shouldn't feel responsible—you hardly even knew her—but I'm her very own brother and I didn't help her out."

"Did she get counseling?"

"No, I urged her to, but she wouldn't listen."

"And Billy's father—couldn't he have seen to it?"

A bite of acid touched his answer.

"No, he'd have no part of that, Detective—he believes one should find the strength to solve one's own problems."

"I'd have thought Nadine might've been a comfort," I continued, not believing that for one little minute, but holding back from mentioning Marc as long as possible.

Aaron Carter gave a little laugh.

"By her mere presence or because you think she'd have been good at consoling her mother?"

"Consoling her," I answered, "talking with her, getting her to share the burden."

"I don't think Nadine went in for that at all. No, I'd never have looked for any help from that source myself."

"How about Billy's uncle, Marc?" I casually asked. "He seems a sympathetic sort—couldn't he have persuaded Thomas to get his wife the care she needed?"

"Another zero there, Detective. Tom can't be influenced by Marc in any way—his opinion doesn't count at all. And Marc knows that and resents Thomas—always has, I'm told."

He put the pipe down without lighting it.

"You called him sympathetic," he said slowly. "Do you really think so?"

"Well, from what I've seen of him he seems friendly enough," I answered blandly, "open, outgoing, so I thought maybe he could've been the one to bridge the gap."

"Interesting," he mused, but said no more.

"There's a great age difference between the Schuyler men," I mentioned affably. "Did Marc follow in his brother's footsteps or did they go their separate ways?"

"Entirely separate, Detective. Marc couldn't even make it through a junior college, unlike Phi Beta Kappa Thomas. And Tom's always lived in his hometown while Marc's lived away from it a lot. Talk about a different life—after he failed college he went off to Hawaii for several years. Can you imagine *Thomas* in Hawaii?"

He smiled broadly at the thought.

"Whatever brought him back?" I asked innocently, using the same light tone I'd employed all along. "I think I might've stayed."

He frowned.

"I don't know. Joyce hinted something happened out there, some sort of trouble but I don't know what it was. I don't think it was very serious but apparently it made him want to leave."

I knew I couldn't talk all day about Marc Schuyler, but I pushed a little further, just to try to wrap it up.

"Did Thomas try to take his little brother into banking? Sometimes, with such an age difference, the big one likes to play protector."

He answered willingly enough, spinning out the words I wished to hear while I sat back and reeled them in.

"No way, Detective Harrod, Thomas lets you make it on your own. When Marc returned, he started out in real estate. Then he left again—lived down south for several years—and now he's back with real estate once more. Banking's not for him and anyway, he wouldn't work well with his brother."

Satisfied, I swung back to Billy's mother without a change in beat and knew my detour to the route Marc's life had taken had been scarcely noticed.

"Again, I'm dreadfully sorry about your sister. She was a lovely woman and I enjoyed knowing her for that brief moment, even though I met her at a time of grief."

"It means a lot to me for you to say that, Detective. Thank you for your concern."

He paused, then went on to something else.

"The case you're up here on—can you tell me anything about it?"

"Only that I had to see a witness in an old investigation," I lied smoothly. "Nothing to concern yourself about. There's not a wanted criminal in your neighborhood."

Then I said goodbye and headed back to San Madera.

I talked to a white-haired woman who'd lived beside the Schuyler boys when they were growing up and to two men who differed vastly in their opinions of Marc Schuyler.

"What kind of boy was he?" I asked Dolly Scott as she watered down her lawn. "Tell me how Marc struck you."

"He was a sweet boy, Miss, and no mistake about it. He got a little wild a little later on, but I could see that coming and I wasn't one little bit surprised."

She pursed her lips, regarded me expectantly, and waited for my question.

"However could you see?" I obliged, showing great interest.

"It was that tartar of a father—would drive anybody wild. Old man Schuyler would not let up on Markie. Always lecturing him, always holding Thomas up to him and saying he should be just like him, and other times just ignoring him like he was dirt. It would discourage any child and cause him to act up."

"What about the mother?"

"Oh, she was just as bad." I could see there'd been no love lost between Dolly Scott and her former neighbors. "The sun rose and set in Tommy and the parents doted on him all the time. They paid no attention to the other boy except to scold and tell him to shape up. And him so sweet. Perhaps he *wasn't* quite as bright as Thomas, but what did that matter? I tell you, Miss, it nearly broke my heart."

I asked if things had ever changed.

"No, never did," she said firmly. "Tom grew up and went away to school and Marc was left at home with them. And became a handful. Cutting classes, racing hot rods, partying a bit too much. But served them right, it did, they reaped exactly what they sowed."

The following day I got out the local yellow pages and started calling realtors, pretending I was head of personnel for a large company in Los Angeles checking past employment on an application for a new position.

I got lucky on the fifth try when Valley Realty told me Marc Schuyler had worked for them for two years, nearly four years ago.

A man named Marvin Kingsford gave a snort when I asked if he'd recommend I hire Schuyler.

"Hell, no. He was unreliable and flaky ... and

couldn't move a property. And then, on top of everything he *didn't* do, he began to try it on with clients' wives. I had one or two complaints and that was it for me. Bingo, I let him go."

I asked Kingsford where Marc had worked before joining him.

"He'd been over in Hawaii—a selling job there, too, he said. I heard later down the line he'd been involved in some sort of dust-up in the islands and that was why he left. I'll tell you one thing—I'm well rid of him and if you'll take my advice, you'll stay clear yourself."

I left Kingsford, phoned Schuyler's office, and asked to speak with him. When he came on the line, I hung up without a word. I called the following day and was told he'd return in twenty minutes. Once again I hung up. I phoned on Friday and got good news at last— he was off till Monday morning.

Thirty minutes later, I walked through the front door and pretended I was shopping for a house. I told the manager I was recently divorced and was thinking of moving here from San Mateo.

"A friend of mine came down not too long ago," I volunteered. "In fact, he's the reason I'm here now. He said to ask for someone called Schuyler, I think it was."

The man's face brightened.

"Marc Schuyler, yes. One of our top salesmen—a real go-getter. Salesman of the month several times. He's sharp and you'll love working with him. He'll find exactly what you're looking for. Unfortunately he's not in today, but leave your name and number and he'll call you first thing Monday morning."

I told him that wouldn't be possible—I was leaving

to visit friends farther south and didn't expect to be back in town for several days.

"But I'll be staying longer then and maybe I'll have decided if I really want to make the move. If so, I'll certainly call your salesman then."

I thanked the man and left abruptly, forestalling any prying questions.

That night I put it all together and saw a mass of contradictions. But as I let it sift and settle, I saw a pattern, too.

I saw a small boy, gentle and good-natured, a small boy ignored and scolded by his father. Then I saw that same small boy become a rowdy teen who grew into a cocky drifting young adult with crafty ways about him.

But I also saw that somehow, somewhere, his life had turned around, away from all that wildness, so that today his boss could call him "sharp" and "go-getter."

Yes, I saw the pattern but I saw nothing criminal in it. Except for one possibility. Hawaii. Two different persons had mentioned Marc's involvement in a problem there—"some sort of trouble," "a dust-up in the islands."

What was it? Did it have any bearing on my case or, at least, on why Marc lied to me? The questions tumbled through my mind and then took hold of me and wouldn't let me go.

The counselor had told me Marc had joined a friend already working in Hawaii. Since he'd barely wet his feet in college before leaving, I'd bet that friend was someone from his high school days.

I'd planned to chat with Molly Blevins's neighbors

as well as people living along Billy's street, to see if anyone could pinpoint the true time of the accident or tell me when Thomas Schuyler had really come home that April night. Instead, I headed for the school library and started leafing through a yearbook twelve years old.

A brash young face with flashing teeth stared at me boldly, and in a candid snapshot section I saw another picture of young Schuyler clowning with two friends.

I flipped backward till I found formal photos of the two and saw their names were Richard Goodin and Robert Day. Goodin's write-up told me nothing, but Bobby Day's gave me what I wanted: "catch a wave," "beach boy forever," and, best of all, one word—"Maui."

I got his address from the listing in the back and drove to Hardin Street. The mailbox name read "Holt" instead of "Day" and no one answered when I rang. I went next door.

A cool brunette, pencil-thin and in a hurry, stepped outside and pulled the screen behind her. No, she said, the Days had moved away five or six years back.

"Did Robert move with them?" I queried, explaining I was a lawyer handling probate of a deceased relative from out-of-state.

"No," she told me, "he left right after high school. Went to Maui where his brother had a dive shop. I sure did envy him."

She no longer seemed in quite so big a rush and her eyes held wistful shadows.

"Do you know where in Maui, Miss?"

"I don't remember. He used to send me cards from time to time, but then he stopped and I haven't heard from him in years."

A DESPERATE CALL

I left her and drove back to the station, hoping Harry Prescott would be in. I knew he spent vacations in the islands and figured he could give me what I wanted.

I found him sitting in the coffee room, polishing his badge.

"Harry, if you owned a dive shop on Maui, where would it most likely be?"

"One of two places, Kate, Lahaina or the Kihei area. Thinking of a family holiday?"

"Not exactly," I responded, and sat down at my desk.

The department wouldn't send me to Hawaii—I knew better than to ask. They'd tell me I was only chasing rainbows, without reason to believe I'd find anything to tie in with my case.

Maybe they'd be right, but I had to make the trip. My digging into Thomas Schuyler could go on hold for several days, till I satisfied my curiosity and got this other matter settled.

I hurried home, packed a bag, and booked the morning flight to Maui.

Chapter Twenty-three

Jon was keeping Tommy while I was away. I'd hired a full-time housekeeper—a white-haired woman with clear blue eyes and a constant smell of fresh-baked cookies—but, though my son had taken to her right away, I wanted him to be with family while I was out of town.

He'd accepted Jon's departure well—far better than I'd dared to hope—and life, right now, seemed to be running on a fairly even keel. I remembered once *I'd* felt the outsider in our family. Now Jon was the one on the outside looking in, but I took no satisfaction from that fact.

He and I were civil when we saw each other—usually when he came to pick up Tommy—but there were no laughs, no levity, and certainly no attempts to get together once again. We were the proverbial "polite strangers," following the rules prescribed by our society for meetings between two people who'd once shared everything but now had little left to say.

Neither of us really knew where we were going. For now, at least, we seemed content just to drift along—to not force the issue but to let it lie easy for a while. I know *I* didn't want to stir things up, because of Jon's threat to fight for custody of Tommy if reconciliation were not possible. Far better this uneasy truce than something much, much worse. . . .

Once the airplane landed, I hurried off, anxious to begin my search. I felt tense, keyed-up, hoping far too hard I'd find the dive shop and the answers that I wanted.

I checked the lobby phone book just to see how many places I'd be dealing with. I'd go to Kihei first, since it was closest to the airport.

Then I saw two words that made me change my plans—the pages for Lahaina showed a shop called "Day Dives." The name could mean the suntime hours or could refer to Robert Day and his older brother. Either way, it offered too much promise to be put off till last.

I picked up a rental car and drove along a road that ran straight and level through large fields of sugarcane. The mountains of West Maui, showing shades of brilliant green and dusky blue, rose sharply on my right, and far in front of me a rolling sapphire sea touched the edges of the land.

Then the road turned north and climbed the cliffs above the sea. The sun, full and summer-hot, hit the waves with points of sparkle and threw a brightness on the hills and the fertile fields beneath them.

I reached Lahaina forty minutes later.

I easily found the shop, set two blocks above the harbor in the older part of town. A husky man with sun-bleached hair bent to pat a sidewalk dog, then walked inside. I followed him. His face looked vaguely familiar.

"Are you Robert Day?" I asked, certain now I faced an older version of the picture in the yearbook.

"Sure am," he answered. "Can I help you with some gear?"

I told him who I was and said I'd like to talk to him about a man he used to know. When I gave the man a name, his eyes snapped wide open and he stared at me for several seconds.

"Haven't heard of him in years," Day told me. "Frankly never thought I'd hear of him again."

"But he *did* work with you on Maui?"

"Sure, right here in Lahaina, when we were in our early twenties. I came over after high school and he joined me the following June. I'm a partner now, but back then we both worked for my brother."

"Did he know Schuyler well, 'cause if he did, I'd like to see him, too."

"Yeah, he got to know Marc pretty good—a hell of a lot better than he ever wanted."

An odd half-smile I couldn't read played across his face, and I was just about to ask him what he meant when an older, taller man came through the door.

"Hey, here he is right now. Meet my brother, Jackie Day."

Jackie Day. A bouncing, stiff-legged terrier and now a suntanned muscled dive shop owner. I hid surprise and laid away the question running through my mind. I'd wait and see what happened—perhaps I'd get the answer without asking. At any rate, now was not the time.

"This here's a lady cop over from the mainland," Bobby Day explained. "Wants to know about your buddy, Markie."

"What's he done?" the older man asked quickly.

"Nothing that I know of," I said calmly. "His brother's child was murdered in the spring and we're getting nowhere with it, so we're checking all those closest to the boy, to see if something in their past gives us any clues. It's a long shot, sure, but it's the only way to go right now."

"And you came three thousand miles just to nose around about a guy who isn't even a suspect? Come on!"

"No," I lied, "I didn't. I'm over here on holiday—staying down in Kihei—and I thought I'd take advantage of the chance to meet and talk."

Not yet sure whose side the Days were on, I stayed low-key and made my visit seem a casual one.

"How'd you know he worked here?"

Again I lied.

"His brother told me several weeks ago, when he heard I was flying over."

"That all the brother tell you?"

"Yes, what else is there?"

Jackie Day frowned.

"I bet he didn't know," he muttered to himself, then he looked at me.

"Okay, we'll talk about the bastard, but it can't be now—I've got work to do and so has Bobby. We'll meet for beers tonight." He looked me up and down. "Or maybe they've got wine if beer don't suit you."

"It suits me fine," I said.

He nodded, named a bar near the Square, and set the time for eight o'clock.

I was early. I sat in back, watched the door, and saw the brothers enter shortly past the hour. They spotted me and motioned to a booth.

"We'll sit here, Detective," Jackie said. "It's just a bit more private."

We settled in, ordered beers, and waited for the girl who brought them to move on to other customers.

"Okay, go. You ask, I'll answer."

"You called the man a bastard, why?"

"Well, Detective, I gotta hand it to you. With that one question you open up the whole caboodle, the whole lousy story of that creep I thought I'd heard the last of."

Jackie Day clapped his brother on the shoulder.

"Let's tell her, Bobby—let's tell the lady dick about the great and good friend you brought to work for me."

He took a swill of beer and eased back in his seat.

"When Bobby came to Maui, I just had a shoestring operation, but by the following spring we were doin' pretty good and I needed some more help. My little brother knew this guy from high school and he sez 'let's get my buddy over here—he's quittin' school and needs a job.' "

"Hell, why not? I knew Marc and Bobby got along okay, so I thought he'd work out just fine. He did, too—for a while. Loved the life and sun and sea and always somethin' going on. And he worked his butt off, too."

"But then he started comin' on to wives of guys we'd take out on dives and once or twice he got caught doin' it. I warned him to lay off. I'd got all my money ridin' on this shop and I didn't want any trouble. It didn't matter if the gals were willing—a complaint or two to the Chamber from their old men would do me in."

"And did he stop?"

"He cooled it down anyway. I doubt he ever stopped, but let's say he got more discreet. Always strictly business when I saw him on the boat and I didn't get any more guff from jealous hubbies."

"And that made him a bastard in your eyes?"

"Oh, no, lady. We're just comin' to the Big One—the one that blew it all away. A family from the south end of the island came up here on vacation and we took them out to dive.

"They had a daughter who was somethin' else—just a kid but knockers on her like you would not believe. She was hot as firecrackers and just askin' for it. Flirtin', teasin', and tossin' that little ass around with every move she made. Excuse my language, lady, but I don't know how else to put it.

"Well, they went out with Marc and Bobby and everything was cool, but that evening, several hours after they got back, the father came by and said he'd left his camera on the boat.

"I took him down there and when we got aboard I heard a sound. We walked astern and there were Schuyler and the girl writhing on a mat. She was spread wide-open and they were goin' at it—they hadn't even heard us come aboard. The father bellowed like a bull and pulled the asshole off his daughter. I was so pissed at Marc I clocked him with a right while Daddy called the cops. They picked him up and booked him."

"On what charge?"

"Sex with a minor, Detective—the missy on the mat was only fourteen years old."

"Ooooh," I said, but I wasn't a bit surprised. "What happened then?"

"He made bail and the case was set for trial. The dad and I were to be chief witnesses against him. The little tramp was what you might call a hostile witness.

She gave her old man holy hell the night we found 'em screwin' and said she'd wanted it just as much as Marc and would never say a word against him. I'd have slapped her mouth shut, but good old Dad just stood and took it.

"Then, as the trial date approached, the whole thing fell apart. I heard rumors half the boys at her end of the island had had a piece of her at one time or another. According to the prosecutor, the parents were afraid of scandal—scared all the dirty stories might come out.

"They suddenly wanted silence, not revenge. Marc had no record, the girl was uncooperative, and then the parents backed off, so the case was dropped. The tart was shipped off to a Catholic boarding school on Oahu."

"Would you have testified?"

"Damn right I would've. I'd have said my piece and hoped that would carry it. I was sick of Schuyler and how he'd jeopardized my business. He could stick his dick in where he liked, as long as it wasn't on my boat with my clients' wives or daughters. I wanted to get him good and send him out of my shop, out of my town, out of my life."

"Did he leave the island then?"

"Sure did—with his tail between his legs. I fired him on the spot that night. He knew I detested him and that I'd pushed hard for the trial to go through. I know he hates me to this day. I heard through mutual friends he bought a dog back in California and named it after me, so he could bully it and treat it mean—sort of make it a stand-in for me."

I felt my face tighten as I thought of that sweet, feisty little animal, and I swore softly. Now I understood the reason for the terrier's funny name. We ordered another round of beers and sat silently for several minutes.

"Well, Detective," Jackie finally said, "I've filled you in on Marc just like you wanted, but I don't see how it's gonna help you with your case."

"Perhaps it won't," I reluctantly agreed, "perhaps it won't, but it sure made an entertaining story. Tell me, do you think he preferred his women underage?"

"Nope, I don't think he went for young ones in particular. He was randy as they come and he just didn't care what age they were as long as they were lookers and they screwed."

I turned to Bobby, who'd stayed quiet while Jackie did the talking.

"Is there anything *you* can tell me about Marc? After all, you knew him longer than your brother."

"No, not much. We ran with the same crowd in high school and always liked the beach and havin' fun. I never knew him to get into any serious trouble, though."

"What about his family? Did he talk about them much?"

"Just his older brother. I didn't even know he had a nephew, but we both knew about the brother, didn't we, Jackie?"

The two men grinned at each other.

"Right, we did," Jackie said. "Marc talked about him all the time—hated him, told us he couldn't stand his guts. Said he was a big-shot banker who thought dive shops were the pits."

Bobby broke in.

"But you know, I think he envied him, too—the money, the respect he got. Wanted to show him some day that Marc Schuyler could be a big shot, too, maybe even bigger than him."

"Well, he sure as hell went about *that* the wrong way"—Jackie gave a throaty laugh and banged the table with his fist—"beddin' down a minor."

"What makes you think so?" I asked Bobby.

"Just stuff he'd say from time to time, even back in high school. I think he felt inferior to Tom and craved to do something really great so he could rub Tom's nose in it and force him to admit he'd been wrong all along about his little brother. That desire ate at him and grew stronger as he got older."

"Hey, lady," Jackie said, cocking an eye in my direction. "I hope we didn't talk too rough for you."

"I wouldn't let it worry you," I answered, "I'm not the tender type."

I paid the tab and walked outside. Rain was falling softly and enveloping humidity brought smells of ripened fruit and earth and fresh salt air. I raised my hand and wiped the dampness from my face. One more stop to make the following morning and then I'd head for home.

I checked in early Wednesday with detectives in Lahaina. As a favor to a fellow cop, they pulled the Schuyler file and confirmed what Jackie Day had told me—the case had fizzled out and they'd never heard of him again.

I talked shop for several minutes, but turned down an invitation to meet at noon for lunch. Instead, I started for the airport.

Chapter Twenty-four

The Delta Tri-Star rose above the Maui mountains and I settled deep into my seat. I felt slightly satisfied, yet keenly disappointed.

I was certain I knew now why Marc had twice lied about his alibi—he'd been with someone's little girl the afternoon of Billy's death, playing doctor, doctor.

He couldn't reveal the truth to me without risking arrest, and if he were arrested, he'd lose the precious foothold he'd finally gained in his quest for the respect and success he desired so very much.

But this certainty didn't take me any closer to Billy's murderer. I felt as if I had two separate crimes running parallel with no connecting points.

What had I expected anyway? To go to Maui and find that Schuyler had committed acts of violence, specifically assaults on little boys? I didn't know—I only knew I felt a letdown, a deep and endless emptiness.

The plane banked and then turned east, and I leaned back and sighed as the island disappeared below me. I ordered vodka-soda and listened to the chatter of the flight attendant as she served the drinks.

She had a crisp, hip personality—slightly on the acerbic side—and she obviously enjoyed the verbal jousting with her passengers. I didn't feel like talking to her, though. I was glum and cheerless, going home with nothing, not even a Maui tan.

I swirled the ice around my glass and thought again about my trip. I'd hoped for more, much more—that was obvious to me now and explained my disappointment.

But I wasn't through with Marc Schuyler yet. I'd pay him one more visit, to tell him I'd talked with Ellen Dancer and sunk his second alibi. If he still refused to level with me, I'd let him know I'd been to Maui and then sit back and watch him squirm. I'd enjoy that thoroughly. I didn't like a bastard who got his kicks from beating dogs and screwing kids.

I waited till the evening following my return. I drove to Morro Street a little after seven and saw his car parked beside the curb. I hoped he'd be alone, though if I caught him with a minor that would have its own reward.

I knocked twice and waited for the barking. It didn't come. A moment later, Schuyler walked toward me from the kitchen. I looked at him and didn't feel a thing.

"Well, if it isn't the pretty lady cop—good to see you. Is there any news?"

"No, unfortunately. I wish there were some. Where's the dog?"

I'd decided I'd go nice and easy. We'd chat around a bit till I got him off his guard.

"Back inside"—he tossed his head behind him—"I just got him from the vet's."

What was wrong with him, I asked.

"Dunno," he said offhandedly. "Something with his

A DESPERATE CALL

leg and ribs—limping really bad. A car must've hit him when he was running loose."

You cruel and callous bastard, I thought hotly, I bet you kicked him till you broke his bones.

He asked me to come in and tell him what was happening with the case. When I reached the hallway, Jackie Day limped forward from the living room to greet me.

The terrier's muzzle had a lopsided look, with the hair on one side hanging lower than on the other. Schuyler picked up a pair of scissors—their silver blades long and lean, their tips sharply pointed—then laid them down again.

"I was just squaring him off a bit," he told me. "Giving him one of those show-dog cuts. A smart-lookin' little bastard, don't you think?"

He grabbed Jackie's face and roughly turned it toward me. I bridled, but hid my anger and bent to give the animal a reassuring pat.

I didn't get the chance. The little dog leapt backward, its eyes sparking, and a growl of high intensity issued from its throat. It braced its front legs wide and glared its master in the face.

"Damn it, Jackie, come off it," Schuyler yelled as he raised a flattened palm. Then he looked at me and quickly dropped it. "He's been like this ever since I brought him home. The vet says it's the medication."

"Could be," I answered, although I had my own theory as to why the dog was snarling. Then I started getting down to business.

"You asked what's happening with the case," I said, making sure I stood well back from him. "The fact is, very little. I'm just touching base as I do from time to time, to see if *you* have anything for *me*."

"Nothing, and believe me, I think about it every single day, trying to puzzle out who'd do that to a kid, especially one as sweet as Billy. I come up empty every time."

I thought about the personal pleasures of the man standing there in front of me and felt disgust, but I kept my feelings to myself.

I turned toward the surfboard photo I'd noticed several months ago. The palm trees and the mountains in the background looked familiar.

"Where was that taken?" I asked innocently. "Looks pretty nice."

"Over in Hawaii."

"Vacation?"

"I lived there for a short time."

He moved uneasily as he spoke.

"Tough life. What island?"

"Kauai."

"Kauai?"

"That's right, why?"

"No reason, except I always wondered if it has as many flowers as the brochures say it does."

"Even more—it's like a garden. You ought to take a break and go there sometime."

I was just about to start to play hardball and bring up the matter of the alibis when Schuyler suddenly pointed to a baseball glove on the shelf above the picture.

"See that glove, Detective? That's a real heartbreaker. I ordered it for Billy and it arrived the week he disappeared. I kept it wrapped for him, but then you found his body and I knew I'd have no use for it. I put it there till I decided what to do with it, but now it's got to go—the sight's just too upsetting to me."

Without warning—clear and clean and blazing out of nowhere—a memory ran through my mind. I stood very still and held my breath, then I asked a question.

"Did Billy know you were getting him a glove?"

"Did he know? You betcha! He was so excited you'd think I was Santa Claus at Christmastime."

The alibis could wait. I made a little small talk, then left as quickly as I could. I needed time to be alone, to take that memory out and look at it.

On that April Monday when I'd questioned Tommy, he'd told me Billy's baseball glove had finally come apart and he'd had to borrow one to play that afternoon.

Billy knew his uncle was getting him a glove. Suppose, suddenly needing it, he'd gone to Schuyler's house, unannounced and uninvited, to see if maybe that glove had come.

And suppose Schuyler and a teenybopper had been rolling in the sheets as I suspected and Billy saw them making love?

He mightn't have understood the meaning of what he'd blundered into, but his uncle couldn't know that and couldn't know the boy wouldn't talk about it.

And if he talked, the life Marc Schuyler was so carefully constructing for himself would fall apart forever.

It was all possible and plausible, and as I realized what could've happened next, my mind reeled and ricocheted with the certainty that I at last had something solid to investigate. The connecting point was made and my separate crimes had come together.

* * *

I hurried home and went directly to the den. Tommy stuck his head through the doorway.

"Play a game, Mom?"

"Not tonight," I said abruptly. "Sorry, kiddo."

He looked at me strangely for a moment. I knew my voice had sounded taut and lower-pitched than usual, and suddenly I felt awful. I went to him and hugged him close, rocking him from side to side. I had to take the time to love him.

"Forgive me, baby, we'll play real soon, I promise."

I took down a city map and spread it open on my desk. I put an "X" where my house stood and another at the Morro Street address, then I studied routes.

To reach his uncle's house from here, Billy could've continued east on Marsh, past the point where he was last seen, for three more blocks and then turned north.

But he could also have reached Morro Street—and just as quickly—by going past his own house on Hollis, turning east for four blocks, and then swinging north. The distance would've been exactly the same and he probably knew the second route better.

So then why had he passed Hollis? And if he'd been told to be home by five and seldom disobeyed that order, why would he have gone at all? Leaving my yard at four-thirty, he didn't have a hope of making it to Morro Street and back to his house in thirty minutes.

My eyes played idly on the map and then I saw the field and woods. A large undeveloped tract lay north of Marsh and east of Hollis.

Billy could've reached it by turning left one block past the vacant lot where the probationer saw him— reached it, traveled it diagonally toward his uncle's, and cut ten minutes off his trip.

A DESPERATE CALL

The shortcut led through waist-high weeds and stands of tall and leafy trees. Most youngsters were forbidden by their parents to go near it, because of the dangers its isolation posed.

But even good kids disobey when they're strongly motivated and, to a nine-year-old, a brand-new baseball glove is a prize above all else.

I swung my chair around and stared unseeing out the window. I remembered the officer had told me the boy was in a hurry—and he would have hurried, because he had to make a long trip and be back home by five. So he ran, and he took a shortcut.

In my mind, I saw the little figure moving down Marsh, turning left and running through the field and woods, coming out the other side and racing hell-bent for his uncle's, hoping against hope his new glove had arrived.

I saw it in my mind and I believed it happened just that way.

I called Carl and Steve.

"Cancel whatever you've got going and meet me at the station—I know who murdered Billy Schuyler."

I couldn't wait to get there. Things were moving at a rapid pace and sitting still didn't suit me. I was pacing near my desk when the other two arrived.

"Thomas Schuyler's not the one we want here," I told them tersely. "It's his brother."

I laid it all out for them—Schuyler's record in Hawaii, his sexual assault on Leslie Jean, the glove that I believed lured Billy to his house, the reason the little boy was killed.

"He'll screw anything that comes along," I said, "and twice that *I* know of, he's messed around with minors. I was already certain that's what he was doing that afternoon in April and why he covered up the truth.

"And then, just by chance, just by sheer luck, I found out about the glove. Schuyler didn't know—had no way of knowing—that Billy's old glove had come apart that afternoon and that *I* knew it and realized he needed a new one right away, so the creep felt safe mentioning his intended gift and telling me Billy knew it was coming."

"Well, well, well, Kate," said Mungers, a slow smile spreading across his face, "I had a feeling you were up to something, but I didn't know what."

"I was playing—just playing to keep my hand in," I answered. "I'd no idea I'd come up with anything at all."

"One thing's wrong, though," Carl continued. "Schuyler *did* have a way of knowing about the glove—Billy could've told him when he went over there."

"Not if it went down the way I think it did. The minute you walk through that door, you can see inside the bedroom. Billy could've come in quietly, and the dog, knowing him, wouldn't even have barked. Billy got an eyeful and very little talk was done. He probably was killed shortly after his arrival."

"Sounds good, it's got a framework, but how the hell do we go about proving it?" Darrow asked.

"We go over the case file bit by bit—every single piece of it. We look at all of it again, with a fresh eye, now that we've got a point of view to bring to it."

They both had ongoing cases with numerous court dates, so I told them I'd get started and call on them to lend a hand when the going got too heavy for me.

Then I left the room, unlocked the metal cabinet, and took down the large blue "murder books" on the Billy Schuyler homicide.

At one o'clock I slammed them shut, disgusted. They hadn't helped me, even though I'd turned them upside-down and inside-out. Worse, they'd raised a question I'd forgotten to ask myself—what about the car?

Schuyler drove a red convertible—the auto seen by Maud Divans, parked by the San Marcos field, was a light-colored sedan. How did I square these two opposing facts? I didn't have the answer.

Perhaps the car Divans saw had nothing to do with the killing or perhaps Schuyler had somehow gotten another car that night. I didn't know, but I wasn't going to let this question hang me up right now—I'd lay it down and work it out later.

I knew patrol had talked with Schuyler on the night of Billy's disappearance. Before today, I'd felt no need to learn about that talk—now, I wanted every single detail. I buzzed records.

"Pull the field activities reports for the night of April twenty and see who logged a stop at 413 Morro Street."

A short time later I was phoning Officer Dunleaven, to tell him to come see me before he went to roll call. He showed up one hour later.

Dunleaven told me he'd talked with Schuyler around eight-fifteen that Monday evening.

"Start from when you rang the bell and take me through it to the end," I said.

"He opened the door right away—him and a snappy little dog he owns. He invited me inside and said he guessed he knew why I was there. We sat down and I asked him if he'd seen his nephew earlier that day or had any idea where we might find him. He answered no to both questions.

"As we talked, I let my eyes roam around, to see if I could spot anything unusual, but I didn't. I instructed him to call us right away if he heard anything from the missing boy, then I left."

"How did he act?"

"Calm, collected, sort of somber—about the way *I'd* act if *my* nephew disappeared but had been gone only a couple of hours."

"Not at all nervous or evasive?"

"No, not at all. I got the feeling he wasn't really worried—that he believed the boy would turn up later on that night."

"Was he alone in the house?"

"I'm almost sure he was. The place is pretty small, so I think I'd have noticed if there'd been another person."

"You said you looked around—you saw nothing a nine-year-old might own?"

"That's what I was looking for, Detective, and I didn't see a thing. Oh, there was a kid's baseball glove, but it was brand new, never used. Schuyler said he'd picked it up as a gift to his nephew that very day, but hadn't had a chance to give it to him. Kinda sad, that."

I felt anger building fast inside me, but I didn't let Dunleaven see it. I asked if he'd spotted any cars in the driveway and he answered no.

"That's it, then?"

"That's it. I went out the door and he went back to do his wash."

Dunleaven sniggered.

A DESPERATE CALL

"What's so funny?"

"He was in the middle of a load when I arrived. The washer and the dryer were both going in the kitchen right beside us and I could barely hear above the noise they made. I was thinkin' I'm glad I'm not a bachelor anymore and that I've got a wife to wash the socks and shirts."

I let Dunleaven go and drew a large round zero on my blotter. Another letdown—he'd offered me nothing to show me I was on the right track.

I thought of Schuyler doing his own wash. I bet he didn't let his lady friends see that domestic scene, so at odds with his macho surfer image.

I remembered Jon, when he'd tried to do the wash one day and how he'd totally botched it. He'd added far too much detergent to the water, then burned his fingers on the inside of the dryer when he began removing clothes before the cool-down cycle started. He'd got the hang of it eventually, but that'd been a funny one.

Then an image flickered through my mind—an image of the inside of a dryer. I saw small holes allowing heat to enter punctuating the interior—small holes the size and shape of those odd marks on Billy's arm.

After murdering Billy, had Schuyler stored his corpse inside the dryer till he moved it to the field later on that night? And had the dryer been so hot it burned the flesh forced into those small holes by the lifeless torso's weight?

No, it couldn't be—no ordinary dryer could operate with such a heavy load.

Then I looked at it another way. Suppose the body had first been hidden somewhere else—in a closet or underneath a bed—and was moved to the machine *after* it was heated up. Perhaps the drying cycle heard by Dunleaven was the very one that revved the heat up high enough to burn the flesh on Billy's arm, even after it cut off.

I felt a chill as I grabbed the phone and called the coroner's office. I asked for Penross.

"Howard, remember those strange marks on Billy Schuyler—the ones you never could identify? Draw a mental picture of the inside of your ordinary clothes dryer. See those little holes that let the heat come out—could pressured contact with the metal that surrounds them cause such marks?"

A long minute passed as Penross turned my question over in his mind. Then he answered.

"I'd have to pull the file and read my notes again, but offhand I'd say yes. If the metal were hot enough, that's exactly what would happen."

I told Steve about the dryer when he got back from court.

"Nice going, Kate, but why would someone stick a body in a dryer when it's already hidden somewhere else?"

"Any one of several reasons—a better hiding place, perhaps, or some idea of rearranging the apparent time of death."

"You're still no closer to proving Schuyler is the killer than you were this morning—nearly every household in this city owns a dryer."

"I know that," I conceded. "My theory may not point to Billy's murderer, but it sure as heck *could* explain those marks."

A DESPERATE CALL

He nodded in agreement, then asked a question I'd been pondering myself.

"How about the girl? How does she tie in?"

"You mean the girl in bed with Marc?"

"Right. You think Billy found his uncle in the sack with some teenybopper and was killed shortly after the discovery. Do you think the dolly was involved in the murder, too?"

"Maybe so, maybe not—that's something we can't know right now. It could've happened either way."

Chapter Twenty-Five

I got up the following morning and headed for the foothills of the Mariposa mountains. I hadn't seen the field since the night of my attack, but suddenly I felt a need to visit it again. This time, somehow, the urgency had to do with Billy, not with me.

I parked beside the footpath and got out. The air was heavy with the still, dense heat of summer. The purple flowers of May had disappeared and the drought had turned the golden grass to brown. I saw that Barrows hadn't tilled the soil. I probably would've left it untouched, too.

I stood for several minutes, looking at the shed shadowed in the morning light, and watched a single crow fly by its roof. I had no desire to go to it but, even though they'd never caught my attacker, I found I was no longer frightened either. I nodded once or twice, then turned away.

"Little boy," I said out loud, "I may be coming close."

On the way back into town, I thought about the field and wondered once again how the killer knew about it and about the lonely shed standing deep within its grasses. I recalled I'd speculated earlier the murderer was probably a city person, because he'd

A DESPERATE CALL

seemed unaware of the rites of spring planting that would soon turn his hiding place into a beehive of activity.

Something nagged at me, but I couldn't pin it down. I went on home, ate my lunch, and tried to trim the roses, but all the while a vague uneasy feeling filled me. I was missing something somewhere—what was it?

Then, like a flash, it clicked in place. I set down my clippers and stared straight ahead. Pete Blackwell told me he'd seen the field four years ago, when he was shopping for a farm—four years ago, when Marc Schuyler worked for Valley Realty. I had to talk with Blackwell right away.

I caught him as he was closing up the hardware.

"Pete, you told me you once looked at acreage where we found the Schuyler boy. What agent showed it to you?"

He shook his head.

"Can't remember, Kate. I dealt with so many of 'em they all run together, and besides, I've never been too good at names."

"Can't, even if you think on it awhile?"

"It wouldn't do a bit of good."

"What realty company, then?"

"Sorry, I just do not know."

Disappointed, I thanked him and walked back toward my car. As I was getting in, I heard him shout and saw him running toward me.

"Wait a minute, Katie, hold on there. I just remembered I kept the cards of the fellas with the farms I liked the best. Guess I thought the wife might come around and I could buy one after all."

"Where are they?" I asked. "At your house?"

No, he told me, they were in the store—stuck in a drawer where he kept his odds and ends.

"Let's go inside," I said, trying not to sound excited.

He unlocked the door and headed for his desk.

"Here we go," he called, pulling out a stack of business cards secured by rubber bands. He shuffled through them, reading notes he'd made on the back of each.

"This is it—'San Marcos farm.' Only one I looked at out that way."

He handed me the card without glancing at its printed side. I flipped it over and caught my breath. It read "Valley Realty Co.—Marc Schuyler, agent."

So he'd had knowledge of the field and of the shed and of a place to hide a body where he thought no one would ever find it.

The car still bothered me. I ached to tie Schuyler to a light-colored sedan, but I could connect him only to a flashy red convertible. Perhaps the auto seen by Divans *was* unrelated to the crime, but I didn't think so.

There was a chance—just a chance—he owned two cars or had sold the sedan and bought the ragtop between the time Billy disappeared and the day I'd first seen it in his driveway three weeks later.

I went to the computer and did some exploring. After asking all the right questions I found that for the past two years he'd owned only one car—the convertible. Damn! I drummed my fingers on the desk in thought.

What about a company car? Did he ever drive one and, if so, what was it?

I phoned the realty firm and pretended I was a student from the local college, doing a paper on the perks of business life. I asked if they supplied autos to their salespeople.

No, I was informed, employees used their own cars and were reimbursed for mileage.

"Is there any time a salesman would get to use a company car?" I asked, pushing to the limit.

"Only if his own broke down and he had appointments to show property or, of course, if he were salesman of the month."

"Salesman of the month?"

"Oh, yes," the voice told me proudly, "we reward our top people with a little bonus and the use of one of our cars during the time they're being honored."

I went back to the computer and pulled up all the autos owned by Schuyler's realty company. There were five of them. DMV doesn't list the color of a car—just the year, make, and license number. I copied down all five plates and left the office.

I cruised slowly past the firm's parking lot and spotted three of the cars right away—two brown Fords and a dark blue Buick. That left two license plates unaccounted for—1NQV647 and 2LKW943. I'd come back another time.

I waited till after business hours, then drove past the lot again. The missing cars were parked side by side, near the southeast corner. I got out and walked over to them. 1NQV647 was another brown Ford. I looked at 2LKW943. It was a light-colored Mercury sedan.

The next morning I was on the phone again, talking with the same helpful person at the realty company. This time, I disguised my voice and told her I was from traffic investigation, inquiring about a minor accident involving one of their cars.

"It's nothing serious," I explained, "just a small fender-bender in a parking lot. Could be your person didn't even know it happened, but a man made a report and we've got to follow up on it—you know how it is."

Then I asked who'd been driving the firm's pale yellow Mercury, license 2LKW943, on Monday, April 20.

Again, she was only too willing to help. I was put on hold for several minutes, then the voice returned.

"That car was on loan to our March salesman of the month, Mr. Marc Schuyler. We awarded him its use for all of April."

"Goddamn it, Kate, don't be so tight-assed careful," Darrow told me as he leaned across the desk. "You've got enough right now to bring him in for questioning—motive, opportunity, the car, knowledge of the place we found the body. What the hell more do you want anyway? Do you want it tied up nice and pretty in a silver gift box with a bow?"

"You got it, Steve, that's just what I want. Motive can be used to prove intent but it can't be part of the corpus delicti, the opportunity is only conjecture on my part, we have no tire tracks or other evidence to tie the yellow Mercury to the crime, and the killer could've driven aimlessly till he stumbled accidentally on the field, so what we're left with looks pretty flimsy.

"Sure, I could bring him in and try to bluff him, but then I risk losing him in the long run, so I want a whole lot more on this one before I take him on. I'll skip the gift box and the bow, but I want it tied up nice and tight with everything in place. I want something solid and I haven't got it yet—all I've got are pointers."

"You're good, Kate, damn good, and you've got balls—I'll give you that—but you're too friggin' cautious. You may lose him anyway if you wait."

"I'll take my chances," I said testily. I was getting fed up with his attitude.

"I'll go with Kate," Mungers intervened. "We've waited this long—a little longer can't hurt."

I turned to him.

"Do you share my gut feeling on this one, Carl? Do you think Schuyler did it or am I barking up the wrong tree?"

"What you've uncovered points to him, but no," he said reluctantly, "I can't feel as sure as you do. I'd like to, but I can't. Wishful thinking gets in the way sometimes, Kate, and we've been hungry a long, long time on this one."

"Well, that's where you and I disagree and I side with Katie," Darrow broke in. "I believe the bastard *is* the one who did it and probably for the reason she says. He was screwing some moist little pussy who was wet behind the ears and he got caught at it. And was scared to death the boy was going to snitch on him."

We talked a little longer and then I went on home. Tommy was waiting on the porch, playing with a model plane.

"Mom," he called out, "when are we gonna get that dog?"

I'd told him after Carmel, in those first few days of harmony following our return, that we'd buy a puppy sometime that summer, but lately it had slipped my mind. Tommy hadn't forgotten, though.

"We'll get one of those stiff little doggies you love so much," he continued with enthusiasm, "even though I'd like a big fluffy one myself."

I stayed silent, not knowing what to say, and in that instant I knew I couldn't own a dog like Jackie Day. I'd drawn back from Marc Schuyler and everything that touched him. Perhaps someday, perhaps never—I didn't know.

I pulled my son close to me and put my arms around him.

"We'll get a fluffy puppy, kiddo—I don't think I want the other anymore."

Chapter Twenty-six

I felt I was so close and yet I couldn't make that final leap, couldn't go all the way. Couldn't get my case on that good straight track, whistling down to its conclusion.

I drove past Schuyler's house, at odd times of the day and night. Like a hunter with his prey in sight but not yet cornered, I stalked him constantly. I had to keep an eye on him to see what he was doing.

I saw him several times, going in or out, nonchalantly whistling as he walked, and once I saw the little dog, trotting smartly on the lawn. But nothing that would let me nail him.

But then it happened. My "something solid" surfaced in an unexpected quarter and gave me exactly what I wanted.

Luck plays a mighty big part in police work and don't let anybody tell you different. Sometimes you make that luck yourself, but occasionally it happens on its own. Like now.

I'd returned from lunch and saw a short elderly man sitting in the lobby. The receptionist nodded toward him as I passed.

"He's here for you, Katharine."

Surprised, I turned to him.

"Detective Harrod, sir. You wish to see me?"

He nodded, stood up, and smiled shyly. He seemed ill-at-ease in these surroundings. Then I saw the woman standing near the water fountain. She walked toward me and held her hand out.

"I'm Dotty Powers, Detective, and this is my father, John DiCarlo. He's got something we think you ought to see."

I invited them to come inside and motioned them through the squad room door. The little man moved forward, smoothing down his cotton work shirt and glancing at his high-topped workman's shoes. His daughter held his arm until we reached the chairs beside my desk.

I asked him what he had for me, and John DiCarlo laid a yellow folder on the blotter, withdrew three color snapshots, and arranged them in a row.

I looked at them and saw a group of preschool children dancing in a circle, waving whistles and wearing pointed party hats.

"This was my grandson's birthday celebration," the man explained. "See, here he is in the baseball shirt."

He pointed to a stocky, dark-haired youngster in the middle of the action. I looked at him, puzzled. What had this to do with me?

"Perhaps I should explain," the daughter said. "Okay, Dad?"

The man nodded.

"My son, Danny, had his fourth birthday party on Monday, April twentieth. We held it outside, on the front lawn, and there was lots of picture-taking. Dad didn't shoot as much as I did and he didn't get his developed till just last week—sometimes a roll will last

Mom and Dad for several months—but when they came back he noticed something funny in three of them.

"See here, across the street? See that little boy skipping past, wearing the jeans and blue-striped T-shirt? Well, we think it looks like the little boy you found murdered."

I scooped the photos off the desk and stared at them. In the background, on the opposite sidewalk, a small figure could be seen moving forward. It appeared to be the figure of a little boy eight or nine years old.

I couldn't say for sure, but the child certainly resembled Billy Schuyler. I got the magnifying glass and scrutinized the prints. The more I looked, the more certain I became.

"What time was this?" I asked abruptly, and I could feel my throat tense and tighten.

"Let's see—the kids arrived at four, we had the cake and gifts, then we played the games. I'd say between four-thirty and five in the afternoon."

I swung toward John DiCarlo.

"Did you see this child in person, sir, or only in the photos?"

"Only in the photos, Miss. I know you haven't got that youngster's killer yet and the wife, her mother"—he nodded toward his daughter—"said I ought to bring them on down."

Where were the pictures taken? I asked—at what address?

"In the front yard of 406 Morro Street," the old man answered. "That's where my grandson lives."

My jaw clenched and tightness filled my chest. I could almost feel my hair rising on end.

"I can't say for sure this child is Billy Schuyler," I

told them evenly, trying not to show excitement. "We'll have to make blowups of the prints and have our lab team examine them before we know. I'll keep you posted on what happens with them."

They rose to go and I cautioned them not to mention the photos to anyone, not even their closest friends. They agreed, said goodbye, and left the station.

Eagerly, I grabbed the prints again and tried to force the magnifying glass to work beyond its capabilities. The face was indistinct, but the size, the shape, the general demeanor looked like the little boy I'd watched play catch with Tommy on many long and hazy summer days.

And if this *was* Billy Schuyler, as I now believed with all my heart, I was looking at a picture of him heading for his uncle's house less than half a block away—a picture of him moving directly toward his death.

Carl and Steve walked in together and I called them over.

"Look at these."

I told them the whole story.

"How're you gonna handle it, boss?" Carl asked.

"We'll have to wait for positive ID. When it comes, we'll pick the bastard up and bring him in."

The photos went downtown marked "Rush." A few hours later, as I was starting to go home, I got the call. The experts said the boy was Billy Schuyler.

I'd planned to bring him in for questioning early on the following day, but sometimes, when luck begins to run, it keeps on going. That night I got its second shot.

I'd promised Tommy we'd go out for burgers and

A DESPERATE CALL

a shake. We drove to the local hangout, walked inside, and found a booth. I went up to place the order, telling him to save our seats, and while I stood in line I passed the time by watching other diners.

A toss of dark hair and a soft and teasing laugh caught my attention, and I saw Nadine, with two teenage boys, sitting on a stool with her back to the counter.

The boys were standing facing her and one was leaning toward her, his hand grasping the hair behind her neck, forcing her head slightly backward. While I watched, he pressed his mouth against her throat, and she laughed again and lightly pushed him back from her.

The other boy moved forward till his thighs straddled her left knee. She bent toward him, ran her tongue across his lips, then pried his legs apart and freed herself.

As I stared, fascinated by her brazen behavior, I saw her place both elbows on the ledge behind her, arch her back, and glance saucily from one boy to the other. Then she laid her right hand on her bare thigh and slowly stroked it, a taunting smile playing on her lips.

I watched the hand, wondering how far this little act would go, and then I saw the wrist above the hand—a wrist encircled by a handsome silver bracelet set with oval turquoise stones. I frowned slightly, trying to figure out why it looked familiar.

And then I remembered, and my mind was slamming, banging, blistering out with the stunning impact of that memory and what it meant. I was looking at the bracelet I'd seen lying on Marc Schuyler's bedside table and I was suddenly realizing who'd been between his sheets the afternoon that Billy disappeared.

Oh, Jesus, I thought, oh, sweet Jesus—his very own niece!

Again, I called Carl and Steve.

"We're not going to pick him up tomorrow after all—something's happened. Meet me at the station right away."

It was early evening so the squad room was empty except for the three of us. We sipped coffee while I filled them in.

"That bracelet is unique," I said. "It's not your usual dime-a-dozen model. I've no doubt whatsoever it's the one I saw beside the bed."

"Oooooh, baby," Darrow chortled as he tipped back in his chair, "screwing his red-hot little niece. I told you she was ripe and ready for the pickin', Kate. But with her own uncle? With so many other studs around?"

I shot a glance at him—I didn't feel like jokes right now.

"If she *was* in bed with Schuyler and Billy saw the action, the bastard knew he had to shut him up for good," said Carl. "The boy would never keep quiet about his sister rolling in the hay with Uncle Marc."

"So what do we do now, Katie baby?" Darrow asked.

"I'm going to talk with her and find out what's going on between them and see if she'll admit where she really was that afternoon. And find out if she was mixed up, in any way, with the killing of her brother."

"You'll have to go real easy, Kate—she's not naive, she'll have her guard up and be as evasive as they come. After all, she's gotta know it's wrong to screw your uncle. And then you've got the father. She's a minor and I can see a lawsuit coming now with one wrong step on our part."

"Don't worry," I assured them, "I'll go nice and easy till I draw it out of her."

"When?" asked Darrow.

"As soon as possible."

Chapter Twenty-seven

I decided I'd get her in her own milieu, lull her with a comfortable familiarity so she'd never think to raise her guard.

I picked up Patti Burke, sensing Nadine would feel more at ease in the presence of two women rather than with either Carl or Steve, and we parked outside the high school. It was close to three o'clock and the doors were swinging wildly with kids anxious to be on their way to somewhere better.

I saw her coming down the path and once again I marveled at the lushness of her sensuality. Just walking down the walk, she laid a visual definition on the word so stunning in its strength it left no doubt as to her nature.

"Let's go," I said to Patti.

We met her as she reached the sidewalk and I gently touched her arm.

"Nadine? Remember me? I'd love to talk to you a minute. Could we sit over here?" I motioned toward a nearby bench.

She frowned slightly and looked from me to Patti, then gave that now-familiar shrug and walked along with us.

"I'm concerned about you," I began earnestly, "and about your dad. How's he doing now?"

A DESPERATE CALL

"He's fine, I guess. I don't see him very much. He's always working or keeping to himself."

For just a moment, I thought I saw a trace of sadness fleet across her mask of insolence and she, for once, looked young and vulnerable. The expression quickly disappeared.

"And what about you? Are you doing okay, too? God knows, you've been through a pretty rough time."

"I miss my mom. I miss my mom a lot. I never thought I would, but sometimes . . ." She let the sentence trail away and once again I saw the flash of sadness. This little girl was not as tough as she let on.

"Sometimes, Nadine, we all need a friend to talk to. Sometimes we all get into situations that get way beyond our control. Situations we wish would go away but we don't know how to make them do that. I think maybe that's happened to you and now you don't have your mom to help you out. Am I right?"

Suddenly she was watching me intently.

"Sometimes. I guess so. I don't really know what you're talking about."

"Let's go on a little further, then. You're an attractive girl—I'm sure you know that. Do you have a boyfriend?"

"Not really—I see several different guys."

The sadness had long since disappeared, and now a vain smile touched her lips.

"I imagine boys your own age want to date you. I also imagine older men admire you and sometimes make passes at you, isn't that so?"

I spoke softly, gently, in a relaxed tone.

"Sometimes. Maybe."

She giggled, and now she seemed even younger than her fifteen years.

"Is there one older man in particular?"

She stiffened, her head jerked up, and a flash of fear passed through her eyes.

"No. I don't know what you mean."

"Nadine, I'm going to tell you something and see what you think about it. I saw you Friday night and you were wearing a stunning silver bracelet—the same one you're wearing now. I saw that bracelet once before, but it wasn't on your arm—it was on a table, apparently where you'd forgotten it. Do you remember where that was?"

A guarded look touched her face and a wary tone edged her voice.

"No—I didn't leave it anywhere."

"I think you did. In early May."

"Where?"

"You tell me."

"I don't know."

"All right, then, I'll remember for you. You left it at your uncle Marc's, in his bedroom, on the stand beside his bed."

A deep flush rose quickly to her cheeks and she bit her lip nervously as her eyes darted from me to Patti and back again.

"So what if I did? I don't get any of this."

Her voice began to crack. I half expected her to get up right then and walk away, to realize we had no right to make her sit and talk with us, but she showed no sign of running. She was probably too naive to know she was free to leave at any time and I hoped she stayed that way.

Patti leaned forward and touched her arm.

A DESPERATE CALL

"Honey, honey, it's all right, we're not going to hurt you. There're just some things we need to understand."

I took up the reins again.

"Now do you remember losing it, Nadine?"

"Maybe so ... maybe for a day or two. I guess I took it off when I was over there with Mom and Dad—maybe to play with the dog and I forgot about it. Then Uncle Marc found it and put it on the table till he could give it to me."

Plausible enough, and if she stuck to that little story, I'd end up striking out.

"I don't think so, Nadine."

"Well, what *do* you think?"

I saw her hands tightly twisting a fold of cloth from her skirt.

"I think you and your uncle are very close—are very good friends. Do you want me to spell it out for you any further?"

She put her head down and looked from side to side, avoiding eye contact with either Patti or myself. I was reminded of a cornered animal. She didn't answer.

"Nadine, let me tell you something right now—no matter what happens, you'll be all right. No one's after you. You're a victim here and you'll be protected."

Suddenly she flared up and lashed out at me, rising from the bench and standing over me.

"You're dirty! You're disgusting! I know what you're hinting at and it's a lie!"

"I don't think so, Nadine—I think you're sleeping with your uncle. I think you took that bracelet off when you made love and laid it on the stand beside the bed and then forgot about it."

"That's not true," she yelled, her eyes dark and

angry and her hair tossing wildly as she shook her head, "that's just not true!"

I waited till she calmed down, then I grabbed a limb and walked way out on it.

"Suppose I told you we had your uncle in here earlier and he admitted the two of you were lovers."

On cue, Patti reached over, took Nadine's hand, and softly told her, "I'm sorry, honey."

Fear and disbelief scored every inch of her young face. Her hands clenched the edges of the bench.

"He wouldn't dare! He'd be the last to tell, he . . ."

Too late, she realized she'd fallen in a trap. She began to sob, and suddenly the hard veneer of polish and sophistication crumbled and she was just a scared little girl with nowhere left to hide.

"It's okay, honey," Patti said, as she stroked Nadine's hair, "it's okay—the worst is over. We just want to ask you a few more questions."

"Will my dad have to know? And Marc, what'll you do to him?"

"We'll try to help you with your dad," I promised, ignoring the last question, "but let's talk now about how it all began, how he got you into this."

Like lightning, her defiance returned full-force.

"Don't you go blaming him! I'm not sorry it happened—whaddya think of that? I loved it, loved everything he did to me, the way he made me feel. I never thought of him as my uncle, ever. He knows just what to do to make me hot and it turns him on to see me beg for it. He calls me his sweet dirty little bitch."

I looked at Patti and she looked back at me.

"How did it begin and how long's it been going on?"

Nadine told us the affair started about eighteen

months ago, shortly after Marc's return from living down south. She'd dropped by his house one afternoon, for help on a paper she was writing on Hawaii.

"I got up to get a drink of water and he came up behind me at the sink. He slid his hands underneath my arms and put them on my breasts. And he rubbed them real hard.

"I loved it. I turned around and kissed him and he pushed my hand down his body and said 'I'm ready for you, baby', and then we went to bed. I wasn't a virgin so it was no big deal."

She'd regained her composure and talked in the hardened offhand manner of a seasoned hooker.

"How often did you meet?"

"Every time we could, but we had to be very careful—usually only once or twice a week unless one of us got really horny. I'd say I was going to the library after school, but I'd go over there instead."

"The neighbors never saw you?"

"I used the door in that little porch that goes off the kitchen. There's a big bush outside, so you're hidden if you time it right."

She laughed, and lit a cigarette.

Then I asked the question I'd been heading toward all along.

"Nadine, were you at your uncle's house on the day your brother disappeared?"

She hesitated, looking for another trap, but saw none. She shrugged.

"What difference does it make? Yes—yes, I was. I went over after school and was there till nearly five o'clock, and when I got home Mom was wondering where Billy was."

"Did you and your uncle have sex that afternoon, right before you left?"

"Yeah, we screwed—in fact, that's all we did from three-fifteen right up to when I had to go. He was really something else that day." She smiled and wet her lips.

"Did you see your brother at all that afternoon?"

"You asked me that a long time ago—I told you no. How could I've seen him if I was fuckin' Marc? Or do you mean sometime earlier?"

"I mean any time after, say, two o'clock."

"No, no time at all."

"Positive?"

" 'Course I'm positive—I'd know my own brother."

I didn't think she was lying. Her face held an honest, open look I believed impossible for Nadine to manufacture. If she was telling me the truth, then somehow Billy must've seen her without her seeing him.

"Tell me something, Nadine," I continued. "When I visited you in May I asked you why you'd been arguing with your girlfriend—what was her name? Janet, Jan?"

"Jan, yes."

"You told me you couldn't remember—do you remember now?"

"Sure I do—it was about Marc. I didn't tell you then 'cause no one knew I was seeing him but her. That bitch said he'd asked her out and I told her she was lying—that's what that was all about."

Now I understood the evasive answers that had puzzled me so much.

"How do you think your dad will take this, Nadine?"

A DESPERATE CALL

"Who cares—I hate him! It'll serve him right if he's upset and all his fancy friends find out. He could never be like Marc—do what Marc does—and I bet he knows that and he envies him. I'm just sorry it has to stop. It's all spoiled now."

"Do you think you love him, honey?" Patti asked gently.

"Love him? No way. I just get hot for him and he gets hard for me. We make each other feel good and it works out fine."

I'd heard enough. Besides, I now had everything I needed.

"I'm glad you talked to us, Nadine. We'll try to help you out in any way we can."

My words sounded good but my tone wasn't very sympathetic. This kid had known exactly what she was walking into and her only regret, even now, was that we'd spoiled her fun.

She mumbled something quick I didn't catch and then she gathered up her books and left us sitting there. I shook my head as I watched her walk away.

"Is 'precocious' the word I'm looking for?" I asked Patti.

"I think it's another one you want," she told me wryly.

I watched her till she turned a corner, then I jumped up and headed for the car.

"Come on, let's move it. You know where she's going, don't you? I'll bet anything she heads straight for him to tell him what's just happened. If I walk in on them and throw him off his guard maybe I can do a squeeze-play on him about Billy."

"Nothing doing," Patti said. "I can't go with you. I've got court in half an hour."

"It doesn't matter. Just drop me near there, then go tell Carl what's up and to meet me at the house in fifteen minutes. I know he's at the station 'cause I left him working on the search warrant."

Patti hesitated. I knew she didn't like it.

"Promise me you won't go in alone?"

"Of course I won't—I'll wait for Carl—but get me over there. I want to see her going through the door."

Chapter Twenty-eight

She dropped me half a block from Marc's house and I walked casually behind a flowery bush and pretended to be searching through my purse. From where I stood, I had a clear view of the bungalow and its side entrance. I didn't have to wait too long to know my hunch was right.

She hurried down the street, up the walk, and through the door. I heard it slam behind her with a quick sharp crack.

I'd give them time to get it going before I barged on in. The more "flagrante delicto" I could catch them in, the better. Ten minutes or so should do it and by then Mungers should be here.

Come to think of it, though, I might find nothing happening in the bungalow. If Nadine told him I was on to him, as I imagined she was doing right this minute, would he really want to jump in bed with her?

Still, it was certainly worth a try. The atmosphere inside that house must be fairly charged by now and such volatility produces tongues that let their guard down.

I checked my watch. Damn it, where was Carl? He should've been here by now. Then suddenly I heard another quick sharp crack and I jerked my head back up. Nadine was rushing down the walkway and her face was twisted with an ugly rage.

Surprised, I felt my disappointment rise and wondered what the hell had happened. Now *I* was the one caught off guard and I was in a quandary. I still longed to face him while his emotions were in turmoil, but my partner wasn't anywhere in sight. Yet if I waited any longer, those roiling feelings would soon be taken under tight control and Schuyler would tell me only what he wanted me to hear.

I bit my lip and thought about it, but only for a moment. I'd always been a careful cop, but I was hungry for this one and I wasn't going to lose the chance. I'd go in alone.

I crossed the road and moved quickly toward the house, throwing one final glance behind me to see if Carl was coming. The street was empty. I went up the stairs, knocked twice, then stood back. The door opened slowly and Marc Schuyler stared out at me.

"I need to talk with you," I said, and silently he waved me past him. I stepped into the little hall and then I stopped so short I rocked back on my heels. I was standing face-to-face with Nadine's little buddy—the blonde I'd seen her arguing with that night so long ago. She dropped her mouth wide open, then looked at me with frightened eyes and fled. The last I saw of her, she was running up the street.

I glanced beyond the hallway and spied the rumpled unmade bed.

"So you were screwing her, too. Just like you screw all the little girls."

"Detective, whatever can you mean?"

He mocked me with a deprecating laugh, but I saw the look of wariness that flashed across his face. In an

A DESPERATE CALL

instant it was gone and he crossed his arms and grinned at me with a boyish cocky stare.

This wasn't going well at all. Instead of finding Schuyler in the flustered state I'd hoped for, I found him totally in possession of himself. I'd have to try another tack if I wanted to unsettle him.

"I'm still not happy with your alibi," I told him bluntly.

The cocky smile vanished. I'd jolted him. He must've thought he'd heard the last of that one several months ago.

"How's that?" he asked.

"You told me you spent that afternoon with Ellen Dancer."

"And *she* told you I'd spent that afternoon with her. Come on, Detective, you talked with her yourself."

"Yes, and then I talked with her again."

He stared at me, his eyes bugging out.

"I talked with her again and she told me she was really up in Reno all that time. And that she did a favor for you giving us not the truth, but what you wanted us to hear."

He sucked his breath in.

"I don't know why she's doing this to me. We were here together, in the sack. You must've got it wrong or else she's lying for some reason of her own."

"I don't get things wrong, and I can easily prove she was in Reno. Charge slips, room registration, phone calls. Do I spell it out enough?"

My voice was tough, edged with steel.

"Okay, okay, you've got me—I was dumb to try blowin' smoke with you—but the alibi's got nothing to do with Billy's death."

He edged into the living room and I followed close behind.

"What's it got to do with, then?"

He twisted back and forth and fiddled with his collar.

"Okay, I'll level with you. I'm protecting someone and I cannot, will not, tell you who that someone is unless you force me under oath.

"It's a gal whose reputation would be ruined if it got out she was seeing me—a married woman here in town whose husband holds a mighty high position. Ellen Dancer's just a whore, so I called a favor from her and had her tell a lie for me, but now *I'm* tellin' you the truth."

"Bullshit!" The word cracked sharply from my mouth. "I'll tell you what you did that afternoon— you were in the sack, all right, but you were screwing your own little niece, Nadine."

His mouth dropped open and a vapid stare filled his face. I'd shot his lies right out from under him and left him with an empty bag.

"Detective," he protested, "that's not true. Why, that's the foulest obscenity I've heard in ages. How could you even think up a thing like that?"

"Very easily," I replied, "when I see the evidence myself and when your niece confirms what I already know to be the truth. And she confirmed it, all right, told me the whole sordid story earlier this afternoon. Why, I thought she'd have told you I was on to you when she was here a little while ago, but I guess she was too upset when she walked in and found you sleeping with her friend. I saw her leave here pretty fast so I guess she didn't have the chance."

"You're lying," he raged. "You're lying or she's lying, for God knows what reason."

I ignored his protests and drove the needle home, moving forward till my face was only inches from him. I should've been more careful, but I was not afraid.

"I know about the door she used to keep your meetings secret, I know about the name you called her so endearingly, and, Mr. Schuyler, I know such behavior isn't new to you. I know about Hawaii."

He blanched and stayed silent for a moment, then he spoke again and the words came growling out.

"That lyin' little bitch, getting me into all of this. You're gonna have to prove this in court before I'll do any talkin'!"

"Okay, I'll do just that—gladly. I'll put sweet Nadine on the stand and she'll name dates, times, and places. She'll paint a cozy little picture of an uncle and his niece. And somehow, somewhere along the line, I'll make sure the Maui episode gets in there, too. Yes, indeed—I imagine this old town will see a very juicy trial."

I let him run that through his mind and analyze its import. He simmered down immediately.

"What if I tell you something *did* go on—not much but something. What then?"

"Well, you've got no record in this state and the DA might decide there'd been extenuating circumstances—it all depends on what we've got to take him."

"Take him this then. We *did* meet once or twice and, God help me, we did have sexual intercourse. Sure, I knew it was wrong, but you've seen Nadine, Detective—you know she's mature way beyond her years.

"She came on strong to me, caught me off my guard, and it just happened. I couldn't help myself. But it's not like I seduced an innocent—she wanted it just as much as I did."

"You say you had sex once or twice. *Was* one of those times the afternoon your nephew disappeared?"

"Yes, yes, Detective," Schuyler answered eagerly, smoothing back his hair with one hand, "yes, it was. That's why I couldn't level with you before about my alibi—because I *was* with Nadine, just like she told you."

"And Billy saw you."

I let it lie there. Just that much, no more. I could almost see his mind whirling as I came out of left field. I'd long forgotten why I'd wanted Carl to be there. I was totally absorbed with what was happening in that room.

He looked at me increduously.

"Billy saw me?"

"That's right. He went to your house that afternoon between four-thirty and five o'clock, found you and his sister making love, and you killed him to keep him quiet."

A clear hard look of cruelty filled his eyes with an intensity I'd rarely seen before and he came quickly toward me. Too late, I realized the danger I was in—the danger I'd embraced so willingly because of eagerness to crack this case.

Involuntarily I stepped backward, hoping I could reach the door, but my foot came down hard on an object lying on the floor and I stumbled, lurching to my left. He was on me in an instant, as I watched the yellow nylon chew-bone of Jackie Day skitter fast across the floor.

A DESPERATE CALL

"Bitch!" he yelled. "You're going to pay for this one." As he wrestled with me, pinning me against the wall with my hands held tight behind me, I smelled it, the faint but certain odor of a man's cologne. I'd come across that cloying scent only once before—on my beaten body that morning in the shed.

My mind reeled and a gasp wheezed through my lips.

"It was you, wasn't it?" I cried and there was no doubt at all he knew exactly what I meant.

He threw me on the floor and sat astride me, then pressed his face down hard on mine until that stinking smell filled my nostrils and seemed to permeate my very being. I began to choke as I coughed to get it out of me.

"Like it, bitch? I wore it just for you that night and now I get to rub it on you once again."

"And the phone call?" I whispered, already certain of his answer.

"What do you think?"

I tried to twist away, to reach my gun inside my jacket, but his body weight held my upper torso tight against the floor. I brought my knee up fast against his back, but he only laughed and slapped me hard across the face.

Let him rape me, I thought desperately. Let that be all he wants to do with me. Let him get it over with and maybe I can see a chance to get away.

My flesh burned from where his hand had struck me and I felt my lip begin to swell.

He eased off a bit and reached inside my jacket, his hand pressing hard against my breast. Then he found the gun inside my pocket and he drew it out and flung it on the sofa.

I struggled to get free, but he slapped me hard again, then flipped me over, running both his hands along the waistband of my skirt. They fastened on my handcuffs and he gave a low mean chuckle. I knew exactly what was going to happen but there was no way I could stop it. Within seconds I heard the clicks and my wrists were trapped behind me.

"We're going to have some fun, you cunt," he whispered in my ear, "and if you want to talk about that nosy little kid, we'll do that, too."

He dragged me to my feet and propelled me toward the bedroom. As he pushed me toward the bed, a glint of chrome from the bureau caught my eye and my gaze fell full on a pair of sharply pointed scissors—the scissors used to trim the hair of Jackie Day. My heart clutched and I looked at them with longing. They might as well have been a million miles away.

He shoved me roughly and I fell upon the rumpled sheets, then he sat down close beside me and caressed my throat.

"What'll it be first?" he asked, as he rubbed me slowly. "Shall we have our fun or a little conversation?"

I was terrified but I fought to keep control of all my senses. I'd never known fear so great as now.

"Tell me about Billy."

I tried to make my voice come out strong and firm, but I could only whisper. I pushed backward and he let me prop myself against the headboard, the handcuffs cutting deep into my wrists.

"Sure, I'll tell you all about him," he said playfully, "but you know why, don't you? Because I'm going to finish off what I started in the shed. You'll never be a fuckin' danger to me after this."

I'd known it—of course, deep-down, I'd known

what he had in mind for me—but to hear him verbalize it made the difference. A deep despair pervaded me, but I knew I couldn't let him see it.

"Was it like I thought?" I asked. "Billy walked in and saw you with Nadine?"

"Of course it was. My own niece, for Christ's sake. What do you think would happen to my life if that got out? Just what you're trying to do to me—they'd crucify me. I'd lose it all."

He paused a moment, eyes narrowing.

"We'd finished and the bitch got up to leave. She went out the side door like she always did and I went through the hall. I saw the kid standing in the corner, near the coatrack. He startled me. I asked him what he wanted and he asked me why I'd hurt his sister—said he'd heard her moaning. Nosy little bastard, he'd seen us going at it and I couldn't trust him to be still. I knew right then he wasn't going out of here alive."

"Did Nadine see him, too?"

"I doubt it—he wasn't in her line of vision. She never said and I never asked."

"What happened next?"

"I calmed him down, said 'let's have a Coke and talk about it.' He started toward a chair and I grabbed Jackie's leash and got him from behind. It only took a moment till he went completely limp, but I kept on twisting to make sure."

A gnawing sickness grew deep inside me and momentarily I forgot about my own predicament.

"Was that all?"

"Hell, no, I wasn't takin' any chances. I laid him on the bed and pressed my hands around his neck until I heard it snap."

I swallowed hard. I was quiet for several seconds, then I spoke.

"A cop came to your house that evening—where was the body hidden then?"

"In the closet. Christ, I thought he'd start to search—scared me half to death. When he left I stuffed it in the dryer till I could move it to the field after dark. Figured no one would ever look in there.

"I'd take it out from time to time and heat the dryer up, hoping it'd slow the rigor mortis—afraid it might get stuck inside if it started gettin' stiff."

I played the gruesome scene over in my mind and my sickness grew. I pushed it back.

"When did you move him to the field?"

"I don't know—well after dark. Maybe ten-thirty, eleven o'clock. I wrapped him in a blanket and laid him on the backseat. After I dumped him, I came home and went to bed."

He grasped my thigh and, bending forward, tried to run his tongue along my lips. I quickly swung my head aside and he spoke menacingly.

"That's the whole story, little sister. And don't you ever turn away from me again."

I hated him. I longed to jump at him and claw him, to put my knee between his legs and crack his balls, to make the blood flow down that stinking face. But of course I could not move. My fantasies of what I'd do to him were shackled, literally, by the handcuffs.

I was silent for a moment while his eyes, cruel and hardened, bore into mine. Then I spoke again. Afterward I wondered why I'd said it. The words came out of nowhere, unrehearsed, unthought of, till a mere moment before I uttered them.

"Your brother should be real proud of you on this one."

I'd hit the nerve. He exploded, rising from the bed

A DESPERATE CALL

and pounding on the mattress. A bulging purple vein ran down his forehead and the venom he'd been storing up since childhood poured out unrestrained.

"That motherfucker? What would I care what he thinks about me? I'm a better man than he is and I'll prove it yet. I hate his guts, that sanctimonious bastard—always on my case, always judging, always finding fault."

It was starting to fall in place for me.

"And you got back at him when you screwed his daughter, didn't you?"

"Damn right I did. Every time I fucked her, I was fuckin' him, too. I wouldn't give a shit if he *did* learn all about it—in fact, I'd look forward to it. I just wish I'd be around to see his face if he ever *did* find out.

"Don't get me wrong—that bitch was great in bed. I told her 'just trust your instincts, little girl', and she sure did. She liked it rough and so did I and she knew how to give me pleasure. But, yeah, you're right—I liked the whole idea of whose kid it was I was layin' down on."

He smiled in satisfaction, lost in his imagined revenge. He'd forgotten all about me and was on a roll. I hoped that I could keep him there as he bared the dark abyss of a sickened human soul.

I didn't have to worry. He'd become crazed ever since I'd mentioned Thomas, and was so caught up in reliving the experience that he talked to me free-flow.

"You know what? I don't care—I don't give a good goddamn. This'll set ol' Tommy right back on his fat ass for good. A double shot—I fucked his little girl and I killed his little boy. He'd never snap back from that one.

"I got him in the balls this time, no doubt about it.

And, yeah, I'd love to see him know I'm the one who got the last laugh after all these years. No matter how it'd end up goin' down for me, I'd say it'd been well worth it. I've been waitin' such a long, long time."

Suddenly I saw my chance and hope began to build in me. I dropped my voice to a seductive whisper, a conspiratorial tone that caressed him verbally the way he'd caressed my throat.

"Let's tell him, then," I said, leaning forward on the bed. "Let's get to watch him while he sees the pictures in his mind. Let's see him writhe in his personal agony while he knows it's all because of how he's treated you like dirt."

His eyes grew excited and his head bobbed up and down. His face held an eager stare while he gazed at some unknown point above my head. He was obviously mesmerized by my suggestion and I felt the pounding of my heart as I began to think I'd found the key to my salvation.

It didn't work. In the splitting of an instant, his expression changed and, like a person coming down from a high induced by drugs, he got control again and knew I'd tried to trick him.

"You conniving cunt!" he yelled. "You don't mean one word of that—you're just tryin' to help yourself."

He ripped my jacket back and tore my blouse from side to side until I lay there nearly naked. Then he sucked on me on one side while his hand squeezed my other breast with cruel ferocity. At first angrily, then slowly and deliberately, he hurt me, then caressed me, in a medley of sadistic pleasuring.

Humiliated, I lay there taking it—there was nothing else that I could do—and I swear I felt my mind begin to snap. I closed my eyes, shutting out the visual aspect of my agony, but the agony itself remained.

How could I ever have been drawn to this beast? How could I have felt a sexual palpitation every time I saw him, so strong and overpowering I'd almost lost control? I was ashamed of the raw hot lust I'd had for him and wondered how my judgment could've been so faulty. Could I ever trust it in the future?

Oh dear God, I thought, there is no future. Soon he's going to kill me. I'll never see my son again.

He drew back abruptly, as if a thought had suddenly crossed his mind.

"I have something for you," he said, in a lilting, mocking tone that seared me with its evil. "If you want to know so much about it all, I think you might enjoy this, too."

He left the room for just a moment, then returned holding Jackie's leash. Again he sat astride me and pulled my head up roughly from the bed. I felt the leather strap slip around my neck and, holding it in both his hands, he crossed the ends, then pulled tight on them as he bent over me.

"This is how I did it, Katie—this is what it felt like when I killed that little bastard. Feel it? Feel what it was like?"

He applied more pressure and, as I struggled helplessly against the strangling, I began to lose my senses. I closed my eyes, then opened them, and suddenly, as I moved in and out of consciousness, I became inordinately aware of the smallest details, such as the way the blinds slanted crookedly across the windowpanes, and the ragged thread hanging from the arm of the maroon sweater tossed across a chair.

He gave one final pull and I thought the end had

surely come, but then he relaxed his grip and let the leash drop beside me on the bed.

"Maybe later, Katharine," he said as he leaned over me, "but not right now." I could feel flecks of his saliva fall upon my face. "We've got to have some more fun together first."

Bruised and dazed, I mentally gave thanks for every moment of life left to me. If I could just hang in there, maybe Carl would come.

I thought of him—of his large florid face, of his strength and calm—and in that instant my own strength began to flow back into me. I'd find some way out of this—I had to.

"Time out, sweetie," Schuyler told me. "Let's make the pleasure last. We're going to take a little break and drink a little wine."

Then he dangled handcuff keys above my head and asked me coyly, "Can I trust you? Can I take them off without you trying any fancy stuff?"

I nodded yes and knew my chance was coming. Somehow I was going to escape. Seconds later, my wrists fell free.

His tone mellowed just a bit as he stared into my eyes.

"You know, bitch, we could've had something once, but you wouldn't come to me. You got scared and pulled away. Well, now you're getting what you *really* wanted all along. Too bad you waited far too late."

As he finished speaking, I heard a whining from behind a nearby door and remembered Jackie Day. Buying time, looking for an opening, I asked if he would let him out.

"Sure, you want to see him? Let's get him in here, then," and backing up, never letting his eyes leave me,

A DESPERATE CALL   347

Schuyler opened up the door, and the little dog darted out and pranced around, then sat down and licked itself.

He leaned across to kiss me, apparently forgetting all about the promised wine, and I tried to wrench away and roll across the mattress.

As he grabbed my shoulder angrily and began to pull me back, it suddenly happened. From out of nowhere, Jackie Day jumped onto the bed and pushed against us, getting under Schuyler's arm.

"Goddamn it, Jackie, get the hell out of here," he cried, and he hurled the little body hard across the room. I heard a thud and then a yelp, and I saw a furry mass leap past me—snarling, barking, biting. I watched the pointed teeth sink into Schuyler's hand, and while he tried to shake the dog away I jumped quickly from the bed and raced across the room.

I wasn't quick enough. Finally free of Jackie Day, my tormentor dove at me and grabbed me by the ankle. As I struggled hard to keep from falling, my hands reached out toward the bureau and closed quickly on the waiting scissors. Mad with fear, I twisted half around and drove them in his neck and shoulder—drove them up and down, up and down, with a strength and a ferocity I'd never felt before.

I saw the silver blades turn red and felt his blood hit my face and chest as it spurted, warm and vibrant, from the open wounds. His grasp slowly loosened and he looked up at me with widened eyes, filled both with pain and with astonishment. Then he collapsed upon the floor.

I stabbed him once again and then again, in the arm and on the shoulder, feeding on a frenzy of hate and of revenge. And then I pulled myself together and forced myself to stop—forced myself to jerk away from that line I was about to cross.

I looked at him as I gasped and fought to fill my lungs with air. Although he was still breathing, he was a threat to me no longer—I was free. Near-naked but not caring, I ran across the room, out the door, and from that house.

They found me on the lawn and covered me quickly with a blanket.

"He confessed," I kept repeating. "He told me how he killed that little boy. Go get him. Dear God, please go get him." I struggled to stand up and go back inside myself but they restrained me.

When Carl arrived only moments later, he took me in his arms and held me close and wouldn't let me go.

"It's over, Kate," he told me softly—"finally, finally over. He's not dead, he's only wounded. He'll live to stand trial for Billy Schuyler's murder."

I pulled away from him and cupped his face in both my hands. I looked into his eyes until my own filled up with tears. And then I wept.

I found out later that Carl never received my message. No one knew where I'd gone that afternoon. A hit-run driver—fleeing, ironically, our own patrol's pursuit—had broadsided Patti Burke, and, though she wasn't seriously hurt, the precious moments lost in the melee that followed delayed till far too late her reaching Carl and rushing him to me. It was a call from a neighbor woman who heard my screams as I stumbled from the house that brought police to the Morro Street address.

I was examined by the department doctor and then, despite the pleading of my partner, I insisted on going home alone.

A moon, nearly full, lit the silent street, and I drove slowly, wearily, through the brightness of the heat-filled night. I was exhausted, drained, spent in mind and body. I needed time for just myself.

I reached for the radio and turned it on, and a powerful rolling song of triumph surged forward and surrounded me—touching me, soothing me, healing my torn spirit.

I stopped the car, grasped the steering wheel, and put my head down. I sat there quietly, overcome by the emotion building deep inside me.

After several moments I drove on, and as I neared my driveway, I recalled another evening not so long ago when I'd pulled up and found Jon and Tommy waving at me from the steps.

Now those steps were empty and the house was dark, and only loneliness waited there to greet me.

Was I happy now? I asked myself. Was this truly what I wanted? I knew it wasn't, but I also knew I didn't want the other either—a life without the work I loved.

Finally, standing in the moonlight with the quiet of night around me, I realized there were no easy answers, no absolutes, no black-and-whites the way I'd once been taught. Life is all a compromise filled with countless trade-offs and it will never, ever, be any other way.

The trick lies in trying to keep those trade-offs small while taking the fullest joy from what is left—pulling the most from every single moment, savoring it until you've wrung it dry.

And, with a building sense of hope and a triumphant pounding of my heart, I felt a blinding flash flood through me and fill me with the sure and certain knowledge that that was exactly what I was going to do. Because without a doubt, without a question, I could live no other way.

⊘ SIGNET   **⬢ ONYX**   (0451)

SPELLBINDING PSYCHOLOGICAL SUSPENSE

☐ **THE RED DAYS by Stephen Kimball.** A brilliant mix of high-tech suspense and old-fashioned gut-churning action, this dazzling thriller will keep you riveted until its final provocative twist. "A tense story of eerie terror."—Ronald Munson
(176839—$4.99)

☐ **GRACE POINT by Anne D. LeClaire.** When Zoe Barlow moves to the coastal town of Grace Point to make a new start of her marriage, she never dreamed of what was to await her. Her son suddenly disappears, and there is no one to trust as Zoe searches desperately, stumbling through a generation-old legacy. Chilling erotic suspense.... "A gripping novel of love, lust, ancient sins and deadly secrets."—Judith Kelman (403959—$5.99)

☐ **NO WAY HOME by Andrew Coburn.** Filled with insight and irony, this electrifying thriller blends roller-coaster action with the sensitive probing of men and women driven by private demons of love and hate, need and desire. "Extremely good ... vivid ... one of the best suspense novels."—*Newsweek* (176758—$4.99)

Price slightly higher in Canada

Buy them at your local bookstore or use this convenient coupon for ordering.

PENGUIN USA
P.O. Box 999 – Dept. #17109
Bergenfield, New Jersey 07621

Please send me the books I have checked above.
I am enclosing $_____ (please add $2.00 to cover postage and handling). Send check or money order (no cash or C.O.D.'s) or charge by Mastercard or VISA (with a $15.00 minimum). Prices and numbers are subject to change without notice.

Card #_____ Exp. Date _____
Signature_____
Name_____
Address_____
City _____ State _____ Zip Code _____

For faster service when ordering by credit card call **1-800-253-6476**

Allow a minimum of 4-6 weeks for delivery. This offer is subject to change without notice.

SIGNET **ONYX** (0451)

NIGHTMARES COME TRUE...

- ☐ **CRIES OF THE CHILDREN by Clare McNally.** Three wonderfully sweet and gifted children won the hearts of the grown-ups who adopted them. But now the three are gone. And on a rescue search that led them to a world ruled by a psychically terrifying envoy of evil, little did the parents realize that the young ones they loved so briefly were now the unwitting possessors of a deadly power to harm.... (403207—$4.99)

- ☐ **WHAT ABOUT THE BABY? by Clare McNally, bestselling author of** *Hear the Children Calling*. Mother, baby, and evil made three. They wanted her dead ... but not until they'd taken her baby—alive. A novel of terror! (403606—$3.99)

- ☐ **DEATH INSTINCT by Phillip Emmon.** A serial killer is loose in Phoenix ... in a thriller with the chill of terror and heat of hell. (172841—$4.99)

Prices slightly higher in Canada

Buy them at your local bookstore or use this convenient coupon for ordering.

PENGUIN USA
P.O. Box 999 — Dept. #17109
Bergenfield, New Jersey 07621

Please send me the books I have checked above.
I am enclosing $_____ (please add $2.00 to cover postage and handling). Send check or money order (no cash or C.O.D.'s) or charge by Mastercard or VISA (with a $15.00 minimum). Prices and numbers are subject to change without notice.

Card #_____ Exp. Date _____
Signature_____
Name_____
Address_____
City _____ State _____ Zip Code _____

For faster service when ordering by credit card call **1-800-253-6476**

Allow a minimum of 4-6 weeks for delivery. This offer is subject to change without notice.

⊘ SIGNET   ⓔ ONYX

INTRIGUING THRILLERS!

☐ **FLIGHT by Fran Dorf.** After twenty years in a catatonic trance, a woman awakens looking younger, slimmer, and more beautiful than she did as a girl of eighteen. What she doesn't remember is her plunging from atop a two-hundred foot cliff and the sensational trial in which her boyfriend was convicted of her attempted murder. Love, betrayal and murder ... a psychological thriller that is "riveting, tantalizing, shocking!"—*Publisher's Weekly* (176472—$4.99)

☐ **DEAD EASY by Arthur F. Nehrbass.** A twisted psychopath turns a South Florida housewife's sheltered life into a nightmare of violence and unimaginable terror. "Gripping, fascinating ... a fast-paced thriller."—Carl Hiaasen (177045—$4.99)

☐ **STONE CITY by Mitchell Smith.** It was a giant state prison peopled by men making their own laws of survival. But none of them were prepared for murder. It was up to one inmate, Bauman, an ex-college professor, to unmask the serial slayer. "A knockout, a compelling, reverberating novel ... impeccably written."—*The Detroit News* (169301—$5.99)

Prices slightly higher in Canada

Buy them at your local bookstore or use this convenient coupon for ordering.

PENGUIN USA
P.O. Box 999 — Dept. #17109
Bergenfield, New Jersey 07621

Please send me the books I have checked above.
I am enclosing $_____ (please add $2.00 to cover postage and handling). Send check or money order (no cash or C.O.D.'s) or charge by Mastercard or VISA (with a $15.00 minimum). Prices and numbers are subject to change without notice.

Card #_____ Exp. Date _____
Signature_____
Name_____
Address_____
City _____ State _____ Zip Code _____

For faster service when ordering by credit card call **1-800-253-6476**

Allow a minimum of 4-6 weeks for delivery. This offer is subject to change without notice.